The Children Of The Night

The Unmasking

Christopher D. Holoman, Sr

The Reading Glass Books
1-888-420-3050
www.readingglassbooks.com
fulfillment@readingglassbooks.com

Table of Contents

CHAPTER 1

The Looming Menace

Charles Sinclair II was having another ill-timed vivid flashback as he sat waiting for his meeting to start. He could feel the heat of the flames, the smell of the burning house, and hear the screams of his wife and children. The look of bewilderment and terror in their eyes burned into his soul as he watched helplessly as the floor collapsed beneath them, descending them into the flames played out once again. He could still see the expectations for him to save them in their eyes and the sudden realization he could not. Sweat beaded on his brow as he gripped his chair's arms, trying to force the visions to stop. He felt himself beginning to hyperventilate, fighting the rage that always accompanied the unnaturally vivid flashbacks. As he began to regain his composure, the pain of losing all the people he had loved and lost almost brought him to tears. He longed to see the faces of the many loved ones he had lost throughout the years. Charles suffered these intense memories that grew more severe with time. Today, lesser forms of Charles's condition would be called Post Traumatic Stress Disorders, but for Charles, they were much, much worse.

Charles wondered if he would ever see their faces again or feel the warmth of their love at the end of life. Charles feared there would be no redemption for him if such a thing as universal

Karma or divine justice existed. Charles was a man of unimaginable wealth and privilege who wanted nothing except the one thing no money could buy, i.e., to grow old and die surrounded by his two children and his cherished Nadine. Memories of his lost family insidiously assaulted his mind no matter how hard he tried to keep them at bay. He fought back the tears that instantly welled up in his eyes every time he thought of his family; he also fought back the rage that always followed the reality of their loss. The rustling of chairs and sidebar conversations conducted by the senior officers sitting around the conference table representing various divisions of his multinational corporate empire snapped Charles back to the monthly 9 AM Friday corporate meeting. However, the murderous rage he felt watching helplessly as his family was murdered was renewed as Charles looked around the corporate table at the faces of men ready to betray him.

The Sinclairs often secretly floated the debts of many Nations but went through extreme measures to hide their activities and actual wealth. However, everyone knew Charles's wealth was immense, and he was a powerful man born into wealth. No one could ever imagine the truth hidden beneath the beautiful clothing and well-manicured man sitting at the head of the table. Charles Sinclair, a first-generation African born in America, his 6-foot-one lean athletic physique adorned in a Navy-blue cashmere-silk hand-tailored suit, custom-made gleaming black crocodile shoes, and a crisp white Egyptian cotton shirt helped highlight his ebony skin. His long black hair fashioned in thin micro braids pulled back and tied in a ponytail that hung to the center of his back, held in place by a solid gold cylinder at the back of his head.

Charles sat gently stroking his finely manicured goatee with his impeccably manicured hands, contemplating the meeting and the many agendas he was being confronted with. Unbeknownst to everyone sitting around the conference table, Charles could read their thoughts and emotions better than their expressions.

Mr. Charles Sinclair had learned long ago how to ignore people's personal and intimate thoughts to avoid going insane. He sat at the head of the large mahogany table surrounded by 12 of his most senior executives in the ostentatious room of precious wood from the floor to the ceiling. One chair to the right of Charles was left curiously empty, causing curious looks when the meeting participants entered the room.

Charles found it ironic that one of the new rising stars in his multinational corporation was foolish enough to investigate his family and friends trying to find a weakness to exploit; he was equally amused to learn how many of the men sitting around the table were foolish enough to join him. Charles needed an outlet for the quiet rage brewing in his soul, and all of the pathetic souls who were imprudent to join the conspiracy against him unknowingly volunteered to be the channel. The average age of the participants in this meeting was approximately 55. Each senior officer was an expert in shipping, banking, construction, investments, politics, media, technology, and many other areas of business and government. One personality stood out among the 12 senior executives: a 29-year-old bold, brilliant, and full of haughtiness Derek Fishman, a 6 foot 2 inch, athletically built, blond-haired, white man with crystal blue eyes. Derek came from the wrong side of the tracks but used his good looks, athletic abilities, and intellect to reach the top.

Mr. Derek Fishman fascinated Charles; Fishman was a prodigy throughout his life and excelled in everything that he did; his only failing was that he was born with psychopathic tendencies. Charles was reminded of his father's admonishment that non-slaves should be treated equally and allowed to pursue their dreams. Sinclair was also warned that given the opportunity, the very people you help would eventually use that kindness to destroy you. While some of Charles's life experiences have proven his father wrong, sitting in front of him was a prime example of his father's advice ring true.

Mr. Derek Fishman believed he was plotting with a rival Corporation to purchase offshore land under the guise of an environmental research group. Unbeknownst to Mr. Fishman, the Sinclair Corporation had secretly purchased the rival corporation and provided the bank loans the conspirators needed to buy into the environmental research group. With control of the area, the research group would acquire permission to drill for oil under a new business structure. The initial news of Fishman's betrayal enraged Charles. Charles had given Derek straight out of college despite his lack of pedigree and the warnings of the corporate recruiters. The recruiters diagnosed Derek's narcissistic and psychopathic tendencies from a detailed background check and the corporation's routine psychological evaluations for senior position candidates. Charles gave Derek an opportunity despite the warnings because many business executives he met shared those characteristics. Charles hoped the opportunities he presented the young man would outweigh Derek's desire to obtain power at any cost.

Hostile takeovers and backstabbing were nothing new to Charles, but Mr. Fisher made a deadly mistake. Derek was dealing with powers he could never understand. Charles was immediately notified of Derek's attempts to investigate his background, seeking an upper hand in negotiations. Charles provided Derek Fisher with resources to lead him in the wrong direction and into a trap. Mr. Fisher began investigating Charles's family and lineage, hoping to find something to use against him. Fisher discovered that Charles was having an intimate relationship with a female leader of one of the major international drug cartels. Fisher gambled that the news of Charles's dealing with such a dark person as Ms. Elaine

Singleton would be something Charles would not want to be publicized. If necessary, Fisher had no problem exposing Charles's love affair with Elaine to ruining his prissy, clean reputation.

Additionally, regardless of what Charles agreed to, Derek had already threatened Elaine by exposing Charles and erroneously linking him to her operations if he was not paid five million dollars, which he expected to receive that afternoon when he met her for lunch. Derek managed to convince the other senior officers to go along with this hostile takeover plan; each one stood to make millions on the deal and to become part owner of the new offshore drilling company. The officers involved in the plot used their Sinclair Corporation stocks as collateral to obtain the bank loans to obtain the funds to buy shares in the drilling company. They were promised executive positions when the company started drilling. However, no one knew of Derek Fisher's blackmail schemes or his investigation into Charles's family. The irony of this was that many of the stocks used to obtain loans were given to them by Charles as gifts for their services. The other stocks they used were allowed to be purchased in an exclusive offer.

Charles opened the meeting with customary greetings and inquiries into the well-being of his officer's families and friends. He then opened the floor to allow his officers to provide relevant updates on the progress of each of their corporations. Charles knew the status of each of their projects. Still, he had learned it was best to allow his employees to present their successes and failures so that they could feel a sense of ownership in their expertise. The meeting continued, but Charles never showed any indication of his knowledge of Mr. Derek Fishman, the plot, or the attempted blackmail Derek intended to threaten Elaine during the upcoming afternoon meeting he was scheduled to have with her. Charles could read the remorse and guilt in the minds of the three senior executives drawn into Fishman's plot. Still, he had to wait until all the facts were on the table before determining their fate. Charles could not help but notice the discomfort of the senior executives who were part of the plot. Senior managers had witnessed Charles's uncanny ability to be one step ahead of his opposition in the past. Still, they were convinced Derek Fishman's plan was foolproof. Regardless of their foolish participation, none of the men sitting around the table were members or agents of the Serapian Order who managed to infiltrate every vital government, religious, and business organization. It would be tough to replace any of them without opening the possibility of recruiting a Serapian who masterly hid themselves in secret societies, religious organizations, and government globally. The constant threat of the Serapians was the catalyst for the Sinclair Corporation's stringent recruiting practices.

Finally, the moment came that he was waiting for, and Mr. Fishman could hardly contain himself in his eagerness to strike a blow to the ego of the elusive Mr. Charles Sinclair.

"Mr. Fishman, I understand you have a matter to bring before the group," Charles announced, leaving Derek Fishman's presentation for the last quarterly business report.

Derek Fishman sat quietly, unable to contain his eagerness to reveal his masterly crafted takeover of the Alaskan offshore property currently protected by the Sinclair estate that promised to make him millions of dollars. Derek knew Charles was a sucker for a good cause, and his new business partner, Mr. George Spanton, assured him that his involvement in acquiring a controlling interest in the philanthropic environmental organization was well hidden. Derek could not wait until he met with Stephany Blair after the meeting to give her the good news and prove that he was more than a Sinclair lapdog. Stephany consumed his mind and actions from the moment he met her. Derek's physique, natural charm, and good looks made attracting women easy. However, Stephany was different. Derek was never so captivated by a woman as he was with Stephany when she looked into his eyes from across the crowded bar he attended one night after work. It was like magic; one moment, she was on one side of the bar, and the next second, she was sitting by his side. He could not recall what he said to Stephany to seduce her to follow him home and eagerly surrender her body to him. He could not remember much at all beyond her biting him while they had passionate sex. However, from that moment, he needed to make more of himself and, with her urging, to take advantage of his position in the Sinclair corporation to seek his riches. It was Stephany that revealed Charles's secret liaison with Ms. Elaine Singleton, the leader of a drug cartel. Stephany had a fantastic insight into Charle Sinclair. He and Stephany devised a backup plan should Charles dare to challenge his business takeover. She provided information to Derek on Elaine Singleton's operations and the damage it would cause Charles if allegations of his involvement in Elaine's illegal business affairs got publicized, giving him the confidence to seek all he deserved. Stephany suggested they confront Elaine Singleton with their knowledge of her relationship with Charles and threaten them with exposure should Derek's takeover plan fail. What Stephany did not know is that Derek had every intention to blackmail Charles and Elaine regardless of the outcome of his meeting with Charles. Derek had already put in motion his blackmail scheme by arranging a meeting with Elaine later that afternoon.

"Thank you, Charles; I will get straight to the point." His casual use of Charles Sinclair's first name shocked everyone around the table.

The senior executives sitting around the table made an audible, involuntary gasp, shocked by Derek's boldness in calling Mr. Sinclair by his first name.

Derek stood up to use his six-foot-two-inch frame to tower over the other meeting participants and to demonstrate his contempt for Charles.

"As I have reported several times, our offshore drilling operations have attracted many interested buyers willing to pay top dollar to acquire the drilling rights and significantly improve our financial standings." Derek started placing one hand in his pants pocket as he pretended to review the papers before him.

"Mr. Fishman, we have gone over that before; I am not interested in selling nor developing any drilling operations that may endanger the fragile ecosystem in that area," Charles stated, baiting Derek Fishman to make his announcement.

"Charles, that decision is no longer yours to make," Derek Fishman boldly said, causing the senior executives who were not in on the plot to gasp again, not only because of Derek Fishman's bold statement but also because of the continued reckless use of Mr. Charles Sinclair's first name.

"I beg your pardon," Charles said, pretending not to know what Derek Fishman was thinking and Derek's next move.

"As I said before, there is lots of money to be made for our shareholders, which seems no longer essential to you," Derek Fishman boldly stated.

"I have taken the liberty, I mean we, to acquire the necessary financial support to gain controlling interest in the environmental research group to whom you solely own the offshore land. We are leaving to create a new company to start drilling." Derek Fishman smugly concluded.

"Is that right, Derek, and what do you mean, we?" Charles asked, pretending not to know who Fishman's co-conspirators were.

"Mr. Sinclair, we assure you that you have our full respect, and we thank you for your generous support over the years, but we had no choice but to seek outside assistance to protect our interest." One of the more senior executives volunteered to try to soften the blow of their betrayal.

"What's done is done; we need to know if you will try to block our efforts to obtain the necessary drilling permits with the EPA." Derek Fishman boldly declared.

Charles sat back in his chair, not responding while listening to Fishman's inner thoughts and marveling at the malice and resentment Fishman harbored for him. Charles could never understand how such hate and loathing could be generated without any actions on his part other than being a man in a position other people envied. Then again, he knew when hiring Fishman that he was ruthless and had unbridled ambition, but Charles had not realized how reckless he could be until now. Yet, something was motivating Derek beyond blind ambition, hatred, and greed hidden from Charles in the inner thoughts of Derek's mind. It was as if a curtain of darkness Charles could not penetrate as he tried to read Derek's inner thoughts. Charles had learned long ago not to underestimate his opponents and to ensure he had the advantage when dealing with people like Derek.

The other senior executive plotters began to speak, trying to explain their reasons for siding with Fishman's efforts to create an independent oil corporation. Charles held up his hand, silencing the room.

"Tell me, Derek, what makes you think I would have to do anything to block your drilling efforts?" Charles asked. The question surprised Derek and everyone in the room.

"Look, we know of your influence with the United States Government and especially the EPA, but you no longer have a controlling interest in the oil corporation," Fishman said.

"I don't think it would be in your best interest to fight us on this," Derek continued with a smirk while looking intently into Charles' eyes to savor the shock and outrage he expected to see.

"Young man, you are very sadly mistaken; you should have looked closer at whom you are doing business. Thanks to you, I now own all the corporation shares you used as collateral, and the money you borrowed came from me." Charles said, enjoying the shock and terror that filled the room, especially the bewildered look on Derek's face.

"Bull Shit!" Derek replied, not wanting to accept Charles' pronouncement.

Charles pressed the intercom button on the phone near him.

"Yes, Mr. Sinclair," a female voice greeted him on the speakerphone.

"Gladys, would you please send in Mr. Stanton?" Charles requested.

The mention of Mr. Stanton's name sent a cold chill down Derek Fisher's spine.

When Mr. George Spanton walked into the room and sat in the empty chair, Fisher knew instantly he'd been duped.

Fearing Charles Sinclair's' retribution, rival corporations alerted Charles of Derek Fisherman's overtures to secure the lands protected by the Sinclair estate. Charles immediately had his chief of security hire help to investigate the threat to his corporation. Mr. George Stanton first approached Derek and floated the idea of a hostile oil corporation takeover. Mr. Stanton helped him convince the other board members to accompany them. Stanton was the one who suggested buying the land under false circumstances once the fake environmental organization had been established. Spanton also found the bank to accept the Sinclair stocks as collateral to finance the hostile takeover of the ecological research investment group.

Derek sat down, trying to wrap his head around what had just happened. Derek was now broken and in debt to Charles Sinclair for over five million dollars. A sudden smile came over

Derek's face as he remembered his upcoming lunch date with Elaine and the two million dollars she would have waiting for him. Stephany was right to advise him to have a backup plan. Derek was more determined than ever to extort Charles Sinclair and Elaine Singleton. Derek knew that would only be the beginning of the money he had intended to squeeze out of her and Charles.

"I don't think introductions are needed for you, Mr. Fisher, but for the rest of you, this is Mr. George Stanton, the new CEO of our offshore oil drilling corporation. Mr. Stanton stood to address the room.

"I look forward to working with each of you. I want to especially thank Mr. Derek Fisher for upholding the Sinclair family's environmental commitment. I am sure you will be pleased to know that you will serve as my administrative assistant.

I look forward to you reporting to work in the morning; I like my coffee black". Mr. Stanton said before taking his seat.

Derek stood up red-faced in rage, slamming both hands on the table, causing his chair to fall backward onto the floor.

"THIS IS NOT OVER YET!" Deck shouted at Charles before storming out of the room.

"Please enjoy your lunch, and don't worry, your office is already cleaned out," Charles said coolly as Derek left the room humiliated.

"Well, gentlemen, if there is nothing more anyone would like to bring to our attention, I think we are done for today," Charles said lite heartily, allowing all of Fisher's co-conspirators to ponder their futures. Charles knew that each officer who co-signed the loan to purchase shares in his secret corporation was now not only his employees but also millions of dollars in debt to him.

The officers stood and quickly left the room before Charles could change his mind. Charles shook Mr. Stanton's hand and thanked him before leaving the meeting room to return to his office suite. As he walked to his office, he could not help but chuckle at the prospects of what awaited Derek with his luncheon with Elaine.

"Lunch with Elaine, what a stupid son of a bitch." Charles thought to himself, laughing and shaking his head, baffling everyone at his sudden outbreak.

CHAPTER 2

Elaine Singleton

Later that evening, instead of his usual helicopter flight, Charles drove home with Elaine in his new Bentley Continental Super Sports Convertible after another enjoyable night at one of his restaurants called the Oasis. Neither Charles's personal security detail, directed by his adopted son's nephew, Mr. Samuel Scales, nor Elaine Singleton's head bodyguard, Mr. Drake Ellisworth, welcomed the news that Charles would not be under their direct observation but understood Charles and Elaine's need for private moments. The elegantly dressed couple enjoyed the cool mid-summer breeze of the air rushing past the open cockpit. Of all the holdings in the Sinclair business portfolio, neither allowed Charles Sinclair to connect with people like the Oasis restaurant nor gave him more joy than sailing on his modernized sailing ship, the La Morena. Each of them gained more pleasure and importance for Charles when Elaine entered his life.

Charles glanced over to his lovely passenger and felt thankful for the companionship she had provided him for the last ten years. He dared to believe that he'd found someone to end his lonely existence after so many years of loneliness after the death of his family.

It had been a busy week, culminating with the meeting to discuss new transatlantic shipping opportunities between China and Africa. This was followed by discussions with the officers of his brokerage firm, updates from the land and architectural development corporation, and the ex-Mr. Derek Fisher's betrayal. All of that was behind him now that he had enjoyed dinner and relaxation at his restaurant with his companion, Elaine Singleton. The transition from the eternally busy streets of Harlem, New York, to the Hudson River Parkway on the way to the suburbs north of the Bronx County line was like leaving one World of mass chaos to ever-growing streams of tranquility. The stars became brighter as they left the noise and artificial lights of the city behind. Charles always enjoyed the quiet serenity of the countryside, and even more so when someone shared the sound of the wind dancing through the trees and the smell of flowers in the air. Elaine lifted her head from her laid-back position. She looked back at Charles with worshiping eyes that made him uncomfortable. He had seen that look many times before, and each time it ended, a piece of his heart was ripped away, but maybe this time, it will last. Perhaps, this time, Dechontee will let him live in peace.

"I am happy to hear your precious offshore environment is still safe from drilling. I enjoyed my lunch with that delicious young man," Elaine said, looking over at Charles without lifting her head from the seat headrest, smiling with satisfaction.

"Did you kill him?" Charles asked.

"No, but right now, he wishes I had," Elaine spoke.

"What do you mean?" Charles asked half, not wanting to know.

"I have put him in time out in a box buried in a steel box in Central Park," Elaine jokingly spoke.

"Oh, that is fucked up," Charles laughingly said.

"I plan to dig him up one day when I need someone to abuse," Elaine joked.

"So he is now infected and will die slowly until you dig him up?" Charles asked.

"Yep, but there was something about him that I had never experienced before," Stephany spoke.

"Something like what?" Charles asked.

"It was as if he was already infected, but that's impossible, right?" Elaine rhetorically stated.

Charles did not immediately respond, but he thought it might explain the hidden motives he could not read in Derek. However, if someone with Charles's condition infected Derek, it would have to be Dechontee or another person she sent.

"No, I found him strange as well. Be careful with that one; he has a snake's instincts and a jackal's ruthlessness." Charles said, trying to dismiss Elaine's concern.

"Don't worry about that fool; he will not bother you again," Elaine said.

"Yeah, but now I got to deal with those fools who sided with Fishman against me," Charles replied.

Charles was always amazed by Elaine's beauty, but her love and adoration for him filled him with dread and sorrow. Elaine's Chinese and African heritage gave her exotic beauty. Her mother was a kidnapped victim forced into sexual trafficking. Elaine's mother went insane because of the abuse she suffered. Her father was one of the many men her mother endured to survive. In Elaine's mother's insanity, she abused Elaine and was powerless to protect Elaine from the same sexual exploitation she suffered. When the sexual traffickers threatened to sell Elaine, her mother finally snapped and killed two of her handlers while trying to escape captivity. Unfortunately, Elaine's mother was mortally wounded while escaping her traffickers and died soon after delivering her to an orphanage. Elaine spent the rest of her life in the foster care system, where the abuse continued until her emancipation.

"Have you given my offer more consideration?" Charles asked.

"Yes, but I have many people to think about other than myself," Elaine replied.

"I realize that," Charles replied.

"Just remember, you do not have to be involved in that business anymore, and besides, you have many people in your organization who could take it over without much conflict." He continued.

Charles and Elaine were complete opposites in many ways; however, he grew to admire Elaine over the years before their union as a frequent customer at his favorite restaurant, the Oasis. Charles was a respected businessman and renowned philanthropist. In contrast, Elaine was the leader of one of the most successful drug cartels in North America. He watched as she ran her organization ruthlessly, never tolerating the slightest disloyalty. Charles could recall how a rival group outside of Philadelphia tried to muscle in on Elaine's territory. One night, she showed up at his restaurant earlier than usual with the leader of the Philadelphia cartel and brought out the bar. Charles thought she was having her last night of fun before going to war with the rival drug cartel, or maybe she was trying to broker a truce with the powerful, thuggish man to avoid conflict; however, the next day's news headlines told the real story. The bodies of at least twenty men were found decomposing in twenty drums of acid. All the bodies were dismembered, and the police could only assume there were twenty bodies because there were twenty sets of clothes and wallets full of money left by each vat of acid as a message and warning. The wallets had the Philadelphia addresses of known high-ranking mobsters from different syndicates. The next night, Elaine arrived alone at her usual time at the club, looking as sexy as ever. She flashed that innocent, seductive smile in Charles's direction, and at once, he knew the ringleader of the Philadelphia drug ring had suffered an agonizing death.

Making love with her was like fucking a tiger. Her raw, no-holds-barred sex tourneys were even shocking to him at times. There was nothing she was not willing to do, and at times, he did not understand what she got out of the sex acts she demanded him to perform with her. One of her greatest delights was to seduce her enemies into going to bed with her. Once she had drained every ounce of sperm out of their bodies, she would sedate them. When the man awakened, he found himself tied necked to a chair with his penis surgically removed. The victim was then tortured to death in front of her as she played with his severed penis.

Charles figured that it took a psychopath with an exceptionally high IQ like Elaine to know that there was something not right about the clean veneer of Charles Sinclair but befriended him anyway. She even provided him with people she wanted to remove quietly, and he was happy to oblige. He guessed that it took a monster to love a monster. While Charles was never part of the financial criminal underworld, he had more reasons than anyone to maintain a well-paid network of police and underworld informants. It was through his information network that a plot against Elaine's life came to Charles's attention. He tried to warn her, but the attack was over before he could reach her. When he found her sexually abused, tortured body lying naked on the floor of an abandoned warehouse in a pool of her blood, urine, and feces, she was near death. It was at that moment he realized that she was more than a mere amusement in his life, and if she died, he would be alone again. He could not let her die, but saving her would mean exposing her to the disease he was afflicted with for all these lonely years. He was not going to trick her into this life as he was. He decided to tell her the truth and let her decide.

As he knelt in the pool of blood and filth, he pulled her into his arms and wiped her blood-caked hair from her mutilated face.

"Hey lady, you know I can't let you die, right?" Charles said in a comforting voice.

Elaine tried to open her softball-sized swollen eyes and painfully smiled.

Charles said," If I am going to save you, I have to make you like me, do you understand?" The slits in her swollen eyes widened, and he could feel her body tense in his arms, and he tried to pull away. A tear formed and mixed with the blood in her eyes, causing a crimson river to flow down her cheek.

Mustering up the strength to fight against the pain, she shook her head no.

Choking back the blood filling her lungs, she mumbled and shook her head.

"No, no, no." Elaine managed to whisper painfully.

Charles pulled her close to him.

"Babe, I will be with you always and take care of you." Charles implored.

"Don't you want to make those mother fuckers to pay for what they did to you?" Charles felt sick to his stomach, knowing he had used her need for revenge for his selfish need for companionship. He knew that was the same line of bull shit Dechontee used to get him to accept this fucking disease.

Elaine stared at him through the swollen slits in her eyes.

"You promise?" She asked.

"Yes, Babe, I promise?" Charles replied, smiling.

"You promise to help me kill those mother fuckers who did this to me?" Elaine said she was finding new strength in her hatred for her attackers.

"Yes, Babe, they are dead, but first, we have got to do this. Are you ready? Charles said.

"Yes," Elaine replied.

It took Elaine months to recover, but when she did, the men responsible for her attack and their families were subjected to horrors that even made Charles sick to his stomach; he could not have dreamt of committing the nightmarish acts of torture Elaine inflicted on those responsible for her attack. Her attackers chose their fate and condemned their innocent family members when they decided to cross a woman like Elaine, and may God have mercy on their souls, Charles thought to himself. Ever since that night ten years ago, they had been inseparable.

The revulsion of those days of revenge had long been forgotten in the memories of their sailing around the world in the La Morena and the countless days and nights of no-hold-barred animal sex they shared. The country roads became less populated with other cars as their anticipation to find a way to exceed their last sexual encounter increased. Charles looked over at Elaine, and she simultaneously turned to look at him with that deadly, seductive smile that made him instantly stiffen. They both laughed, knowing how easy it was to read each other's minds.

"I just want you to know you can leave that business whenever you are ready." He said in a comforting voice.

"I know that, Baby, but I just want to ensure my people will be alright before I leave," she said as the stars twinkled in her dark emerald green eyes.

As Charles turned his attention back to the road ahead, he noticed a distant set of headlights in his rearview mirror that disappeared as he continued down the tree-lined, twisting country road. The roads twisted left and right and became narrower as he approached his Westchester estate. Charles rechecked his rearview mirror and saw nothing, then eased back into his seat, listening to a live recording by Sananda Maitreya in the fresh summer air. In the rearview mirror, a sudden flash of headlight turning around the last bend on the road snapped Charles out of his peaceful trance. Judging by the rapidly increasing brightness of the lights behind him, Charles knew the trailing car was catching up with him quickly.

"Oh my God, this can't be happening. Why is she fucking with me now?" Charles thought to himself.

If Dechontee was behind Derek's actions, Charles knew she could be petty and vengeful, that her plan did not work, and that she would try to hurt Elaine to punish him.

Charles had few enemies, but the ones he did have were ruthless and beyond the law, i.e., the Serapians and the woman responsible for his nightmarish condition, Dechontee. Charles knew that if Dechontee wanted to find him, it would be useless to run from her. He only hoped she would not find Elaine a threat and let them live peacefully. If it was another kidnapping attempt by the organ-snatching Serapians, Charles knew he and Elaine were more than a match for them. Charles maintained his rate of speed to allow the trail car to catch up and to keep the element of surprise.

"What's the matter, Babe?" Elaine asked as she sensed Charles's mood change.

"Just relax and do not say or do anything," Charles said in a comforting voice, trying to hide the sheer terror racing through his soul.

"Are we being followed?" She asked.

"I think so, but I am not sure. It could be nothing," he said, trying to reassure her.

The pursuing Mercedes Benzes followed dangerously close behind Charles's Bentley for several miles along the isolated country road. Charles intentionally drove in the opposite direction of his estate, hoping this wouldn't be another intimidation session with Dechontee and she would leave, never knowing where he lived. The Mercedes, with nearly black-tinted windows, pulled alongside Charles's Bentley, and the darkened windows rolled up.

"Why are you so nervous? Babe, you are making me scared". Elaine said.

Elaine had never seen Charles show fear in the ten years she had known him. Others trembled in fear once they saw Charles's hidden nature.

"Don't worry, Babe; it's just that bitch I was telling you about."

Charles's words, while filled with bravado, were not reassuring. Elaine, while still new to the life she now shared with Charles, was aware of how dangerous Dechontee was and how powerless Charles was in protecting her if things got ugly.

The Mercedes rushed forward and cut in front of the Bentley, forcing the car off the road into the embankment.

"This is some bullshit," Charles thought to himself, making sure he controlled his anger not to give Dechontee any reason to escalate the violence.

All the doors of the Mercedes opened, and four well-dressed armed men rushed out and surrounded the Bentley. Two of the two gunmen had handguns, but the others had AK-47s.

"Damn, we are being carjacked," Charles stated while laughing out loud.

Elaine also smiled, relieved that they only had to fear the loss of the car and not their lives. One of the passengers rushed over to the driver's side of the vehicle, holding his handgun in the typical Hollywood gangster style to Charles's head.

"You know what the fuck this is, so get the fuck out of the car!"

The man shouted in his most intimidating voice.

Charles could not help but smile as he unbuckled his seat belt and prepared to exit the Bentley.

"Damn, that bitch is bad"! One of the two Hispanic carjackers proclaimed as Elaine stepped out of the passenger seat, exposing her long, sexy legs.

"Hey, stupid mother fucker don't you know better than to bring some badass bitch out into the woods in the middle of the night all by yourself with mean ass wolves out here?" One of the carjackers said, trying to add insult to injury.

"Look, just take the car and leave," Charles said disinterestedly.

"Mother fucker, you better be lucky I don't take your car, your bitch, and your mother fucking life!!!" The white carjacker said, holding an AK-47 assault rifle.

There was something familiar about the theatrically dangerous man who looked out of place trying to play ghetto thug that Charles just could not put his finger on.

Charles looked closer and recognized the man as one of his restaurant customers. He remembered the man being escorted out of the restaurant for being too aggressive with one of his servers. He then realized this might not just be a simple carjacking but something much worse.

Once again, Charles sensed a veil of darkness similar to Derek's as he tried to read the man's intentions. Another assailant brandishing an AK-47, which Charles assumed was a Jamaican because of his long dreadlocks, reached out and grabbed Elaine by the arm. Before Charles could stop her, she spun and bit a gaping hole in the assailant's neck.

The assailant grasped his neck in a useless attempt to stop the blood rhythmically gushing into the night's air. Elaine, now in killer mode, grabbed the terrified carjacker by his dreadlocks, yanking his head backward and exposing his throat. Her wide gaping mouth exposed razor-sharp elongated canines swimming in the victim's blood. She savagely bit down into the man's exposed throat, causing his body to convulse uncontrollably as blood and urine ran down his leg. The dying man's friends stood in shock at the horror they were witnessing. Their minds tried to find a context to understand what they were seeing. This beautiful sexy goddess, who they were hired to rape in front of this punk ass nigger, bit the shit out of their boy. Now she is giving him some mean ass kiss on his throat that he is not enjoying.

Elaine slowly lifted her head from the throat of the dead man and smiled seductively at the next closest carjacker. She allowed the dead man to fall to the ground like a rag doll. She seemingly began to walk slowly towards her next victim. Still, her movement was so fast that the attackers' minds refused to believe what their eyes were witnessing. As if in slow motion, Elaine snaked towards her next target. Elaine licked the dead man's blood from her fingers, allowing her exceptionally long tongue to slowly wrap around each finger before sticking them into her mouth. Her eyes rolled back into her head as she enjoyed the warm and salty taste of the dead man's blood on her perfectly manicured hands and blood-red lips. As she approached the next victim, he was dumbfounded, confused, aroused, but most of all, terrified. His mind screamed to run, but his body was paralyzed and wanted to be in her death embrace. He turned to take the first step to run, then turned back to look at the horrible, beautiful, sexy beast seeking to hold him in her arms. His ears ached from the sound of his beating heart as his mind screamed to run but could not move. He was paralyzed with fear and lust as he could now smell the sweet perfume of her body and the stench of blood on her breath as she held him locked in her arms. Against his will, he leaned his head to the side and awaited her sweet kiss. He felt her hands crushing his arms into his ribs and pulling him to her as his gun fell from his hand. A sharp pain, then the warm, soothing sensation of high-grade heroin, rushed through his body as his body went limp and all faded to black. To Elaine's two victims, it seemed their experience with her lasted several minutes. Still, it was only seconds after the first man touched her.

The carjacker closest to Charles turned his head in disbelief at the speed of Elaine's attack. He instinctively started shooting, hitting Charles in the center of the chest and knocking him backward. Charles fell back against the Bentley and quickly rebounded and, with even faster speed than Elaine displayed, rushed forward and decapitated the man who shot him. The final assailant began to shoot his AK-47 wildly, hitting Elaine and knocking her back onto the ground. Charles rushed to get Elaine out of the line of fire, but in the process, he was shot eight more times, knocking him into Elaine's arms. Elaine could feel the gushing blood pouring from the multiple gunshot wounds in Charles's body.

The surviving carjacker took advantage of Elaine's concern for Charles to get away in the waiting Mercedes, leaving the bodies of his dead friends behind.

"Hold on, Babe; you're going to be alright," Elaine said as if she had some magical healing powers. In her heart, she knew Charles was in trouble. They were no fairy tale creatures of the night who were impervious to bullets and hated crucifixes. They could die if they lost enough blood or suffered too much trauma. The one significant advantage of the disease was that their circulatory system was transformed genetically to produce embryonic stem cells instead of blood cells. It gave them the ability to heal from impossible injuries if they got an immediate transfusion from another person afflicted with the same illness. The injuries that Charles had suffered would require a transfusion, and the blood donor would not survive.

Charles lay dying in Elaine's arms on the lonely, deserted country road. He could not help but smile thinking back on those years so long ago when Dechontee found him dying in a similarly deserted place in the deep South and offered him a chance at life that, if he fully understood the implications of the gift, he would have turned down. Long had he struggled with his love for God and his hunger for blood. He often was tempted to commit suicide to end his damnation, but his faith and hope for redemption forbid the taking of one's life. Here now was his chance to end his suffering and hope that God would remember who he was before being tricked into becoming the monster that he was now.

Charles felt his life slowly slipping away, but he was brought back to consciousness by Elaine's sobbing and shaking him.

"Babe, please don't leave me like this!" Elaine begged.

"Come back to me, Babe; you know I can't live like this without you," she continued. Charles, you promised me that you would never leave me," Elaine stated, crying uncontrollably.

Charles looked up at her and remembered why he chose her as a mate. Yes, she was a natural-born killer, but her capacity for sincere love and vulnerability is what drew him to her. Elaine could be ruthless, incredibly sexy, and innocent all at the same time. Yes, she was a psychopath, but Charles knew she was a creation of the environment in which she was born. She was also generous and agreed to share his affliction without judgment or remorse. He did promise to stay with her as a teacher, mentor, and lover as a pre-condition to spending the unknown years with him in search of a cure for his affliction. Now, that promise was slipping away, and the only way he could keep it was to end the life of one of the most unique souls he ever had the privilege of knowing.

"Charles, Charles, you got to take my blood, or you are going to die!!" Elaine yelled.

"My sweet lady, it would kill you, and you know I could not do that." Charles managed to whisper.

"Without you, I am already dead; I can't live like this without you, Babe; please don't do this to me." Elaine implored.

"Charles, you promised me," Elaine stated in a soft, desperate voice.

To honor your commitments was one of his father's chief admonishments. "When you give your word, it enters the ear of God and will be used to judge the worthiness of your soul at the end of days." His father drilled into him so many years ago.

Besides, he knew in his heart that Elaine had long regretted her decision to join him on his lonely, slow ride to hell but stayed loyal to him, suffering in silence. Charles looked up into Elaine's tear-filled eyes and smiled.

"Ok, Babe."

Elaine gave him that innocent smile that he loved so much. Cradling him in her arms like a mother preparing to breastfeed her infant, she exposed her neck. Charles reached around to pull himself close, burying his face between her breasts, and breathed deeply to savor as much of her scent as he could one last time. Shameless tears filled his eyes and began to roll down his cheeks. Elaine kissed his forehead cheeks and then gave him a long, soft kiss on his lips. She then leaned forward to whisper into his ear.

"Thank you; everything is going to be alright, Babe. Don't worry; God will allow us to see each other again." She said.

Elaine then kissed him one last time before reaching up with her free hand and slit open her jugular vein and forcing her exposed neck into his mouth.

CHAPTER 3

Paul Blacksmith

Meanwhile, Paul, the surviving member of the ambush on Charles and Elaine, pushed the Mercedes hard to escape the nightmare he had just witnessed. He frantically dialed a number from his cell phone repeatedly, never getting an answer.

"What the fuck was that? What the fuck!? He yelled out to his non-existent passenger.

He wiped the sweat-soaked hair from his eyes as he drove more than 120 miles per hour, cutting off anyone who got in his way. Paul took another drag of the marijuana-filled tobacco leaf that looked like a fat cigar, trying to burn out the nightmare images from his mind, not caring if anyone saw him or if the police were anywhere around. He would welcome their company now.

"What the fuck was that!? What the fuck was that"!!? Paul kept screaming as he tried to understand what he had just witnessed.

He took another long drag from his marijuana cigar. He chased it down by guzzling down Hennessey from the bottle he and his now-dead friends were drinking before the attack. What in the hell was he going to do? He thought to himself.

"I can't go to the cops and tell them that I and my boys were hired to rape, carjack and beat up some loudmouth punk bitch, and now they are dead," He thought to himself.

"That fucking bitch took out Louie's throat!" Paul yelled to himself, still in disbelief.

He finally reached the city's safety as he drove recklessly at a high speed. The tightly packed storefronts, tenement buildings, and the city's bright lights seemed to swirl past him in a kaleidoscope of lights, shapes, and colors as he raced the Mercedes through the narrow city streets. As he lifted the bottle to his lips for another long guzzle of Hennessey, a pedestrian walked out in the middle of the road, forcing him to swerve to avoid hitting the pedestrian at the very last second but slamming into several parked cars, but he dared not stop. He had to get home and secure himself behind the safety of his apartment door. After an eternity, Paul finally reached his West 34 Street tenement building and carelessly parked in front of a fire hydrant. Exiting the car, he grabbed the AK-47 and placed it under his jacket along with the remainder of the Hennessey bottle.

Paul Blacksmith always presented himself as a man of mystery to his working-class neighbors on the West side of 34th Street. He would use almost a jar of hair moose to get that slicked-back gangster look. Paul's designer knock-off clothing fooled only himself, but Paul would strut about as if he were at the center of everything happening in the streets. Chain smoking and always seemingly on edge was the fake gangster image he carefully crafted for all to see. The fact was that Blacksmith and his now-dead friends were college dropouts and sons of upper-middle-class parents from Rochester, New York. The only connection Paul had with the principal street players of New York City was as a low-level drug mule carrying drugs onto college campuses to destroy the lives of other rebellious middle-class college students. Usually, Paul came home with his shifty-looking friends, the African American who wore dreads, and his two Puerto Rican friends to play loud music, smoke marijuana, and entertain an assortment of women all night. That night, Paul came home alone, drenched in sweat. His usually groomed hair was flopping about his face like a dirty mop; he rushed past his strait-laced neighbors, trying not to make eye contact. Paul didn't even wait for the elevator to take him to his third-floor apartment but ran up the stairs as quickly as possible. After reaching his apartment, he fumbled for his keys and was forced to use two hands to insert the key into the lock because his hands were shaking out of control. Entering his apartment, he ensured all the windows were closed and locked and the curtains were drawn. Paul went into the kitchen and drank an unfinished beer before going to his bedroom, carrying the AK-47 in one hand and the bottle of Hennessey in the other. He sat on the edge of his queen-sized bed covered in a leopard print sheet and held his head in his hands.

"I should have never left home," He thought as he lifted the bottle of Hennessey and emptied its contents into his mouth.

CHAPTER 4
Damage Control

Back at the crime scene, after calling his estate for help, Charles struggled to gather enough strength to move the three dead men onto the road and Elaine's dead body back into the Bentley. Fighting against the urge to blackout, Charles then fired several rounds into Elaine's' neck and upper body to hide the exact cause of death. Charles also fired several rounds from the AK-47 into the front and side of the Bentley to make it appear that he and Elaine were shot trying to escape from the carjackers. He positioned the three men in the middle of the road sitting, then accelerated the Bentley as fast as he could before running them over and running his car into a nearby tree at full speed. Charles gathered Elaine into his arms while struggling to stay conscious, awaiting medical help to arrive. The blood transfusion Elaine had given him was still not entirely out of danger of dying of his wounds. Charles trusted his adopted son and personal doctor, Stanley Johnson, to save his life and hopefully get there in time to save Elaine. Charles faded into unconsciousness.

Clair Sinclair, a sixty-five-year-old African woman in charge of the Sinclair Estate, was not accustomed to receiving 3:00 AM phone calls, especially not from Charles, and this call would be one she would never forget. Charles had called to inform her that he had been shot and that Ms. Elaine Singleton was near death.

Clair was one of Charles's adopted family members who lived with him on his estate. Charles watched Clair from an infant to adulthood, and she became one of the few people he could trust with his secrets. Long lost was the distinction between Charles Sinclair and the descendants of the formerly enslaved people Charles helped escape to the North during the Civil War. On the Sinclair estate, everyone was family and entirely loyal to Charles as a family member and benevolent benefactor. Charles requested that she call the police and contact his adopted son and personal physician, Doctor Stanly Johnson, immediately and to have him prepare for surgery.

Charles went out of his way to avoid public attention, and the people in his innermost circle fanatically aided him to keep his secrets safe. Mr. Frederick Lawrence, Aunt Clair, and his adopted son, Dr. Stanley Johnson, all knew and assisted Charles in maintaining his deception. Charles learned how to avoid public attention, and he found that as long as his public relations department provided a plausible story, they would go away satisfied. Charles could not allow the Paramedics to examine him. Charles knew it did not take a rocket scientist to understand that the gunshot wounds should have killed him. Luckily, his doctor was well-trained to meet his needs. Many years ago, Charles rescued him from the streets of Port Du Prince Hattie when Stanley Johnson was an abandoned little boy. Charles took him in and ensured he received all the finest things in life, including a world-class medical education from Harvard University. To show his gratitude, Stanley specialized in researching rare blood disorders to try to find a cure for his adopted father and benefactor.

Dr. Johnson shared the fifty-year deception Charles would perform on the public and friends to hide that he was not aging like everyone else. When Charles's family members and colleagues would enter their middle years of life, he would announce that he was traveling overseas to handle a business affair. Through correspondence and phone conversations, Charles would reveal he had fallen in love, married, and fathered a male child named after his father, Charles. Upon his return, Charles would share birthdays and other constructed information about his fractious wife and offspring with his family and friends, always promising to bring him to the United States in the future. As the aging disparity between Charles and his contemporaries became apparent, he would arrange an overseas emergency requiring his appearance. News of his fictitious wife's death and his sudden change in health would soon follow his arrival overseas. Charles would conduct his business remotely, staying out of sight for several years. Before faking his death, he would arrange for his return in the guise of his fabricated son, who was to inherit his family's vast fortune. Charles had successfully pulled this off three times, and now it may be time for him to pull it off again. Only Dr. Stanley Johnson and a few others knew of Charles's deception. Charles confided with Stanley and told him his secret. Still, others like Auntie Clair Sinclair and Frederick Lawrence, the fourth-generation head Butler for the Charles estate, were born into the deception. Frederick Lawrence's family was also purchased and freed by the Sinclair family hundreds of years ago, who swore eternal allegiance to the Sinclairs for their generosity. Charles suspected other older family members knew as well. Still, they ignored the truth and played along with the deception.

The head of Sinclair Estates' security, Mr. Samuel Scales, Dr. Stanley Johnson, Hamilton Lawrence, and a security detachment were the first to arrive at the scene. They found Charles unconscious, holding Elaine's lifeless body wrapped in his arms. The two men quickly bandaged all of Charles's wounds, placed him into his private, fully medically equipped van, and transported him back to his estate. Meanwhile, a well-trained security detachment made the final touches on the crime scene to mask the actual events that had taken place. The Doctor accompanied Charles in their private ambulance to the nearby Sinclair Estate for medical attention and to prevent Charles's unique physical characteristics from being discovered by the City's paramedics. The Doctor determined it was pointless at that time to try to help Elaine because she had been dead for more than one hour. Dr. Stanley had stumbled upon a theory on how to restore people with Charles's affliction even after death; however, the procedure required massive amounts of the infected blood to attempt it, plus the process required laboratory equipment is still under development. Charles needed his immediate attention now. To his regret, Dr. Stanley had only enough of the blood type to save Charles from his massive injuries. The chief of the Sinclaire Estate security, Mr. Samuel Scales, Frederick Lawrence, the Estate's head butler, along with trusted members of the Estates security staff, stayed behind to ensure all the evidence at the crime scene supported Charles' account of the attack and to provide Charles' information to the police.

The following day, police detectives and disappointed news reporters seeking information descended upon the Sinclair estate. Charles was still in a medically induced coma and under the direct care of Dr. Johnson. Without the identity and location of the lone surviving attacker, there was no one to challenge the rendition of the night's events provided by the Sinclair estate spokespersons concerning the attack on Charles nor Elaine Singleton's death.

Dr. Johnson gave the police and the news media a statement that Charles Sinclair had suffered gunshot wounds and was in serious but stable condition. He also gave a simi-factual narrative of his efforts to save Elaine. He expressed his regrets about his unsuccessful attempts to revive Ms. Elaine Singleton before leaving her lifeless body in capable medical hands and rushing Charles to the estate for emergency lifesaving surgery. Charles

Sinclair became an uninteresting footnote as the media focused their attention on the death of Elaine Singleton, the notorious drug kingpin.

Charles awoke from his coma Monday evening, relieved to find himself in the familiar surroundings of his bed chamber. The gunshot wounds Charles barely survived on Friday night caused waves of pain when he tried to sit up. Aunt Clair rushed to his bedside and gently laid him back down.

"Thank God you came back to us," she said, not trying to hide the tears of joy and concern in her eyes.

"Elaine, where is Elaine?" He struggled to ask.

"You don't worry about that right now," She said in a motherly voice.

"Where is Elaine?" Charles asked again, already suspecting the answer.

"I'm sorry, Charles, she did not make it," Claire said, stroking his face.

Charles turned his face from her to hide his tears. "Claire, I need to be alone right now," He said.

"Of course, Charles, I will let Stanley know you are awake," She said as she opened the drapes covering the large windows, allowing the moonlight into the room before leaving.

"Claire," Charles gently called out.

"Yes, baby," Claire responded as if she knew he would have one more request before he could rest. Claire's concern moved Charles, which reminded him of her great-grandmother Kate.

"I think it is time for us to plan a trip on the La Morena, don't you agree?" Charles asked.

"I will get everything ready for your journey; now, get some rest," Clair gently stated as she closed his bed chamber's door and exited.

CHAPTER 5

New Reality

One month later, Charles allowed his awakening from a coma to be announced. Soon after, he received an unexpected visitation request from Elaine's former second-in-command, Mr. Drake Ellsworth. Drake was an enigma, a professionally dressed middle-aged white man and Elaine's most trusted lieutenant in her organization, but he was not a career criminal. Drake had a reputation for being ruthless, emotionless, and efficient. In his former life as an Army Special Operations Officer serving in Iraq and Afghanistan, Drake learned the value of reading his opponent's intentions through their body language and subtle changes in their facial expressions. Missing a person's body language or not picking up on subliminal messages could result in death. When Drake first meets Charles, he became suspicious and concerned for Elane's safety when he could not read anything from Charles.

However, Charles could read beneath Mr. Drake Ellsworth's hard exterior. He could tell that Drake Ellsworth was a conflicted man pretending to be something he was not. Ellsworth arrived at the Sinclair estate with two other men less familiar to Charles, carrying two briefcases each. One of the men he later learned was another ex-Special Operations Soldier, Mr. Joseph Bowser, Drake's enforcer and right-hand man. Charles had known men like Bowser over the years; he found them to be neither good nor evil but ruthlessly efficient and deadly. If they were your ally, your victory was assured, but if they were your enemy, your only choice was to kill them.

Charles wanted to make sure that Mr. Ellsworth understood that his social relationship with Elaine was not transferable to any of her associates. Charles wanted nothing to do with the illegal business she left behind; however, having access to Elaine's vast empire would be a great asset in helping him track down whoever had anything to do with her death and make them pay dearly. He instructed Lawrence to bring Drake to his office for the meeting.

He sat behind his ornately carved large mahogany desk, wearing silk pajamas and a satin robe. Intravenous bags filled with fluids hung from both sides of Charles's chair, along with a variety of health monitoring machines to maintain the image of a person recovering from a life-threatening event. The oxygen tube running beneath Charles's nose completed the expected appearance of fragility he wanted to present for the urgent meeting he had to have with Elaine's associates.

Mr. Ellsworth and his associate placed the metal briefcases on his desk.

"What is this"? Charles asked.

Charles could see the resentment and hostility in Drake's eyes as he and his men approached his desk. Charles knew Drake blamed Elaine's death on her association with him. Elaine's refusal to allow Drake to provide security for Elaine on the night of her death was due to her need to be alone with Charles. Charles knew Drake expected him to protect Elaine, and he failed.

"Ms. Singleton instructed us to deliver this to you if anything should happen to her," Drake said in his usual flat, emotionless voice; however, he could not hide his hatred and resentment for Charles.

Charles found the sound of Elaine's last name being used by Drake amusing, and the anger Drake felt was understandable. Drake did not know Charles was the deadliest creature on the road that night. However, he was saddled with the guilt that Elaine's death was because of her association with him.

Charles opened one of the attaché cases full of one-hundred-dollar bills. Charles estimated the money in the four cases to be approximately two million dollars, which would have impressed anyone without Charles's vast wealth.

"What am I supposed to do with this?" Charles asked.

The men looked at each other, confused by Charles's question.

"Ms. Singleton instructed us to take our orders from you should anything ever happen to her," Drake explained; the money was the weekly profits.

The last thing Charles needed was to have one penny of Elaine's drug money linked to his legitimate business empire. He understood her foresight to get Charles to assist in the leadership transition within her organization to avoid a bloody power struggle in the event of her sudden demise.

Charles studied the man standing before him, dressed like a Wall Street executive, his shoes black and polished like glass. He could sense that he was a natural leader and a trustworthy Soldier. However, Charles felt that Drake had no ambition of becoming Elaine's new drug operation head. Charles ignored Drake's resentment and reluctance to continue his affiliation with the criminal underworld. Charles knew it would be impossible for Drake to disassociate himself from Elaine's empire just by turning his back on it. Charles decided to use Drake to help distance himself from Elaine's drug empire and to find out who was behind the attempt on his life and Elaine's death. Drake's participation would justify Charles promoting him above his peers and gradually transferring Elaine's business to him.

"Drake, I want you to take this money and put it out on the streets to find the man who killed Elaine and anyone else who had anything to do with it," Charles instructed.

Drake's heart sank, realizing Charles would not take over Elaine's business, leaving him as the inheritor.

"Mr. Ellsworth, you are now in charge of all operations, and I hope the next time you come to my house, you will have the names of those responsible for this nightmare. Once you have found the people responsible for her death, contact me, and if my health is up to it, we will meet." Charles said in an authoritarian but polite voice.

Charles decided to use Elaine's organization to help locate the man he recognized during the attack that resulted in Elaine's death before the police could find and question him and make Elaine's killer wish he were never born. Charles knew Drake did not want to continue his affiliation with Elaine's organization. If Drake were successful in helping Charles unmask the hidden threat, he would help Drake find a new life away from the criminal underworld.

"One of the dead shooters was kicked out of one of my restaurants called the Oasis. I will tell my security people to release the videotapes to you." Charles continued.

Charles could see a newfound respect shine through Drake's shark-like dead eyes. Charles knew the commitment to street justice from a well-respected businessman like Charles Sinclair took the two men by surprise. Secondly, Drake did not think Charles took his relationship with Elaine seriously; after all, Charles was one of the wealthiest men in the world. What could he find in a relationship with Elaine beyond the cheap thrill of sleeping with a female underworld boss?

CHAPTER 6

Drake Ellsworth

Two weeks later, Drake Ellsworth received the first report in his Upper Westside apartment overlooking Central Park from his trusted lieutenant, Mr. Joeseph Bowser called to announce that he and three other men were arriving at his apartment with a detailed report. While Drake awaited Bowser's arrival, he looked out of his eight-floor balcony window at the construction crews setting up barricades and warning tape below. Drake remembered notices were given to the occupants of Drake's apartment building apologizing for the construction work to repair a water pipeline in front of Drake's building.

"New York City is a city that never sleeps nor undergoing construction," Drake thought.

Drake watched enviously as the men unpacked their equipment, placing warning signs and barricades.

"What wouldn't I do to have such a simple life"? He thought.

He imagined a brutal workday and a routine trip to a bar with his fellow workers to end the day. Drake fantasized about what it would be like to return home to a family with too many bills to pay and to have Elaine as a loyal wife to struggle with. Drake wondered how he had gotten entangled in such a dangerous situation.

Since Elaine's death, Drake's life has become more stressful, causing his PTSD symptoms to intensify. Many nights, he awoke dripping in sweat, screaming commands to long-dead comrades trying to prevent a massacre and to save his men's lives in a post-traumatic stress nightmare. The recurring nightmare always ended with his men and the civilians they were trying to protect dying engulfed in flames. As a member of the US Army Special Forces, Drake had risked his life on the battlefields of Iraq and Afghanistan, but this danger was much worse. The enemy he fought in the deserts and the mountains posed no threat to his family or the people he loved. Elaine's enemies were ruthless and were known to target the family members of their rivals.

Drake found it ironic that his seeking a new purpose for his life after leaving the Army led him to be hired by Elaine as a bodyguard shortly after the murder of her husband. Drake wondered how he would keep his parents and siblings safe while untangling himself from his late boss's business and trying to return to the straightforward, boring life he joined the Army to escape. Drake had to admit to himself that it was more than pay that kept him employed by Elaine; he was attracted to her exotic beauty. However, he knew she would never fit into his life nor be accepted by his Mid-Western family, not to mention that she was a cold-blooded killer. Elaine's relationship with Charles Sinclair surprised him. Drake never thought Elaine would find support and love with Charles. He believed she could not be the high society woman Charles expected her to be. Drake found it ironic that Elaine lost her life not because of her dealings in one of the most violent occupations known but because of her relationship with Charles Sinclair. Drake was brought back to the present by a call from the front desk concierge announcing the arrival of Bowser, a man he would later learn was named Fred Smith, and the other men.

Drake answered the door and escorted the men to the living room. Before he could speak, Bower started rattling off all the details of the unbelievable information he had discovered about the perpetrators of Elaine's death.

"Fred gave us the shooter's name, and Fred had all the information we needed to find him. Now ain't that some shit!" Bowser pointed to Fred Smith, who stood nervously, trying to keep his composure. Smith nervously looked around the room for the reaction on the men's faces as Bowser delivered the news to Drake.

"Who is he?" Drake asked.

"Paul Blacksmith is a petty drug dealing college drop-out," Fred said.

"Who were his friends, and who did they work for?" Drake asked.

"They were all from his neighborhood from upstate," Fred answered.

"College boys from upstate?" "That does not make much sense," Drake said.

"Who were they working for?" Charles asked again.

The question caused Fred's heart to freeze, "He used to work for me for a while, but I knew nothing about this shit!" Fred volunteered nervously.

Drake turned to look at Bowser, now understanding why he and the other men escorted Fred Smith to his apartment to deliver the news.

"What in the fuck do you mean they were working for you?" Drake asked in a controlled voice, barely masking his rage.

"Wait, before you answer that question, Bowser, take Mr. Smith here for a walk and meet me in the park in one hour alone with your report," Drake said, suspecting Smith may be wearing a police wire.

"Mr. Ellsworth, I swear on my mother's soul, I didn't know they were going to do this," Smith desperately said as the two men by his side grabbed his arms to leave.

"Mr. Smith, I am sure you will cooperate to help us bring this man to justice, and I thank you for your visit," Drake said, still suspecting law enforcement eavesdropping.

"Mr. Bowser, please arrange a meeting with Mr. Smith and me once Mr. Blacksmith is contacted," Drake said, secretly conveying that he wanted Smith alive for additional questioning.

Bowser understood the hidden message not to trust that Smith was not being secretly monitored, and he did not want anything to happen to Smith until they got all the information they needed.

"Go to Blacksmith's apartment to see if we can assist him, and please invite him to speak with me," Drake said as Bowser and his men escorted Smith out of the apartment.

Alone again in his apartment, Drake poured half a glass of whiskey from the fully equipped bar by his apartment's terrace sliding doors overlooking Central Park; he then swallowed its contents in one shot. Many thoughts raced through his mind due to the revelation he had just learned. Was there an internal threat to the organization? How could Paul Blacksmith not know that Smith worked for Elaine? More importantly, the men involved in the shooting were too dumb to pull this off themselves; Drake concluded that there had to be someone else behind all of this. He could trust that Joseph Bowser would get to the bottom of this by the night's end, and Paul Blacksmith would be in his hands in a few hours.

Drake returned to the large window and looked down with envy at the construction crews' simple life working outside his building.

"I better call home tomorrow; it may be a while before I have another moment of peace for the foreseeable future," Drake thought to himself as he poured himself another drink.

CHAPTER 7

Detective Julio Rodriguez

Meanwhile, Detective Julio Rodriguez, a thirty-five-year-old olive-complexioned Puerto Rican who was a third-generation New York City Police Officer, learned to laugh off the jokes of him being an undercover Irishmen due to his family's long lineage with the New York Police Department, or NYPD, as it is better known. Despite his troubled youth, it was pre-ordained that he would follow his family's footsteps into the NYPD. Julio's adolescent years on the mean streets of the hidden inner cities of New York gave him insight into the criminal mind. Due to his childhood affiliation with many of New York's prominent crime figures and drug laws, Julio understood their methodology and motivations. Like Julio, many of his friends seemed destined to follow in their father's footsteps but, unfortunately, into lives of crime.

Unlike many of his fellow Police Officers who came from outside the City to join the NYPD, Detective Rodriguez did not view all criminals as people beyond redemption. Julio watched his childhood friends struggle to avoid the curse of their fathers, only to be dragged into lives of crime by circumstances beyond their control. One of those events finally sealed Julio's fate to become an NYPD Detective. Like his friends, he tried to find his way in the world. Still, unforeseeable circumstances led him to follow in his father's footsteps. One fall night at the Latin Quarter Night Club, Julio and his friends were attacked by a group of rivals from a Dominican neighborhood. The attack left one of his friends and one of the attackers dead, and all of their lives changed forever. Julio's friends didn't have family in the NYPD nor the money to afford competent legal counsel to help them make a deal to save them from jail time. However, true to their friendship with Julio, they never revealed who made the fatal shot that saved their lives but resulted in the attacker's death. Julio's friends kept silent and went to prison and started their indoctrination into their fathers' profession. To get his father's assistance and avoid jail, Julio had to accept a plea deal to join the Army and, if he survived the first Iraqi invasion, agree to become a New York Patrolman like his ancestors.

That was two divorces ago, and like his father, the only consistent home he came to know was the NYPD. His adult daughter hated him, his eldest son from his first marriage avoided him, and wife number three was on the fence about deciding if she wanted to become ex-wife number three or hold out to see if the renewed efforts to save their marriage would work. One thing he was determined not to do was allow his job to turn him into one of those lonely older men sitting alone on the bench feeding pigeons.

For months, Julio and his wife Melissa had planned a romantic night to rekindle their romance. He had worked overtime and traded weekends and holidays to ensure he had the time to focus on his wife and marriage.

It was another joyless hump day morning when Detective Rodriguez entered the noisy and chaotic NYPD Homicide Unit. He went to his desk camouflaged under mountains of files and loose paper. No one could figure out how Julio could find anything under those stacks of paper on his desk. Still, he could miraculously reach under a pile and produce documents without looking.

"Hey Julio O'Bannon, you are up for a triple homicide?" Matthew O'Bannon asked before Julio could put down his black coffee cup and sit in his castle of paper.

Matthew O'Bannon, a thirty-five-year veteran of the NYPD, was Julio's partner and lead jokester. Matthew was sixty years old but looked much older. The long workdays and hard drinking had taken their toll on him. Now, all he had to show for his life was a wife lost to cancer, a strained relationship with his adult children, and his NYPD job. Still, most of all, he was one of the men Julio could trust with his life.

Like Julio, Matthew came from a long line of NYPD Policemen. He was nearing mandatory retirement and made it his business to point out every little mistake Julio made. Julio understood it was the old Irishman's way of ensuring he did not commit an error that would get him killed when he was no longer there to watch his back.

"Bullshit, I'm not up on rotation yet Motherfucker," Julio shot back emphatically. "Oh yes, you are Leddy, Brown called out sick today, and there was a break in this month-old case, and it has been turned over to the next available Detective; that makes it our sorry asses," Matthew said in a very sarcastic voice.

"What the fuck is wrong with him now?" Julio angrily asked.

Julio suspected that Brown was using the money he was getting under the table from drug dealers and other criminal scum to pay the Desk Sergeant to tip him off when complex cases were posted so he could avoid taking on unsolvable cases and keep up his closed case numbers. Julio knew Brown would get nowhere on the month-old triple homicide and elected to play sick to avoid getting assigned to the case.

How the fuck would I know? Do I look like his mother to you, Leddy?" Matthew shot back.

"What I do know is you better get your smiling ass to the assignment desk to get the details of this fucking mess." Matthew continued.

"Mother fucker," Julio sat back in his chair in disbelief, thinking about all the plans he had with his wife that he had to cancel. One homicide could take months to unravel, but three would keep him busy.

"Hey, cheer up, Leddy. We are not the lead in this case. We are helping the State police solve this one. A beat cop already found the car identified leaving the crime scene; you see, the luck of the Irish is still with you," Matthew said jokingly.

What are the chances we will find enough evidence in the car that will lead to a quick arrest and conviction? Julio thought to himself.

"Yeah, great; where the fuck is it?" Julio replied, still thinking of the shit he was going to hear when he got home.

"But don't get your hopes so high, partner. Word on the street is that this guy has a two-million-dollar hit on his head. At this point, we are more likely to find him with his brains painting some fucken wall than alive," O'Bannon said in his usual wet dream-killing voice.

Detective Rodriguez and O'Bannon drove to the location where the suspect's car was found at their usual suicide speed of 100 mph through the narrow streets of New York City with the sirens blaring. Partly because they wanted to get there before the evidence in the car was contaminated by some wannabe Detective, but O'Bannon was also an adrenaline junkie who loved the suspense of driving that close to death's door. If someone pulled in front of them, no way in hell would they be able to avoid a fatal collision, but that was half of the thrill, the other half he never allowed himself to admit.

CHAPTER 8

The Trapped Rat

Smith went out of his way to provide Bowser with all his information on Paul Blacksmith. Leaving Smith in the care of the other two men, Bowser, accompanied by two additional henchmen, drove off to capture Paul Blacksmith before the police could get their hands on him. When they arrived at the address provided by Smith, they noticed a Police patrolman speaking with an older woman pointing in the direction of Blacksmith's building as he investigated a damaged black Mercedes illegally parked and decorated with several parking tickets pinned on the windshield outside the residence.

"If this were a poor neighborhood, the car would have been towed weeks ago," he thought, but he was grateful it remained to point him to his target.

Bowser viewed the police as soldiers in a different uniform; he had no love, hate, or fear of the police. Bowser figured if they did not get in his way, he would not have to kill them. The lone patrolman was no match for Bowser and his two trained assassins. Bowser and his two trusted henchmen casually exited their car and entered Paul's building. The Patrolman glanced at them as they passed but could not see anything unusual with the three well-dressed businesspeople except the hard life each man had lived etched into every line of their faces. Usually, men who could afford the elegant suits they men wore displayed the soft and privileged life they lived and showed no signs of the stresses of life the commoner had to endure. However, these men's faces told a different story, but looking hard and weather-beaten was not against the law. The old rat-faced woman playing the role of the neighborhood busybody smiled and gave them a nod of approval for their professional appearance as they entered the building.

Julio sat in the passenger's seat, disinterested in O'Bannon's high-speed driving, lost in the excuses he would have to tell Melissa for missing their date night. He could not believe his bad luck when a break in the month-old triple robbery-murder case came up, and that bastard Brown called off leaving this shit on his lap, but maybe his luck was changing. It was an incredible stroke of luck when Patrolmen finally recognized the illegally parked car that fitted the description of the Mercedes described in the Sinclair murder case in which the fourth suspect escaped. The Patrolman was smart enough not to touch the vehicle but to call it in and stand guard over it so that no one else disturbed it. Rodriguez and O'Bannon finally arrived at the scene, parking in front of the suspect car with a blaring siren coming to a screeching stop.

"God, I'm going to miss this job," O'Bannon thought as he exited the car.

Patrolman Anthony Martin approached the detectives and began to debrief them. Patrolman Martin was a tall, athletic Hispanic male in his late twenties. Detective Rodriguez could not help but wonder if he had looked as good as Patrolman Martin did in his uniform many years ago. One thing was sure: Julio was never in better shape than this young Patrolman. Nor was he as sharp; he would have looked for clues in the car before calling it in to present evidence and bring attention to himself. He was not intelligent enough early in his career to realize his actions could result in the guilty going free. The Patrolman was approached by an older woman who claimed to know who parked the car in the current location. Not only did the old lady know who the person was, but she also knew which apartment he lived in. The woman had called the Police several times to report the illegally parked car and to make a noise nescience report against Mr. Blacksmith and his strange friends. Now that the police had finally responded to her complaints against Blacksmith, she was more than willing to escort the detective and his police officer to Mr. Blacksmith's door. The rat-faced older woman always knew Paul as a no-good Punk who would end up on the wrong side of the law one day, and it filled her with great satisfaction to bring the law right to his door.

Paul Blacksmith had spent the weeks after his nightmare with Charles and Elaine in his apartment under blackout conditions in a self-medicated semi-coma. He had consumed most of the drugs he was given to transport or sell; many of the drugs he took for the first time in his attempt to not deal with the images of horror locked in his mind. Many times Paul tried unsuccessfully to overdose, only to awaken in a deeper pool of piss and vomit. For days, Paul attempted to recite the Lord's prayer. Feeling frustrated and dammed, he could not get past "Our Father," which he continuously repeated, bursting into tears for not remembering the rest of the incantation against evil.

He was jerked halfway back to the land of the living by a loud banging on his door. He sat upright, terrified, in his bed, still wearing the same filth-infested clothes he had on the night he came face to face with death.

His heavily sedated mind reeled with images of an agonizing death and the need to find a way to escape. His eyes filled with tears, and he tried to hold back the trembling words he was mumbling, "Momma, Momma, I need you to come get me."

Bang, bang, bang, the knocking continued. "Open up! We know you are in there!!" The mysterious voice demanded from the other side of the door.

"Oh, sweet Jesus, they found me; please don't let them have me."

Paul whispered his desperate prayer, hoping the devil on the other side of the door could not hear him. He looked around the darkened room, disorientated and momentarily not knowing where he was or how he got there. The streaks of sunlight that slipped between the tightly drawn curtains helped him identify his once stylish studio apartment as the filthy rat trap Paul would now die in. He had abandoned all hope of survival, having witnessed, with his own eyes, how the creatures moved like a blur, and even when shot, they kept coming. How could he hope to get out of this?

Bang, bang, bang, another round of heavy knocking on the door; shaking hysterically, Paul jumped with each bang and pointed the AK-47 at the door with both hands on the barrel of the weapon. Paul reached over to the assortment of drugs littered on a table by the bed, grabbed a handful of heroin, and shoved it into his face. Breathing deeply, he hoped this time he would not awaken back into this nightmare; maybe this time, it was enough to give him an overdose. Paul preferred to slip into a never-ending opiate comma than to have the monsters at his door rip him to shreds as they did to his friends. The drugs were not working fast enough, and he began to sob loudly. He did not notice the warm-rank fluid soaking his pants and bed and did not care.

"Open up, Mr. Blacksmith; this is the police!" "We know you are in there." A loud authoritarian voice said from the other side of the door.

Never had those words filled him with such relief. Restored visions of hope and the redeeming powers of Jesus raced through his mind. Paul broke down and cried uncontrollably, barely able to catch his breath between the heavy sobbing and prayers of gratitude to the God his mother always would be there for him if he only prayed with a sincere heart.

"Oh, thank you, Jesus!" Finally catching his breath, Paul cried out and rushed to the door, dragging the AK-47 behind him.

The overwhelming stench of Paul's darkened apartment assaulted the Patrolmen when Paul opened the door. The smell of fesses, urine, vomit, and Paul's unwashed body caused Detective Rodriguez to gauge. Secondly, they were shocked by his wild and frantic appearance. Paul began to speak wildly and incoherently as he dangled the AK-47 by the barrel with a white-knuckle grip of desperation. He didn't understand why the police were wrestling him to the ground and putting handcuffs on him. Paul frantically tried to tell his story about the Bentley, car chases, beautiful woman, and demons to the arresting officers, who were too busy trying to hold him down until the paramedics could arrive.

Bowser and his companions watched helplessly as the police took away Paul Blacksmith. They were seconds away from apprehending him when the lobby suddenly filled with police looking for Blacksmith. Trying to take Blacksmith by force with so many law enforcement officers now on the scene could have resulted in the death of Blacksmith and the secrets he held.

"I knew that man and his darky friends were up to no good," said the old rat-faced woman to Bowser.

"I am glad I could help them put him away." She continued. Bowser smiled at her as he imagined the neat red hole his 9mm would make if he shot her between the eyes.

Detective Rodriguez could not believe his luck; not only did he find his suspect, but he also found what was sure to be the missing AK-47 and the getaway car. Even O'Bannon pitched in to assist him with the paperwork so he could leave the station house in enough time to make it home to his wife. Still, there was a lingering feeling of dread hovering over him. Never had he seen a man wanted in connection with a triple homicide so happy to be arrested. Maybe it was the drugs, or perhaps he was genuinely crazy, but one thing was sure: someone or something scared that fool out of his mind. Julio could not shake the crazy stories the suspect was trying to tell: demons, the woman attacking them, the man moving like the comic book superhero, and, to top it all off, Charles Sinclair being bulletproof.

"Wow, drugs can do some fucked up things to a man's mind. This guy should be the poster child for drug prevention". Julio thought to himself.

CHAPTER 9

Julio's Matrimonial Bliss

Detective Julio Rodriguez moved out of the City to a suburban home on Long Island shortly after joining the police department. He hoped to live the American dream of a home with a white picket fence, a two-car garage, and two or three children. Julio now lived in a one-bedroom house without any children. Still, he paid all the living expenses for his first two offspring, who did not even have the decency to call him on holidays or his birthday. Julio often wondered if his two adult children knew of all the men their mother had slept with while Julio was putting his life on the line to support his family, would they still resent him? Julio had no illusions of perfection; he recognized his faults like any other man, but at least he had the decency not to get caught three times in the act.

Julio met his current wife, Melissa, while on a hospital visit to check on his partner, Matthew O'Bannon, who had landed there after being injured during an arrest. If you let O'Bannon tell the story, you would believe he was responsible for Julio and Mellissa meeting each other. Mrs. Melissa Ortiz-Rodriguez, an attractive 30-year-old Registered Nurse at Belleview Hospital, still looked like she was twenty-five. She had those perfect genes that enabled her to eat all the fattening Latin dishes and never gain a pound. Julio knew he had dodged a whole world of hurt by making it home for dinner that night. Melissa had reached deep into the Latino cookbook to complete the night's meal. The heavy aroma of garlic, cilantro, epazote, cumin, roast pork, and baked chicken could be smelt as Julio walked up to his local driveway.

When Julio entered the house, Melissa was busy at the stove with her back turned to the front door.

Julio wrapped his arms around his wife's waist from behind, pulling her close and kissing her affectionately.

"I'm glad you could make it home for a change, Papi," Melissa said with her back to him while finishing preparing the evening meal.

"Why don't you relax and get a beer while I finish cooking? It will be ready in a few seconds," She said.

"I have some good news to tell you," She said, giving him a longer-than-usual kiss before returning to her cooking.

Julio sat at the kitchen island behind the stove where Melissa was cooking. Their modern open floor plan house enabled Julio to watch the evening news on the television on the living room wall. Melissa was in a more than usual upbeat mood. He figured she would tell him about a new dress, a promotion on her job, or a great deal she got on a vacation package that he had to pretend to be excited about.

"You would not believe what happened today," She said.

That was his cue to drift off to his happy place until she stopped talking, but his mind drifted back to Paul Blacksmith.

"Well, you know when you get that feeling that something just isn't right?" She rhetorically asked.

The evening television news began to broadcast a report on his earlier arrest, and he could not help but pay attention to the evening news being broadcast just over Melissa's shoulder. He tried as hard as he could to listen to her never-ending stories of needles, tests, dumb doctors, and hard-to-deal-with nurses. Still, her voice faded further into the background as details of the arrest began to dominate the broadcast.

"Why don't I just shut the fuck up, Julio?" Melissa said in a sharp, sarcastic voice.

Julio immediately snapped back to Melissa, who was now looking at him. "Oh fuck! I will hear about this during our next counseling session," he thought.

"I'm sorry, Mommy, but that was my bust on the news," Julio said apologetically.

"Who gives a shit Julio!?" Melissa shot back, now standing in that pissed-off Latina pose.

"What the fuck, does that have to do with me being pregnant, Puta!?" Melissa shot back.

Julio sat back in his chair, shocked. "Oh, fuck me," he thought to himself. His mind drifted to black as Melissa went into a protracted stanza of rage.

CHAPTER 10

Dr. Johnson's Abduction

As the adopted son of Charles Sinclair, Dr. Stanley Johnson had access to the billions of dollars the Sinclair estate had to offer; however, Dr. Stanley Johnson chose to live a simple life dedicated to his medical research. He refused to be pampered or treated differently than the commoner. Unfortunately, the recent attack on Charles caused Dr. Johnson to work extra hours to produce the plasma Charles needed to recover. He worked late into the night, ensuring the treated donated plasma could benefit Charles's recovery. After putting away his specialized equipment at the hospital lab, the doctor went to the elevators to take him to the parking levels. Walking down the empty hallway, he felt someone was following him; he turned and saw nothing. The doctor continued walking to the elevators, but this time, the presence behind him was undeniable; he turned, ready to face whatever it was, but there was nothing there again. The doctor laughed, thinking how his long work hours made him imagine things. The doctor reached the elevators and pressed the down button. The doctor thought he could hear the faint sounds of drums in the darkness.

"I got to stop working so hard," the doctor said to himself, believing the feelings of dread and the sounds he was hearing resulted from work fatigue.

As he waited for the elevator to arrive, the lights at the far end of the corridor went out, and the sound of the drums increased. The doctor attributed the light going out to a burnt fuse or a timed shutdown to save energy but could not find a logical reason for the drums' sound.

Despite the doctor's efforts to remain objective and calm, nervousness crawled up his spine. He turned back to await the elevator's arrival, trying to ignore the growing sounds of the drums. The doctor turned to look down the hallway, and a second set of lights approaching his location went out with a thumping sound that made him jump. The doctor could not see anything in the darkness, but he could feel the presence of an evil entity approaching. Now, the doctor could hear the unmistakable sound of chanting accompanying the beating of the drums. The doctor could hear heavy footsteps that vibrated the floor could be heard from the end of the pitch-black hallway approaching his position. With each heavy footstep crashing into the ground, another set of lights went out as the drums and chanting intensified. The next set of lights getting closer to his location went out with a loud thud as the darkness and hidden menace became undeniable in the approaching blackness. The growling of whatever was approaching hidden in the darkness sounded like a lion or some other sizeable man-eating beast. The elevator's display lights above the door indicated the elevator was ascending in rhythm with the approaching darkness. The sound of the chanting and drums was deafening, and the growling of the hidden danger was now only a few yards away from him. The doctor frantically pushed the elevator call button as only the light above him shielded him from total darkness and death. The final light went out, leaving the doctor in blackness. Finally, the elevator reached his floor, and while the doctor waited for the doors to open, he could feel the hot breath, smell the stench, and hear the growls of something huge in front of him, drowning out the sounds of the chanting and drums. The elevator doors opened, and the brightness of the interior temporarily blinded him. The doctor rushed into the elevator only to find Stephany standing before him. She grabbed him and pinned him to the elevator wall by the neck.

"So, you are Charles' little brat, " she said, flashing her long canines as she pressed the elevator's down button.

The following day at the Sinclair estate, Lawrence stood outside Charles' office, mindful of Charles' fragile condition. Lawrence entered and carefully delivered the disturbing News that Charles Sinclair's' adopted son, Mr. Stanley Johnson, had not returned to the estate and could not be found. Charles received the news in a quiet and composed manner reserved for extremely perilous situations like this.

Providing extra security for Dr. Stanley Johnson did not seem necessary. The Doctor had no direct affiliation with Elaine, and few knew of the nature of his relationship with Charles other than close family members.

Mr. Samuel Scales was the first to notice the Doctor's absence and had tried unsuccessfully to locate him before reporting his disappearance to his uncle, Lawrence. Mr. Scales scrubbed every city hospital, jail, and morgue, attempting to find the doctor, but was unsuccessful. It was as if he was there one moment and vanished without a trace. Lawrence knew that not only was Charles concerned as any parent would be, but he also relied on Stanley for a steady supply of fresh blood that he needed to survive. Charles's injuries caused him to use more of his stockpile of blood than he usually would consume. Based on his current consumption rate, he only had one week's supply of blood left. Charles knew there was a provision of blood hidden at the Oasis restaurant. Still, the blood required special treatment before his consumption that only his son, Dr. Johnson, knew. Otherwise, only the ingestion of blood directly from a living victim would keep him alive. Charles wanted to keep Dr. Stanley Johnson's disappearance quiet. Still, he knew the Doctor's absence would not have gone unnoticed by his colleagues at work, and soon, the police would have come to investigate if he had not acted first.

Charles had not received any information from Drake using Elaine's underworld contacts concerning Stanley's disappearance. However, he was disturbed to learn that none of Elaine's' enemies believed she was dead, and members of rival drug cartels were seen at his restaurant, the Oasis, looking for her. Charles was relieved that his lawyers had arranged to contact the police and make a missing person's report like an average person would. He also thought it would be best to have Mr. Scales increase surveillance of the underworld activity to ensure their presence at the Oasis restaurant would not cause him unintended consequences.

CHAPTER 11

Two Blind Monkeys

Far away, south of the Mason Dixon line, in an abandoned department store on the outskirts of Birmingham, Alabama, FBI Special Agent Wanda Jackson and her team secretly listened in on a conversation conducted in the Pigs Head bar and grill, a few storefronts down from their location. Agent Wanda Jackson, a 35-year-old single black female and ultimate professional, inherited her family's hatred of the KKK. She was one of the few field Agents who were also Lawyers. Her radiant jet-black skin and exquisitely beautiful features were a novelty in her family and the source of many subsequent conversations with her friends. The 16th Street Baptist Church in Birmingham, Alabama, was bombed on Sunday, September 15, 1963, years before FBI Special Agent Wanda Jackson was born. Still, the savagery of the Church bombing shaped her life just the same. Her parents were survivors of the attack, and the ritual retelling of the event led her to join the FBI to prevent future acts of hatred and to avenge the innocent. Agent Wanda Jackson's dedication to the Bureau had resulted in many failed relationships, and she prayed her current assignment would not end her latest friendship with Los Angeles District Attorney Brian Shabazz. She was determined to provide the evidence that would lead to the arrest and conviction of the murders of Army Sergeant Cross and his wife. For months, she and her team were trying to find proof that the bar under surveillance was the watering hole for the local area Klan responsible for the military couple's deaths. Agent Jackson's team consisted of three Probationary Agents and her. Someone seemed to have a good sense of humor when Wanda filed a request for assistance in the investigation. Her request was granted in the form of three newbies to babysit. To Wanda's surprise and relief, the three Agents proved very resourceful. The three agents were called the Mod Squad after a 1968 television show about three young undercover police officers. Agent Todd Bostic, 27, a White male born in the state of Oregon, had already identified most of the members of the local KKK. The other two agents assigned to Wanda were Agent Glenn Baker, 28, Black male, born in NYC, and the newest Team member, Susan Cruz, 25, Puerto Rican, born in Riverside County, LA. The two agents developed personal attachments after the many nights spent in spider holes deep in the woods of the old South, photographing and documenting the Klan secret assemblies.

For three months, Wanda and the three assigned probationary Agents had been trying to find evidence of which members of the local KKK were responsible for the military family's murder. She and her team had deciphered most of their operations and identified most of its members and officers. However, there were activities unknown to most of the local Klan members, according to one of their paid FBI informants within the organization.

Inside the Pigs Head bar and grill, Mr. Floyd Harrison, a middle-aged, casually dressed married white man, sat at the counter drinking a beer. If there were another drinking hole in town, Mr. Floyd Harrison would be there in a heartbeat. Unfortunately, the Pigs Head was one of the oldest bars in Alabama and could trace its origins well before the Civil War, and It was the only bar on his side of the town. Like its patrons, this bar was passed down from generation to generation, and the interior and décor were a testament to that fact. The acid aroma of beer, vomit, and pine disinfectant floated on the thin clouds of cigarette smoke that lingered in the air of the dark interior. The Pigs Head bar still had its original counter forever stained by the many spilled drinks, cigarette burns, and human handprints soaked in over the centuries. Behind the bar counter, the usual assortment of liquors faded cheap Confederate portrait prints and other dusty Confederate memorabilia, large jars of pickled eggs, assorted pig parts, and sausages almost entirely covered the old dingy mirror on the wall.

"You want another refill, Floyd?" Bob Belington, BB to all his neighbors and friends, asked in a high-pitched voice with a thick Southern accent.

Mr. Floyd Harrison could trace his lineage beyond his family, landing at Pilgrims at Plymouth Rock. He taught American history at the local high school and was considered an expert on Alabama's culture and history. Floyd's wife, Carol, shared his distaste for the irrational bigotry of their neighbors. Still, like Floyd, she learned how to smile to present the illusion of agreement when the most biased and racist things were said in front of her.

Since Floyd's legal separation from his wife Carol, he had been spending more time at the local watering hole than usual. Each day of their separation grew harder for Floyd to endure, and he was ready to participate in couples counseling Carol demanded as a prerequisite for their reconciliation. Carol demanded to know more about Floyd's mysterious activities none of the wives of his Masonic Lodge husbands participated in. Floyd struggled to find a way to convince Carol his late meetings had nothing to do with another woman or could jeopardize their marriage. However, unlike his participation with the Masonic Lodge, he knew sharing his involvement in the Serapian Order was impossible. Carol was his soulmate and only source of sanity, living in a community that was nostalgic for the days of legalized oppression against non-white people. The Pigs Head bar was the only watering hole in town for Floyd to go to drown his sorrows.

Floyd pretended to be fully engaged in watching the news to avoid talking to the bartender, Bill Billington. The News broadcast featured the recent arrest in the murder case involving Charles Sinclair and the death of Elaine Singleton. One of the News anchors jokingly suggested that Charles Sinclair had enough wealth to bribe the angle of death. Upon hearing the name Sinclair mentioned, Floyd became laser-focused on the news broadcast. He was immediately reminded of a story that became folklore for the Serapians. The story was told of a Sinclair born hundreds of years ago who survived equally life-threatening injuries and lived to fight for the Union Army against the South during the Civil War and finally died mysteriously in Africa.

Floyd was also the Grand Master of the local Masonic Lodge called Society of the Sacred Cross Lodge Number Sixteen of the Ancient and Accepted Order of the Irish Scottish Rite. Floyd begrudgingly inherited his father's position on the City Council and was considered a leader in his little town. However, Floyd never really felt that he fit in. Floyd knew all the right things to say and do to make people believe that he was indeed a son of the old South, but the truth was that he could not stand the ignorance and self-righteousness of most Southern Rednecks. Floyd practiced the warm smile and chuckled to hide his contempt for the people who so admired his long Southern lineage. Floyd's father's dying wish was for him to take his father's position in the ultra-secret society called the Serapians, which his father and forefathers had before him. Ever the dutiful son, Floyd reluctantly took on his family obligations and committed to the organization's wishes. At first, it seemed like another excuse for older men to play dress up.

However, he later realized that the Serapians took their activities much more seriously than his local Masonic Lodge did. His father never revealed any secrets about the organization to him, even after he agreed to take over his seat in the group. Floyd could not remember a day when he was not fulfilling his late father's dreams and ambitions. Floyd found it ironic that the one dream his father had for him to pass on the family name would never come true now that he was separated from the only woman he desired to have children with.

A year after his father's death, Floyd was visited by a total stranger who invited him to a clandestine late-night meeting. It was on that dark, moonless night when Floyd was first introduced to the secretive organization. Unlike his introduction to the Masonic Order, there was no fanfare or group participation. Later, Floyd learned that he had been under surveillance by the Serapian Order to ensure that he was a worthy candidate for admission to the Order.

Floyd felt alone and vulnerable as he drove along a narrow, unpaved road through the thick forest to a secluded two-story family house void of light. Once inside the dark interior of the house, Floyd made his way to a candle-lit room. The few candles obscured the faces of the people sitting in the shadows interviewing him. The one question the interviewers ask Floyd would never forget was if he could live forever, would he be willing to sacrifice a life for the gift? He remembered answering no, but secretly, in his heart, he knew of a few people he would not mind sacrificing, and one of them was standing right in front of him. However, Floyd could not have imagined that it would be his marriage would be the price of his admission to the Serapian Order. Floyd was determined to find a way to get back with Carol, the only woman he had ever loved.

"Hey, Floyd, do you want another glass or what?" BB asked Floyd, who was mesmerized by the news on the television over the bar above the dirty mirror behind the counter.

Bob Belington was a walking stereotype of a Southern Redneck. He consistently sported denim overalls over his impossibly swollen gut. His remaining teeth and every shirt he wore had been permanently stained with the pungent drippings of chewing tobacco.

"Hey Floyd, you hear me talking to you?" BB asked in an annoyed voice.

BB's nagging brought Floyd out of his fixation with the story about Charles Sinclair's miraculous survival and the capture of Paul Blacksmith.

Floyd hated Belington and thought he was dangerous to the Serapian Order or the Bishops of Christ philanthropic Charities, as they were publicly known. The Serapian public camouflage allowed them access to medical institutions and their patients' information. Access to medical records enabled them to identify people with matching genotypes and blood types for organ and blood transfers. Floyd was told the Bishops of Christ's activities were philanthropic efforts to help severely ill people needing organ transplants or blood transfusions find the necessary donors promptly. However, only the highest Priest of the Serapian Order benefited from the genetic information. A neophyte like Floyd was not told the Serapian Order was responsible for the disappearance of people who matched the genetic matches they needed. Nor were people like Floyd made aware of the identity of the High Priest, who was rumored to be immortal.

People like Belington attracted the attention of the FBI and other law enforcement organizations. The Serapians hid in Masonic Jurisdictions and other secret organizations worldwide.

It was Floyd's misfortune that the Sacred Cross Masonic Lodge also had racist, murderous members of the Ku Klux Klan in its ranks. Floyd never could imagine the racist ranting of some of the members would lead to the death of an innocent man and woman. Floyd did not doubt that members of his Lodge were responsible for the Black Soldier and his wife, who were on leave from Fort Benning, GA, and that they were now under surveillance. The Serapians used their political connections to keep their hidden member out of the FBI investigation of the military couple's death. However, rednecks like Belington have managed, in their ignorance, to cause more attention to be attracted to the Sacred Cross Masonic Lodge, where Floyd was hidden. Fortunately, the Serapian members within the FBI controlled most of the investigation. Floyd was sure the Order would not allow the KKK to expose his presence, nor were they going to let the local rednecks interfere with their support for the crucial research the Bishops of Christ was providing for vital medical treatments.

"I can't believe what I am seeing." He said to himself, loud enough to let BB think he was paying attention to him.

"Don't surprise me one bit," BB proclaimed; "Those niggers are always killing each other and blaming it on the White man," BB continued in the typical ignorant poor White trash fashion. Floyd's skin crawled with every word Bob Billington spoke.

The news suggested to Floyd something BB or most of the members of his lodge could not imagine or believe. For years, the secret hidden society within Lodges was their involvement in scanning the globe for candidates with genes and blood types. The primary goal of the donations to the Bishops of Christ is to support medical genetic research. It was also used to look for evidence to validate the incredible story of a monster who slaughtered an entire town despite being shot multiple times. Legend has it that this monster killed the inhabitants and used some survivors as food before disappearing forever, or maybe until now.

"Well, do you want anuthern, or not?" Bob asked in that high-pitched squeaky Floyd could not stand.

"No, Bob, I think I had enough for today," Floyd stated as he pulled away from the bar.

"Hey Bob, you wouldn't know how much we have in the Lodge treasury, would you?" Floyd asked.

Floyd always regretted allowing Billington to be elected lodge treasure. Still, he was obligated to seek assistance to obtain the funds to confirm his suspicion that there may be more to the story concerning Charles Sinclair.

"No, can't say I do; why are you asking?" Bob responded in a voice that conveyed that Floyd needed his approval to receive the money.

"I just might need to borrow some," Floyd replied, barely able to hide his disdain.

"How much are you going to be needing?" Bob asked, still trying to get Floyd to gravel.

"All of it," Floyd responded sternly, finally fed up with Belington's false sense of authority.

"All of it?" Bob asked, puzzled, realizing that he had stepped over the line.

"Yep, all of it," Floyd responded sharply as he walked to the door.

Once again, BB was offended by the high and mighty attitude of Floyd Harrison and his college-educated friends. BB knew they were up to something, and he wanted to be a part of it no matter what it was. He felt he had every right to join their inner circle after all he had done for the Lodge. He even killed that uppity Nigger Soldier and his black bitch for daring to strike a white man just for grabbing that Nigger bitch's coochy. BB could not remember any of those smart-ass college boys ever showing that much determination to keep the Niggers in their place. BB reached under the bar and took out the lodge checkbook.

"For Floyd's Pleasure Trip to NYC," he made an angry note in the check ledger. BB wrote a ten-thousand-dollar check and made it out to Floyd Harrison.

CHAPTER 12

A Night On The Town

Charles learned long ago to allow his Lawyers and Publicists to speak for him and shape whatever narrative suited his purpose. Charles was amazed to see the makeshift memorials of bundles of flowers constructed near the attack's site and the get-well card he received every day. The Sinclair House staff were overwhelmed by phone calls from world leaders wishing Charles well and offering assistance. Charles laughed and thought, how many people would want him well if they knew who and what he was? Charles was still recovering from the gunshot wounds he had suffered two months ago, while the loss of Elaine was beginning to sink in. Long ago, longevity lost its' thrill for him. Charles witnessed everyone he loved die one by one, knowing he had the means to keep them with him forever. However, Charles loved them too much to subject them to the never-ending hunger for blood he despised. Charles had always been a family man and remembered how long it took him to find Elaine. While she had her faults, she provided him with a glimpse of what it felt like to be loved and needed. Trips around the world, fantastic nights out on the town followed by long days of savage, no-holds-barred sex were the memories that came to mind when Charles thought of Elaine. Now she was gone, and he was alone again.

He could recall one night he and Elaine got out for a treat. That was their pet name for fresh blood; most of the blood they consumed was provided by Dr. Johnson, who always had an ample supply due to his research. However, occasionally, they desired to savor fresh blood rhythmically pumping into their mouths and the erotic terror of their victims. Charles would wear expensive designer clothing these nights and flash a costly watch and rings. Elaine would wear the sluttish dress she could find. They would find a seedy bar in the highest crime areas of New York, New Jersey, Philadelphia, or equivalently dangerous parts of town worldwide to set their trap. One night in New York, they had hit the jackpot; the bar was filled with all kinds of wannabe pimps, whores, drug dealers, and their customers.

Like moths to the flame, Charles's apparent wealth attracted the woman in the bar. All sized up his assets and began their mental calculations on how to take Elaine's place. At the same time, the men's eyes were all fixated on Elaine. Charles could read the resentment and jealousy on their faces. Sitting in a regular cup-shaped lounge sofa in the club's most secluded and dark part, they awaited their first volunteer. A group of men turned their backs to the bar and gawked in the mysterious wealthy couple's direction. Charles's hypersensitive hearing was unnecessary in understanding what the people were talking about, but Charles pretended not to notice. Boldest and loudest of the bunch, made sure Charles knew he was looking at Elaine and talking about him. Typically, by hoodlum rules, if a man did this in front of you, it was a sign of total disrespect, and a formal challenge to a duel to regain your street credibility or honor was obligatory. Elaine would encourage the victims' attention by pretending to sneak a smile in the man's direction while Charles was not looking. When Elaine took out her lipstick, it was Charles's cue to go to the bathroom and leave

Elaine alone in their booth. Like clockwork, the man swaggered to the booth when Charles entered the bathroom.

"Hey, sweet thing. I could not help but notice you smiling in my direction," the overconfident victim said, leaning over Elaine.

"Is that your man?" He asked.

"No, we are just friends," Elaine replied encouragingly.

"Well, I want to be your friend too, if that is alright with you, Baby." The victim continued.

"Why should I want to be your friend," Elaine asked coyly.

The man standing over Elaine looked in the direction of his crotch to draw her eyes in that direction and smiled at her.

"Looks like you didn't put away all of your socks," Elaine said, toying with him.

"Babe, it can be your toy; I want to be your friend with benefits," the man said, encouraged by Elaine's willingness to accept his disrespectful behavior.

"Slide over, Sweet thing; let me make it plain to you," he said as he sat close before she could answer.

"Are you sure you want to be my friend?" Elaine asked shyly.

"Oh yes, Baby doll, friends with all kinds of benefits," the man said, leaning close to whisper in her ear.

Elaine suddenly turned, facing the man and looking deep into his eyes. The victim noticed something terrifying in her eyes for the first time but was bewildered why he had this cold chill run down his spine. His first instinct was to draw back, but the hustler rule precluded him from doing what nature had programmed every dumb animal to do when in danger. Elaine grabbed the man by the shoulders, crushing her mouth into his and shoving her unnaturally long tongue down his throat, busting his lip in the process. Her tongue pushed deep down his throat and injected the neurotoxins in her saliva into the victim's bloodstream. The feeling of danger was immediately replaced with a soothing opiate high. The man sank back into his seat as Elaine continued to inject the man with neurotoxins orally. The man's friends looked on in disbelief and cheered him on, giving each other high fives. While Elaine was sedating her victim, she was unzipping his trousers.

Pulling away from the heavily sedated, Elaine whispered into his ear. "Pull down your pants, honey; I want to suck your dick."

The drugged, now terrified but unable to resist her commands, man moved slowly. He complied with her demand, pulling his pants and underwear down to his ankles. Seeing this, the people at the bar were beside themselves with envy and admiration for their friend's ability to not only pull that chump's woman but to talk her into giving him a blowjob right here in the club.

Elaine went down on her knees between the man's legs. Hidden in her hand was a small razor-sharp knife long enough to reach the descending aorta in the drugged man's thigh. As she plunged the sharp blade into the man's thigh, he momentarily lurched forward in pain, but Elaine quickly placed her open lips over the wound as the hot, salty liquid gushed into her mouth. As she sucked the life out of her victim, the neurotoxins in her saliva made it impossible for the man to gather enough strength to stop her sucking every drop of life out of him.

Charles came out of the bathroom and sat at the bar next to the dying man's friends. They all turned and laughed at him.

"Damn, man, your girl is a freak!" One of the soon-to-be-dead man's friends mocked, causing a new round of laughter.

"Shit man, if I were you, I would be all up in that mother fuckers shit right now." The man continued, followed by more laughter.

"Of course, we would have to kill you for fucking with our boy, but I'm just saying." The man stated in a mocking voice.

The group of men all laughed louder, giving each other high fives and slapping one another on the back.

"Yo braw, that is your woman, right?" The ringleader continued.

"No, we are just good friends," Charles replied.

"But still, she should have more respect for you than that. Hell, at least take the mother fucker out in the ally to suck his dick." The man loudly said, bringing another round of humiliating laughter.

"Shit, mother fucker, since she isn't your bitch, you won't mind if I have next then." The man said, joking, bringing his audience back into hysterical laughter.

Charles smiled and thought if only he could introduce this fool to Elaine. Charles could read the man's intentions to do him more harm than insult his pride. Charles noticed the man making eye contact with a woman at the other end of the bar, giving her a signal with a head nod in Charles's direction. The woman looked overused and dressed like a streetwalker.

The bartender placed a drink in front of Charles, "Compliments of the young lady," The man said.

Charles could sense the bartender's compassion and regret. Charles knew the bartender would warn him not to take the drink if he could, but doing so would cause immediate retribution from the criminals in the bar.

Charles smiled, "Thank you," as he accepted the drink.

Unknown to the bartender, Charles thanked him for his humanity despite his inability to put his life in danger to stop him from taking the drink.

The woman was neither young nor a lady. Charles had learned to size people up over the last two hundred years, and he knew this was not a rescue but the wolves responding to the sound of a sheep in distress.

Charles accepted the drink and gave the woman a nod of gratitude. From the first sip of the glass, he could recognize the aftertaste of the date rape drug Rohypnol. Minutes later, he faked drowsiness, and instantly, the woman was at his side.

"Are you alright, Baby?" The fat woman smelled of semen, sweat, cigarettes, and reeking of cheap perfume, looking like she was on break from prostitution, asked, pretending not to know what was wrong with him.

"I'm just feeling a little dizzy," Charles replied.

The men continued their taunting. The punk ass Nigger can't hold his liquor, and he can't hold onto his bitch!!

The mocking men held onto anything they could to stay on their feet from all the laughter.

"Come on, Sugar, let's sit over here," The woman said as she led Charles to another secluded seating area to begin her robbery.

Charles pretended to need her assistance to walk into her trap. Once seated, the woman moved close to him to avoid anyone seeing her go into his pockets. As she moved in, Charles suddenly lifted his head and looked into her eyes. The woman was shocked and paralyzed with fear like a deer staring into oncoming headlights.

"Do you want to help me?" Charles asked.

"Yes," the woman unconsciously answered.

"Then kiss me," Charles instructed.

Usually, the woman did not kiss her Johns due to the emotional connotations of kissing, but she suddenly wanted to be in his arms. She had forgotten the lethal dosage of Rohypnol she and the bartender put into his drink. Now, all she could think of was the warm waves of pleasure flowing through her body as this man held his mouth against hers. The crushing grips of his hands on her body made her vagina throb and ache for penetration. She didn't notice his mouth on her neck as her mind followed the rivers of ecstasy into the blackness. On cue, Elaine showed up at the lounge chair where Charles and the woman were seated and pulled the dead woman away from Charles. Elaine slapped the dead woman to give the impression that she knocked the woman out, who was now lying dead on the floor.

Elaine then pretended to be uncontrollably enraged with jealousy, forcing Charles to drag her out of the club. The occupants all laughed, not realizing what had just happened. To the mocking audience at the bar, their boy was sleeping off a fantasy blowjob, and the woman was temporarily knocked out from a bitch slap. As for the strange couple driving away into the night, it was the best meal they had had in a long time. Charles remembered how Elaine would clownishly imitate the sorry lines the victim used to get himself killed. Elaine could always find a way to make him laugh, even after taking the lives of two not-so-innocent people. She was gone now, and he would have to prowl the streets of the world alone once again.

Thanks to Drake Ellsworth, Charles now knew the name of one of the men responsible for her death. However, the master mind's identity was still a mystery.

CHAPTER 13

The Deaf Detective

The time it took for Paul Blacksmith's arrest, booking, and arraignment for capital murder was a new NYPD record. Detective Rodríguez could not believe his luck, but something did not sit well with him. Blacksmith's court-appointed Attorney had been calling him all morning with a request to visit his client. The detective had all the information he needed to put Blacksmith away for life without the possibility of parole and had no incentive to speak to him again. However, that gut feeling would not go away. If the man is not insane, as his lawyer is suggesting, then he must have been on some unique drug to make him think he saw the things he said transpire on the night of the murders. Blacksmith's story was impossible to believe, i.e., the woman moving so fast that she killed two of his friends before he could get a shot off. Paul admitted he was the one who shot Charles Sinclair in the chest with a burst of fire from his AK-47 and claimed Charles continued to attack. The most incredible is that Charles Sinclair is still alive, at home, fully recovering. Paul Blacksmith was up to something, and now he is trying to get out of spending the rest of his life in prison, the detective thought to himself, but just for shits and grins, he decided to take the lawyer's invitation to speak alone with his client. Who knows, maybe the crazy son of a bitch will help identify the unknown person rumored to be behind the attack on Charles Sinclair and the late Elaine Singleton during his visit with Paul in prison.

It was late in the afternoon when the detective arrived in the segregated wing of Ricker Island. Despite the daily use of copious amounts of disinfectants, mops, and gallons of water, the jail reeked of fear, pain, and hostility. Its interior was extremely utilitarian and void of life, i.e., anything other than free rodents, roaches, and caged humans. As he walked by the heavy cell doors, he could see the faces of the incarcerated peering out of the eight-by-eleven fortified Plexiglas for any sign of hope for freedom or their next victim. They all looked at him with the same air of contempt and hostility. All wished they could have just one moment with the representation of everything they hated and loathed. The detective ignored the loud sounds of the hundreds of proclamations of hate and unnatural sex acts promised to be visited upon him if they ever got out of their eight by ten feet holding cells. Detective Rodríguez and his escorts finally reached Paul Blacksmith's cell.

The Detective was informed that Paul was on suicide watch and had to be forced-fed since he arrived at the detention center. When Paul's cell door slid open, he immediately ran to the furthest corner of his cell, fell to his knees facing the wall, and began to scream, "No, no, I'm not ready, I'm not ready!"

The guards rushed in and subdued him. One of the guards sent a coded message over the radio; the detective translated it as sending the restraining team immediately. The detective stood clear of the chaos to allow the Correctional staff to do their job. The riot unit arrived quickly with someone who looked like they had read at least one medical book and was carrying a hypodermic needle. Once Paul Blacksmith had been subdued, the medical person injected him. After a few moments, the guards were able to remove him from his cell and take him to a padded cell to prevent self-injury.

"Yeah, right, he ain't crazy," Detective Rodríguez thought. Just the same, he came all this way, and he could wait for a few moments to let the drugs calm Blacksmith down long enough to learn what was so important that he had to come to this shit hole to hear it.

An hour later, the Detective was escorted to the jail's psychiatric wing. When he arrived, Paul Blacksmith sat slumped over with his hands and feet strapped to a metal chair. Paul's head was clean-shaven; his scrubbed pale white skin seemed transparent as he sat heavily sedated, wearing an open-back hospital gown. Whatever type of drug they gave him could have been reduced ten times and still knocked out a horse.

"Hello, Paul, you asked to see me," the detective said, trying to get Paul's attention. When Paul looked up, the detective was frightened and shocked to see how much the man had seemed to age but now resembled a restrained, starving predator. His unnaturally black eyes appeared sucked into dark eye sockets to the back of his head by some strange internal vacuum. Paul's skin, which had been pale initially, was now pasty white and clammy.

"You got to get me out of here," Paul demanded in a pathetic, feeble voice.

"Is that what you dragged me here to say?" Julio asked in an annoyed voice.

"You don't understand, man, they are going to get to me in here," Paul replied, almost in tears.

"Who is going to get to you?' Julio Rodriguez asked.

"That dude with the car, he is going to kill me," Paul now whimpering.

"In that case, maybe this is the safest place for you." The detective responded.

"No man, when he comes here, I will be trapped like a fucking rat," Paul now becoming more agitated.

"How in the hell is he supposed to get past all these guards just to get to you? It's time for you to drop this crazy act and tell me what the fuck you got me here for!" Julio demanded.

"I am telling you the fucking truth, man. I shot the mother fucker dead in the chest with my AK, and the mother fucker kept on coming, man!" Paul emphatically stated.

"Yeah, I shot the bitch too, but it was too late for my boys; I'm telling you, man! When he comes for me, and I am trapped in here, none of these fucken guards is going to stop him!" Paul continued.

The Detective could not believe Blacksmith's story and thought it was time to see if he could trick Paul into giving up his accomplice.

"You say you and your friends were only trying to rob and scare them, right?" Julio asked.

"Yeah, man, I ain't no fucking killer, man, I was only trying to make a little money, and that was all." Paul emphatically stated.

"If you tell me who was paying you, I will see what I can do to get you out of here," Julio stated, never intending to fulfill his promise.

The news of the plot financier's freedom of mobility caused Paul to involuntarily jump out of his seat, nearly ripping the chair's restraining bolts off the floor.

"You mean you have not arrested that bitch yet? And she is out there running around free, too!?" Paul stated in panic.

Paul's terrified reaction to the news that the ringleader was still unknown and free took everybody by surprise. The orderlies quickly rushed in to regain control of Blacksmith, who now seemed to have superpowers. Luckily, the metal chair bolted to the ground together, preventing Blacksmith from lunging at Julio. Blacksmith fought like a caged beast, breaking the chains of one of the handcuffs attached to the chair. It took six people to get the

Blacksmith into restraints and bandage the gashes in Paul's risk caused by the handcuffs. Julio had never experienced anything like what he had just witnessed. He quickly tried to regain his composure and control of the situation. As Julio looked around the room, the detective saw the same bewilderment in the faces of the correctional officers and medical staff. Julio decided to use the fear he witnessed Blacksmith display to learn more about the unknown accomplice.

"If you tell me who she is, we can at least get her off of the streets and make it safer for your return," Julio suggested, knowing Paul would probably die in prison.

"I can't tell you her name, man." Paul struggled to say as he was held in a forearm chokehold by one of the correctional officers.

"Tell me, and I will make sure we get her off the streets," Julio said, feigning a genuine concern for Paul.

"Ha, ha, ha, No, you don't want to know her name!" Paul shot back after laughing hysterically.

"You let me judge that, but I can tell you one thing. You will never see the light of day unless you cooperate with us." Julio said as if it mattered.

"You mean you will let me go if I tell you her name?" Paul responded through his heavily medicated state.

"You have my promise that I will do everything I can to get you out right away," Julio said, knowing there was nothing Jesus could do to free this bird.

"You shitting me, man"? Paul slurred.

"Paul, tell me her name!" Julio demanded.

"The bitches' name is." As Paul began to speak the name of the unknown accomplice, he began to cough uncontrollably. Paul's coughs became more and more violent as he struggled to say the name of the unknown accomplice. His coughing caught the attention of the medical staff as they raced to him to release him from his shackles and to render first aid. After placing him on his back on the floor, they tried to find what was obstructing his breathing. Paul began to convulse uncontrollably; as he seized uncontrollably on the floor, Paul never broke eye contact with Detective Rodriguez. Blood started to rhythmically gush out of Paul's mouth as the medical staff looked at one another helplessly. The pool of blood spread over the interview floor; Paul's convulsions seemed to quiet down. Paul was desperately trying to say something as blood continued to flow from his mouth like lava from a volcano.

Frantically, Paul motioned with his eyes and nudged his chin to direct Julio's attention to his right hand. The detective followed Paul's eyes to where his hand was now only partially restrained and saw him write a name in his blood.

DECHONTEE

CHAPTER 14

Agent Wanda Jackson

The Boars Head Tavern stakeout was long and frustrating. Listening to hours and hours of what she called redneck gibberish made Agent Jackson want to bang her head against the wall—the long hours working so close to one another also affected two of her agents. The two FBI Agents, Glenn Baker and Susan Cruz were always on the same monitoring assignments and had been spending more hours off with each other. Baker and Cruz dedicated their lives to becoming FBI agents. They never took the time to develop a personal life outside the agency. It was a relief for both to work with each other. The third Agent, Todd Bostic, was her resident geek and source of treasured research ability, but he was also young and career-driven.

Wanda Jackson and Todd Bostic continued to casually listen to the gibberish being spoken at the Boars Head Tavern. The two agents listened to the conversation between Floyd Harrison and Bill Billington; they recorded Floyd instructing Billington to withdraw all the money to the Masonic lodges account. Why would any of them require all that money? Was this an attempt to escape?

The Masonic Lodge had registered as a 501c3 to raise public funds for charitable purposes; thus, spending funds violated Federal law. The news of the possible financial abuse was the break

Wanda was looking for to justify obtaining a search warrant to enter the tavern and find the evidence to prove the hate group's connection to the death of a soldier and his wife from a nearby military base. Agent Jackson was surprised at how quickly the search warrant was issued and found Wanda and her team at the door of the Boars Head bar and grill the following day. When Agent Jackson and the warrant team arrived, Bill Belington was the only occupant in the bar. She delighted in the fact that Belington was offended and disgusted that a black woman and other people of color dared to enter his sanctuary of hate. Agent Jackson professionally approached Belington and presented him with the search warrant.

"Mr. Belington, you are registered as the lodge's Treasurer and bookkeeper, right?" Agent Jackson asked, already knowing the answer.

"So, what if I am?" He responded by launching a wad of tobacco and spit into an overused bucket near his right foot. Billington did not try to hide his contempt for Agent Jackson and her fellow agents. As far as he was concerned, she and the men who had invaded his bar were what was wrong with America.

"The warrant states that you are to turn over your books and any other financial records to me immediately or face arrest and possible prosecution for obstruction." Agent Jackson said professionally, barely masking her delight at seeing the fat man squirm.

"Does Sheriff know you Nig? I mean, you people are here?" BB demanded angrily, hoping his co-conspirator in the murder of the military couple could prevent the disclosure of the lodges' financial records.

"This is a Federal search warrant, and your Sheriff will be served soon enough." Agent Jackson shot back.

BB reluctantly conceded to the search and presented the books for inspection. After all, there was nothing to hide, and it was just the fact that these agents of the nigger president were in his bar violating his rights as a red-blooded American citizen that he found most distasteful. Agent Jackson knew what she was looking for in the lodges' financial record but pretended to be randomly looking over the registers so that BB would not be tipped off that she had prior knowledge of the lodges' financial transactions.

"Mr. Belington, can you tell me about this entry?" She pointed to the check notation made out to Mr. Floyd Harrison for a pleasure trip to NYC.

BB laughed in a stomach-turning, high-pitched voice and said, "Hell, that there was me being funny, that's all." As he looked around the tavern filled with stone-faced FBI agents seeking to find a face that shared his humor.

"Where is Mr. Harrison now?" Agent Jackson asked, already knowing the answer.

"Well, I don't rightly know," Answered Belington, now beginning to understand the gravity of the notation he had made in the lodge's official financial records.

CHAPTER 15

Ghouls of New York

Meanwhile, at the city morgue, a well-dressed woman and two men approached the back entrance of the New York City Morgue behind Belview Hospital on 1st Avenue and 26th Street. An NYPD Patrolman approached the group who entered a restricted area of the morgue and was quickly dispatched by the woman with a blow to his head that was so violent it broke his neck. The woman's two accomplices dragged the body of the patrolman to a hidden location so it would not be found. They proceeded to the basement of the morgue. One of the morgue attendants stopped them again, warning them they were in a restricted area. The woman grabbed the man off his feet and plunged her canine teeth into the man's neck, causing him to convulse and then become limp and docile violently.

"Where is the body of that bitch, Elaine Singleton?" the woman asks the now compliant mortuary worker.

"Elaine Singleton? I do not know," The man replied.

"Find her!" the woman demanded.

"Yes, yes, I will find her." The man replied.

The attendant went to a computer terminal and searched the database for the location of Elaine's corps.

"I found her," the man proclaimed.

"Take me to her," the woman demanded.

"Yes, I will take you to her," the man replied.

As the trio, along with the attendant, navigated the narrow halls of the morgue, the unfortunate attendants, who came across on their way to Elaine's body, suffered the same fate as their escort, only this time at the hands of the two men who accompanied the woman. A trail of dead bodies littered the morgue hallways leading up to the refrigerated unit where Elaine Singleton's body was stored.

Upon opening the mortuary fridge, the woman looked down on Elaine's body with contempt.

"Ok, pack the bitch up, and let's get out of here," the woman said.

Alarm bells and announcements of intruders began to blast from the PA system. The woman and her companions were taken to a mortuary truck by the man first bitten by the woman and made their escape past the arriving police and ambulance units from the nearby hospital.

Detective Rodríguez welcomed the long drive to work the next day; it gave him time to compartmentalize his thoughts. Melissa was pregnant; how did that happen? Yeah, they had been having a lot of makeup sex, but what great fucking time for his soldiers to all of a sudden show-up and storm her uterus. There goes any hope of retiring anytime soon. He thought to himself.

Something told him he should not have gone to see Paul Blacksmith, and now his mind was all fucked up from what he had witnessed. Who in the hell is Dechontee? The Detective was now convinced that Paul was not putting on an act or trying to pull a fast one over on him, but why had her name never come up in any police report nor reported by any confidential informant? He pulled out a piece of paper and looked at the name again: Dechontee.

On his drive to work, the Detective, lost in thought, had not realized that he had arrived at the Midtown police station. He navigated past the sea of humans to park in the station's parking lot. He walked into the usual noise and organized chaos as he pushed past men in handcuffs, people trying to make a complaint, and officers coming and going in and out of the station. Julio stopped off at the makeshift coffee break area to pour a cup of coffee of questionable age before climbing the stairs to the homicide division on the second floor.

"Julio, my man, thanks for the solid the other day; too bad it was all for nothing." Greeted Detective Brown as Julio entered the open bay homicide division work area.

"Yeah, right, mother fucker, we caught the son of a bitch in record time." Julio shot back as he navigated past the well-used wooden desks with stacks of case files piled on each one.

"Glad to see that dick you had up your ass did not keep you out too long," Julio responded, igniting a round of laughter from his fellow detectives.

"Top of the morning to you, my boy," O'Bannon greeted him in a loud, cheery voice before he could sit down at his desk and hide behind the buttresses of case files on his desk.

"Oh shit," Matthew said, putting his palm on his forehead.

"What is it now, Matt?" Julio asked, knowing he would not like what he was about to hear.

"I thought I should be the one to tell you we will have to let your crazy boy go."

"What in the fuck are you talking about, Matt?"

"You know, your friend Paul Blacksmith," Murphy continued.

"How the fuck is it that we got a clean confession and the murder weapon? How in the fuck is he going to walk?" Julio demanded.

"It seems, my boy, that someone lost the dead girl's body," Murphy stated, not wanting to believe it himself.

"Murphy, I am not in the mother fucking mood for your bull shit today, alright. I am telling you, today is not a good day to be fucking with Me.!" Julio said, getting very annoyed.

"I shit you not, Leddy, the dead girl's body, along with the evening attendant and night watchmen, went missing from the morgue last night, and without the body, the Judge had to make him qualified for bail." "His new lawyer posted his bail, so Blacksmith is being released."

Julio remembered that Paul Blacksmith came from a middle-class family and assumed they mortgaged their home to bail him out.

Julio could tell by the look on Matt's face that he was not joking.

"Well fuck the shit out of me," Julio said as he sat in his chair in disbelief.

Julio saw Detective Brown sitting across the room, gloating over the bad news. Julio imagined himself punching him in the face.

"It wasn't our case anyway, so fuck it," Julio said in a false attempt to distance himself from the case.

The fact that Paul Blacksmith was in prison had little consequence for Drake Ellsworth. If he wanted to, Drake could have used Elaine's connections to have him killed no matter where Blacksmith was; prison only made it more accessible. When Drake learned of the disappearance of Elaine's body and Paul's eligibility for bail, his first reaction was admiration for whoever came up with the idea as a means of beating a murder rap. However, Drake's primary concern was the package he received earlier. The package was a wrapped empty box with a note inside instructing him to provide the head of Elaine to prove that she was dead or his own. He did not have to know who the package was from to realize that the news of Elaine's death had already attracted the attention of all her rivals. Ellsworth realized he had to apprehend Paul Blacksmith very soon and make an example to everyone considering taking advantage of Elaine's death to muscle in on her territory. He would ensure his men were waiting for Paul Blacksmith at the prison gates when he was released. He imagined the shocked look on the face of whoever opened the box and discovered their flunky head instead of Elaine's. Drake put his hand on one of his 45 caliber automatic pistols in its shoulder holster. The touch of it reminded him of his father, who had given them to him as a graduation gift when Drake had completed Army Ranger school. The M1911A1s had been passed down from his grandfather, one of the Army Rangers who assaulted Pointe du Hoc during the WW II Omaha Beach invasion of France. Ever since the automatic pistols had been passed down as a talisman against harm and death, every Ellsworth man had used them in anger. A wave of homesickness came over Drake, and he decided to call home while he could.

Drake dialed his family's home phone, and after a few rings, his mother answered.

"Hey Ma, this is Drake," he announced.

His mother let out a squeal in delight, hearing her son's voice.

"Drake, where have you been, and what took you so long to call?" Drake's mother, Lillian, asked.

"Sorry about that, Mom. I have been swamped, but I am calling now. How have you and the family been?" Drake asked.

"You know, when you don't call, it worries me sick," She said.

"Are you still in New York, and when are you coming home to visit?" She continued.

"Carl, Carl, it is Drake on the phone!" Drake's mother called out to his father before he could answer.

Drake could hear joyful sounds in the background and imagined the smiling faces of his younger brother and sister. It did not take his father a minute before he was on the phone.

"Hey Ranger, where have you been?". Drake's father, Carl, asked.

Drake's bond with his father was unshakeable. Drake followed in his father and grandfather's footsteps by joining the United States Army Rangers, strengthening their bond.

"I'm still in New York, Dad wishing I was home." "How are Luis and Brenda doing? I could hear their big mouths in the background". Drake said, feeling the world's weight lift off his shoulders with each moment spent talking with his father.

"Hold on, I will put them on the phone." Drake's father said.

"No, Dad, not now," Drake said before his father could call his siblings to the phone.

"Dad, I have gotten myself into a cluster fuck here, and I am afraid it might follow me home," Drake said, getting straight to the point.

"What do you need me to do, Son?" the old soldier responded.

" I own a house on the Hawaiian Island of Maui. The house is fully furnished and supplied. Please take the family there ASAP. The traveling arrangements and airline tickets will be delivered to you by the end of the week." Drake said in a tone easily recognized by anyone who had spent time in the Army Rangers.

"Will do, Son. Please make sure you meet us there." His father replied, trying his best to hide the fear of never seeing his son alive again.

"I've got to go now and tell the family I will call back soon to talk with each of them. Dad, please tell Mom I love her and will call more often."

"Roger that, Ranger. Please don't make me a liar, Son. I love you." Carl Ellsworth said, choking back the tears.

"I love you too, Dad," Drake said before ending the call.

Drake felt a wave of guilt knowing his ambitions to leave his family home in search of adventure had resulted in his family being uprooted and placed in danger. How could he have known things would end up this way? Drake returned to the French doors leading to a balcony overlooking Central Park. He poured himself a drink as he looked down at the busy construction workers below. Drake watched people enjoying the vast park, walking here and there, cyclists riding to and fro, and envied them all. Drake dreamed of the day he would put up his guns for good and promised himself that if he were blessed with a son, he would do everything he could to convince that child would never be a soldier.

CHAPTER 16

Paul's Prison Nightmare

Paul received the Rikers Island jail notice that he would be released. The news filled him with dread. The jail provided him with security and protection from the monster he encountered on the road. However, despite his fear and appreciation, he craved seeing Dechontee again. He felt like he was addicted to her, but unlike a drug, he didn't know of a cure. The fear of falling asleep was Paul's immediate concern. A recurring nightmare made falling asleep terrifying to Paul. Pounding his fist against his legs, he hoped the pain would keep him awake just a little longer to avoid the terror that awaited him in REM sleep space.

"Five minutes to lights out." The correctional officers announced they would give the inmates time to put away whatever they were doing before the jail cell lights were turned off, with only the hallway lights remaining on.

"Oh God, please don't let me fall asleep." Paul prayed silently to himself. Paul stared through the small Plexiglas on his cell door at the hallway light that stood sentry against the lurking demons waiting in his nightmare. It had been four days since he last slept, but the visions in his reoccurring nightmare were still vivid in his mind. His eyes grew dark as the warm sensation enveloped him, signaling the beginning of sleep. Panicked, he shook himself awake, admonishing himself for being so careless. With renewed vigor, sitting on his bed, Paul looked out of his cell door window at the light in the hallway, determined not to fall asleep. Suddenly, the cell door slid open, and he sat up on high alert. He could see and hear people and cars passing by his open cell door.

"What the hell is this?" Paul asked himself.

Paul nervously walked to his cell door and looked out into the night on a busy city street.

"Where in the hell did all these people come from, and how did they get here?" he thought, bewildered.

"Hey, Bro, where have you been?" It was his best friend Brandon who suddenly appeared out of the crowd, but Paul watched him die that night.

"I thought you were dead," Paul said.

"Do I look dead to you, mother fucker?" Brandon said in his usual upbeat manner.

"You're the one who looks like someone in need of a good time," Brandon said.

"Come on, my brother; there is someone I want you to meet," Brandon said as he placed his arm around Paul's shoulders like they did when they were kids.

Brandon continued to talk as Paul tried to make sense of what was happening. Paul was always envious of Brandon's swagger. As Brandon walked, his long dreads swung in rhythm with his long strides.

"Hey, man, the fellas and I have missed you. What has kept you away?" Brandon asked as they continued down the busy New York City street.

Paul allowed himself to relax and take in the sounds and sights of NYC nightlife. The yellow taxi cabs racing up and down Broadway, the thousands of people pushing up and down the streets, and the loud sound of many voices were momentarily drowned out by the sound of emergency vehicle signees passing by. But something was not right.

"Where are we going?" Paul asked.

"Going? We are already here," Brandon replied.

All the people and cars vanished from the streets, leaving the city vacant except for Paul and Brandon.

"I told you, man; she wants to see you," Brandon said, no longer smiling.

Paul noticed they were in front of the nightclub where he first met Dechontee, and his blood ran cold.

"She is waiting for you inside," Brandon said as Paul watched rivers of blood begin to flow down his friend's neck. His radiant brown skin turned a sickening shade of gray while it rapidly decayed and fell away from his face. Brandon's eyes sunk back into his skull as the flesh of his face as magots ravished his dead flesh.

Paul moved away from Brandon in horror, and against his will, he found himself reaching for the doorknob.

"Why are you going in, you fool?" He thought as he pushed the door open and stepped inside the darkened nightclub.

Inside, the club was silent and void of patrons. A spinning disco globe illuminated the dark and empty nightclub with momentary flashes of red illumination.

Paul entered the club; he noticed a lone woman sitting in a darkened booth and immediately knew it was her.

His body became frozen with fear and arousal, but he could feel himself floating towards her as if on a conveyor belt. The woman's broad-brimmed black hat blocked her face. Her voluptuous breasts and long, lean legs were easily recognizable in the short, skin-tight, low-cut dress that clung to her body like the skin on her tantalizingly perfect body.

"Have a seat, my love?" She seductively said.

Her voice made him tremble with fear and gave him an erection at the same time. He began to motion to the seat across from her.

"No, lover, come sit next to me. I have missed you, my love." She said in a soothing, sexy voice as she slid over, making room for him to sit.

Sitting beside her, he felt like a mouse getting into bed with a hungry snake but could not resist her every command.

He had to do something; perhaps if he could explain what happened, she would realize that none of this was his fault.

"Dechontee I." As Paul spoke, she quickly placed her ice-cold hand on his mouth.

"Didn't I tell you never to speak that name, my love?" She said in a very soft, gentle voice.

"Yes, but please let me explain what happened out there," Paul stated, desperate to end his suffering.

"There is no need to explain, my love; I only want to hold you in my arms again and feel your warm kiss on my lips," she said as she turned and softly placed her arms around him, drawing him closer.

Paul began to relax and close his eyes, remembering the heroin-like sensation he experienced the last time he kissed her. A cold chill ran through his body, and he forced his eyes open to find Elaine coming in for the kill with her mouth wide open, flashing her enormous fangs. Paul tried to push her away, but she held him in a constricting vice grip he was unable to break. His strength was quickly fading as he could feel her hot breath against his neck and her saliva running down his cheek. Paul managed to cringe a little away from her. Elaine pulled away and slapped him across the face, knocking him to the floor and knocking him semi-conscious. With blazing speed, Elaine straddled him while pinning his head to the ground with her forearm. Paul struggled with all his might to free himself as he could feel her fangs sink deep into his neck and her tong and lips sucking the blood from his body. Paul continued to fight, determined not to let her finish him off like he had witnessed her finishing off his friends. As his mind went blank, he could hear someone calling his name and a light shining in the distance.

"Blacksmith, Blacksmith, wake the fuck up, you are having a nightmare." Paul continued to fight until his mind cleared. He found himself surrounded by a room full of correctional officers who had restrained him to the floor, and he began to cry uncontrollably with relief.

"I will be glad when this mother fuckers bail is posted, and he is transferred out of here; I can't take much more of this bullshit." One of the restraining guards said.

"Yeah, I hear that." Replied another guard.

As Paul's mind cleared, he became aware of the loud noise the other inmates of his cell block were making.

"Would somebody please shut that crazy mother fucker up?!" was the most frequent demand.

CHAPTER 17

The Serapian Trap

Drake's prison informants reported Detective Rodriguez's interview with Paul Blacksmith and gave him the name Paul claimed to be the mastermind behind his actions the night of Elaine's death. Drake had never heard of anyone called Dechontee and concluded that Elaine's killing was not random but contracted by someone not trying to muscle in on their territory. Elaine's contract killing and the thief of her body still mystified him. Why were there no records of the woman named Dechontee in any police record anywhere? Who would benefit by stealing Elaine's body?

Drake knew the information verifying Elaine's death not being at the hands of one of her drug cartel rivals did not matter. He knew her absence would be like chum in shark-infested waters. Drake was determined to ensure he eliminated whoever was behind Elain's death before he became the next victim. Luckily, Drake purchased the property in Maui to be used by Elaine if she had to disappear. Drake could not have known it would be his family utilizing the property for the same reason.

It was time for him to call upon his trusted ace and battle buddy, Mr. Joseph Bowser, to discover the Dechontee's identity.

Meanwhile, back in Mississippi, Floyd Harrison thought about how he always enjoyed traveling. He jumped on any opportunity to get away from the small-minded people he was forced to deal with daily and rejoin the rest of the world. He needed something to clear his head, find a way to explain his secretive behavior to Carol, and not give away his sworn oath to the Serapian Order.

Floyd was pleasantly surprised to learn his airline ticket had been upgraded to first class, and the money he had spent on his ticket had been fully refunded to his checking account. After nervously enquiring about the change in his itinerary, he was convinced it was not an error and accepted the upgrade. Now, more than ever, Floyd was reminded that this was not a pleasure trip and had to stay focused. He cringed his neck as the aircraft finished its final approach to LaGuardia International Airport in New York City. He looked out the airplane window to see the magnificent New York skyline.

Floyds' mind drifted back to his last meeting with his Serapian master before he departed for New York. He was summoned to another late-night meeting. Floyd remembered feeling annoyed by the Order's disregard for his personal life. It was this kind of last-minute meeting that caused Carol to ask for a legal separation, and if he did not do something, his marriage would end in divorce. A hooded and masked regional council member met with Floyd and the three other local members of the Serapian Order late one night in yet another remote location late one night. Dressed in their dull gray monk-like robes, they began the proceeding. Floyd recalled them as men who had little to live for and found a purpose for their lives by living out dungeons and dragon fantasy. Why else would grown men enjoy meeting in the woods late at night?

"Honorable Brethren, I am sure you are all aware of the sensational story coming out of New York," Floyd rhetorically said, not expecting a reply.

To honor his late father, Floyd played the role of a believing member the best he could.

The three senior members sitting in a circle nodded in agreement.

"If it is true, needless do I have to tell you the significance of this story."

He continued, "We have the historical testimony of a distant Sinclair surviving injury that should have killed any other human being, and now it seems another has inherited the same gift." The members looked around the circle at one another and then nodded in agreement.

"I proposed that you send me to New York to investigate this man to determine if he truly has the traits that so many have dedicated their lives to find," Floyd concluded.

"What you ask can prove to be very dangerous." One of the hooded men stated.

Floyd could hardly contain the impulse to laugh at how seriously the hooded man took his involvement in this costume play.

"What do you know about the previous investigation of the Sinclair family?" another asked.

"I have read that the inquiry was inconclusive," Floyd answered.

"Inconclusive?" The elder of the three hooded men asked.

"Yes, the record stated that the investigation of Mr. Charles Sinclair's forefather, escape, and subsequent death in Africa ended the investigation," Floyd responded.

"What else did the record tell you?" Brother Harrison? Asked the third hooded man.

"It also spoke of mysterious deaths, but what I found interesting was the report of the missing Brothers," Charles sincerely concluded.

"This doesn't give you alarm, Brother Harrison?" The senior hooded figure asked.

Honored Brethren, that was almost 150 years ago; I am sure we are living in a safer time," Floyd said, trying his best not to show how humorous he felt watching these three grown men taking this treasure hunt game a little bit too seriously.

"What do you think happened to the investigators?" The second speaker asked.

"We all loved your grandfather; your father was a great champion for our cause. We would be remiss if we did not share our concerns with you." The second speaker stated before Floyd could answer.

Floyd wondered why the man had tried to obstruct the other Serapians' inquiry.

"What do you mean our concerns?" Floyd asked.

"We believe the investigators were murdered because of something they found." The first speaker reluctantly stated.

Floyd took a moment to allow the words to sink in. Have these fools murdered while playing dress-up in the past? Floyd asked himself.

"Murdered, who and why would someone feel it necessary to kill someone investigating a theory?" Floyd asked.

The hooded assembly moved away from the table enough to be out of Floyd Harrison's listening range to have a private discussion. For the first time, Floyd began to feel apprehensive. He did not like the implications of the line of questioning he was engaged in and wondered just how seriously these men took their fantasy play.

Away from Floyd, the three men quietly spoke.

"Do you think he can pull this off without getting himself killed?" One of the hooded men asked.

"If he follows our instructions, he should be ok." One of the trios said.

"Has anyone gotten an indication the mysterious women our brothers warned us of had been detected in New York City?" The first speaker asked.

"No, but one of those Witches seems to show up every time we get a good lead directing us to the Challis of Life," the second speaker said.

"What should we tell Mr. Harrison about them?" The third man asked.

"Let us not forget; he was chosen because of the limited importance of his Chapter and the improvability of him revealing anything about the inner workings of our Order should he be captured by one of those witches." The Senior member stated.

"He knows too much already, and we don't know if we can trust him with the full truth yet; besides, we don't have any useful information to provide him with." The Senior member continued.

"As long as he follows our instructions, he should be able to complete his investigation and lure out the witches before anyone gets the wiser. Besides, he will be protected by a member of our guards, the Serapian Eidikoi Frouroi (SEF)," The third man said.

The three hooded men nodded in agreement and returned to address Floyd.

"We are approving your investigation and your trip to New York. Members of the New York affiliation will support you. You are to limit sure investigations to Mr. Charles Sinclair only. Please understand that we cannot guarantee your safety, and we are instructing you to end your investigation immediately at the first sign of trouble." The first speaker stated.

These people took themselves way too seriously, Floyd thought to himself as he left the house. The news of people being murdered over the theory that there was some elixir for immortality was disturbing and almost laughable. After all, we no longer live in a world of superstition and witchcraft. It would take a person addicted to conspiracy theories and games like Dungeons & Dragons to feel the need to kill somebody over a notion that could not be true. However, the rumor concerning people disappearing after being identified with specific genetic and blood types by the Bishops of Christ caused Floyd discomfort. However, he refused to associate the disappearances of people with the medical facilities the Bishops of Christ sponsored with the Serapian biological research. Still, the talk of sacrifice for immortality did not make him feel well.

Floyd's first-class flight to NYC was impressive and uneventful. Still, the opportunity to leave his small redneck town was exhilarating. He tried not to reveal his excitement while watching the massive city from his window as the aircraft approached JFK International Airport. After disembarking from the plane, he joined the sea of humans rushing in all directions while he made his way to the baggage claim area. Floyd was surprised to see a well-dressed man holding a sign with his name.

He approached the man, not entirely sure if the man was there looking for him. After all, he had never received that kind of attention before.

"I am Floyd Harrison." He announced to the man.

"Mr. Harrison, don't worry about your bags. I will deliver them to your hotel suite. Your driver is waiting for you outside," the man explained.

Floyde found a woman standing in front of a Lincoln town car limousine, holding another sign with his name, waiting for him outside the airport terminal.

"Mr. Harrison? A woman in a black business suit wearing one-inch heel shoes greeted him. She held the limousine passenger door open, inviting him to enter. The attractive woman could have easily been a supermodel. However, her calm, professional demeanor made it clear she was no one to be taken lightly.

"My name is Rachel Horne, and I am your concierge."

"Yes, I am Floyd Harrison." "Where are you taking me?" Floyd asked.

"To your hotel, Sir." The female concierge answered, puzzled by the question.

Floyd felt embarrassed and did not want to give away how dumbfounded he was by the level of support he was receiving.

"Do you have my hotel reservation number?" He asked.

"Of course, Sir, you have already been checked into the penthouse in the Waldorf."

"There must be some mistake." He said, making it clear that he would not be responsible for this type of lavish expenditure. He replied, giving them another chance to determine if this royal treatment was for him.

"No, Sir. You are Mr. Wu Choi's guest, and everything has been taken care of," the lovely Rachel Horne replied as they pulled away from the airport.

Seeing NYC from the perspective of a VIP gave Floyd a profound respect for the city.

His mind raced through the Rolodex of New York City hotels that he knew and crashed into the Waldorf Astoria on Park Avenue, one of the most expensive hotels in the city. He knew that his chapter of the Order could not afford this expense.

Floyd knew the Order had many affluent members. He never had the opportunity to experience the organization's full power. To ensure their secret activities would never be exposed to the public, the many branches of the Serapian Order intentionally isolated themselves.

Floyds sat in the gorgeous limousine interior as his out-of-place luggage got in the trunk, his mind filled with many questions. He and the lovely young woman pulled away from the curb of the airport arrival terminal; he noticed one black Cadillac leading them in the front and another trailing the limo in the rear.

His mind reached increasing degrees of excitation while driving through the busy streets of NYC. Upon arrival at the

Waldorf Hotel, Floyd was ushered past the reception desk in the lavish lobby to the elevator to the hotel's exclusive penthouse. The colossal grin across Floyd's face revealed how impressed he was, no matter how he tried his best not to show it. He thought about reaching for his wallet to tip the lovely young concierge who escorted him from the airport, but that would be the final proof that he was some country boy way in over his head. Before leaving, Rachel handed him a cream-colored linen paper envelope. His name, written in a fancy italic print embedded in gold, never looked so important.

"Your butler will be here shortly to unpack your luggage and to assist you with any concerns, Mr. Harrison," the lovely concierge said.

"Thank you, Rachel." He wished he had the words or a snowball's chance in hell to have a woman like her in his life. However, he did have Carol, and if only he could share this experience with her, she would realize the benefit of his affiliation with this mysterious organization.

Later that morning, Floyd received a phone call.

"I hope I did not disturb you, Mr. Harrison," Racheal said.

She informed him a suitcase and other packages were waiting for him at his hotel door. She asked if he required additional assistance.

"No, that will be all, and thank you for the wake-up call." He spoke.

"Your car will be waiting for you when you are ready to leave, Mr. Harrison, and I hope the tailor matched your measurements correctly." She stated that as she concluded the phone call,

In the foyer leading to his hotel suite, Floyd noticed the packages. Placed on the packages was an envelope with his name on it. After retrieving the packages, Floyd opened the envelope, dreading the possibility of finding a bill inside. The note read,

"Brother. Floyd Harrison,
Your visit honors us, and your quest overjoys us.
Please join us for dinner at:
The Yi Lan Halal Restaurant.
Your driver will pick you up.

Sincerely,
Your Eternal Brother Wu."

By its wording, Floyd was convinced that Mr. Choi was a senior member of the Order, yet still, he had to be cautious. He was looking forward to meeting his generous benefactor and brother.

"I better find out something about this Sinclair guy." He thought to himself.

After showering, Floyd decided to get some sleep before meeting his benefactor.

Floyd Harrison awoke to a knock on the door. After wiping the sleep from his eyes, he checked the time on the clock on the nightstand by his bed.

"Dang, it's 4:00 PM, I must have overslept." He said to himself.

Floyd jumped from his lavishly large bed and put on his robe before going to answer the door. He stopped to look in the mirror to ensure the power nap was not showing on his face. After all, he wanted to make a good impression on the lovely Rachel even though he did not have a chance to impress her.

Floyd opened the door, trying to project a Tom Cruise coolness. He was shocked to see an exotic, stern-faced middle-aged man, who he would later learn was the result of Nigerian and Japanese heritage.

"Good morning, Mr. Harrison. Mr. Choi sends his regards; my name is Isoba Miyako." The man said.

"Oh, hello, I was expecting Rachel; please come in," Floyd said, regaining his composure and trying to conceal his embarrassment.

"I will be helping you with your research while you are here in the city." Mr. Miyako said.

"That's great. Can I get you something to drink," Floyd asked, trying to stall to figure out just how much this man knew about him and his research.

"No, but thank you." Mr. Miyako said as he sat in the suite's living room.

"Do not worry, Mr. Harrison, or may I call you Floyd? Mr. Miyako said, sensing Floyd's reluctance.

"Yes, by all means," Floyd responded.

"Mr. Choi has briefed me on your assignment here, and we stand ready to assist you." Mr. Miyako stated.

The "we" reference indicated to Floyd that Mr. Miyako was affiliated with the Serapians.

"Mr. Choi is my Bishop and mentor. I will provide security and administrative support while you are here." Mr. Miyako stated.

"That's great. Since we are on a first-name basis, how should I address you?" Floyd asked.

"My friends call me Iso." Mr. Isoba Miyako said.

"Well, Iso, when do we get started?" Floyd asked, still not sure why security was mentioned.

CHAPTER 18

Frederic Lawrence

All day, Mr. Frederic Lawrence continued monitoring Charle's physical and mental condition at the Sinclair estate. He grew more concerned with each passing day and wondered how long Charles could contain the beast that hid within him.

"Charlie, are you OK," Lawrence asked, trying to jolt Charles out of his trance.

Several times, Frederic had found Charles trapped in a living nightmare, digging his nails into a chair's armrest, staring wide-eyed into space, and drenched in sweat. However, the recent events left Charles more distressed than Frederic had ever seen him before, but they became more frequent and intense.

Charles knew by Lawrence referring to him so familiarly that he was genuinely concerned and was grateful to have a friend like Frederic who knew how to break him out of the mental hell he often found himself in.

"Frederic, I am okay," Charles lied, but what else could he say? How could Charles describe the horrors that visited him without warning? How could anyone understand the horrible, vivid smells of blood, the burning heat of the flames, the screams of pain he was increasingly experiencing while still awake? If a psychiatrist diagnosed him, he would have been given a diagnosis of severe schizophrenia or post-stress disorder syndrome. However, these were not hallucinations; they were memories of a hundred years of a living hell, all coming back to haunt him.

"Is there anything I could do to help you, Charles?" Frederic asked.

"No, Fred, you have already done all you could do; please let me have some time alone," Charles said.

Reluctantly, Frederic Lawrence conceded, leaving Charles alone in his study.

Once Charles was alone, he went to his desk and dialed Drake.

After the phone had ringed a few times, Drake answered.

"Yes, Mr. Sinclair."

"I have learned that our mutual friend will be released from prison shortly; please make sure we do not lose track of him," Charles directed.

"Yes, Mr. Sinclair, I am already aware of the situation," Drake stated in his general matter-of-fact tone.

"Let me know as soon as you hear anything." Charles requested, admiring Drake's efficiency.

"Yes, Mr. Sinclair, will that be all?" Drake asked.

"Yes, and we need to meet soon," Charles stated before he hung up the phone.

Drake sat alone in the dark, trying to make sense of the news he had just received. More importantly, he was intrigued by a new side of Mr. Charles Sinclair that Drake had noticed since Elaine Singleton's' death. That still did not explain why he got the chills and the urge to fight or fight whenever he interacted with Charles. Drake had remembered Elaine Singleton before she met Charles Sinclair. Yes, she was your ordinary Psychopath back then, but she got much worse after she met Charles Sinclair. Drake remembered first meeting Elaine after returning from Iraq and leaving the Army. Drake was without direction or purpose when

Elaine hired him as her security chief. He was aware of her criminal reputation, but that made her no different than the pedophiles and drug lords he guarded for the United States government. He was trained in the art of death as a Ranger and Green Beret while serving in the Army. During his final deployment, he and his best friend, Master Sergent Joseph Bowser, were the only survivors of a failed mission that resulted in many civilian deaths and his entire platoon being wiped out. He returned to the States disillusioned and good at only one thing: killing. He knew where he stood with Elaine when she hired him and trusted her to keep him out of her illicit businesses. Unfortunately, as time passed, he found himself in numerous questionable positions on both sides of the law. Initially, the multiple attacks on Elaine's life required him to use his firearm more than he wanted to. Eventually, as the chief of security, he became the target of the attacks and was forced to go on the offensive more than once. Drake had to face the harsh reality that now his fate was tied to Elaine, and he desperately needed to find a way to escape Elaine's' shadow.

The attack on Charles' life was under the jurisdiction of the State Police. In comparison, the theft of Elaine's body fell under the purview of the New York City Police. Unbeknownst to Detective Rodríguez and Detective O'Bannon, they were assigned to the case at the request of the Sinclair estate. Having the two detectives assigned to the case reduced Charles's exposure and kept them under Charles's control. Finally, It would reduce the amount of damage Charles would have to clean up if they discovered a connection between the attack on his life and the doctor's disappearance.

The detectives requested an opportunity to visit Charles Sinclair to look at the bulletproof man to see if he had any idea who would want to steal his dead friend's body. Charles approved the detective's request for an interview to learn more about the men he was allowed to intrude into his life.

On the interview day, the Sinclair estate bursts into view from the many twisting tree-lined roads Detective Rodríguez and his partner Detective O'Bannon navigate to interview Charles Sinclair. It was sunset in the late afternoon when they arrived at the estate. Still, the sprawling grounds of the estate were impressive.

"This doesn't look like drug money, but you never know," O'Bannon said as they drove through the front gate onto the property.

Rodriguez did not answer, knowing Matt O'Bannon had the mental condition of seeing potential crimes in everything, as most law enforcement officers shared after many years on the job. The Detectives parked their car in the semi-circle driveway with a giant bronze statue of a rearing horse surrounded by a bed of multi-colored roses. Lawrence Hamilton greeted the two men at the door. He escorted them to the dining room the size of half a basketball court, where Charles liked to meet people he was trying to win over.

The long walk through the marble atrium, the extravagant library, the sitting room, and finally, the dining room was to impress the visitors. The walls were covered with various rare, expensive oil paintings, portraits of people the detectives assumed were dead Sinclair family members, and many of a beautiful African American female from the 1800s. The inspectors were amazed to see how much each member of the Sinclair lineage looked like one another. Rodriguez also took notice of an assortment of Civil War-era swords, knives, and pistols, as well as other instruments of death from other proceeding wars, on one of the library walls and wondered if any of the devices of death had ever been used by the long-dead Sinclair's.

"Mr. Sinclair will be with you shortly; gentlemen, please make yourself comfortable," Lawrence stated as they entered the large dining room. A large family portrait framed in an elaborately carved gold frame hung from the wall behind the head of the table. Judging from the dress style of the man, woman, and two children, plus the plantation scenery in the painting, Julio estimated the portrait was commissioned before or during the American Civil War period. The wealth of the family took Julio aback in the picture. He was accustomed to seeing photographs of enslaved Africans and field workers in history books and in the media representing the lifestyle of Africans in America during that period. However, the large lithograph portrait on the wall told a story of African American wealth and privilege Julio never imagined existed during that period. The detective could not calculate how much it must have cost to make a lithograph with such clarity back in the 1800s. In fact, until that moment, neither man knew an African American could afford it.

"Would either of you gentlemen like a refreshment?" Lawrence asked.

"Yeah, single malt scotch on the rocks for me; how about you, Leddy?" O'Bannon stated, knowing Rodríguez would decline.

"No, nothing for me, thanks," Rodriguez responded while glancing at Matt sternly.

After Lawrence had left the room, O'Bannon said, "Leddy, are you mad? Are you not taking advantage of getting some of the best booze in the world? What is the matter with you?"

"I just don't want to have to be dragging your ass out of here," Rodriguez responded.

"Just a little bit of top-shelf scotch wouldn't kill ya, you know," Matt said.

"Ya gotta untie your panties once in a while, Leddy," Matt concluded.

Lawrence returned with a tray with Matt's drink.

"Mr. Sinclair will be with you shortly. Is there anything I can do for you?

Lawrence stated as O'Bannon turned up his glass, emptying it all into his mouth.

"No, thank you anyway," Rodriguez said, giving O'Bannon a long hard stare. The noise of the door opening announced Charles's arrival. Charles was wheeled into the dining room by Clair, who also steadied the drip bag connected by an intravenous tube into Charles' arm. The two detectives stood as Charles arrived. The two detectives glanced at each other to verify their amazement; they could not believe how much this man sitting in front of them looked identical to all the males in the paintings in the estate and precisely like the man staring down at them from the photo hanging on the wall behind him.

"Gentlemen, gentlemen, please be seated," Charles stated as Claire pushed closer to his visitors.

"Please excuse me for not standing," Charles said, pretending frailty.

"It is understandable, Mr. Sinclair," Rodriguez stated.

"Thank God the bullet missed all my vital organs, and it is a miracle that I escaped with my life." Charles volunteered.

"A miracle indeed," Rodriguez said as he recalled Paul Blacksmith's account of that night's attack.

"I understand that you have arrested my dear friend's killer," Charles said, probing for the reason for the visit.

"Well, yes, but a complication has developed," Rodriguez answered.

"Complications, I don't understand," Charles stated.

"It seems that we have misplaced your friend, Ms. Elaine Singleton's friend's body, without a body, "Julio confessed.

"Without her body, we had nothing to deny bail for Mr. Blacksmith, and his bail got posted. We had to release him from prison," Rodriguez said.

Charles was aware of the theft of Elaine's body, but the thought of it still enraged him and gave him a sickening feeling in the pit of his stomach. He imagined the perverted hands of the Serapian Order dissecting his beloved Elaine to find the secrets to extend their lives or Dechontee using it to inflict more pain and suffering.

"What the hell do you mean? You misplaced Elaine's body!" Charles demanded," Charles demanded pretending to have no previous knowledge of the situation. Yet, he hoped the NYPD had discovered the information he could not obtain.

"All we can tell you at this time is that the night staff at the city morgue are missing along with the body of your friend, but I assure you we will get to the bottom of this, recover it, and put anyone who had anything to do with her body's disappearance in jail." He continued with false conviction.

Charles pretended the news of Elaine's missing body caught Charles totally off guard; he requested the interview be terminated. While Lawrence escorted the two detectives from the estate, Charles's mind was filled with murderous rage as he tried to imagine what Dechontee, or the Priest of Serapes, could want with Elaine's corps.

CHAPTER 19

Hidden Agendas

The months of investigations and surveillance in the back woods of little redneck town had taken a toll on FBI Agent Wanda Jackson's relationship, or at least that is what she was calling it. Otherwise, Wanda would have to describe it more accurately, i.e., her reliable booty call partner. Now that she and her team had written a detailed report concerning the murder of the Soldier and his wife to include Mr. Bill Billington, the town Sheriff, and other suspected members of the Masonic lodge, and request for the New York State FBI field office to be aware of Mr. Floyd Harrisons as a flight risk, Wanda thought she would take advantage of the break in the action to get reacquainted with Gerald. The night before, Wanda had received a much-needed phone call from Gerald to inform her that he had finished his caseload early and was catching the first flight out to see her. The news helped Wanda shake off the frustration of the investigation. She found a new lease on life as she lost herself in preparation for her reunion with District Attorney Gerald Shabazz. The thought of Gerald's arrival awakened suppressed desires to have a life with Gerald. She knew trying to make a life with Gerald would demand sacrifices, but Wanda dared to dream that their love could prevail. Wanda promised to find the courage to invite Gerald to her parent's house for dinner during his visit. Her parents, happy to hear she was dating again, pressured her to bring him home to meet him. Wanda knew her mother would love Gerald, but her father was not welcoming of any man who came calling on his daughters. Wanda was reviewing the list of things she needed to get done before he arrived, i.e., nails, hair, a new outfit, and the dreaded bikini wax torture. Wanda needed Gerald's visit to help her reconnect with what was decent in life and remember what it felt like to be in the comfort of a man. Her thoughts were interrupted by a phone call that put a knot in her stomach, requesting her to immediately report to the Alabama FBI Bureau Chief in the morning. She wondered who she had pissed off or what she could have done now to warrant this urgent request to meet with the State Bureau Chief. Wanda stayed up all night reading, reviewing, and re-reading her case notes to see if there was anything that she had missed that would warrant a meeting with the Bureau Chief, but she found nothing. The news of her summons to the Bureau Chief's office was a precursor to death. Wanda spent the remainder of the weekend at the local FBI Bureau reviewing all aspects of her case. She noticed her fellow agents treated her like she had suddenly become the most contagious person on the planet while others offered their halfhearted support. Her appointment was for Monday at 0700, but Wanda arrived at 0630. While sitting across from a young male receptionist outside the Chief's office, she noticed military members and other unknown men and women entering the Chief's office for the meeting.

"This can't be good if members of the Military are involved; this must be a National Security matter," she thought to herself.

"Agent Jackson, the Chief is ready for you now," the young man announced, wakening Wanda from her thoughts.

Entering the room, she could see the Bureau Chief sitting at the head of a mini-conference table surrounded by an Army two-star general, a Navy Rear Admiral, a female two-star Air Force general, and four other unknown people. Judging by their age and ranks, she suspected they were senior members of whatever agency they represented.

"Agent Jackson, thank you for joining us on such short notice; please sit down." The Bureau Chief said as she walked into the door. Like most other men, the Bureau Chief was cold and calculating. His smile and twinkling blue eyes masked a professional ruthlessness no cold-blooded reptile could match. The other committee member remained stone-faced and silent as she made her way to the only remaining seat with a name placeholder, her name on it facing out on the table in front of it.

"We understand that you oversee the investigation into the death of Specialist Kenneth Jones and his wife. Is that right?" The Bureau Chief asked.

"Sir, that is correct." She answered, puzzled at the level of interest her investigation was receiving.

"Please tell us how your investigation is going." He asked.

"Sir, we have identified two definite suspects, Mr. Bob Belington and the town's Serif, Mr. Jack Baines, and other possible accomplices," she stated.

"Who is Floyd Harrison?" The Bureau Chief asked.

The question took Wanda by surprise.

"He is a member of a local Lodge that our primary suspects belong to." She answered.

"Do you know where he is?" He asked.

"Yes, sir, I filed a report stating our suspicion that he misused non-profit funds for a pleasure trip to New York City as the pretext for the search warrant, but I suspect he may be trying to escape." She said, confused that he would ask a question about the foundation used for her search warrant.

"What have you learned about his affiliation with Mr. Wu Choi?" He asked.

"Sir, that name has never come up in our investigation." She answered.

The committee members began to speak to one another, ignoring Wanda's presence. "Are you telling this board that during your wiretaps, you never came across the name of Mr. Wu Choi?" A steely-eyed middle-aged woman asked.

"That is correct, Madam," Wanda replied.

"Young lady, can you tell us why he is meeting Mr. Choi in New York?" The gray-haired Navy admiral asked.

"Sir, I have no idea," Wanda replied.

"Agent Jackson, you will be provided a joint mission brief to familiarize yourself with en route to New York via military transport. Upon your arrival, you are to take the lead in investigating what Mr. Floyd Harrison is doing, but more importantly, what the connection between Al Qaeda and the Ku Klux Klan is. However, you are not to interfere with his actions or activities. You are dismissed."

"Al Qaeda and the KKK, how is that possible, and if it were true, why wouldn't they want her to stop whatever they were up to?" Wanda thought as she left the conference room, dazed and confused.

"Fuck, can't a woman get a break"? She thought to herself as she tried to figure out what to tell Gerald this time.

Outside the conference room, she was met by several agents and high-ranking military members who began escorting her to a briefing room while speaking in various jargon. Now that the prospects of her demise had been lifted, she was warmly greeted by her fellow Agents who had avoided her moments ago. Wanda returned their greetings with the same fake smile and cold-hearted affection.

CHAPTER 20

The Serapian Master

Later that evening, Floyd was picked up and taken to his hotel for his dinner date with his mysterious benefactor. The ride to the Yi Lan Halal Restaurant seemed longer than the 45 minutes it took him to travel from midtown New York to Long Island City. On the way, Floyd could not help but be amazed at the precision of his new suit of clothing and his perfectly fitting new shoes. He tried to figure out when anyone had gotten close enough to get such precise measurements of his body and feet before he could figure it out. At the hotel, he looked up the restaurant as any good member of the Priesthood would try to determine anything he could about his hosts' personalities and interests. Who would have figured one of the highest-rated Chinese restaurants in New York City would be a Muslim restaurant?

What could he surmise about his host from his host choice in restaurants? Chinese and Muslim in New York City, he found himself stumped.

Floyd was given the now familiar VIP treatment and secretly wondered how it would feel once this fairy tale assignment ended. He was taken to a secluded section of the restaurant where Mr. Choi received him. Mr. Wu Choi was a senior man with questionable but distinctive Asian origins. Floyd fought the urge to laugh at his inner thoughts, which reminded him of how Mr. Choi looked like that old guy from The Karate Kid.

"Mr. Harrison, thank you for accepting my invitation on such short notice." Mr. Choi stated as he rose to greet Floyd.

"I hope you found your accommodations to your liking, Mr. Choi continued while an army of waiters and busboys tried to outdo each other to meet Mr. Choi's every wish.

I still am not sure you have the right man." Floyd honestly answered.

"Mr. Harrison, I assure you that you are the right man and have the full support of all the regional chapters of the Order to assist you in your investigation," Mr. Choi offered to try to put Floyd at ease.

"But before we continue with the business, please let me introduce you to the splendid cuisine offered here."

With a wave of his hands, Floyd was surrounded by a multitude explaining the menu and all the restaurants had to offer. People were pouring water, moving flatware, and making other adjustments at the table. After an endless course of dishes and many changes in service settings, Floyd found himself again alone with Mr. Choi.

"Mr. Harrison, I hate to inform you of a complication with your investigation of Mr. Charles Sinclair. Mr. Sinclair's doctor has been reported missing, and any attempt to contact Mr. Sinclair at this time may bring unwanted attention to our Order." Mr. Chow announced.

Mr. Chow secretly feared the doctor's disappearance could be the work of the witches who appeared during the Sinclairs' investigation.

"Mr. Harrison, did you know that the Sinclair family has been brought to our organization's attention in the past?" Mr. Choi asked.

"Yes, I believe it was just after the Civil War," Floyd answered.

"That is correct; we assumed his ancestor's rumored ability to survive injuries that would kill the average man indicated that he may have the secret we seek flowing in his veins.

However, his subsequent death in Africa forced us to end our investigation of his family," Mr. Choi stated.

"Yes, not to mention the disappearance and presumed death of all the investigating members of the Order by unknown assailants before Sinclair's great-grandfather died in Africa. With the investigators disappearing and all the members of the Chapter killed, the investigation was dropped after Sinclair ancestors' death; after all, the man they were looking for could not die," Floyd volunteered to demonstrate his knowledge of the inner workings of the Order.

"That is correct; your family has served the order for many generations. We hope that you will be able to be the first member of your lineage to reach the rank of Bishop. That is why you were selected to come to New York to head up this investigation," Mr. Choi said.

Floyd didn't know that the news of his family's final acceptance into the higher ranks of the Sons of Serapes filled him with great pride and fretfulness. However, Floyd still does not realize he was chosen because he is expendable.

"Tell me, what do you know about our Order?" Mr. Choi asked.

The question surprised Floyd: he did not expect his knowledge of the organization to be on trial.

"Every first male child has been initiated into this society for as long as anyone could remember," Floyd answered.

"Yes, we know that, but what do you know about our objectives?" Wang asked.

"We are searching for descendants of Jesus of Nazareth who may hold the secret of the location of the chalice of eternal life within their DNA," Floyd answered.

This was the story given to all neophytes to the Order to justify the clandestine keeping of medical records of people from around the world.

"Did you know our organization existed 323 years before the proclaimed birth of the mythical Jesus?" Wang asked.

The order began during the reign of the bloodthirsty king of Macedonia, Alexander," Wang continued.

"I have always wondered why we are called the Sons of Sarapis, not simply the Sons of Christ," Floyd answered.

"We Sapiens were the first Christians. Most educated historians only know of the Roman Emperor Hadrian's conflict with our brothers during his reign. As a result of Emperor Hadrian's correspondence concerning the Serapian Order, Christians have struggled to hide the fact our ancient brothers were called the Bishops of Christ and our god Serapis, the Christ.

"Ha, ha, ha, most Christians today don't know that they worship our beloved founder, Ptolemy Lagi I, who was surnamed Soter, which means Savior. Ptolemy was born circa 366 BC, the son of Lagus and Arsinoe, a concubine of Philip of Macedon. In 305-304, he defended the Rhodians against Demetrius Poliorcetes, forcing the latter to raise the siege--hence, the title "Savior." The uneducated masses unknowingly worship Ptolemy in many forms to this day," Wang joked.

Some say the pursuit of immortality motivated Alexander's burning desire to conquer Egypt, or Kemet as it was known then in 333 BCE," Wan continued.

"Haven't you ever wondered why the capture of the libraries of Egypt and the establishment of the library of Alexandria was so important to the Macedonian king?" Mr. Choi continued.

"My young friend was seeking the same thing we are today. Before Alexander's death in 323 BC, the throne of Egypt was entrusted to one of his most trusted friends, Ptolemy I Soter. Ptolemy I was entrusted with persecuting the secret of immortality from the Priest of Amon Ra," Mr. Choi stated.

"However, Ptolemy Soter learned of the deception the Kemetic priest had played on Alexander after defeating Mazaces, the last Achaemenid satrap of ancient Egypt, during the late reign of Darius III of the 31st Dynasty of Egypt. Alexander was given an elixir that improved his health but denied him the object of his desire. Not understanding the spiritual concept of immortality, he thought he would live physically forever and demanded he be proclaimed a god like the Pharaohs of the old kingdoms. Ptolemy Soter demanded the people of Egypt provide him with the real elixir of life and proclaim him a god, as they had done for all African-born Pharaohs before him. At the point of his sword, he forced the Kemet Priest to consecrate him as the god Serapis, now referred to as the Anointed One or Christ." Mr. Choi concluded by searching Paul's face for his reaction to the information he was being told.

"Did Ptolemy get the elixir?" Floyd asked.

"No, he too was deceived, and after the deaths of many Kemet Priest, he learned the elixir to extend life was secreted out of Kemet deep into the African interior." Mr. Chow answered.

"I don't understand; if we are looking for an elixir, why then all the pretense of seeking out the descendants of Jesus of Nazareth?" Floyd asked.

"We have discussed much today; why don't we leave something for our next discussion." Mr. Chow said to avoid Floyd's question.

"Tell me, Mr. Harrison, what would you be prepared to do to obtain the gift of immortality?" Wang asked.

Floyd remembered being asked that same question during his first interview before joining the Order, and the question still did not leave a comforting feeling in his mind. He searched for this fabled secret of immortality, like searching for lost Aztec treasure or any other impossible task designed to pass on tradition and foster father and son bonding. As a historian, Floyd was familiar with the historical record of Alexander of Macedonia. Still, Mr. Chow's revelations concerning the motivation of Alexander and Ptolemy took him by surprise. The unanswered question concerning the gathering of medical records did not make sense. What could be found in the medical records leading to the elixir Mr. Chow spoke about?

"If it existed, I do not know," Floyd answered honestly.

"Then we shall see." Mr. Choi stated.

The conversation turned to other subjects, but his last words on his research troubled Floyd. The man before him believed that such a thing as immortality was achievable. He was willing to invest vast sums of money to aid Floyd in his research. Floyd only prayed that he could deliver something at the end of his investigation to justify the expense Mr. Choi was incurring.

CHAPTER 21

Stephany Blair

Drake could not think of anyone who would think of stealing a dead body other than Elaine, who was already dead and now missing. However, the early release of Paul Blacksmith came as welcomed news to Mr. Ellsworth and his associates, who were still reeling from their last failed attempt to capture Paul Blacksmith. Paul Blacksmith was diagnosed mentally incompetent and was released to the Psychiatric medical facility at Belleview Hospital, still under doctors' care for psychological and medical observation. Drake's police informant informed him that Paul Blacksmith would be transferred to Belleview Hospital mental ward for evaluation but warned that Paul could sign himself out of the hospital upon being diagnosed as not being a threat to himself or others. Drake dispatched Mr. Bowser and two of his men, who waited parked at a safe distance outside of New York's Central Booking facility at 100 Centre Street for the medical transfer. Knowing the destination, the ambulance could quickly be followed through the busy city streets. Upon arrival, one of Bowser's associates disguised himself as a medical attendant at the hospital to find out what floor and room Paul Blacksmith was assigned to, and he noticed no increased police presence. Now, they had to patiently wait until the hospital's reduced night shift to settle down and make their move. Mr. Bowser and his men spent several hours planning Paul Blacksmith's abduction. The trio sat and watched as the hospital staff changed shifts, then allowed the overnight shift to settle in for the evening. Mr. Bowser sent his two associates through an unlocked back door in the receiving area of the hospital they discovered earlier that day. Dressed as Orderly's, they went upstairs via the back stairway to Paul Blacksmiths' ward. The hospital hallways were abandoned and eerily silent except for an occasional outburst by some unseen mentally disturbed resident or a janitor signaling his approach by the numerous dangling keys on his belt as he patrolled with a mop bucket. One of the two men stood guard at the corner intersection leading to Paul's room while the other entered the room holding a medicine tray with a silencer-equipped gun hidden under it. Entering the darkened room lit only by the cloudy moonlit sky shining through the half-opened window blinds, the man saw Paul lying in a chemically induced sleep in a hospital bed in hand and leg restraints. He also noticed the smell of cigarette smoke as he entered the room but made nothing of it.

"Oh, this is too easy." The man thought to himself.

He approached the bed and allowed the door to close behind him.

"What took you so long?" asked a woman sitting in the shadows behind the door.

Dropping the medicine tray to the floor, the man spun, aiming his silencer-tipped weapon toward the mysterious woman. The woman remained sitting with her long legs crossed, holding a cigarette casually in her hand with her elbow resting on the arm of the chair. The flash of the lighter allowed the man to see the woman's lean body wrapped in a white dress that looked painted on her. The nipples of her firm breast protruded from beneath the stretched fabric that caused her cleavage to bulge out of the

V-neck of her low-cut dress. The woman took a long, slow pull on her cigarette, making her eyes glow red in the darkness.

"Who the fuck are you?" The man demanded as he pulled back the hammer of his 9mm Beretta.

"There is no need for that, my love. I need your help to get Paul out of here." The pasty white-complexioned woman said as she seductively rose from her sitting position in the shadows. Her face briefly lit as she slowly drew from her cigarette.

"Move into the light and keep your fucking hands where I can see them." The man demanded.

"Anything you say, my love." As she appeared to float into the moonlight.

The man was stuck by her perfectly chiseled body, unnaturally white skin, jet-black hair, and blood-red lips. He dreaded the idea it would be he who would send this goddess to her grave. Her face was momentarily exposed as the moonlight broke through the cloudy night sky, revealing the face of innocence and the eyes of a demon. The clouds obstructed the moon once again, and the man lost sight of her, but he instantly felt her breast and body pressing on his back. He tried to turn, but she held him firmly with one arm around his chest and the other down his body as she massaged his crotch.

"Get the fuck off me bitch." He demanded as he struggled to break her steely grip.

"Oh no, my love, we are just getting started." She said and spun him around like a rag doll and slammed her mouth into his, busting his lip, then shoved her long tongue down his throat, causing him to gag. The man felt his body go limp as his mind drifted in a warm, soothing mist of ecstasy. His gun made a clicking sound as it fell to the floor, and semen ran down his leg from an apparent instant ejaculation.

"I can't help you; they will kill me." The man managed to say as he fought against the neurotoxins running through his body.

"No, my love, it will be me who will kill you. Stay still now so I can kiss your neck and taste you." The woman whispered in his ear.

The man tilted his head as instructed, then felt a sharp pain in his neck as her neurotoxins rushed into his body and instantly realized he would never be free of this woman. After what seemed to be an eternity, the woman finally released her grip, and the man fell to his knees.

"Get up, my love; we have not all night." The woman said in a soft, gentle voice.

"Do you have a car ready for us?" She asked.

"Yes, it is at the back of the hospital," the man responded as he staggered, rising to his feet.

"Splendid, my love, now call your friend who is waiting for you in the hallway. I want to meet him," the woman said as she sat back down behind the door.

The mesmerized gunman turned to leave.

"My love, don't forget your gun. You will need it," The woman instructed as she crossed her legs in her spider trap.

The dumbfounded gunman picked up his weapon and left the room as told.

The planned abduction of Paul Blacksmith should have taken less than thirty minutes. It was now ten minutes overdue, and Mr. Bowser was increasingly concerned. He had previously lost the opportunity to grab Blacksmith and was determined not to return empty-handed this time. Bowser listened throughout the operation; no disturbance was reported over the police monitor, which was reassuring, but what could be keeping them so long? As he began to exit the car to investigate, the loading bay door opened.

He saw his two men leaving the cargo bay door while towing a man in a hospital gown that he assumed was Paul Blacksmith.

Bowser sighed in relief and exited the vehicle to make an identification and open the car trunk to stow his captured prize. He noticed a woman in white following them. At first, he thought it was an unfortunate nurse who witnessed Paul's abduction, but then he realized that she was not wearing a uniform but a white dress. As the men got closer, Bowser noticed that they had blood on their shirts, and they had a bizarre and distant look in their eyes. He instinctively knew something was wrong and tried to draw his weapon, but before he could bring his weapon to bear, one of the two men carrying Paul Blacksmith raised his gun and fired in full automatic, hitting Mr. Bowser in the chest and face. The force of the bullets knocked Bowser back onto the waiting sedan and the floor. Mr. Bowser blacked out momentarily and awoke to see the two men put Paul Blacksmith into the car. The woman walked over to him and kneeled over him, exposing her naked vagina that smelled like a rotting corpse close to his face.

"What a shame. I would have enjoyed the taste of a man like you; what a waste," she said as Bowser drifted into blackness.

CHAPTER 22

The Blind

Agent Jackson wasted no time acquiring all the information she could on Mr. Floyd Harrison and Mr. Wu Choi. Her intent for gathering information on Harrison and Choi was to find the financial link, if it existed, between the Klan and Al Qaeda. Gaining knowledge of Harrison and Choi was very easy, and nothing in their financial records or correspondence provided evidence that either was an active member of the Klan or Al Qaeda. Like many white men from the old South, Floyd only had a casual affiliation with the KKK. Then why would these two men be associated with no real ties with either organization or be meeting here in NYC to investigate Charles Sinclair? Wanda pondered on her flight to NYC inside the massive empty C-130 Cargo military aircraft cargo hold. Agent Jackson learned that Mr. Harrison was picked up by Mr. Wu Choi's organization employees and booked into Astoria. Confidential informants at the hotel alerted the FBI that the two men would meet for dinner that night. She arranged to have a surveillance team stationed outside the restaurant equipped with a high-tech listening device to eavesdrop on their conversation and discover the reason for their affiliation. After landing at JFK airport, Agent Jackson was met by other FBI agents and transported to her Holiday Inn hotel on an Army base in Brooklyn. The room was excellent; it reminded her of all the other hotels on military bases the government preferred, but it was no Waldorf Astoria.

Wanda could not make sense of the recorded conversation between Choi and Harrison earlier that evening, which she had listened to while sitting in the back seat of the government sedan on her way to her hotel.

"Dang, another secret boy club!" She thought to herself.

At least now, she could prove that Belington misappropriated the nonprofit funds to finance this trip and use the evidence to broaden her investigation into the Lodge's activities.

"Who in the hell is Mr. Charles Sinclair?" She wondered if these fantasy role players believed what they said on the tape.

"Agent Bostic, please send all our information on Mr. Charles Sinclair to my hotel room in the morning." She asked Agent Bostic, sitting in front of her in the passenger seat.

"Yes, Madame." Agent Bostic responded.

Wanda smiled and thought, "Wow, a girl could get used to this."

The following day, Agent Jackson read the thin file Agent Bostic had gathered on Mr. Charles Sinclair and his business ventures.

"Todd, is this all the information we have on Charles Sinclair? Wanda asked.

"Yes, Madame, we must obtain court-ordered subpoenas to get more." Agent Bostic responded.

"Well, get on it right away," Wanda replied.

Little information was released after a day of various legal roadblocks and a special warrant request. This man was well-connected and protected, but from what? All his assets were lawful and very transparent; she could trace every dime of his estate back hundreds of years, so why was there such a need for such secrecy? More importantly, why was Mr. Floyd Harrison so interested in him? She was also given the name of the first NYC

Detective who was investigating the assault on his life and the death of his associate, Ms. Elaine Singleton. Agent Jackson could not understand the foundation for the relationship between the late Elaine Singleton and Charles Sinclair. Charles Sinclair came from a privileged background, but Elaine was born into a life of cruelty and horror. Elaine's late husband was the former leader of a small drug dealing operation that she inherited when he was murdered during a drug sale that went wrong. Elaine's husband's death forced her to inherit his insignificant illicit drug business, and she turned it into one of the largest illegal drug distribution organizations in the world. Agent Jackson suspected that it was one of her rivals that had her killed. Wanda decided to try her luck on the internet to see if she could find any additional information on Mr. Charles Sinclair III that may have leaked.

Wanda found it interesting that there were very few mentions of the Sinclair family.

"That's interesting." She thought to herself, most rich people want the world to know how rich they are, so why is the family so secretive? She found a link to images of the Sinclair family; she was shocked when the link opened to a page full of pictures of an elegant African woman who looked just like her. Others were of the entire family before and after the Civil War. She looked into the eyes of the man identified as Charles Sinclair I. She felt she had seen him before, or perhaps it was his masculine profile she admired in all dominant men. She was looking forward to meeting this man's great-grandson very soon.

CHAPTER 23

Growing Confusion

The murder of Elaine Singleton and the attempted murder of Charles Sinclair had taken more twists and turns than Julio could ever imagine, and now the FBI has gotten involved. He prayed Agent Jackson's subsequent request was not to meet with Paul Blacksmith, who checked himself out to the hospital and disappeared without a trace. Detective Rodriguez collected all personal items belonging to Paul Blacksmith left behind at the hospital, including Paul's cell phone. He did not see why he should report the items voluntarily abandoned by Paul Blacksmith to Paul's lawyer or anyone else until he got all the information the phone could provide.

The investigation was starting to take its toll on his marriage as well. He tried to leave his work at the office but found himself thinking about it more and more at home. His pregnant wife was beginning to complain about his lack of attention to their marriage and, in particular, his lack of attention to her. Paul Blacksmith's allegation of being attacked by the late Elaine Singleton and his assertion that Charles Sinclair was somehow bulletproof didn't stand up to the evidence. The latest twist was the security footage of Paul Blacksmith being escorted out of the hospital by two known associates of the late Elaine Singleton's organization, along with an unidentified white female. The shooting of Mr. Joseph Bowser was not caught on camera, but he knew Paul's disappearance had something to do with it.

"There you go again, Julio." The Detective was brought out of his trance by his wife sitting on the other side of the dinner table.

"Fuck!" Julio thought to himself.

"Julio, you promised me that you would leave that shit at work and spend more time working on our marriage," Melissa said, fighting back her tears.

From experience, he knew the first trimester of her pregnancy would bring emotional highs and lows, and the last thing they needed was this outside interference to add fuel to the fire.

"Babe, I am sorry; this thing drives me crazy," Julio said.

Melissa had never seen her husband so wrapped up in a case before, and she began to fear for his sanity.

"Couldn't they give you more help on this case?" She asked.

"They are sending in the FBI in the morning," He said.

"¿Qué demonios, Julio, who are these people you are investigating?" Melissa asked. "Babe, I do not want to mention their names in our home. I don't want the devil to know where we live." He spoke.

The following day, he met with Agent Jackson at his midtown precinct; he and his partner O'Bannon were amazed at how much she looked like the woman they saw in the paintings at Sinclair estate. He immediately recognized her choice to meet him on his turf, designed to clarify who was now in charge. After the customary handshakes and greetings intended to provide only information on a need-to-know basis, she requested to be introduced to Mr. Charles Sinclair.

Julio wondered why Agent Jackson wanted to meet with the victim, Mr. Charles Sinclair, and not review all the evidence he had on Paul Blacksmith first; however, he was more than happy to have the FBI take over this case, and maybe he could finally get out of this tangible episode of the Twilight Zone.

CHAPTER 24

Billington's Dilemma

It didn't take Belington long to notice that he was out of favor with his Lodge and, more importantly, with the Klan. He, of all people, should have known that for all the rhetoric, white brotherhood, and cross burnings, the Klan's significant contribution is to allow frustrated poor white men to dream of a world that will never return. Now, when he needed their support the most, Billington found himself the target of their hate and vengeance. Billington and his family had been receiving death threats and cold shoulders now that he was the target of an FBI investigation. The same hypocrites who hailed him as a true Knight of the Sacred Southern Cross for standing up for the white man's rights now call him a traitor and government agent. On yet another hot and humid sweltering night, Belington's family took to sleeping on the floor of their ranch-style home, waiting for his so-called white brothers to spray his house with bullets and fire as he had done to others who were deemed a threat to the white race in the past. Billington had to figure out a way to save himself and his family. Knowing he was a co-conspirator of the murder of the Soldier and the soldier's wife, he could not make a deal with the FBI; he was equally concerned that the Serif would use his department to exonerate himself and place all the blame on him. If only he did not give the money to Floyd for that fucking trip to New York, but how was he to know it was illegal to write a joke in the ledger?

"That's it!" he said out loud, rising from the mattress and lying on the floor beside his wife. "BB, what in tarnation are you shouting about?" his equally fat woman asked, not bothering to turn over to look at him.

"Sweetie pie, I need to go to New York to get the money back from Floyd Harrison," BB said.

"BB, have you lost your mind? Don't you think you have caused this family enough trouble already?" his wife asked, now upright and facing him.

"Pudding, you don't understand. If I get the money returned, there will be no reason for the FBI to investigate the Lodge," BB said.

"BB, you know damned well they do not care about that money. They are trying to find out who killed that nigger Soldier and his wife." She spoke.

"And you swore to me that you had nothing to do with it, didn't you?" She stated.

"Well, Pudding, I may have had a little more to do with it than I told you, but I swear I was only trying to make sure you could walk down the streets and not have to worry about being assaulted by some crazy nigger." BB pled.

"Bill Belington, what have you done?" His wife demanded.

"It wasn't my idea, it was the Serif, and he went crazy when the nigger kept trying to attack us," BB said in a not-so-convincing tone.

"The Serif killed those niggers?" She asked.

"Yeah, and now they are trying to pin it on me," BB said.

BB's wife knew there was something he was not telling her about his involvement in the murders; however, if the Serif was indeed the killer of the Soldier and the Soldier's wife, it may be best that Belington gets out of town for his safety.

"You go on to New York BB and try to get Floyd to return with the money; we will be alright here until you return." She said, resigning herself to an uncertain fate.

CHAPTER 25

The Menace Revealed

The rhythmic sounds of beeps and the intense pain in his chest and face brought Mr. Bowser back out of the darkness. He struggled to open his eyes to find out where he was. Through swollen eyes, he was able to make out that he was in a hospital room connected to multiple machines. When his vision fully cleared, he saw Mr. Drake Ellsworth sitting by his bed.

"Welcome back, Joe." Said Drake.

Bowser grunted a response. Hearing Ellsworth referring to him by his first name told him that the failure to capture Paul Blacksmith would not be held against him. After all, the men selected for the assignment were Drake's choice, and their betrayal was on his head.

"Luckily, you were wearing your vest that caught most of the rounds, but unfortunately, it didn't protect your face. You have several broken ribs and a flesh wound to your arm." Drake added.

"Get some rest; I am going to need your help when you get back on your feet," Drake said, reassuring Joseph that he had not lost any stature in his eyes due to Paul Blacksmith's botched capture attempt.

"We have a copy of the video surveillance footage from the hospital, and we need you to tell us anything you can about the woman seen with our men at the hospital," Drake said as he rose to leave.

Bowser did not have anything to add concerning the mysterious woman, but one thing he did know; that bitch and her two backstabbers were going to die as soon as he could get back on his feet.

Leaving the hospital, Drake could not help the chilling feeling he'd been feeling ever since he reviewed the security tapes from the morgue where Elaine's body was stolen and the hospital footage where Paul Blacksmith somehow turned his men and almost killed one of his most capable operatives. On both tapes, the people just seemed to join some sick conspiracy and walk off their jobs along with a thin white woman whose face was blurred on the video recordings by some technical glitch. He struggled to understand it, but the events made him remember that it had been long since he went to Church.

At the Sinclaire Estate, Charles received only an envelope marked for your eyes from Drake at the Sinclair estate. He opened the envelope, discovered a DVD, and sat alone at his desk to view its contents. Charles was told the DVD captured the footage of Paul Blacksmiths' disappearance from the hospital and the theft of Elaine's body from the morgue. He secretly hoped he could not identify the mysterious woman whose image was reportedly on the disk. However, in his heart, he knew who it was, but he prayed that he was wrong. The footage captured the two men dressed in Orderly uniforms entering the empty floor and one of the men entering Paul Blacksmith's room. After a few minutes, the second man opened the door and gestured for the other man to come to the hospital room. When the door opened, the two men left the room, and Paul Blacksmith walked with them. Then he saw her; even with her face obscured, his blood went cold.

"Stephany." He said under his breath.

Now, all of the events of the past month made sense. With the confirmed sighting of the closest thing Dechontee had to a sister, he knew that Dechontee had to be responsible for Dr. Stanley Johnson's disappearance, but he could not figure out why. Charles was aware that Dechontee was not interested in obtaining a supply of blood from the doctor. Perhaps she was hoping to use him as a bargaining chip to force him to be her little pet again or only to kill the doctor because she knew how much he cared for his adopted son. Why did Dechontee have Elaine killed and then steal her dead body? Knowing how her twisted mind worked, he could not put anything past her. The one thing Charles did know was this would be the last time that twisted bitch or her girlfriend would cause him or anyone he loved pain. It is time for them to die.

CHAPTER 26

The Gateway to the Pass

Charles found Detective Rodriguez's visits amusing and very beneficial to helping him keep his secrets. It was comforting to be around people who had secrets. Charles had learned to read the inner thoughts of individuals and found people with dark secrets fascinating. Detective Rodriguez's meticulous investigative approach and professionalism were used as body armor to hide something Charles could not put his finger on. He did not find Julio's inner thoughts threatening but rather amusing. Charles was sure whatever secrets the Detective was keeping were important enough for the Detective to keep hidden away. Still, they paled in comparison to his own. Charles was also amused by how Julio tried to build trust between them by telling him anecdotes about his relationship with his wife and the difficulties a Detective brought to his marriage.

Charles laughed at the Detective's attempts to get into his head, giving him much credit for his sophisticated approach. Charles found it rather refreshing to play a mental chess game with the Detective to see who found the other's hidden secrets first, and of course, he would win.

When the Detective requested another visit, Charles did not hesitate to accommodate him, especially when he needed information on Paul Blacksmith's whereabouts. Charles was informed that he was bringing the FBI agent who was asking so many questions about him and his family. Charles was eager to size up this new threat to determine how many resources he had to use to get them out of his life. Charles had heard that the FBI agent was a young woman and decided to overwhelm her with a display of his wealth and sophistication to distract her from her investigation of his family and finances. Six months have passed since the attack on Charles and the death of Elaine. His recovery was beyond ordinary thanks to his son, Dr. Stanley Johnson's care before his disappearance, and Charles's unnatural healing ability. Charles was mindful to keep up the appearance of being a man recovering from multiple gunshot wounds. He hoped his pretense of needing a cane to limp about his home would inspire her sympathy.

While waiting for Detective Rodriguez and his mystery guest to arrive, Charles's mind drifted back to the night his life was turned upside down. He was filled with rage to think that the pretentious son of a bitch escorted out of his restaurant was the cause of so much trouble in his life. The thought of that scum bag that killed Elaine being sent by Dechontee, now free and missing, enraged him. It was bad enough to have the NYPD coming to his house but now the fucking FBI. He felt himself slipping back into the wrath experienced in the summer of 1866. Charles fought not to allow his anger to cause him to make a mistake, complicating his life further. However, he vowed that there would be no expense or sacrifice too great to get his hands on that low life and that he would give him a long and painful death that would even shock his recently dead lover.

It was Detective Rodriguez's first sight of the Sinclair Estate in full daylight. He was even more impressed by the well-kept, manicured grounds and gardens. However, what surprised him the most was the number of children and people who lived there.

He never took Charles as a family man, so he was stunned to see many old and young people on the estate grounds. Special Agent Wanda Jackson was also taken aback by the friendliness of the well-dressed and mannered children who grabbed her by the hand to drag her away to play with them. A particularly adorable little girl dressed in a simple sundress, about four or five years of age, beckoned her to bend down to whisper into her ear. The little girl asked in a whisper, "Are you going to be Uncle Charles' girlfriend?"

Wanda smiled and answered jokingly, "Maybe." After all, she thought, I will need a new man if I don't spend more time with Gerald.

The Detective and Wanda laughed and continued up the paved walkway to the mansion's main entrance, trailed by a curious platoon of children. At the manor's entry, they were greeted by five or six older adults lounging, enjoying the sunshine on the patio, and being served cool drinks by white-gloved house servants dressed in white.

"Y'all better come in out of the sun," One of the ancient-looking women commanded as if speaking to one of the young children circling the visitors.

Charles could remember when Clair Sinclair was born into the Sinclair clan and watched her grow into a loving woman with her grandchildren.

Clair asked the children, "Don't you have something better to do than to bother these nice people?" "Run along and play before I take a switch to all of you!" She threatened, which only brought out more laughter from the children.

The elderly family members at the door's entrance gave the large woman moral support, "You children run along now and listen to Auntie Clair, and I am not going to tell you again." The senior woman said in a soft, almost whisper.

Aunt Clair called out, "Peter, Betty, I am going to tell your father how y'all were acting up when he gets home."

The children's mood stiffened, and they immediately stopped their clowning and reluctantly ran off to return to their carefree life of fun and games.

Detective Rodriguez could not distinguish who the employees and family members were, but everyone was happy. Julio and Wanda were met at the door by Lawrence and led to the main dining room. Charles was brought out of his trance by a knock on his master suite door.

"Charles, your guest, has arrived," announced Lawrence.

"Are you sure you are up to this?" Lawrence asked.

Lawrence was his sir name, and his first name was Frederick; the Lawrence family had worked for the Sinclair family for hundreds of years, and the position of head Butler was passed down from father to son. Understanding the toll of Stanley's disappearance and the recent murder of his close friend Elaine Singleton had on Charles, Lawrence felt an increased need to protect him.

"I will be fine, Frederick," Charles answered reassuringly.

"You are under no obligation to keep meeting with them, and I strongly suggest that you let your public relations people handle this," Frederick Lawrence said.

"Yes, I know, Frederick, but hopefully, they will have all of their questions answered soon, and we can get back to our lives," Charles stated as he made his final inspection of his appearance in the mirror.

Like most employees of the Sinclair's, the Lawrence family had learned to keep to themselves and mind their own business in exchange for salaries that exceeded most doctors and lawyers, not to mention the outstanding health benefits and educational opportunities for their children. However, this was the first time Frederick had seen Charles sick or injured. While his physical state seemed to be improving nicely, there was an apparent wound to his soul. Charles had taken the death of his friend Elaine very hard, and no matter how he tried to put on a brave face, Frederick could see the pain her death had caused him.

"Very well then, Sir, I will tell your guess that you will be with them shortly," Frederick stated as he left to prepare for Charles' lunch engagement.

Charles smiled when Frederick called him "Sir," knowing it was a sign of respect and a ringing declaration of his objection to Charles allowing so many visits by the NYPD. Frederick Lawrence was instructed to lay out the best china and gold and silver flatware in the main dining room where he planned to meet his new guest. The fifteen thousand square foot dining room was chosen because of its two-story glass vaulted ceiling, hand-carved gothic wood panels, and life-sized statues of demons and saints. The table is set in Victorian style, with natural flower arrangements in every third location. Charles knew the sunlight would cascade off the commissioned Waterford crystal glasses perfectly placed around the table. Charles checked his appearance in the full-sized mirror near the bedroom suite's main door. He adjusted the lapels of his embroidered velvet burgundy-colored house coat. His oversized tailor-made silk-cashmere blend cream-colored pajamas flowed like air over his skin. The full-legged pajama pants draped to the floor, almost covering the Burgundy-colored Gucci slippers that adorned his feet.

He selected a slim black walking stick with a golden lion's head for the handle to complete the image of a noble gentleman on the mend. After aspirating himself with citric-based cologne, he exited his chambers. He slowly limped to the dining room where he had arranged to meet his guest, ensuring his theatrical show of pain was in keeping with his audience's expectations. Making his best-crippled entering into the dining room, Charles found Detective Rodriguez alone. Somewhat disappointed at wasting his best theatrical on Detective Rodriguez, he was puzzled about the other threat in his house.

Detective Rodriguez, how good it is to see you again; I thought you had a guest with you," Charles said in a warm and welcoming voice.

Rising from the large ornate dining table, Detective Rodriguez rose from the elaborate wood-carved dining chair to meet Charles. Despite his reservations, Julio found himself admiring Charles Sinclair and secretly hoped that he would never find evidence to have to put him away. After all, Charles was still the victim and not a suspect yet. However, he wanted to see Charles's reaction when he met Agent Wanda Jackson for the first time.

"Good afternoon, Mr. Sinclair. I see you are getting around much better," Detective Rodriguez returned the greeting.

"Where is your companion?" Charles asked.

"She had just left to use the restroom," Detective Rodriguez replied.

"The old semi-legal home search excuse." Charles thought to himself.

"I guess we better make ourselves comfortable," Charles said, pretending not to know the real reason for her absence.

"I hope she does not run into my little nieces or nephews out there; she will never be seen again," Charles said jokingly.

The two men laughed; Charles asked, "Did you have lunch yet?"

Ever the true professional, the Detective declined the invitation.

"So, how goes the investigation?" Charles asked, trying to make small talk. Perhaps the police had found out where Dechontee was hiding.

"The families of the two of the dead men have hired private investigators to investigate the deaths of their sons, and they are applying political pressure on the Mayor to reopen the case. I guess they do not want to accept that their little boys were involved in crime despite their high-class upbringing." Julio reported.

The knowledge that his attackers did not know about Elaine's underworld activities helped Charles realize how Dechontee had enticed them into attacking Elaine and him. Anyone who knew anything about the real underworld of New York City knew Elaine was the last person you wanted to cross. Even if their plan to steal his Bentley or rape her had succeeded, they still would find themselves dead by the end of the day, that is, if they were lucky. However, the news of even more people scrutinizing his life did not bring him any joy. To avoid revealing how much information Charles already knew, he did not ask about the sudden disappearance of Paul Blacksmith; besides, he probably knew more about the perpetrators than the police did.

"Please give my warmest sympathy to their families and let them know I am willing to assist them in any way I can," Charles said in a well-rehearsed show of compassion and support. He hoped the Detective could read the hidden message that he would pay them all to go away.

"How is the recovery of my friend's body going?" Charles asked.

"Unfortunately, Mr. Sinclair, we do not have any new leads, and our primary suspect in her murder…" he began to reply but was interrupted by the squeaking sound of the massive dining room door opening, signaling Agent Jackson's return.

The agent trailed behind Lawrence and emerged from her concealed position just feet from Charles.

The well-rehearsed smile and greeting Charles had used hundreds of times to disarm friends and foes alike fell from his face. He tried to speak but could not find the words. Time seemed to stand still, and he could not hear anything but his pounding heart. He tried to talk again, but the only word that came out of his mouth was Nadine.

CHAPTER 27

Nadine

In the summer of 1845, Charles and his father visited a nearby plantation to discuss the purchase of enslaved people to help clear land recently acquired by the Sinclair family. The Sinclair were members of Dakadonu, the royal bloodline of Agassu of the Kingdom of Dahomey, modern-day Bénin. His Great-ancestor was a Prince of Agassu who became the king of one of the most prosperous regions of the Kingdom by waging a relentless war of conquest on his neighbors. His warriors often returned from raids on their enemies with hundreds of captives, livestock, grains, and gold. Unlike many other African Kingdoms, the Dahomey Kingdom first participated but then resisted trade in enslaved Africans with the Arabs and Europeans because of a warning from a Chief Priest of Kpo called the Agasunon. The Agasunon Priest warned that he had received a dream vision of a great leopard being trapped in a pit, drowning in blood, being tormented by faceless devils. The Dahomey resisted participation in the slave trade for a while. Unfortunately, the lust for wealth and foreign goods later corrupted the Kings of Dahomey, who returned to the human flesh trade. The dream vision of the Agasunon Priest proved prophetic; the destruction of the cultural foundation of the Dahomey Kingdom due to the demand for enslaved people and the depopulation of West Africa brought about the destruction of their kingdom. The tremendous wealth of the Agassu kingdom first attracted the attention of Arab merchant traders, whom the Portuguese replaced. Other nations of men with different skin colors and tongues came to the shores of West Africa for trade and conquest.

The one thing all the nations of Dahomey had in common was the need to be rich and the fortitude to achieve their goals. At the apex of Charles's ancestors' wealth, their armies were second to none in arms and strength. Still, his ancestors were wise and understood that their kingdom's wealth could not rely only on conquest. They realized their armies had to travel further to find villages with enough people to provide captives. Regardless of the strength of the village, the men always fought back, forcing the warriors to kill them, which was not good for business. Wounded men did not bring a reasonable price on the slave market. Wounded captives were not worth feeding or storing space in the kingdom's slave pins. If a significant building was being constructed, the bodies of the weaker prisoners were used in the foundation to bring luck to the inhabitants. Other times, they could be used for target practice to help the younger warriors perfect their use of the new rifles and traditional spears. Targeted for severe and brutal reprisals were the Kingdoms that resisted the Dahomey aggression. The men were killed, and the woman was subjected to rape. Those women who were already pregnant were cut open, and the fetus was speared, still dangling by its mother's umbilical cord. During reprisal raids, all male children were killed to make sure they could not one day rise to challenge the Dahomey Kingdom.

The Dahomey King Akaba was as intelligent as he was cruel; he became concerned over the shrinking number of captives and the further distances his warriors needed to travel to find people to conquer. The King and his counsel concluded that they should change the way business was being conducted and demand to be included in the end sale of the captives in the new world. To achieve this, The Dahomey King sent his son Prince Do-Aklin, Charles Sinclair's grandfather, to America to establish a business foothold in the new world on a ship they purchased called the Sinclair. After acquiring thousands of acres of land in the Mississippi colony of America, the Dahomey Prince established a plantation he named after his ship, the Sinclair. With their uniquely brutal motivational techniques, Prince Do-Aklin cleared land and began plantings in record time. The Princes' cruel motivation methods resulted in abundant harvests and a constant need to replenish their labor pool faster than the surrounding European plantations. Surrounding plantation owners would often threaten their underperforming captives with the prospect of being sold to the Sinclair plantation as a means of motivation, which frequently resulted in a frantic display of loyalty and willing servitude. After a generation, the Agassu family came to be called the Sinclairs due to their association with the Sinclair plantation and the Sinclair shipping company. Charles' father and grandfather, Prince Do-Aklin, never let him forget his lineage. They taught him that while he should associate with his fellow Plantation owners, he was royalty and was expected to stay above his neighbor plantation owners, whom his father called their inferiors or Iyase.

Charles lost his mother soon after childbirth. His only mother figure was an older enslaved woman named Auntie Kate. His mother never recovered from giving birth to him. His mother was not in good health before her pregnancy. The physical demands and the stress of childbirth made her more fragile. His mother suffered from sudden pain attacks, dizziness, and jaundice. Her health continued to decrease until her death before Charles's first birthday. Kate was his wet nurse and his father's reluctant bed warmer; she had a love-hate relationship with the Sinclair family. Her love for Charles was unquestionable. However, she had no love for Charles's father, who had sold her first daughter when the child was only four years old. Kate never forgave the senior Sinclair but held no animosity against Charles. Charles' father was stern with Charles, trying to instill the notion that enslaved people could not be trusted and that they had no rights beyond the benefit of being alive. Prince Do-Aklin II would find his son, Charles, sitting and conversing with the enslaved people on the plantation and treating them like friends more than their property. Prince Do-Aklin II was worried that upon his death, these same enslaved people, which Charles consistently argued to be treated more humanely, would turn on him and slit his throat in his sleep.

Charles was fourteen years old when he accompanied his father on a business trip to a neighboring plantation, where he first saw the woman who would change his life forever. Charles could still remember how dumbstruck he was at the sight of Nadine. Her lean, regal appearance overshadowed the fact that she was enslaved. Charles watched her as she walked about with a bucket of something on her head with a grace he had never seen before, her back straight, head held high with an air of silent defiance. Dancing rainbows reflected across her black, ebony skin. At the same time, her close-cropped, wooly hair seemed to explode with millions of stars in the sunlight. The wind was knocked out of him when she turned and politely smiled, revealing the whitest ivory God had ever produced in the mouth of this radiant goddess.

Charles was broken out of his trance by his father, who nudged him and told him he would purchase the girl for him if he wished. Charles was excited about having her for himself, but he was also repulsed to think he would do anything to destroy the spirit that had just captivated his heart. Charles knew the affection he wanted from her was not for sale. Charles knew about the plantation owner, Mr. Benjamin Greenburg's fetish for young enslaved women and feared that if she remained enslaved on that plantation, the spirit he witnessed would be lost in the act of violence and perversion sooner or later. He felt compelled to protect her, so Charles agreed to his father's offer to purchase her.

Charles could not wait until his father's business trip was concluded to return to the Sinclair Plantation to see Nadine. Charles could not understand why he had never felt this way about any other woman. Yes, there were other young enslaved women on this plantation and free-born women who all bided for his attention. Still, none had the effect this beautiful stranger had on him. The return trip back to the Sinclair Plantation took an agonizing eternity. Upon his return, Charles immediately went to the slave quarters to ensure Nadine's living quarters were upgraded. His father was amused by his son's-stricken state. The elder Sinclair thought he understood his son's feelings; however, he misjudged Charles's feelings for Nadine as teenage lust and failed to appreciate his son falling in love with an enslaved woman at first sight.

The negotiation for the sale of Nadine was more complicated than the Prince anticipated, but his father knew such a young beauty would fetch a high price; after all, slavery had its nocturnal benefits, and by the reluctance of her former owner, he was sure those benefits were days away from being fulfilled. The elder Sinclair added that the girl must be delivered un-soiled, unsettling her previous owner, Mr. Benjamine Greenburg. However, Prince Do-Aklin II had to ensure that the young lady met all of Charles' fantasies for the lesson he anticipated Charles would learn from the experience of having his gentle advances rejected, leaving brute force and dominance as the only means to achieve his carnal desires.

Unknown to Charles, his father's health was deteriorating rapidly, and his father did not know how long he had left. Perhaps purchasing this slave girl, whom his young, gullible son was so enamored by, will teach him Charles that enslaved people are incapable of returning the love of a child the royal house of Agassu deserves.

Unfortunately, his father's concerns over Charles's abnormal relations with the enslaved people and his increasingly lousy health were the least of his troubles. For years, the rumors of secession from the Union grew with intensity. The Sinclair's' once tolerant relations with his fellow plantation owners became increasingly tense. Would his property rights be protected if the South seceded from the North? More frightening of all was the notion that his young, naïve slave-loving son would be forced to face this uncertain future without his assistance. His only consolation was like his ancestors; he was vigilant and constantly monitored international and national business trends. The Prince diversified his family's business ventures beyond agriculture and slavery and continued developing his family's shipping business in the North. The Sinclair shipping company, plus their land, real-estate companies, and mining activities in Africa, would ensure Charles's future regardless of the political aspirations of his fellow enslavers.

A week had passed, which seemed like an eternity to Charles, and the delivery of the newly purchased enslaved people arrived. He watched as the head overseer led them to their living quarters. The overseer was an exceptionally cruel white man who delighted in his work. He was adept at locating any sign of defiance in the slave population. He used his bullwhip to overkill the notion of rebellion. Charles made it a point to instruct him that this load of enslaved people was not to receive his customary whipping welcome ceremony. Charles stood just close enough to ensure Nadine moved into the quarters he had prepared for her but not close enough for her to see him. Charles noticed something different about her; she stood tall and defiant, but the light of life no longer shined over her. A dark cloud of sadness blocked the sun as she stood proudly but somehow diminished. Seeing her in this state infuriated Charles, thinking someone had done something to her during or after her purchase. He immediately sought out Auntie Kate and demanded that she examine Nadine to see if she was violated in any way. Thoughts of rage and blood lust raced through Charles's mind as he envisioned Greenburg's filthy hands and mouth on the body of his beautiful goddess. Auntie Kate finally understood why one of the new slave quarters was lavishly prepared. She was pleased to see the young man she raised reach this stage of maturity; however, Kate was afraid for Charles because she understood that love could not be purchased, nor could it be demanded. The shameless display of concern for this young girl was more than infatuation. His old hand nurse was afraid that the young man that she practically raised as her child would commit a horrible act when his affection was not returned.

Auntie Kate quickly raced to the slave quarters to find Nadine. When she arrived at the peculiarly lavish cottage built for Nadine, the door was slightly ajar. Peeking inside, she could see Nadine was sitting on the bed crying with her head in her hands.

"Lord have mercy, child, what seems to trouble you so?" Auntie Kate asked in a genuinely concerned, motherly voice.

Nadine continued to cry, not acknowledging Auntie Kate's question. Auntie Kate gently approached her and sat down beside her on the bed.

"Come on now, child, not a soul is going to bother you here," Auntie said as she wrapped her arm around the young girl, motherly pulling her close.

"Child, did somebody touch or harm you in any way?" Auntie asked as she raised Nadine's tear-soaked face to look into her dark, almost black eyes.

Nadine shook her head no and seemed comforted by Auntie Kate's sincerely warm nature and genuine concern for her well-being. Auntie Kate smiled, realizing why this beautiful young girl smote her young master. Auntie Kate could see the innocence and purity of this girl's soul, which shined like beams of light from her eyes; however, this young woman had a strength that Kate had not seen in a long time. Auntie's fear for Charles began to grow.

"Don't you worry, none child, I am going to take care of you, so don't you go messing up that beautiful face with all them tears." Auntie Kate said, trying to calm Nadine's fears.

"I bet you did not know you have a secret admirer." Auntie Kate said, trying to test the waters.

"I don't care about no admirer; I want my mother!" Nadine demanded.

The young girl's demand struck Auntie Kate straight in the heart. Kate fought back the tears as the memory of her forced separation from her daughter so many years ago resurfaced. Now, in this gilded cage, Kate saw a reflection of her suppressed pain in its raw and sublime state. Auntie Kate silently held Nadine by the shoulders. She looked deeply into her tear-soaked eyes, selfishly sharing the young girl's pain and grief. She pulled Nadine close, wrapped her arms around her as tight as she could, and imagined Nadine was her child who was never seen again. The two women held each other, fusing their grief into a new kinship, and cried the tears only a mother and lost daughter could understand.

Later that evening, as Charles and his father sat at the dinner table, Auntie Kate noticed the great anticipation for her report on the young master's face but pretended not to notice. As the servants placed the trays of food on the table, Charles took little notice of the roast beef, the baked chicken, the candy yams, and other succulent food items being served. His eyes were fixated on Auntie Kate for any sign of what she would tell him about his newfound love. Charles could not take the anticipation any longer. Just as he was going to ask Auntie Kate what she found out, his father said calmly, almost disinterestedly, "So Auntie Kate, how are the new arrivals settling in?"

Charles was infuriated; who cares about some damned field hands? He thought to himself, "I want to know about Nadine. The senior Sinclair and Auntie Kate went on and on about plants, peeling paint, a broken door, a sick mule, and the growing tobacco color. Unknown to Charles, they both knew about his request to Auntie Kate and dragged out the conversation just to upset him. Charles could not stand the anticipation any longer, and he rose to his feet, turned to his father, and said in a controlled, tense voice.

"Father, I believe Auntie Kate has something she needs to tell me."

Faking shock and disbelief, the father turned to Auntie Kate and asked.

"Do you have something you need to tell my little boy?"

With her hands on her wide hips, Auntie Kate turned to Charles and gave him a look she reserved for him when he had been caught doing something wrong.

"The young lady is doing just fine, and nobody done nothing to her except for taking her away from her family; other than that, she is just peachy." She said in a defiant voice that only she could get away with.

Charles was relieved to hear that she was not molested. Still, as Auntie Kate's words began to sink in, he realized that bringing Nadine here meant taking apart her family. What a fool he had been; why didn't he understand that only getting her here without her family may have been the cruelest thing anyone could have done to another individual? The many years of buying and selling people as property had numbed him to the pain Charles and his family had inflicted on hundreds of families like Nadine's. He sat back in his chair without an appetite.

The next day, the enslaved people and overseers were surprised to see Charles personally supervising the daily activities of the plantation. Charles did not make his interest in the new young enslaved woman oblivious. Still, everyone knew about his interest in this young woman before she arrived. Usually, the slave quarters were one to two cramped room shacks that housed entire families, contrasting with the two-room cabin he had prepared for this young lady. She had her own stove, a real bed, and a bathtub; her quarters were even better than most of the overseers on the plantation.

"How yawl doing, Jim?" Charles greets one enslaved person.

"When is that baby due?" He inquired of an enslaved woman late in her pregnancy.

Charles went out of his way to demonstrate his kind and humane treatment of his captives to Elaine. She continued to ignore him and worked hard alongside all the other enslaved people. For days, he sat helplessly on his horse, watching Elaine for some sign of her appreciation for him buying her and providing her with more luxury than she had ever known.

Kate had noticed a change in Charles ever since the arrival of Elaine. He was more like a son to her than anything else, and she hated seeing him in so much pain. One night, she came across him sitting in front of the fireplace, staring into the fire in the entertainment room.

"What's troubling you, Child?" she asked in a soothing, motherly voice that instantly disarmed him.

"I don't know what to do, Kate." He replied.

"What do you mean, Child?" Kate asked.

"I did all I could do for her, and she won't give me the time of day." He replied.

"Child, you did not think you could buy her affections, did you?" Kate asked.

"No, but at least she could acknowledge that I am better than the rest." He responded.

"Better, then who?" Kate asked.

"Better than those who would rape her, then sell her off once she is robbed of her beauty." He responded.

"No boy of mine that I have raised ever think about doing something like that!" Kate said. "But Child, did you ever stop to think that that young girl has a family that she loves too and that you took her away from the only people she has ever loved?" Kate asked.

"Yes, I thought about that, but what was I supposed to do? I could not let her stay there", Charles said.

"Child, my heart goes out to you. You have fallen in love, and while I am so proud to see the man you have become, I fear for you, Child." Kate said.

"Kate, I did not mean to hurt her; I only wanted to protect her," Charles said.

"What can I do to make her understand?" Charles asked.

"Have you tried talking to her Son?" Kate asked.

The thought of explaining his actions to an enslaved person violated everything his father and other slaveholders taught him. He was educated to believe that his actions were beyond question by an enslaved person. Yet, his only hope may be to reach the object of his affection, words, and actions.

"Talk to her; what would I say? He asked.

"Let your heart guide you, my Son; it has not let you down yet," Kate answered.

Kate came near and drew him into her arms as she had done so many times before when he needed love and assurance.

"I am so proud of you, Child, and I don't know what God has in store for you, but trust Him, and He will guide your way," Kate said as she rocked him in her arms.

The love, warmth, smell, and comfort of Kate's loving arms always soothed Charles, and he felt himself drift back to the days when he looked up at her as he sucked on her breast, thinking she must be God.

Nadine was surprised to find Charles at her door the next day when she left to join the other enslaved people on their way to the planting fields. She immediately dropped her eyes and assumed the passive slave stance, awaiting Charles's following command. She had feared this day because every young woman in bondage knew if the enslaver took a particular interest in you, it would not end well. Her quarters and special treatment usually showed that her master expected her to do most of her work after hours on her knees or her back. She would instead pick all the cotton in the fields in Mississippi than be subjected to the ultimate humiliation of being an enslaver's sex toy. She could not help but notice Charles watching her, and despite all efforts not to respond to his attention, she found herself secretly admiring him. As much as she tried to maintain her hatred for him for taking her away from her family, something about him intrigued her. If she were to be an enslaver's mistress, she could do much worse than young Master Sinclair.

"I beg your pardon." Agent Jackson responded, bringing Charles back to his senses.

"I apologize; please forgive me; it's just that you remind me of someone very precious to me that I had lost long ago," Charles stated, still regaining his composure.

"I see, Mr. Sinclair. My name is Agent Wanda Jackson, and I hope you can answer a few questions for us." Agent Jackson stated in an emotionless, professional tone.

"Yes, of course, Agent Jackson, I will be more than happy to assist you," Charles said as he theatrically struggled to sit back into his chair.

Detective Rodriguez never witnessed this side of Charles Sinclair. He had always felt Charles' defenses were impenetrable, but now he saw them fall like a stone. He sat back and listened carefully to any information that could help him make sense of the events surrounding his attack and the death of his friend Elaine Singleton.

"First, I would like to offer my condolences for losing your friend." She sincerely stated.

"Thank you," Charles said, his eyes still locked on her.

"I have a few questions I would like you to help us with if you are up to it." She spoke.

"Yes, of course, anything I could do to assist," Charles said with conviction.

"Mr. Sinclair, have you ever heard of a man named Mr. Floyd Harrison or Mr. Wu Choi?" She asked.

"No, I can't say I have," Charles answered.

"What do they have to do with my friend's death?" He asked.

"We do not have any reason to believe they had anything to do with it." She responded.

"Then what is this all about?" He asked.

"They seemed interested in you, and we wanted to know if you knew why," she said.

"I have no idea, but men in my position often attract many types of people." He answered.

"Well, we thank you for your time, Mr. Sinclair." She stated as she began to put away her notepad.

"Is that it?" Charles asked.

"Yes, Mr. Sinclair." She stated as she began to rise from her seat.

"Perhaps one of my business associates knows more about these men than I do; I would be happy to look into it and provide you with the information." Charles quickly volunteered.

"That would be great, Mr. Sinclair; here is my card. Please let me know if you come up with something." She spoke.

"Tell you what, Agent, what did you say your name was again?"

"Agent Jackson." She responded.

"Agent Jackson, do you have a first name?" Charles asked, never looking at her card.

"It's "Wanda," She replied.

"I will be in touch, Agent Wanda Jackson." He playfully stated.

"Thank you, Mr. Sinclair." She responded, offering her hand to shake his hand goodbye. Charles eagerly reached out to receive her hand. The touch of her skin pressed against the palm of his hand made him warm all over his body.

"Can I come back too?" Detective Rodriguez jokingly asked, trying to take advantage of Charles's exposed flank.

"Julio, you are always welcome to my home, and I cannot thank you and your department for all you have done for my family and me in these trying times," Charles stated, using the detective's first name for the first time.

Detective Rodriguez was unsure if Charles was genuinely casual with him or if he used his first name to give the beautiful, hot FBI agent the impression that he was a good man.

Charles suddenly realized he was still holding Wanda's hand when speaking to Detective Rodriguez and quickly released her hand.

"Please forgive me, Agent Jackson. I have not been myself since the death of my dear friend," Charles said as he adjusted his night coat.

"That is very understandable, and no harm was done." She said before turning to exit the dining room.

"I almost forgot to ask." Agent Jackson stated as she turned back and faced Charles.

"Have you ever heard of the Bishops of Christ or the Sons of Serapis?" She asked.

The question surprised Charles and Detective Rodriguez for different reasons. The name made Charles's blood run cold, but he quickly regained his composure.

"Sounds like some college fraternity, but I am afraid to say I never had." He lied light-heartedly. However, he was unsure if this crafty FBI agent detected the minute shift in his composure when she blindsided him with the question.

He thought that is precisely what Nadine used to do to get him to obey her every desire.

Detective Rodriguez now had the name of a mysterious organization to associate with the two other names he had learned from the FBI's interview with Mr. Charles Sinclair. Unfortunately, nothing still made any sense to him.

Lawrence, who was remotely monitoring the interview, opened the dining room door and escorted the Detective and FBI agent out of the estate. Upon his return, he found Charles still sitting where he left him in the dining room.

"Lawrence, I want to know everything you could learn about that FBI agent and her family," Charles said, not looking at him.

"Charles, aren't you concerned about the Order?" Lawrence asked.

"It doesn't sound like a full-fledged Priest is investigating me; more like one or two of their apprentices are on my trail."

"It may explain Stanley's disappearance and the stealing of Ms. Singleton's remains," Lawrence added.

"No, my dear friend, unfortunately, I believe there is someone much worse than the followers of Serapis we have to thank for that," Charles said.

"They could be just as dangerous, Charles," Lawrence said.

"You are right, Lawrence. Also, keep an eye on the two men." Charles conceded.

Charles sat alone in the large dining room, reliving painful memories he had never successfully repressed. Charles could not get over how much Wanda Jackson looked, sounded, and felt like his long-lost love, Nadine. He smiled, reminiscing how Wanda caught him off guard with the question concerning those Serapes idiots. It was the same way Nadine would catch him off guard when she wanted to get her way. His mind returned to the day he found the nerve to expose his true feelings for her. The conversation was still crystal clear in his mind. That day, he rose early and waited along the path Nadine traveled on her way to work in the kitchen.

"Nadine, can I have a word with you?" Charles asked.

"Yes, Master," Nadine said, her head and eyes lowered.

"How are you being treated?" He asked.

Nadine had never been asked about her feelings by any master or overseer. She was perplexed and struggled to find an appropriate answer.

"Fine, Master." She replied.

"Do you know why I brought you here?" He asked.

Again, another question Nadie had only stories of pain, suffering, and humiliation to use as a reference to answer.

"To pick cotton?" Nadine answered, hoping to plant an alternative suggestion other than being purchased as a sex toy.

Charles remembered how he broke out into hysterical laughter. His laughter took Nadine by surprise. Nadine had never witnessed her previous owners laughing so openly. She was confused about the reason for his laughter. Was he ridiculing her? Did she sound funny or ignorant? Nadine thought.

"Do you think I have gone through all the trouble of setting you up in private quarters if I only wanted you to pick cotton?" He asked.

Charles' response made Nadine's body tense up at the prospect of her being violated by the man in front of her.

"Here it comes, Nadine thought; finally, the beast in silk clothing is going to reveal himself," She thought.

"I brought you here to protect you." He said.

"To protect me, protect me from what, Master?" She asked, confused.

It was his turn to be taken off guard. He realized Nadine did not know how beautiful she was or how men reacted to her beauty. Charles knew many of his neighboring plantation owner's daughters, who were always dressed in their finery. Still, none came close to Nadine's natural beauty.

"From men like me." He answered, barely able to hide his shame.

Nadine stood silent and confused, unsure what to make of her conversation with her new owner.

"Tell me why you always look so sad," Charles asked.

"Master, I miss my family," Nadine answered.

"If I brought your family here, would that bring back the woman I saw at the other plantation?" Charles asked.

Nadine's eyes came alive with hope and shame. She knew she would be willing to submit herself to any humiliation to be with her family again.

"Yes, Master!" she answered enthusiastically.

"Ok then, I will see what I can do." He spoke.

But before he could complete the statement, she fell to her knees and began to cry tears of gratitude. Nadine's raw emotions brought tears to Charles's eyes, and he had to quickly turn his head away so she would not see how much her happiness meant to him.

CHAPTER 28

The Fly in the Ointment

Floyd Harrison sat on the edge of the large bed in his hotel suite, reviewing the information he could collect on Charles Sinclair and the Sinclair family. So far, nothing has stood out except Sinclair's' charitable contributions to Africa. He was surprised to see the strong connection the Sinclairs continued to have with Africa, given their rumored association with the slave trade. However, most Fortune 500 corporations could be traced back to the slave trade, so Sinclair's connection would not be any different.

Floyd's mind drifted back to his conversation with Mr. Choi when he first arrived, leaving him uneasy. What if this chapter of the Serapian Order believed obtaining immortality was possible? He thought to himself. He hoped they would not blame him when they found out that Charles Sinclair was just as mortal as anyone else and the reason for his survival had more to do with a bulletproof vest than with some magic potion. The ringing of the hotel phone by Floyd's bed broke him out of his deep contemplations.

"Mr. Harrison, we have Mr. Belington here requesting an audience with you. Shall we send him up?" the voice from the reception desk asked.

"What the hell?" Floyd thought to himself.

What the hell? This cannot be happening. Floyd's mind raced, trying to find a way to make Billington disappear before his Serapian brothers discovered him.

"No, tell him I am not in, and leave a message." Floyd quickly responded.

"Very well, Sir." The voice had answered before they hung up the phone.

What the hell is he doing here? Floyd thought to himself. Floyd instantly realized the danger BB was bringing with him. He knew there was no way the authorities investigating the death of the military couple would not read that he and BB had come to NYC to avoid prosecution. His family had kept the secrets of the Order out of the hands of the non-initiated for hundreds of years, and now, in the lobby of the Waldorf Astoria stands the idiot that could end his family affiliation with the Order and his hope of becoming a Bishop.

Floyd's cell phone rang. Floyd raced to answer it before it went to voice mail.

"Floyd Harrison here; how may I help you?" He said, answering the cell phone.

"Floyd, where are you?" Belington asked frantically.

"BB, what the hell do you want!?" Floyd asked, not trying to hide his irritation.

"We got to talk; the FBI is asking for the money you took from the Lodge," BB said.

"First of all, Belington, I didn't take anything from the Lodge; you issued me a check for the trip," Floyd emphatically answered.

"Yeah, well, I didn't know you were going to use it for no vacation," BB stated.

Floyd immediately understood why Belington was there.

"BB, what did you do now?" Floyd asked, irritated.

"I gotta get the money back to get the FBI off my back," BB stated.

What a fool; if he thinks the FBI gives a rat's ass about some unauthorized expenditure, then he is more of an idiot than I could have ever imagined, Floyd thought to himself.

"Ok, Belington, where are you staying?" Floyd reluctantly asked.

"Aren't I staying with you here?" Belington asked.

"Belington, the Lodge would have to save every dime it collected for a hundred years to afford this place; go find a Hojos, then call me to tell me where I can meet you!" Floyd stated.

"You don't have to take that tone with me, Floyd!" Belington shot back.

"You aren't no better than me, so don't you go acting so high and cidity because you are staying in some fancy blue belly Yankee Hotel," BB stated before hanging up the phone.

Floyd laid back on the bed with his eyes closed, trying to think of a way to get rid of Belington and disassociate himself from the white trash that he found himself in bed with.

What would he be willing to do to obtain immortality? He could not answer but knew what he was ready to do to eliminate Belington.

Belington ignored the stares and not-so-veiled glances of disdain as he left the hotel lobby. Belington made sure the African-American doorman in the fancy uniform felt his contempt when he refused to allow him to call a cab for him by walking away without acknowledging him as he offered his assistance. Entering onto the busy NYC Street, Belington was unaware of the FBI agents who had been tailing him since he left his southern home and now walking the busy, incandescent-lit night in New York City.

Mr. Samuel Scales had taken the disappearance of his uncle, Dr. Stanley Johnson, very hard. He had not gotten more than four hours of sleep a night since his uncle's apparent abduction. As the head of security of the Sinclair Estate, he felt personally responsible for the series of lapses in security that resulted in Charles's injury and Elaine's death. He had received a call from a friend in the FBI about a private investigation that mentioned Mr. Charles Sinclair. He was given the name of one of the people investigating Charles Sinclair. He was warned that Mr. Floyd Harrison and Mr. Bill Billington, who were also affiliated with a KKK group, were responsible for the murder of a military family in the South. Stanley was disturbed to learn that Mr. Floyd Harrison, who had questionable affiliations, was now in NYC. Samuel also received many courtesy calls from official FBI Agents and the NYPD.

Mr. Samuel Scales could not get any leads on the mysterious woman in the videotapes. However, Floyd Harrison was easy to find. Mr. Scales went to Floyd's hotel and blended with the visitors and residents. He stopped when he noticed the FBI agents stationed in the vestibule. Sam did not want to make any additional connections between the Sinclair Estate and Floyd Harrison than what had already been established and the FBI and began to exit the hotel lobby when a curiously underdressed, red-faced fat man entered the lobby. The poorly dressed Fat man loudly demanded to speak to Mr. Floyd Harrison at the reception desk.

When the obese man received some unwanted information, he had to be escorted out of the hotel after becoming loud and angry. Samuel waited until the men in dark business suits who followed the large man to the hotel exited the lobby before attempting to get a tail on his possible lead to recovering his beloved uncle. Outside, the fat man had a heated argument with someone on his cell phone before walking away from the hotel, followed by the FBI Agents. Samuel signed his waiting car and instructed the driver to let his target get a safe distance ahead before following him. The fat man did not go far before hailing a taxi and squeezing himself into it. The two men following him did not have to signal their car that pulled up, and they quickly got in to follow. Samuel had finally gotten something to fix his mind on to help determine where his uncle was and who would have to pay for his disappearance, but unnoticed by Samuel was another vehicle pulling out a few cars behind him to join the caravan following Belington.

The South Bronx of New York City was once the seat of one of the most active industrial parks in the Northeast. Over ten square miles of large factories once produced every kind of goods sold worldwide. Globalization and the shipping of the manufacturing industries overseas for cheap labor created a massive South Bronx industrial park ghost town, populated with giant hulks that once employed thousands but now only provide income to illegal metal scavengers and a place for crack whores to take their Johns.

NYPD Patrol car 87 crept in the shadows of the abandoned monoliths; its headlights turned off to avoid detection by those practicing their illegal trades during the hour of darkness.

The two rookie Patrolmen were just off supervised training and eager to obtain their first unsupervised arrest. The two young, ambitious police officers's patrol car silently crept, waiting until they had an unobstructed view of a crime before turning on the car's searchlight, illuminating the night, hopefully catching their target off guard. After five hours of searching, they only produced a ticket for vagrancy and a summons of public intoxication. As the excitement of their first unsupervised patrol ebbed to boredom, the Patrolmen on the passenger side noticed the reflection of a large vehicle's taillight deep inside the pitch-black factory floor.

"Richards, stop the car." The passenger said, keeping his voice low.

"What is it, Frank?" The driver asked after stopping the car.

"I thought I saw something back there." He spoke.

"Ok, let me back up."

After backing up a few feet, he turned the car so that the headlights would be facing in the direction his partner instructed. Turning on the patrol car headlights' high beams, they saw one mortuary wagon and a hospital ambulance parked deep inside the abandoned factory floor beyond the forest of steel beams holding up the building. They drove their patrol car slowly between the rusting steel beams holding up the ceiling of the massive dark structure until they arrived close enough to make out the license plates of the abandoned vehicles. Fighting to control their excitement, they called in the discovery of the missing mortuary vehicle and the license plate number of the ambulance and another car discovered next to it. They decided not to wait until backup arrived, hoping to capture any suspect associated with the abandoned vehicles single-handedly.

"Shit, by the time backup gets here, our suspects will be long gone," Richards said.

"Yeah, fuck that; let's take a look around to make sure they don't get away," Frank said.

The two Patrolmen exited the vehicle and began their search for any criminal responsible for the abandoned cars in the area. With weapons drawn, they carefully made their way behind the cars to a pitch-black stairway. They went up the stairway to the factory's second floor using flashlights. Their flashlight revealed walls with flaking paint and water-soaked floors. They noticed a red light coming from the bottom of a door towards the end of the long, dark hallway. As the two officers quietly approached the door, they heard strange sounds like chanting and moaning. Taking up tactical positions on both sides of the door, one of the patrolmen slowly opened the door before they both rushed in.

"What the fuck!?" Richards managed to say.

The officers were dumbfounded by the vision of a massive pile of squirming human flesh, including legs, arms, heads, and torsos, all moving in a squirming serpentine manner. Males and females rubbed against each other in a red syrup-like substance. A female slowly surfaced out of the pile of squirming human flesh. Her black skin was covered by the red liquid of the human snake pile from which she emerged.

The two officers stood mesmerized as the nude woman slowly approached.

"God damn it, shoot the bitch!!!" An unknown voice commanded, snapping them out of their shocked state.

"This is the police; you are all under arrest," Richards said, not knowing why.

A massive blow hit him on the side, knocking him over his partner, who, for some reason, was kneeling and holding his stomach. He felt two more blows and thought it funny that he could smell gunpowder and burning flesh as he faded into blackness.

Paul Blacksmith slapped the seated and bound Dr. Stanley across the face with the hot 9MM pistol he had just killed the two patrolmen with.

"My darling, is that any way to treat our guest?" Dechontee said as she looked at the two dead men in front of her.

"What a waste. I would have enjoyed them, my love." She spoke.

"We are running out of time and should prepare my gift for my true love." She continued.

"My good Doctor, are you ready now to help me?" She asked Dr. Stanley.

"What you are asking is very dangerous." He responded.

"I am desperate. Charles will never forgive me if I don't bring her back." She said it so convincingly that he almost believed her.

"You are not doing this for him; this is another one of your sick schemes," Stanley said defiantly.

Secretly, she feared that her neurotoxins would degrade his thinking abilities and jeopardize her chances of creating the one weapon with which she could control Charles.

"Stanley, my love, you should think of me like family; if it were not for me, Charles would already be dead." She said.

"Dechontee, just let me go and forget this foolishness." The doctor said.

"I can't do that, my love, and now that those two darling young men have found us, it will not be long before their friends come looking for them." She spoke.

"Paul, go get our guess out of the freezer and place her into the bath our good friend Stanley prepared," Dechontee instructed.

Paul and several of Dechontee's servants not involved in the blood orgy immediately complied. The bath Dr. Stanley Johnson prepared was in a Plexiglas bathtub tank filled with a gelatin-like white color substance designed to raise the body temperature and retard any further decay. The revival tank was based on Dr. Stanley Johnson's research, which Dechontee had secretly stolen long before his abduction. The medical equipment assembly told the Doctor that this was not a random act and could be successful with terrifying results. Elaine had been dead for more than six months now, and regardless of the frozen state her body was stored in, decay was inevitable.

"Stanley, my dear, how is your lovely nephew doing?" "What was his name? Oh yes, Samuel, am I right"? Dechontee asked.

Chills ran down his spine, hearing his nephew mentioned by this monster.

"Samuel, yes, that's right. Samuel is his name, right?" She asked toying with him.

The doctor remained silent, trying not to give Dechontee the satisfaction of smelling the terror reeking from his pours.

"You know, he has not taken your vacation way from home very well." She spoke.

"My servants have been telling me Samuel has been looking all over town for you," Dechontee said.

"Should we bring him here to visit us?" She asked.

The thought of his only surviving blood relative being turned into a mindless food supply by this monster enraged him.

"Ok, Dechontee, have it your way, but don't say I didn't warn you." Dr. Johnson said.

"Thank you, my love." She said as she leaned forward and kissed him on the cheek.

The doctor cringed and tried to move his face away, and the touch of her cold lips on his face made his skin crawl.

"Paul, my darling, it is time for you to give me the gift you promised me, my love. Go get the others ready; we must move to our final location." She said like a child preparing for a birthday.

CHAPTER 29

Demons of the Past

That evening, Melissa Rodriguez tried her best to understand her husband's new obsession with demons, vampires, and secret societies. Her years of studying science and medicine to pass her Nursing exams challenged many ideas she had been taught as a child in Catholic school and Church.

Now, her husband was staying up nights searching the internet for information on weird stuff. He had grown distant and was spending unexplained time away from home on an investigation he would not share with her. Even after being told that the case was being transferred to the FBI, she found him on the computer late at night researching cold case files, or at least he was telling her. One day, when she was cleaning out the pockets of his suit before taking it to the cleaners, she found a piece of paper with a woman's name on it: Dechontee.

"Now who is this bitch?" She asked herself out loud.

She remembered their early days of marriage and how one old girlfriend after another kept creeping up until they were on the brink of divorce. She remembered his many secret lives and his reluctance to share them with her until they went to marriage counseling. She decided to keep the discovery of the woman's name to herself. She hoped he would explain it to her very soon without her having to ask him about it, or she would put his cheating ass out when she caught him in a lie.

Meanwhile, Wanda sat at her desk at the Manhattan FBI office, struggling to finish her weekly progress report. She was warned to limit her investigation to the parameters she was given at the onset of her assignment. Agent Jackson left the Sinclair estate with more questions than answers. During her pre-interview of Charles Sinclair, Wanda was struck by Charles's close resemblance to his ancestors. Yet, there was something familiar about Charles that disturbed her. She could not shake the feeling that she had seen Mr. Charles Sinclair before, or maybe her familiarity with the information the agency could obtain on him gave her that feeling. There was something Wanda could not put her finger on. She also recounted his reaction when she mentioned the Serapians. Her female intuition told her he was holding something back from her, but what could that be? Mr. Floyd Harrison and Mr. Choi belonged to some secret society that went out of its way to stay hidden, but that was not a crime. Yet, how could two men with different backgrounds and affiliations belong to the same organization? Their fascination with Mr. Charles Sinclair did not make sense unless there existed another layer of secrets she had yet to discover. As far as she could tell, their activities posed no threat to the public. However, she was given the impression the agency was more interested in learning if anyone other than Harrison and Choi was interested in the Serapian investigation of the Sinclairs, like the KKK or Al Qaeda, which did not make any sense to her. Wanda could not imagine what either terrorist organization would benefit from learning anything about Charles Sinclair. Wanda knew there was something the agency was not telling her. Other bizarre coincidences that were beyond reasonable occurred around Mr. Sinclair, like the disappearance of his physician, Dr. Stanley

Johnson, and the mentioning of Mr. Paul Blacksmith's criminal boss, Dechontee. When she mentioned Dechontee in her weekly report, she was told to disregard the suspect and the disappearance of Dr. Johson. Wanda was told anything Paul Blacksmith told Detective Rodreguez was hearsay until the suspect, Dechontee, was identified by the New York Police Department, and starting an investigation before that was a waste of FBI Agency resources. Secondly, Dr. Johnson's disappearance was being treated as a missing person, not a kidnapping, due to the lack of a ransom note or any communication with a suspect connected with his disappearance.

Elsewhere, Charles sat alone in his office at the Sinclair estate, contemplating the sudden change in his fortune. Over one hundred years ago, Dechontee had saved his life and, in the process, condemned him to this hellish condition. He knew she did it out of loneliness, thinking he was a natural-born killer like her, but she was wrong. Charles knew she would never give him up, and Dechontee would always resurface, bringing havoc to his life. Charles remembered the days before Dechontee, before the war, and the only time in his life that he was happy.

His father's death brought both sadness and a joyous change to his life. Charles recalled the sense of freedom he experienced after the grief of the loss of his father. He was now free to run the plantation the way he saw fit, and Charles was especially free to pursue the love of Nadine without his father's interference. Charles still remembered how his heart ached for her and still did. Nadine gave life a new meaning and elevated him from an enslaver to a human being. Charles had always planned to purchase Nadine's family upon his father's death. The previous owner thought he was exploiting the young, inexperienced Plantation owner. Mr. Greenburg, or Mr. Green as he liked to be called, felt it was foolish to buy a man and woman growing too old to work the field and to produce children for sale. Every enslaver knew not to buy intact families because they tended to try to escape.

After seeing what Nadine's family reunification meant to her, Charles never mentioned it again. However, he could see she was going out of her way to demonstrate her value as a servant. Knowing she could not conceive him as a fellow human doing something decent and noble broke his heart. He was forced to see himself through her eyes and felt ashamed of the inhumanity reflected in them. He remembered with pride the day she was reunited with her family. The purchase of Nadine's family from the Green plantation was kept a secret from her. Almost every day, Charles sat on his horse beneath a large tree to watch her return from her daily duties. He knew she could tell he was looking at her even though she never raised her head to return his glance or look in his direction. He watched her as she opened her cabin door and entered. Nadine screamed with delight to discover her family waiting inside for her. The reunited family was joyful as they laughed, cried, and danced with unmasked jubilation. To hear Nadine's cries of joy lifted all the dark memories of his father's passing and revealed her proper warm and loving personality for the first time since arriving at the Sinclair plantation. He remembered how affected he was by the raw show of human emotions Nadine and her family displayed. He decided at that moment that he could no longer be a part of a society that denied other human beings the simple joy of a family reunion. It would not be enough to reunite her family, but she had to have the choice of freedom before he genuinely revealed his feelings for her.

Charles was brought back to the present by his private telephone line ringing.

"Hello, this is Charles." He answered.

"Mr. Sinclair, I may have a lead into Uncle Stanley's disappearance," the caller said. Charles instantly recognized it as Samuel.

"That's great news, Sam," Charles replied.

"I am following a man who tried to gain access to Floyd Harrisons' suite and was denied. Perhaps he could tell us why Harrison is here and if he had anything to do with my uncle's disappearance". Sam stated.

"Be careful, Sam; I do not want to lose any more family members." Charles cautioned.

"Yes, Mr. Sinclair," Sam replied.

Hearing Charles refer to him as family swelled his chest with pride. Stanley was uncertain of Charles's confidence in his ability to secure the Sinclair estate and personnel. The death of Elaine, the disappearance of Dr. Johnson, and the attack on Charles's life all happened under his watch, which made Mr. Scales doubt his abilities. Unlike most of the third and fourth-generation residents of the Sinclair estate, Sam was brought on as a young boy by his uncle, Dr. Stanley Johnson, after he had lost his family in a fire that ran through the small town Samuel lived in with his uncles' brother back in Haiti. Stanley only knew of his uncle from the stories told by his father. He imagined joining his wealthy uncle in America. He felt guilty about his dream coming true at the expense of his parent's lives. Samuels' uncle Stanley tried to get him to follow in his footsteps in the medical field. Still, his uncle was just as supportive when Samuel told him his wish to join the military. Samuel was determined to find his beloved uncle and to repay Charles for the confidence placed in him when he was appointed as the head of security of the Sinclair estate.

"Sam, I need you to come with me to Africa," Charles announced.

"Africa, Sir?" Samuel responded.

"Yes, I know you are busy with our security concerns, but would you give Clair a hand planning the voyage when you can?" Charles asked.

"Sir, I will get right on it," Samuel responded.

"One more thing, my employees and enemies must call me Mr. Sinclair or Sir. My family and friends call me Charles." Charles said, conveying his support and trust in Samuel's ability to address the many threats to the Sinclair estate.

"Yes, Charles, I will get right on it," Samuel said, expressing his gratitude for his position in the Sinclair Empire and Charles's continued confidence in his ability to do the job.

CHAPTER 30

Princess Dechontee Houegbadja

Floyd received an unexpected visit from Isoba that evening at the Waldorf Astoria Hotel. Floyd worried that the Serapian Order would notice Billington's arrival and terminate Floyd's investigation due to the risk of exposure Billington represented.

"Floyd, it is my unfortunate duty to inform you that there have been some complications," Isoba said.

Oh fuck, what has BB done now, pissed on the sidewalk or got beat to death by a mob of young Black men, Floyd thought to himself.

"Your associate, Mr. Belington, has attracted the attention of the FBI, and his visit here last night has caused additional interest in your activities here," Isoba stated.

"Shit, I was hoping you were going to tell me that he has been beaten to death." He said sarcastically.

"Yes, sometimes our hiding places become more trouble than they are worth. We are managing the situation. We need you to try to get Billington to go home or, at the very least, stay away from you while you are here." Isoba spoke.

"I will see what I can do," Floyd responded, relieved to hear his assignment was not immediately terminated.

"We understand that there is a matter of ten thousand dollars involved; please see that he gets this," Iso stated as he stood to leave and handed Floyd an envelope.

"I will get right on it," Floyd said, placing the envelope into his robe pocket. As he walked to the door, Isoba gave Floyd a Spartan business card with his name and telephone number.

"I will return at 1 p.m. tomorrow to pick you up. We should visit Charles' favorite restaurant to get to know the man better; how do you feel about that?" Isoba asked.

"Sure, that sounds great," Floyd responded, still wishing it was with Rachel that he was having lunch.

The following day, a solemn mood hung over the police precinct. The burnt remains of the two murdered Rookies and other unidentified remnants were recovered from the smothering remains of an abandoned factory by the New York Fire Department. The head city coroner was examining the victims located in the burned-out factory due to two of the victims being police officers and the high probability of foul play. The remains of medical supplies were also discovered in the burnt remains of the factory, where they did not belong. The Coroner determined the two dead policemen were the victims of gunshot wounds. Still, Detective Rodriguez eagerly awaited the full results of the medical examiner's autopsy of the other unidentified bodies found at the crime scene. The preliminary coroner's report cited the unidentified bodies all were drained of blood with no other apparent cause of death. Julio had a growing sick feeling in his gut that warned him the findings would only add fuel to the evidence he gathered, leading to an illogical conclusion.

During his off hours at home, Julio researched dozens of cold case files going back hundreds of years involving death by unexplained blood loss without signs of trauma. He discovered victims of cold cases that could not be described as murder due to a lack of evidence of a weapon that could cause the wounds that resulted in the massive blood loss of the victims. The most infamous case he thought was an urban legend. Julio researched the urban legend online and found a link to a story from the late 1800s. The story was as follows: on a foggy, moonless night, a derelict ship drifted into the New York harbor on Manhattan's Lower East Side. The Harbor report stated the ship emerged out of the fog on the evening of August 15, 1851, and came to rest in the middle of the harbor. After numerous attempts to hail the crew, a rowboat was sent to investigate. The boarding party reported the stench of death was so overwhelming many of the boarding party members began to throw up before they reached the darkened ghost ship. After climbing aboard, they saw dead bodies, both black and white, lying everywhere. Holding their lanterns high with one hand and handkerchiefs over their noses and mouths with the other, they made their way to the cargo hold, hoping to find anyone alive. They discovered a mass of dead black bodies piled against the back wall of the cargo hole as if the dead people were trying to escape something before their deaths. The boarding party went to the Captain's cabin to retrieve the logbook and learn where the ship came from and who could claim the ghost ship. Upon entering the cabin with their lanterns held high, they were shocked to find a healthy young African girl sitting on the captain's bed with her legs folded. The ship's manifest listed the infamous Slave port of the Cape Coast Castel in Ghana with 250 humans bound for slavery and 20 deckhands. None made it to the shores of America alive except the surviving passenger, whom the ship manifest described as the daughter of a prominent African chief on board as a passenger, not as an enslaved person. The City's surgeon attributed the death of the crew and the enslaved Africans to an unknown pathogen that resulted in spontaneous explosive ulcers causing massive blood loss. The young girl's name entered the passenger's manifest as Princess Dechontee Houegbadja. Researching later New York City newspaper articles, the detective found unsolved death cases involving death by unexplainable massive blood loss in the same area listed in the coroner's office.

Upon further investigation of the slain victims, Julio discovered the Blair's, a prominent New York family financial ledger, recorded that they purchased a young African female. Despite the listing of the young girl as the daughter of African royalty, the courts decided she could not prove she was born a free woman. The Blair family owned the port; they claimed salvage rights on the ghost ship she arrived on. The court document listed the young lady's name as Dechontee Houegbadja. The Blair family claimed the young African girl and gave her to their eighteen-year-old daughter, Stephany, as a gift. The Newspaper article reported the Blair family was found dead from what the doctors were calling an epidemic of a mysterious disease the medical doctors attributed to spontaneous anemia; however, the young African girl and Stephany disappeared without a trace. There was no further documentation of the fate of Ms. Stephany Blair nor of the young African female named Dechontee. However, the anemia epidemic ended with the two young girl's disappearance. Julio's instincts told him there was a connection between the missing young woman on the internet and the mysterious woman he saw on the surveillance videos from the morgue and the hospital. At the same time, common sense told him the relationship was impossible.

CHAPTER 31

Billington's Obsessions

The next afternoon, in a cheap hotel near midtown New York, A heavy aroma of sweat, mildew, unwashed bodies, and sex hung in the air as Belington watched the male prostitute dressed as a woman apply massive amounts of makeup on his face to give his next customer some remotely plausible deniability of his true sexuality. Belington delighted in the fact that he tried his best to hurt the nigger as much as he could when he violently slammed his swollen flesh into the sex worker's backside in an attempt to draw blood and cause permanent damage. He felt vindicated in the fact that he could buy a nigger for just fifty dollars and make him submit to his will. He fantasized what it must have been like to own as many niggers as he liked. He imagined himself as the owner of a large plantation with hundreds of niggers at his mercy. Belington wondered what it must have been like to be an enslaver and legally force his will on all women and men alike. He imagined that nigger Soldier he killed as his slave; BB fantasized himself forcing that nigger soldier to his knees and fucking him in the ass in front of his woman like he just fucked the nigger in the bathroom.

"Hey, you in there, I did not say you could use my fucking bathroom!?," Belington yelled out to the male prostitute.

"Can't a girl get herself fixed up before she leaves?" The transvestite replied.

"What, girl?" "Get your fucking black ass out of here!" Belington demanded to try to project as much disrespect as he could.

The male prostitute quickly assembled his things and rushed out of the door before the fat man could roll himself out of bed.

He sat dripping with sweat, sulking in his small room in the transient hotel, trying to figure out how Floyd Harrison could afford to stay in such a fancy hotel while he had to find a place to stay in this run-down flop house. Belington hated the nigger city and all the Yankees who lived there. BB felt it was Floyd's obligation as a member of the Lodge to provide him a place to stay as he did for himself and not to abandon him to fend for himself in this mongrel city. BB always knew Floyd was an untrustworthy brother of the Lodge and could not wait to return to expose him for the profane that proved himself to be. Belington's cell phone rang to the tune of Dixie, and after several attempts, he managed to roll over to answer it.

"Yeah," Belington said.

"Belington, this is Floyd; I have the money. When do you want to meet?" Floyd said, getting right to the point.

"Well dang, what about today," Belington happily answered.

"I will call you later this afternoon to arrange a meeting place," Floyd replied.

"Sure thing, brother, I will await your call," Belington replied.

"Belington, stay put and look out for my call," Floyd demanded.

"You bet, and.." BB had said before the phone call abruptly ended.

"Well, I'll be damned!" Belington said to himself.

He was shocked that Floyd could come up with that kind of money quickly. BB wondered what sort of business Floyd Harrison was involved in and how he could get a piece of the action. Belington was tired of being the workhorse of the movement. After all, it was he who had proven his commitment to the cause of the white race by helping to kill that nigger and his wife. What had Floyd ever done to prove his worth? Why should Floyd get all the glory and rewards that he justly deserved?

"Yeah, buddy, I will wait for your call, brother, but you will not get rid of this country boy so easily," Billington said to himself.

Back at the New York City FBI Headquarters, Agent Wanda Jackson was surprised to learn that additional supervision was assigned to her as she sat in the midtown FBI office after mentioning the Serapian in her audio evidence report. Additional wiretaps of Floyd Harrison were also denied, and her request for more agents to assist her in her investigation of Mr. Floyd Harrison and his associates was met with resistance. When she asked for additional assets to investigate the Serapes organization, she was harshly denied and ordered to halt all inquiries into the organization and destroy all information and records she had obtained. Wanda was warned to limit the scope of her investigation and avoid mentioning the secretive organization in future reports. She learned early in her career not to question the decisions made by the Bureau and not to stick her nose where it didn't belong. After all, it made perfect sense not to include the Secret Boys Club in her official record, which would be thoroughly scrutinized by the defendant's defense attorney at trial. The last thing they needed was to have a reference to an organization whose existence was hard to prove and whose motives were too bizarre to believe. However, with the arrival of Bill Belington and his visit to Mr. Floyd Harrison, she was obligated to find out what Belington's motivation was to come to New York City. She found it hard to believe that he would think that coming here to recover the money he gave to

Floyd Harrison for his trip would somehow end her investigation of him for the murder of the military couple. She had a meager opinion of Belington but could not believe he would be that stupid. Wanda received a phone report from a surveillance team sitting in an unmarked sedan down the street from Billington's hotel entrance. The FBI surveillance team reported Billington's solicitation of a male prostitute and the prostitutes leaving the hotel. Wanda's stomach turned when she visualized the red-faced fat man naked.

"Dame, that's fucked up." She said, causing Agent Todd Bostic and the three other two male Agents in the surveillance car to laugh.

CHAPTER 32

Mr. Isoba Miyako's Assignment

Meanwhile, New York City's Chinatown always seemed busy day or night. The crowded Canal Street has been particularly busy during the afternoon hours. The tightly packed open storefronts, markets, merchants, shoppers, and tourists shoved up and down the avenue. Mr. Isoba Miyako loved Chinatown for its amalgamation of Asian culture and the blending of humanity.

Meeting with his mentor, a high-ranking Bishop of Christ, Mr. Choi, was a bonus to his trip to Chinatown. They had chosen to have lunch there to discuss the recent events and challenges their Chapter now faced.

Entering the restaurant, with the two large ornate red dragon carvings decorating the entrance, Mr. Isoba Miyako was greeted by two lovely young Asian women in tight black dresses. After informing them of his reservation, they escorted him to a private room in the back of the restaurant where Mr. Choi was waiting. Rising from his seat

Mr. Choi greeted his apprentice.

"Iso, how are you, my friend?" Mr. Choi warmly said.

"Master, I am well. How are you?" Isoba responded.

"Time is running out for me, my young friend, but I have renewed hope based on the recent leads we have found." Mr. Choi responded.

"How was your visit with our guest?" Mr. Choi asked.

"Interesting, but I do not think Mr. Harrison fully understands what he is getting into," Isoba said.

"Yes, I share your concerns, but by using him, we will keep our Chapter safe, and if anything goes wrong, we will not be held accountable." Mr. Choi stated.

"You are most wise, my Master; have the FBI's investigation been dealt with yet?" Isoba asked.

"Yes, our brothers made sure that was halted, and now all we need to do is ensure that the filth that followed our brother here gets his money and goes back home," he replied.

"Master, is it true that one of our Chapters disappeared without a trace while investigating one of Charles Sinclair's ancestors?" Isoba asked.

"Unfortunately, I have assigned you to watch over our brother. You and your team must keep him safe if you can. Please remember, Mr. Charles Sinclair may not be the one we are looking for, but somehow, his family is connected to our goal." Mr. Choi said with a voice of grave concern.

"And what of the woman in the video surveillance tapes?" Isoba asked.

"We are not sure." Mr. Choi replied.

"Should we add her to our investigation as a person of interest?" Isoba asked.

"No, we have other teams on that already; however, we suspect they will make themselves known once Mr. Harrison starts his investigation." Mr. Choi replied.

"I don't understand; what am I to do if Mr. Harrison and I find out who she is or where she is located?" Isoba asked.

"No, my son, she will detect you long before you learn who she is, and if you should ever come across her, we advise you to run." Mr. Choi bluntly stated.

"But enough of that, let's have something to eat." Mr. Choi said, changing the subject before any more questions could be asked.

"Master, I must decline. Floyd and I will visit Charles Sinclair's restaurant later this afternoon, and I must be on my way to prepare for the meeting." Isoba said.

"Always on the job, you will make an excellent Bishop one day." Mr. Choi said with pride.

"Thank you, Master; I will not let you down," Isoba said.

"You never have." Mr. Choi said as he rose from his chair to shake his apprentice's hand before he departed.

Once alone, Mr. Choi reflected on the woman's question on the surveillance tape. What he could not tell Isoba was the last report made long ago by the missing Chapter before their disappearance. In historical records only accessible by the highest-ranking members of the Serapian Order, a historical account reported the sighting of a mysterious white woman who helped an ancestor of Charles Sinclair escape from the South and reunite him with his family here in NYC. The investigating brothers' last entry was a note that they would attempt to interview her to obtain more information on how Sinclair managed to survive the attacks on his life and escape capture in the South. The woman's name was listed as Stephany Blair, but she vanished along with the investigating brothers. A cold chill ran down Mr. Choi's spine as he contemplated the possibility that the woman viewed in the video surveillance tapes was linked to the same woman recorded in the missing Chapters logbook. Perhaps the woman in the video was a member of an unknown rival organization seeking the same thing as the Bishops of Christ because the facts point to more than one person being involved. However, if she were the same woman reported by his distant brothers, that would make her immortal. The primary goal of the Serapian Order genetic research was to capture an immortal and learn the secret of immortality. However, If she was the same woman who dispatched the brothers who investigated Charles Sinclair's distant ancestor, Mr. Choi had to ensure Brother Floyd Harrison did not know enough to endanger him or the Serapian Order if captured.

Back at the Sinclair estate, the security dogs' barking grew increasingly loud and annoying as Charles began to feel the hunger pains from going without adequate blood nourishment. Once Charles's blood supply stockpile had been depleted, and without his son's assistance to obtain a fresh supply from the blood bank, he knew it was just a matter of time before he would be forced to seek out a victim. Already, Charles could feel his temper growing shorter and his agitation level increasing. His wounds had almost completely healed, but Charles had to maintain the image of a man on the mend to avoid suspicion. If his son were not found soon, he would be forced to seek out living sources of the vital life-giving fluid Charles needed.

Samuel Scales' report of one of Floyd Harrisons' associates' location seemed promising. Still, he was noticeably irritated and confused when Charles instructed him not to engage his suspect until further notice. Charles assigned Samuel and his security team to keep a 24-hour eye on Mr. Floyd Harrison and learn as much as possible about his associates. Samuel was angered when Charles secretly relayed the information to Ellsworth for investigation. Samuel did not know that Charles did not want anything to happen to his son's nephew and feared what would happen to him if he fell into Dechontee's hands. Charles had not fully revealed his secrets to Samuel but knew that Dr. Johnson's the nephew was no dummy. It was only a matter of time before his nephew would discover his secret. Still, he was not ready to let another person into his minuscule and dedicated inner circle. Secondly, it would be harder to trace one of Drake Ellsworth's men back to him should they get captured by the police or Dechontee.

The information Charles provided to Drake could help him bring the people responsible for Elaine's murder and his son's disappearance to justice or retribution. Drake Ellsworth was more than happy to receive the news and was equally as eager to find someone to pay for the death of his boss and the disappearance of his men. More importantly, Charles knew that Drake had to ensure Elaine's organization's efficient ruthlessness was maintained now that he was in charge.

Any sign of weakness displayed by Elaine's drug syndicate would encourage the rival crime syndicates to continue to muscle in on her territory and target him and his men for elimination. Drake had to make a bloody example of the people responsible for the attack on Elaine's organization without any further delays.

CHAPTER 33

Billington's Abduction

Later that afternoon, Bill Belington had renewed confidence after receiving the $10,000 from Floyd Harrison. Billington walked down the streets of New York City with a renewed sense of arrogance as he wondered how many other pedestrians had $10,000 in their pockets. Indeed, Yankees walking up and down the busy city streets had fine suits and exciting lives. Bellington convinced himself that no one he passed on the streets was as rich as he was, even if it was not his money to spend. Receiving the money from Floyd Harrison only fueled Belington's curiosity; he now wondered how much more Floyd Harrison had at his disposal. Based on what he had seen, he calculated that Floyd Harrison had access to much more money than anyone could have imagined. Bob Billington had always suspected that he was being denied access to the legendary wealth of the Masonic organization at its disposal. He was determined not to allow this opportunity to slip through his fingers.

As he walked down the streets of New York, he fantasized about what type of nigger he could buy with 10,000 dollars? He imagines he could buy just about anyone he wanted to. With 10,000 dollars, he would not have to settle for a burned-out nigger prostitute. He could afford any one of them that he liked. Walking down the street, BB played a mental game of auctioneer and imagined that every black person he encountered was for sale. He chuckled as he put prices on the men and women who walked by. A block from his destination, Belington noticed a tall, elegantly dressed white woman wearing a large brim hat covering her face leaning on a black limousine. Belington tried to put a price on her. Belington was frustrated, realizing that he did not have enough money even to contemplate purchasing a white woman like that. Nevertheless, it did not stop him from imagining bending her to his will. The thought of the woman being beyond his reach only infuriated him, changing his playful mood into that of a vengeful white knight hell-bent on bringing all the arrogant Yankees like her to their knees.

Passing the woman, trying not to look at her to conceal his feelings of hate and lust, he was startled when Stephany spoke.

"What's the matter, handsome, can't just say hello?" Stephany said.

Belington looked around in confusion.

"Yes, good-looking. I am talking to you." Stephany proclaimed.

Belington tried to make sense of the situation. He turned to look at the woman, attempting to hide his bewilderment.

"I'll be damned, she ain't nothing but a high-class whore." He thought to himself.

"Come on over here, Sugar. I won't bite you yet," Stephany said.

"How much is this going to cost me?" Belington asked.

Stephany laughed, "Sweetie, I am not after your money; just having you in my arms will be payment enough."

Belington always knew Yankee women could not resist Southern white men, and he was told the city bitches were hotter than the ones he had forced himself on down south, but this was beyond his wildest expectation.

Still, he hesitated because he sensed some unexplained danger. Stephany approached, took him by the arm, and escorted him into the limousine's back seat. Once in, Stephany handed him a drink as the car pulled away from the curb. Belington sat back, looking over Stephany's toned body with greedy eyes as he gulped down his drink. He chuckled to himself, thinking that she was going to be disappointed if she believed she was getting more than that burned-out nigger he fucked got.

"Where are you taking me?" He asked.

With blazing speed, Stephany closed the distance between them and shoved her mouth on his, shoving her long tongue down his throat. Belington gagged and tried to push Stephany off him but found himself locked in a steel-like vice grip between her hands that were digging their nails into his biceps. He struggled as a warm, soothing feeling began to engulf him; more profound, he sank into the relaxing pool of bliss as his body melted into the limousine seat.

Stephany released him and pulled away, and Belington, panicky, reached for her to kiss her again to feel that moment of instant bliss again. Stephany pushed his hands away.

"Not now, my pet; if my sister is pleased with you, you will get a lot more than that," Stephany said as she crossed her long, shapely legs, causing Belington's glazed eyes to become fixated.

Agent Todd Bostic did not mind the many days and long hours spent alone on surveillance with Agent Cruz. Not only was she one of the most intelligent women he had ever met, but she was also one of the most beautiful. He tried his best to keep his feelings for her professional, but he found it harder and harder not to notice her beauty and sexuality. He thought he had caught her gazing at him once or twice but could only wish her feelings for him were growing as he was for her. The radio broke the silence.

"Delta two, this is delta one." Agent Cruz picked up the radio.

"Go ahead, Delta One." Be advised that the suspect is heading in your direction on the Northwest side of the street; how copy?"

"That is a clear copy delta one…delta two out." She said, ending the radio communication.

"I see him." Agent Cruz said, looking at the side mirror.

She watched as the round man proudly walked towards their parked location. Suddenly, he stopped to talk with a well-dressed woman standing by a parked limousine.

The Agents were caught off guard when Belington suddenly entered the limo, and the car expectantly pulled away into the busy NYC traffic. The radio came alive with reports of Belington's sudden and unexpected departure. Agent Cruz and Bostic pulled into traffic and made a dangerous U-turn across multiple traffic lanes to pursue the limousine carrying Belington, which disappeared around the busy street corner, barely missing the pedestrians crossing the streets. The two agents turned the tight New York Street corner in time to see the limousine speeding towards the West Side Highway. The agents had to risk revealing their hidden surveillance presence to avoid losing the limo in the heavy traffic. Half a city block ahead, Agent Cruz and Bostic watched the limousine turn onto the Westside highway. The perusing surveillance car's engine roared as Agent Bostic accelerated to ensure they reached the Westside highway intersection without losing sight of the limo.

Agent Todd Bostic slid the car sideways as the agent's car turned the intersection of the West Side Highway. The last thing Agent Bostic saw was a massive cement truck that seemed to appear out of midair, violently striking the pursuing FBI car broadside on the driver's side. The impact of the truck instantly killed Agent Todd Bostic, painting the driver's side window with brain and blood. The collision momentarily knocked out Agent Cruz as the cement truck continued to push the vehicle down the highway, using it as a battering ram. Agent Cruz regained consciousness, still in shock; she knew by the amount of blood and brain tissue on the smashed driver's side window that Todd Bostic was dead. Agent Cruz struggled to free herself from the twisted car as it was being pushed down the busy West Side Highway. New York Police patrol cars witnessing the collision joined the other pursuing FBI Agents trying to get the truck's driver to stop first by voice commands over their loudspeaker, followed by the police firing at the truck's tires.

The tires of the FBI car being pushed down the highway came off their metal rims, causing sparks that ignited the fuel leaking from the car's ruptured gas tank. The car burst into flames as the now burning truck continued to use the burning car as a battering ram, smashing into any vehicle unfortunate to be in its path. A swarm of NYPD patrol cars fired hundreds of rounds of ammunition into the truck's driver's compartment, trying to bring the rampaging truck to a halt. Agent Cruz's screams could be heard as the FBI car filled with smoke and flames. The truck finally made a long right turn, smashing the burning FBI agent's car into the parked cars along the highway, causing them to jump the sidewalk, and crushing the bewildered pedestrians into the side of a building. The burning truck's engine continued to roar as it smashed the FBI car and human remains into the wall of the building. Black, white, and red color smoke billowed from the burning cars and the trucks still spinning wheels. The city fell unnaturally silent when the vehicle's engine suddenly stopped. The sound of screams and the distant herald of the arriving fire trucks broke the silence. The flames and enormous billows of thick black smoke engulfed burning cars and cement truck, forcing the NYPD officers to await the fire department's arrival to begin a futile rescue attempt for anyone trapped between the burning truck and the wall. The door of the truck cabin unexpectedly opened, revealing the armed driver engulfed in flames, firing his weapon as he exited the vehicle.

A patrolman was hit in the chest as he stood to stare in disbelief. A hailstorm of bullets knocked the burning man back against the burning truck and finally to the ground. After the fire had been extinguished, the armed law enforcement officers approached the charred body of the driver with their weapons drawn, expecting the blackened corps to jump up and start firing his gun again. Only after the weapon had been kicked away from the dead charcoal-black body with crimson-red rivers of blood and white fluid oozing out of dozens of bullet holes did anyone dare to drop their guard. The bodies of the two FBI Agents were finally cut out of the mangled remains of their vehicle. The bullet-riddled burned remains of the truck driver were also removed and taken to the morgue for identification. The limousine carrying Belington used the confusion to escape the FBI detail. Still, it overlooked the Sinclair Security Team, led by Mr. Samuel Scales, who weaved through the traffic to avoid the accident and take up trailing positions behind the limousine.

CHAPTER 34

The Revival of Elaine

Dr. Stanley Johnson meticulously scrutinized the preparations for Elaine's reanimation in an industrial factory in Astoria, Queens, New York. His addiction to science led him to engage in the project despite his fear and loathing of Dechontee. He did not recognize the location of the building, the large industrial bay in which he constructed the medical laboratory. Dr. Johnson preferred it over the last area, an abandoned structure. At least this facility was not an abandoned factory like the one he was first held in the Bronx. The six-story red factory building in Astoria Queens was recently utilized and is in reasonably good condition. He inspected the re-animation tank he had constructed to ensure everything was working. The multitude of machines, tubes, and monitors that sunk beneath the surface of the opaque milky white slimy substance led to the lifeless body of Elaine. The shadow of her body could be seen two feet below the surface. Dr. Johnson navigated around the clear Plexiglas container, giving the electrical connectors one more inspection before igniting the re-animation sequence. Paul Blacksmith watched every move he made as if he understood the complex and innovative medical breakthrough he was about to perform. Paul, now totally transformed by the virus Dechontee infected with him, made Dr. Johnson more nervous than ever. He knew that if he were of use to Dechontee, she would keep her pet Vampire away from him, but he feared what would happen to him once the doctor was no longer helpful to her. Stanley hoped her desire to unite with Charles would encourage her to make sure he came to no harm. Still, the way she was willing to play with the dead body of Elaine proved that she was capable of anything.

The doctor inspected the re-animation tank he had constructed to ensure everything was working. The multitude of machines, tubes, and monitors that sunk beneath the surface of the opaque milky white slimy substance led to the lifeless body of Elaine. The shadow of her body could be seen two feet below the surface. Dr. Johnson navigated around the clear Plexiglas container, giving the electrical connectors one more inspection before igniting the re-animation sequence. Paul Blacksmith watched every move he made as if he understood the complex and innovative medical breakthrough he was about to perform.

"What are you doing now?" Paul asked.

"Tell Dechontee that I am ready to begin." Dr. Stanley responded.

Paul flashed the smile of a hungry animal at the sound of the dinner bell. He quickly departed to tell Dechontee the news.

While waiting for Dechontee to arrive, the doctor disconnected the tubes delivering blood and other fluids to Elaine's body.

He suddenly felt nauseous, and a cold shiver went down his spine, signaling the arrival of Dechontee, trailed by newly infected victims, hungering for another fix of her neurotoxins.

"I have brought many volunteers to help provide the special blood Elaine is going to need once she is out of your tank, "Dechontee said, pointing to the half-dead people surrounding her.

Paul strolled confidently beside her now that he was no longer in need of her blood to ease the pain of his transformation. Still, now he had a burning hunger for anyone's blood he could get his hands on.

"Stanley, my love, are you ready to show me my present?" She asked if he was a willing suitor.

The doctor fought the urge to regurgitate as he looked upon the half-dead victims, uncontrollably worshiping the monster that took away their lives.

"Dechontee, I must warn you against this; you do not know what she will be like if we successfully revive her." The doctor advised.

"My dear Stanley, I am touched by your concern, but as you can see, all my children adore me." She said as she slowly sank her teeth into the neck of a young woman standing near her, allowing some of the blood to run down the victim's neck and in between her young, firm breast.

Paul shifted nervously, licking his lips at the sight of wasted blood running down the chest of the young woman.

"Stop it; you are killing her!" The doctor demanded.

Dechontee lifted her head and let out a long, ridiculing laugh.

"No, my dear, I am going to let my pet do that," Dechontee said, mocking the Doctor.

"Paul, come here, my love, and finish this for me," Dechontee instructed.

Paul flashed across the room faster than the doctor had seen anyone move before; immediately, Paul pounced on the young woman, knocking her to the floor as he bit into her neck, feeding on her.

"You filthy bitch!" The doctor said he no longer feared for his life.

"Come now, my love. You do not want to be next, do you?" Dechontee asked in a coy, seductive voice.

"Let's just get this fucking thing over with!" He shot back.

The doctor turned to walk and was quickly stopped by Paul, grabbing the doctor by the leg.

"Where the fuck do you think you are going?" He asked, looking up at the doctor from his straddling position on the dead girl's body.

"Someone needs to turn on the electrical generator." The doctor shot back, looking down at Paul with disgust and contempt.

"No, you wait here. I will do it," Paul said, dismounting the lifeless body of the young woman on the floor.

The doctor secretly hoped that some part of the woman he knew as Elaine would emerge out of the tank and help him escape Dechontee.

Paul turned on the main power switch required to power the doctor's medical equipment, which also powered the lights in the large industrial workspace. This temporarily blinded the doctor and cast light for the first time on the entire floor on which he had constructed his experiment. The gauges and monitors associated with the electrical status lights of his research came alive. They flashed from red to amber to green, indicating that all systems were activated and ready.

Dr. Johnson was surprised to see the painful effects the lights had on Dechontee and her victims. It took them longer to adjust to the lamps; their eyes never seemed to accumulate to the brightness. The doctor made a particular note of this and stored it away for future use.

"Quickly, Doctor, get on with it!" Dechontee demanded, no longer trying to be smug or clever. The doctor silently prayed for forgiveness and pressed the first button on the control panel before him.

"I don't see anything happening," Dechontee said.

"I have to increase the power slowly to avoid causing any further damage." The doctor responded.

Dechontee shielded her eyes and watched as the physician slowly increased the power. A low-pitched hum grew in amperage as the doctor increased the power. The sound volume increased as small flashes of electricity began to streak within the white fluid. The laboring sound of the electric generators raised to a loud whining noise as the smell of ozone and burning electrical insulation filled the air. Large bolts of neon blue electric plasma flashed across the holding tank, followed by a loud bang that made everyone jump in fear. The plasma flashes increased in intensity as the smoke in the air became more and more visible.

Elaine's body began to shake and convulse uncontrollably. The doctor turned up the power to the maximum setting, causing some of the electric connectors to catch on fire as Elaine's' body continued to convulse in the electrified solution.

Finally, the doctor turned the power off, and the flashes of electrical current slowly died down, leaving the air filled with the smell of burnt rubber and ozone. Elaine's body lay motionless in the tank. The silent heart monitor was left on; all other machines were systematically turned off.

"Perhaps I have not properly motivated you, Stanley," Dechontee said as the machines went silent.

The doctor began to back away from her. "Charles will never forgive you if you let anything happen to me." He warned.

"Stanley, my dear, Charles and I were lovers long before you were born and will be lovers long after you are dead." She declared as she moved slowly towards him.

"You've got to give me one more chance; let me adjust the equipment so it works," he demanded, still backing away.

With backs turned away from the resuscitation tank, no one saw the needle of the electroencephalography jump. Everyone was fixated on watching the Dechontee slow death walk towards the doctor.

The needle of the electroencephalography began to fly up and down, creating a broad black, unbroken line on the readout.

Paul leaned his back against the holding tank with his arms folded, laughing as he imagined the taste of the doctor's blood in his mouth.

No one paid attention to the silent rhythmic flashes of the heart monitor that increased in intensity. Stanley did not see Dechontee move any faster, but suddenly, he found himself locked with her hands, crushing his arms into his ribs. She lifted him off the floor quickly and tilted his face close to hers. He could smell and feel her hot, putrid breath on his cheek as he turned his face away from hers and cringed, awaiting the kiss of death.

Without warning, Elaine exploded out of the tank, letting off a terrifying pain-inspired scream. Paul turned, but it was too late; Elaine grabbed him with one hand on his head and the other on his shoulder and almost ripped his head half off his body; she slammed her dagger-filled open mouth on his gushing descending aorta and savagely sucked him dry.

Dechontee's creatures tried to escape, but Elaine was quicker than all of them, and she tracked each one down; Elaine seemed to appear on the neck of another victim as if by magic and drained them of blood.

The doctor saw that Dechontee was shocked and frightened by what she witnessed. Elaine suddenly stood trembling as she stared at Dechontee and the doctor. The dark red blood of her victims streamed down her chin onto her naked breast, mixing with the milky white fluid from the reanimation, causing a cascade of color from red to pink. Her eyes were black and lifeless, yet they could sense unbridled malice radiating and braced themselves for her attack. Elaine tried to step in their direction, then collapsed onto the floor. Dr. Stanley approached cautiously and checked if she had a pulse.

"She is still alive." He spoke.

Dechontee cautiously picked her up and moved her into a furnished she had prepared the hospital room for Elaine with a reinforced door that could only be unlocked from outside.

The survivors of Elaine's awakening did not speak of what they had witnessed. The doctors' warnings fell extremely short of the nightmare played out before their eyes.

Dead bodies lay everywhere, and Dechontee feared the monster that she had created. Her mind raced to find a way of controlling Elaine or a way to kill her if she could not.

The shock of Elaine's resurrection was broken by the alarm signaling the return of the limousine Dechontee had sent out earlier to capture one of the Bishops of Christ that had come to her attention.

Dechontee had planned to infect the doctor regardless of whether he succeeded in reviving Elaine or not; however, after witnessing Elaine's unexpected behavior, she feared that he would need to find a way to destroy her if necessary. Dechontee had never known fear until then, and the sensation thrilled and frightened her. Dechontee now had the bargaining chip she had hoped for when she sent the late Paul Blacksmith and his now-dead friends to kidnap Elaine. Dechontee never intended for them to kill Elaine nor to try to kill her beloved Charles.

With Nadine's revival, Charles must speak with her, and she can finally make him understand how much he needs her and that it is useless for him to continue to try to live without her. She will show him that he could have his pet Elaine and any other woman he wanted, but he must pledge his heart to her and her alone. After his transition, Dechontee remembered how sentimental he was and thought the change would also bring out the killer instinct that had attracted her to him. She was disappointed at his reaction to realizing what the gift of life she had given him meant. She had tolerated his brooding for the last hundred years. It is time for him to come to his senses and accept that he could never return to the life he once knew. No matter what fantasy life Charles surrounded himself with, the reality is that he and his ancestors had always been the predators of men, and not even his death would change that.

"It is time for you to go home, Stanley, my love, and tell Charles about the good news." She spoke.

The doctor could not believe his ears and had difficulty believing she would let him go.

"When you see Charles, please give him my love and tell him we will be together real soon." She said, trying to mask the fear in her voice.

"Please go downstairs and tell the driver where you would like to go unless you would like to spend a little more time with me, my love." She spoke.

The doctor did not answer.

He rushed to the stairway door and ran down the stairs and to the waiting car as fast as he could. On his way to the car, he brushed past a large white man and the dreadful Stephany.

"Watch where you are going, nigger!" A large red-faced man said he ran into trying to get to the limousine.

"Don't worry about him, sugar; I got something nice waiting for you upstairs," Stephany said as they continued up the stairs.

The doctor almost felt compelled to warn him, but then he thought, fuck him, I am out of here.

Meanwhile, Lawrence watched Charles unnoticed from the library door. He became more and more concerned for Charles's health because he noticed that Charles no longer slept and became increasingly short-tempered and isolated. The groundskeepers did all they could to stop the usually silent watchdogs from constantly barking and howling day and night. Lawrence instructed the house staff to give Charles privacy and not contact him without permission. Charles sat alone in the library, lost in thought and impervious to his surroundings. The phone rang in Charles's office, startling Lawrence, who rushed to answer it.

"Mr. Sinclair, this is Drake; did I catch you at a good time?" The caller said.

"This is Mr. Frederick Lawrence. Mr. Sinclair is indisposed now; can I help you?" Lawrence responded.

"I have vital information for Mr. Sinclair, and he instructed me to contact him when I had the information he requested," Drake replied.

"Very well, please hold on," Lawrence said.

Knowing the importance of the information provided by Mr. Drake Ellsworth, Frederic carefully approached Charles to alert him concerning the phone call.

Lawrence knew Charles had become more distant and introspective since the night of Elaine's death. He approached Charles to make as much noise as possible to avoid abruptly taking Charles out of his dark thoughts.

"Charles, Mr. Ellsworth is on the line; he stated that he had important information to give you," Lawrence announced.

Charles rose and walked past Lawrence towards his office without speaking. A chill went down Lawrence's spine as Charles passed. Lawrence had known Charles all his life and never felt any hint of danger while in his company. Yet, an undeniable sense of danger had continued to grow in him with each passing day. Lawrence was not the only one sensing the threat; the generally quiet guard dogs now barked endlessly at a hidden danger within the Sinclair mansion. He hoped Dr. Stanley Johnson would be found soon to administer the drugs to Charles that kept the concealed beast he held within at bay.

"This is Charles," he stated, answering the phone.

"Mr. Sinclair, I believe we have located where the doctor is being held," Drake said.

"When will you know for sure?" Charles asked.

"I have a team on their way there now," Drake responded.

"Tell them not to go in and wait for my arrival," Charles instructed.

"Mr. Sinclair, I don't think you being involved would be a good idea," Drake said.

"Just do what I tell you, Drake," Charles stated.

Hearing Charles being so short and direct with him took Drake by surprise, and he was taken aback by the sudden change in Charles's personality.

"Yes, Mr. Sinclair." He immediately started making mental calculations to ensure that nothing happened to Charles when he arrived.

The late-night ride home was one of the most terrifying experiences of Dr. Stanley Johnson's life. Sitting alone in the limousine's darkened passenger compartment, the Doctor mentally prepared himself for the next sadistic prank Dechontee had in store. When he gave the limo driver the address where he wanted to be taken, the doctor was surprised the driver never turned to face him but constantly looked forward. There was something strangely anatomic about the driver's behavior. Reluctantly, the doctor allowed himself to feel optimistic about his situation. Dr. Johnson began to recognize familiar landmarks along the moonlit route to freedom. The unusual sound of the estate's dogs barking uncontrollably reassured the Doctor and filled him with dread. The car stopped at the Sinclair Estate gate, and the driver seemed to fall asleep, slumping over the steering wheel. After waiting for someone to open the door or to tell him what to do, he attempted to open the car door. To his surprise, he found the door unlocked.

He opened the door, stepped out, and walked briskly to the access control box to gain entrance into the Sinclair estate. Out of the blackness, two sets of headlights flashed about 500 meters from the entry of the gate; additional spotlights turned the night into day. The Doctor quickly entered the access code and rushed onto the Sinclair Estate. He could see the security detail rushing forward, allowing his full emotions to surface for the first time. At the gate, the limousine stood motionless with its engine running. A hidden police public address system pierced the silent night, issuing commands and warnings. The police carefully approached the vehicle, crouched with guns trained on the drivers. The police tactical unit sprang into action; all the windows were knocked out. The consecutive blast of stun grenades preceded a blazing domination assault on the unresponsive vehicle driver. The motionless driver was snatched from the car, tackled facedown to the ground, and handcuffed. The driver, lying flat on the ground with knees on his back, was thoroughly searched; however, when the driver was turned over, he was dead. Everyone was perplexed to find a cause for the suspect's death; no gun wounds nor extreme trauma were witnessed during the suspects' apprehension.

Detectives Rodriguez and O'Bannon were notified when the limousine used during Bill Belington's disappearance was spotted at a bridge crossing that led to the Sinclair estate. On a hunch, they raced to the estate.

"Wasn't that one of the creepiest things you have ever seen"? Julio said after searching for the corpse for weapons and a pulse. Using a flashlight, they looked over the body for any sign of injury. After turning the dead man's head to one side, Rodriguez noticed gaping wounds on the dead man's neck.

"What do you make of this?" Julio asked his partner.

"Fuck if I know, and where the fuck is all the blood?" O'Bannon replied.

CHAPTER 35

The Oasis Restaurant

The Oasis was an upscale restaurant and lounge. Floyd immediately understood Charles Sinclair's attraction to the place. The restaurant's decor was North African-inspired and elegantly adorned.

The menu supported any changes or additions the guest wished. The chefs were virtuosos in the culinary world who used the Oasis as a retreat and collaborative lab to discover new cooking and presentations.

Floyd enjoyed one of the best meals of his life, i.e., flounder stuffed with crab, lobster, prong, scallion, and other magical herbs and spices, all covered in a buttery light Alfredo sauce over a bed of linguine.

Floyd leaned forward. He whispered, "OK, how do we interview the man himself?"

"We have friends in the news industry, and they have arranged for us to tag along as media members for the next media interview with Mr. Sinclair." Isoba casually stated.

"You've got to be kidding me; it can't be that easy," Floyd stated.

"Not only easy but tomorrow," Isoba said.

"You aren't shitting me, are you?" Floyd began to believe he was the subject of some attempt at humor.

"Haven't you heard the Sinclair family doctor was found alive and unhurt?" Isoba asked.

"Come on now, this is no longer funny," Floyd stated, getting tired of the joke.

Isoba passed Floyd his smartphone and replayed the news broadcast.

"OK, what time should I be ready?" Floyd said, getting right to the point.

"Your driver will be at your hotel at 8:00 AM to bring you to my office," Isoba instructed.

"Well, I will be damned." Floyd stated as he sat back in his seat in disbelief."

Isoba's thoughts drifted back to his earlier conversation with his mentor, and his Mentor admonished him to run if confronted by the mysterious woman. He wondered just how far this Mr. Harrison would be willing to go to find the truth and what he would do once he had uncovered it. Isoba was guilt-burdened by Mr. Choi's warning that he could not share with Floyd. He wondered if this tested his loyalty to the Serapian Order and his ability to keep their secrets. Isoba was determined to give Floyd every opportunity to be successful in his investigation and to stay safe.

Unknown to the two apprentices, the restaurant was also being visited that day by a group of well-dressed men from Philadelphia. The two parties eyeballed each other, not knowing why the other seemed out of place.

With the payment to Bill Belington Floyd, he felt he could finally get down to business and return to his investigation of Charles Sinclair. There was a lot to learn about Charles Sinclair, and with the help of Mr. Choi, he could finally get to the bottom of the Sinclair mystery. He was confident that there was a scientific explanation for how Charles Sinclair survived the attack that led to the death of his companion, Elaine. Yet he still could not entirely dismiss all the stories he heard about the Sinclair family, starting with the elder Sinclair, who had survived a similar attack many years ago. Upon returning to his hotel, Floyd was instructed to wait until Isoba could obtain press credentials to set up an interview with Mr. Charles Sinclair under the guise of New Reporters.

CHAPTER 36

Wanda's Confusion

The following day, many thoughts ran through Agent Jackson's mind as she sat waiting for a briefing from the NYPD homicide division chief detective on the death of her agents. Death was a natural component in the life of the FBI. Still, no one was prepared for the brutal death of the two officers who were following Belington. The fact that the driver turned out to be the missing city coroner only added to the impossible circumstances. All the evidence pointed back to Charles Sinclair, but none made sense. Why would the city coroner steal Elaine's corpse? What motivated the same man to be willing to kill and commit suicide to prevent the FBI from following a man who was the primary FBI murder suspect? Was Floyd Harrison involved in the killings, and why was he here in NYC investigating Charles Sinclair? The most intriguing aspect was that she was summoned to the regional FBI director's office earlier that morning to explain why she had contacted NYPD to get additional information about Charles Sinclair. What were they trying to hide, and why would they ignore the questionable connections to Charles Sinclair? She owed the families of Glenn Baker and Michelle Cruz an explanation of why their loved ones died and the reassurance that the perpetrators would be brought to justice.

Deep in thought, she had not noticed the briefing had begun. At the podium stood a middle-aged man who looked like he had slept in his clothes. His two-day-old beard indicated he had not gotten much time off or sleep.

The police lieutenant in charge of the homicide division at the 10th Prescient tried to hide his bewilderment during the morning's operations briefing as he read the name of the truck driver who was shot and burned to death earlier that week. He tried to find a way to make sense of the information he had to read to the Detectives of his Division. He immediately addressed the issue with the matter-of-fact voice he had practiced using in such situations.

"Ok, ladies and gentlemen, Listen up, the perpetrator in the vehicular manslaughter of the two FBI agents has been identified as Dr. Richard Pike, who was reported missing from the City Coroner's office last month," The Lieutenant said.

"We have no other leads; Detectives Rodríguez and Murphy are to conduct the investigation and determine if there is a connection between Dr. Pikes' disappearance and the suspect the FBI Agents were following." The Lieutenant concluded.

The events of the previous night didn't make it any better. The Lieutenant reported on the missing person who died at the scene after delivering Charles Sinclair's missing personal physician to the Sinclair estate.

A wave of nausea started in Detective Rodriguez's stomach, giving him the sensation of being on the verge of throwing up. He did not have to investigate anything; he knew there was a connection but did not want to be the one to find out. He did not want anything more to do with this case and tried to think of a way to escape it. On his way out of the briefing, Agent Jackson stopped him.

"Detective Rodriguez, I expect to receive all your information on this case delivered to my office immediately." She said in a cold, professional voice.

"And good morning to you, Agent Jackson." He sarcastically replied.

"Look, Detective, I lost two good people yesterday, and I am not in the mood for any bull shit, just get me the damned files!" She said as she turned and walked away.

"That's all I need, a bitch on the rag." He commented to his partner, Murphy O'Bannon.

"Yeah, it just keeps getting better," Murphy responded.

For some unknown reason beyond his comprehension, Julio did not tell Agent Jackson that he possessed Paul Blacksmith's cell phone and was identifying the last people Paul had contacted before he went missing. Julio left a phone at home to clearly state that he did not have the phone if asked and would be technically telling the truth. However, he was ready to give it up and planned to give it to Agent Jackson at the Sinclair as soon as possible.

That evening, Agent Jackson sat alone at her desk in the empty office of the NYC FBI, still in disbelief at the video of the missing and assumed kidnapped relative of Charles Sinclair being returned unharmed in a limo driven by a Deadman. Not just any Deadman either; he was once a prominent industrial real-estate agent who went missing a month ago. She wondered if the property of the agent the last working on belonged to Mr. Charles Sinclair. Wanda leaned back in her desk, reviewing all the files her team had compiled. She mentally organized the folders into stacks as they related to each other.

"Let me see here." She thought to herself.

"I'm going to call this group Laurel and Hardy," she said as she moved the two folders to one side.

The phone rang, breaking her concentration.

"This is Jackson." She answered.

"Hey, it's been a long time," a male voice stated.

"Oh, Hi, baby," Wanda replied.

"I just wanted to call to check on you." The Gerald Shabazz continued.

Wanda struggled to resist the urge to allow herself to psychologically give in to the temptation to seek comfort in the male voice. All the events of the last few days came crashing down upon her. The deaths of Agents Roger Bostic and Michelle Cruz, as well as the dreadful occurrences, made her desire to escape into Gerald's embrace now more than ever.

"So, how are you enjoying the Big Apple?" Gerald asked.

Gerald could sense something was wrong with her. He had all come to terms with her career as an FBI agent and knew that there were some things that she could not tell about. However, he was not used to hearing her so quiet and perceptibly disturbed.

"I can't wait to get away from this place." She responded.

"I lost two people yesterday, and to tell you the truth, I don't know what for." She stated.

"I know, are you okay?" Gerald asked.

"I will be as soon as I find out who was responsible and lock them up until the sun no longer shines." She stated defiantly.

"Baby, just be safe and come back as soon as you can," Gerald said.

"I am trying to wrap this up as soon as I can, and I hope we can get away to our favorite spot when I return." She stated.

A flashing light on the phone indicated that another call was coming in.

"Hey babe, another call is coming in, and I will talk to you later," Wanda stated.

"Okay honey, call me when you can," Gerald said just before Wanda switched over the phone lines.

The Agent received an urgent message instructing her team to dispatch to the Sinclair estate to investigate possible infiltrators masquerading at tomorrow's official Sinclair press. Floyd Harrison and another unknown person were identified as the potential infiltrators. Following receipt of the phone briefing, she sat quietly at her desk.

"What the fuck now, Mr. Sinclair?" She said to herself.

As if things could not get more complicated, Wanda also mentally reviewed an earlier report of increased underworld activity centered on the late Ms. Elaine Singletons" criminal organization. Several of her former gang members were found tortured and drained of blood around the city. It was speculated that the Philadelphia crime syndicates were taking advantage of Elaine's death to make a move on her organization. So far, she has not been able to tie any of the late Ms. Singletons' activities to Mr. Sinclair. However, Charles was contacted by the illusive Mr. Drake Ellsworth, who, because of his top-secret security clearance he obtained while serving as a Special Operations Soldier, had been a person of interest to the Agency since the beginning of his affiliation with the late Elaine Singleton.

Wanda's thoughts drifted to the parents and families of the two former agents. She wished she could do something to help them through the pain and loss of their loved ones. Agents Roger Bostic and Michelle Cruz were not only colleagues but trusted her with their lives, which abruptly ended in a fiery death on the West Side Hwy in New York City. Agent Jackson swore to avenge their deaths and to bring anybody who had anything to do with it to justice. She was looking forward to her morning visit with Mr. Charles Sinclair and was taking off the gloves this time. Regardless of the warnings and consequences, it was time for Mr. Sinclair to come clean and tell her what all these events linked to him meant. Wanda had to get Charles to reveal what the Serapians wanted from him, which could have led to her agents' deaths.

CHAPTER 37

Melissa's Pandora Box

The following day, after another wave of morning sickness, Melissa Rodriguez housecleaned to take her mind off the discomfort and help her discover what the universe left in her path to uncover. She noticed a cell phone in his pocket while preparing her husband's suits for the cleaners. Turning the strange phone on, Melissa reviewed the contact list and realized she did not know anyone. Not one of the names was familiar as she strolled down the contact list until she recognized the name Dechontee.

Who in the fuck is this bitch!?" She asked herself out loud.

"Pinche idiota, Julio, I fucking told you that you are not that fucking smart!" She continued. She pressed the call button, and after a few rings, a woman answered.

"This can't be my baby, who are you?" The unknown woman answered.

"I'm his fucking wife!" Melissa responded angrily.

"Hey, honey, there is no need to be rude." The unknown woman replied politely.

"Fuck you bitch, what the fuck is your number doing in my husbands' phone!?" Melissa shot back.

The unknown woman laughed. "Sweetheart, I have a lot of men who love me; maybe your husband is one of them!?" The woman suggested.

"I know your name bitch, and if I ever catch you with my husband, I'm going to kick your bitch ass, you fucking whore!" Melissa stated angrily.

"You know my name? Honey, how did you learn that?" The woman asked.

"Listen, Dechontee, or Dede, or whatever name you and my husband think I am too stupid to figure out, the next time you fuck with my husband, you can keep his dumb ass," Melissa replied.

"Don't be stupid, my dear; perhaps we women can work this out. Why don't we meet to get to the bottom of this?" Dechontee stated.

"The only thing that is going to be worked out is my foot from out of your whore ass!" Melissa stated.

"Ok then, let me give you my address," Dechontee suggested.

After taking down the address, Melissa Rodriguez opened the hallway closet. She pulled out the 9MM pistol her husband stashed on the top shelf. Julio had taught her how to use it and instructed her never to draw the weapon unless she was ready to use it. On this day, she was not only willing to confront his mistress but to shoot him if his dumbass was stupid enough to be there when she arrived.

Meanwhile, at the midtown police precinct, the morning briefing started with less banter than usual. No one could sense the activities in the last few weeks. Agent Jackson sat quietly alone with the one remaining member of her team, Agent Todd Backster. Neither of the agents spoke of the incident from the previous nights nor the death of their colleagues. The room fell silent when the police commissioner entered. Julio knew his presence was confirmation that things were getting out of control. The commissioner spoke about dedication, perseverance, rules, and regulations but could not make more sense of the bazaar occurrences than anyone else. After the Police Commissioner had finished his obligatory pep speech, it was the captain's turn to try to refocus the law enforcement officers in the room.

"Listen up, people, I don't want to hear any more talk of ghosts and vampires; what I need are suspects we can arrest and present to the District Attorney for prosecution." The Captain said in a stern voice.

"The Sinclair news conference will go on without a hitch, and all of you need to get your heads out of your asses and do your jobs." The Captain continued.

Julio welcomed the Captain's approach. He needed something to refocus his mind and distract him from feeling way over his head. He and his partner had received that assignment to oversee the Sinclair news conference and to continue to work with the FBI in the investigation into the murder of Ms. Elaine Singleton, the disappearance of Dr. Stanley Johnson, and the attempt on Charles Sinclair's life.

After the morning briefing, the room was noticeably glum. It insulted the professionalism of the detectives not to be able to find a motive, suspect, or crime, yet people are missing and dead. He was looking forward to the new conference to get a chance to observe the interview of Charles Sinclair and see if he could learn anything more about the investigation.

He noticed Agent Jackson at the back of the room looking more intense than usual. Julio knew the pain of the death of her two Agents was still fresh and decided to give her space to grieve for her lost colleagues as he and the other officers were grieving for their dead.

Julio was not looking forward to following Agent Jackson's instructions. Still, he hoped the Feds would play their trump card and take complete jurisdiction over the case. Julio was already very irritated that he was not allowed to interview Mr. Floyd Harrison and Mr. Isoba on how they got access to the upcoming Sinclair interview and their interest in Mr. Charles Sinclair. As much as he wanted to get this assignment over, the unexplainable experiences he witnessed were addictive in some strange, sick way.

"Ready to hit the road?" O'Bannon asked, breaking Julio and bringing him back to the situation at hand.

"Yeah, but it would be great to be allowed to do our fucking job," Julio stated as he rose to his feet.

"Good Morning Detectives." Agent Wanda Jackson said as she approached the two standing men.

"Good morning, Agent," Julio replied.

"Did you get the green light to interview Harrison and Isoba? I can tell you one thing, those two didn't fucking work for the local news yesterday!" Julio continued.

"What's this bull shit we're hearing that we can't ask them? What the fuck are they doing there?" Julio continued.

"Gentlemen, I don't like this any more than you; we leave in five minutes." Agent Jackson stated as she continued to the briefing room door.

"I guess she fuckin told you off, didn't she?" Agent Brown stated sarcastically in passing, walking to the briefing room exit door and drawing laughter from the other patrolmen and detectives close enough to hear the exchange.

"Go fuck yourself, Puta!" Julio replied.

Come on, Leddy, let's get the car." O'Bannon stated, trying to get Julio out of the Station as soon as possible.

Julio immediately noticed a change at the Sinclair Estate when the grounds appeared. A thick cloud seems to have lifted from over the property. Thank God those dogs finally stopped barking, Julio thought as they navigated between the many New Vans and their support trucks and vehicles parked all along the access road and front lawn.

Later, at the Sinclair estate, Floyd Harrison wasn't ready for the acting job he had to pull off, not to give away the fact that he and his fake Reporter, Isoba, did not belong there.

Floyd could not tell if his act was fooling the uniformed and non-uniformed police and security detail; one well-dressed Hispanic detective had been paying particular attention to him and Isoba since their arrival. He lurked around like a cat, ready to pounce. The Detectives' warm smile and the "Oh, by the way," question all nurtured the notion that he and Isoba were simply mice caught between the paws of a hungry alley cat.

"Excuse me, Mr. Harrison, right? Julio asked as he approached Floyd and Isoba.

"Yep, still my Daddy's boy!" Floyd responded cheerfully and immediately regretted it.

"What News Network did you say you worked for again?" Julio asked, already knowing each name and Network affiliation from the access list printout.

"XBS, of course," Floyd responded, still trying to maintain his bright Southern optimistic masquerade.

"Hey, thank you very much, Mr. Harrison. Floyd, right? Julio asked.

"Do you mind if I call you Floyd?" Julio asked cheerfully.

"No, I don't mind if you do. And what is your first name, if I may ask?" Floyd responded in a similar joyful tone.

"Detective," Julio replied coldly.

Julio knew he was flirting with a suspension at best and losing his job for interfering with Mr. Floyd Harrison or Isoba unless they were in the process of a criminal act. Presenting press credentials to interview Mr. Charles Sinclair did not entirely fall within the crime category; however, whoever was their inside fix, Julio wanted Harrison to know not every cop in the room could be manipulated.

Floyd felt his knees buckle like he was hit cleanly on the jaw with a right cross. It took all of his strength not to show any of the mental and physical nightmares he was feeling.

The desired effect of Julio's probing mind game on Mr. Floyd Harrison, or whoever he was, caused the Detective to single out Floyd as the weak link. Julio had to figure out how to get his new buddy, Floyd, to provide him with more information.

"Ha, ha, ha! You should have seen the look on your face!" Julio said after watching Floyd squirm.

Julio was brought out of his hunter's stalking instinct by his cell phone ringing his wife's ringtone; "Oh Fuck, not now, Melissa!" He thought to himself before rejecting the call.

"You need to lighten up; you are wired too tight." Julio continued, placing his arm around Floyds' shoulder.

"I'll tell you what to show how much of a great guy I am. Why don't we all go out for drinks after work, and it is all on me?" Julio continued, knowing his invitation would only make Floyd more uncomfortable.

O'Bannon, standing just over Julio's shoulder with his back turned involuntarily, coughed, thinking of how they would get the Department to reimburse them for an investigation they were not supposed to be having.

The sound of Melissa's ringtone playing for a second time suggested that he answer before she showed up at the station.

"I'm not taking no for an answer," Julio stated before looking for a quiet place to answer Melissa's call.

"Sorry about that, Honey, but you have caught me at a bad time; is everything O.K.?" Julio stated as he answered the phone, trying his best to hide his frustration.

"That was so sweet," the foreign and unrecognizable cold female voice answered on the other end.

"Who the hell is this, and why do you have my wife's phone?" He demanded.

"That's funny. Your wife had to tell me who you are, but you already had my name in your pocket and my lover's cell phone your wife used to track me down." The woman stated.

"What the fuck are you talking about?" Julio asked.

"Is this some kind of sick joke; did Melissa put you up to this?" Julio asked, hoping that it was true.

"Hold on, Sugar, I think your wife has something she wants to say to you." The woman calmly said.

The scream of an animal in agony and pain caused Julio to drop his phone. He quickly bent to recover it and immediately could associate the horrible screams with that of a human, a human female. However, his beautiful Melissa could not make such pitiful, perverted sounds.

"Please don't hurt my wife." Julio pled as he slowly put the phone close enough to make his gentle plea.

"Oh, it is too late for that, my love." The woman stated just as coldly as she had begun.

"What do you want?" Julio asked, trying to find a way to gain control of the situation.

"I am glad you asked. You see, Sugar, I already have the Fat one, but he can't be the brains of the operations, and I was hoping you could bring us the other one." The woman continued.

"What the fuck are you talking about? Julio shot back.

"Oh, I see; you are the blind one." The woman stated.

"Look, bitch, I can't help you if you don't tell me what you want!" Julio responded, relieved that he now had a dialog that could lead him to his wife.

"Julio, you are so amusing; you insist upon acting like you don't know who I am." The woman continued.

"Tell you what, why don't you give me a clue," Julio stated sarcastically.

"Well, love, the first time you saw it, it was written in blood." The woman said.

"DECHONTEE?" Julio asked, as his blood ran cold and his knees weakened.

"You can call me Deedee as your wife does; I kind of like it, don't you?" Dechontee said cruelly, toying with him.

"Listen, De or whatever you want to be called; If you lay one hand on my …" Julio was interrupted by new agonizing screams blasting through the cell phone speaker.

"Wait, hold on, OK, please don't hurt her anymore; I understand, I get it." Julio plead.

Julio noticed he now had an audience and waved away the other Detectives who came in closer to assist him.

"Can you at least tell me the name of the man you are talking about?" Julio continued to plead.

"The Fat one called him Floyd Harrison," Dechontee stated and hung up.

Julio looked up, and his eyes immediately locked with Floyds standing beyond the mass of humanity assembled at the other end of the large Sinclair dining room. Julio looked to his right and into O'Bannon's eyes.

"It's bad, an 'it? O'Bannon asked.

Julio did not answer but turned and headed in Floyd's direction.

CHAPTER 38

Wolves in Sheep's Clothing

Ellsworth hasn't remembered many good mornings since the death of Elaine Singleton; this was not one of them. His network could retrace the limousine that dropped off Charles Sinclair's doctor back to the abandoned factory where he was held. It was time for some payback. Ellsworth was determined to send a message to whoever had anything to do with the stealing of Elaine's body and punish all those who betrayed his organization. It was time to inform everyone that Elaine was dead, and no new Boss would be appointed. Still, no threat to any surviving organization member would go unanswered. Drake was looking forward to the live interview with Charles Sinclair's doctor to learn something that would help him put the finishing touches on his plan of retribution.

Drake made his traditional phone call before making his final weapons check. He tested the upper assembly of his two 45mm automatics. His father gave him the automatics when Drake graduated from Ranger school. The military was a proud tradition in his family, and he often wondered how he got into this business. He was hired as the head of security for the late Ms. Elaine Singleton. Still, time after time, he found himself in situations he had never dreamt of. Today was a prime example; he knew if he did not retaliate effectively, his life and family's life would be endangered. He had already lost ten men since Elaine's death and had been given an ultimatum to produce Elaine's head as proof of death or prepare for war. For Ellsworth, the solution was simple: go on offense. After holstering his two pistols, he stopped at the full-length mirror to give himself a final inspection. Looking over his navy blue business suit and black shoes, Drake looked into his blue eyes to find the innocent young man he was once. Today, many people will lose their lives, but this is the life they have all chosen. Drake made his way down to the lobby of his apartment building and immediately noticed his two personal bodyguards strategically positioned to cover all entrances and exits. Drake hoped the bandages on the face of one of his private guards would not cause more stress on his negotiations than what already existed. Still, he had to be sure that every man could be trusted beyond any doubt, and Bowser had long ago proved trustworthy. Drake had noticed the heightened level of security as the current situation developed, but he expected nothing less. After thoroughly screening their military backgrounds and criminal records, Drake hired each of them. He knew they had spent the night cleaning their weapons and reloading ammunition. They all had that rationally edgy look in their eyes that said that they were ready to do battle.

Drake gave each of them a quick glance before exiting the building. His driver immediately pulled up to the front of the 962 5th Avenue building, chosen because of its scenic vistas and corner location. Now that Drake was at ground level, he could see the faces of the construction crew he enviously admired from above. Drake expected to see defeated men who had come to terms with their station in life, but instead, he could see the gleam of a predator in their eyes. Instincts told him to pull his weapon immediately. However, he could hear the sickening hiss sound of an approaching RPG before he could react. The rocket blast killed two of Drake's men and knocked him and others to the ground. Drake realized the construction crew members had set up the ambush in plain sight. They had constructed scaffoldings beyond the park's boundary walls to support heavy machine guns and other weapons. A barrage of RPG rounds followed by a hail storm of bullets fired from heavy caliber machine guns from multiple locations. The quiet Central Park West neighborhood was suddenly transformed into an urban combat zone. He watched in horror as each of his five sedans, fully loaded with his heavily armed men, went up in flames and explosions from multiple direct hits by RPGs and heavy machine guns firing from scaffolds behind the short stone wall across the street from his building. While selecting the building, he had assessed that the drop on the wall's far side was too high to make a large-scale attack like this possible. He was now witnessing the price of his miscalculations. His men fought back as best they could, but the attackers had the element of surprise and heavy crew-served weapons. Drake could see the attacker's support vehicles coming in both directions to finish him off.

Drake and three of his surviving men fought a running gun battle to the corner of 77th Street and 5th Avenue to get out of the kill zone and to avoid being trapped by the approaching SUVs. They ran West on 77th Street, trying to reach the 77th Street Subway. The pursuing black SUVs fired as they weaved through the oncoming traffic, trying to get a clear shot at the fleeing men. The 77th Street subway was another three blocks away from the men. They systematically provided cover for each other the best they could, ensuring none of the pursuing SUVs got in front of them to cut them off. Finally, an NYPD patrol car joined the battle but immediately shot one of Drake's men; instinctively, Drake returned fire on the police vehicle, killing the police officers shooting from the patrol car window. One of the pursuing black SUVs pulled up alongside the patrol car and began shooting through it, trying to kill Drake. The Patrolmen driving the vehicle were immediately killed and reduced to red liquid chop meat by the volume of the automatic heavy gunfire coming from the black SUV. Drake hit the ground for cover and crawled forward out of the direct path of the gunfire but could not find a next covered position that would not put his fate in the hands of Jesus. The moment he had been trained to embrace had finally come; it was time to rush the machine gun, the ultimate Hail Mary pass. He checked the ammunition in both of his vintage 45mm automatic pistols and braced himself to attack as soon as he heard any one of the guns stop to reload. Drake inched high enough to get a visual on his point of attack. Surprisingly, he noticed Bowser, maneuvering behind the black SUV, had miraculously survived the initial ambush. Drake immediately began firing from his hidden position to draw the gunmen in the SUV fire in his direction. Drake again hit the ground from the gunmen's firing angle of attack. Drake then heard several controlled gunshots that temporarily silenced the gun battle. Bower was able to sneak around to the blind driver's side of the vehicle to attack and kill its occupants. More police cars began to arrive and engage the other pursuing SUVs; Drake and Bowser put away their weapons and blended into the mass of people who had gathered to watch the spectacle of death. Drake and Bower walked in silence to the 77th Street subway station. Both entered the subway platform without stopping at the booth to obtain subway passes and walked to the end of the station.

"You didn't get back a second too soon, Joe," Drake said to his bandaged gunman.

"Yeah, I wouldn't want to miss this shit for anything in the world," Bowser replied.

"That's the same bull shit you said in Baghdad," Drake replied.

"Why the fuck did you think I took this job?" Bowser asked.

"I know wherever your ass is, the fire could not be far behind," Bower said jokingly, causing both men to burst out laughing.

Detective Rodriguez fought through the mass of people separating him from Mr. Floyd Harrison. Julio had no idea what to say or do when he got to Floyd. However, Floyd's only hope to continue living was his assistance in the safe return of Julio's wife and unborn child. Suddenly, the room erupted with a radio broadcast of shots fired, officers down, and a possible terrorist attack on 77th Street, Central Park. Every law enforcement officer in the room immediately began making plans to join their brothers in blue in combat. The path to Mr. Harrison was now clear. The two men's eyes locked onto each other, and Floyd could not understand the new level of hostility he now saw in Detective Rodriguez's eyes, but it immediately made him fear for his life.

Just as Julio reached Floyd, a firm hand gripped his right shoulder, shaking him out of his trance and causing him to spin around.

"What the hell do you think you are doing!? O'Bannon angrily asked.

"They got my wife!" Julio shot back.

"Who has gotten your wife, Julio? You are not making any sense," O'Bannon stated in a calm but firm voice.

"How the fuck would I know? I got a call from a soon-to-be-dead son of a bitch, telling me to give them this mother fucker in exchange for my wife's life," Julio stated as he struggled to break free of O'Bannon's grip.

"You've got to be fucking kidding me, but we can't do it this way, Julio." O'Bannon compassionately stated.

"We know where the Fucker lives, and the fucking FBI will not let us get out of here with him anyway." O'Bannon reasoned as he pulled Julio away from Floyd.

Elsewhere, at the Sinclair Estate, the cancellation of the news conference came as welcomed news to Charles. The last few days have taken him on an emotional roller coaster ride. His beloved little boy, Dr. Stanly Johnson, has returned home safe and sound. Charles never toyed with the idea that Stanley was dead because he feared what he would become if he had to face the death of not one but two of the people who meant the most to him. That out-of-control rage catalyzed what he is today.

The news of Elaine's resurrection was too unbelievable for him. He had always known Dr. Stanley Johnson was a genius, but Dr. Frankenstein smart?

The one downside to the news of his beloved Elaine's return to life was she was now in the hands of Dechontee, and only God knows what is at the heart of that mad woman's mind.

The news broadcast provided all the news he needed to know Elaine's empire was under attack, and perhaps the only man with any potential leadership qualities may now be among the reported dead. Equally disturbing were the reports of out-of-town organized criminals frequenting the Oasis and asking questions about his and Elaine's past relationship. The news of the Midtown attack enabled him to avoid the interview, which he was forewarned had been infiltrated by members of the Serapian Order. He now knew who they were and could easily avoid them until they got tired or went to play elsewhere.

First, he needed to get to the hidden blood supply at the Oasis. He thought of the irony that his favorite restaurant served human blood. He postponed his trip to the Oasis until Mr. Drake Ellsworth asked him if he had survived the midtown violence.

His skill sets would be needed if things got out of control with the out-of-town interest seeking information about Elaine.

Dr. Stanley Johnson entered the lounge area, breaking Charles out of his trance. Charles rose and gave him a bear hug, lifting Stanley off his feet. Stanley remembered these hugs since he first saw his beloved benefactor, father, and friend. It pained the Doctor to see the only man he ever knew as a father look weak.

"Charles, you are being overly cautious; Samuel and I could retrieve the necessary supplies you need from the Oasis because I am sure the police and the FBI still have it under surveillance," Stanley said.

"We need Ellsworth's help on this," Charles said.

"Samuel and his men are ready for this." Stanley stubbornly replied.

"I know they are my friends, but I fear we will need them for things much more important than this," Charles replied sadly.

"Besides, I just got your back, and I will be damned if I ever lose you again, young man!" Charles stated in a fatherly tone.

"What you could do is to make sure La Mujer Moreana is ready because it looks like we will need to see her sooner rather than later," Charles stated.

"But Charles, don't you realize you need the blood now! What are you trying to do, kill yourself?" Stanley shot back.

Charles took a long, deep breath before answering.

"Stanley, my son, I wouldn't expect anything less from you. At least we now know you are not some Stanley clone." Charles stated, causing both men to laugh.

"Trust me, Stanley, I know what I am doing, but please make sure the La Morena is ready to sail at a second's notice," Charles said, ending the discussion.

Meanwhile, as Floyd and Isoba drove back to Floyd's hotel, they discussed their recent experience at the Sinclair Estate. The sudden cancellation of the Sinclair interview caught everyone off guard. However, it greatly relieved Floyd to get away from the suspicious gaze of Detective Rodriguez.

"Did you see that shit!?" Floyd asked Isoba after they got to their vehicle.

"I hope Charles Sinclair doesn't influence to orchestrate that kind of a situation to get out of an interview," Isoba stated.

"No, the way the Detective looked at me!?" Floyd shot back.

"What the hell are you talking about?" Isoba asked, totally unaware of why Floyd would be so paranoid.

"His partner had to stop him from attacking me; it was like he lost his mind," Floyd said, not believing what he was telling himself.

"Wait, a minute, are you suggesting that Sinclair can remotely cause people to lose their minds and start shooting each other and influence an NYPD detective to try to attack you simultaneously?" Isoba asked in disbelief.

"No, that is not what I am suggesting," Floyd responded.

"That is what it sounds like to me; it is like you suggest this guy has that kind of power?" Isoba asked jokingly.

Floyd laughed, "No, I guess not; it's just that Detective made me feel uncomfortable and a sense of danger that I don't understand nor can explain," Floyd said. "I just hope we won't be seeing him again," Floyd concluded as they drove away from the Sinclair estate, unaware of the unmarked police car trailing them.

CHAPTER 39

The Beginning of the End

Back at the Sinclair estate, Charles could not shake the image of Elaine helpless in the hands of Dechontee. He knew what her final wishes were, and now even that was taken from her by that bitch. The location for the resurrection laboratory Dr. Johnson was forced to construct for Dechontee was determined from the description of the buildings and reverse path analyses of the road of travel to the Sinclair estate conducted by Samuel's security detail. Charles knew he did not have much time before Dechontee would change locations and perhaps disappear for hundreds of years, knowing what that would do to him.

His thoughts brought him back to a time when he could call himself human, a time when love didn't equate to pain and suffering, back to a time when he was alive. He recalled when the last inhabitants of the Sinclair Plantation were evacuated to the Sinclair estate before the Civil War, except for a few volunteers who stayed behind to guard the plantation. The first years were magical, but storm clouds of war threaten the horizon every day. His Northern neighbors, who once supported the financial opportunities of the slaveholding South, now suddenly openly questioning Charles Sinclair's commitment to the Union. The public could not help but notice that Charles Sinclair was once again one of the wealthiest men known despite his extreme efforts to hide his many holdings. The closer the nation came to war, the more public demand grew for Charles to demonstrate his allegiance to the North. Charles noticed free men of color were being pressured to show their support more than other citizens whose loyalty was assumed. Many young African men living on his estate felt compelled to volunteer to join the Union Army as soon as the opportunity presented itself. The Sinclairs contributed financially to the war effort by helping equip many African volunteer regiments underfunded by Congress. Charles also provided financial support for many freed African families whose sons, brothers, and fathers died on battlefields to preserve the Union. However, in the end, only the offering of his blood on the battlefield quieted his feeling of guilt for his family's involvement in the destruction of hundreds of thousands of African lives.

The battles Charles fought while serving in the Army of the Potomac were bloody and loud. It was the first time he witnessed just how cruel a man could be to a man. To enslave a man was a terrible thing to do; however, to run him through with a bayonet was much worse. The butchery and suffering Charles saw during the war caused him to pray for a clean, quick death. However, the battles fought after the declaration of peace caused the most horror. He felt a growing feeling of anger, remembering how naive he was and the cost of his belief in law and justice he and his family paid for with blood and death. At the end of the war, Charles received legal notices challenging the legal ownership of land held by former slaveholders in Confederate-held territories. Landholders who sided with the Confederacy were subjected to having their lands confiscated by the provincial governments placed over Southern regions. The Carpet Baggers had an exceptional talent for finding the best real estate to claim for Southern economic development under shadow companies that they controlled. The Carpet Baggers used dubious laws and regulations to obtain prime lands at the Federal government's expense and to rob the Southern landowners of their property. A group of these Carpet Baggers first contacted him, demanding that he prove ownership of the land and his allegiance to the Union. Charles immediately prepared to return to his southern property to stop the challenges to his estate. He tried to convince his beloved wife Nadine to stay in the North, where her safety was assured. Still, she insisted on being with him and refused to submit to the fear of the recently conquered Confederacy. What neither Charles nor Nadine could imagine was that the threat would not come from the defeated South but from the victorious North.

Upon arriving at the Liberty Mississippi train station, he was immediately struck by the level of destruction of the town and the damage the train station had sustained during the war. Charles and Nadine were met by a young man who identified himself as John Lawrence. John Lawrence and another man loaded the Sinclair's luggage onto a waiting wagon. At the same time, Charles and Nadine were directed to an open coach for their ride to the Sinclair plantation. Liberty City had been turned into a Union military barrack with a sea of blue uniforms prancing about among the oppressed, defeated boys in gray. The level of open hostility between the occupiers in blue and the town folk could not be missed. While the official policy was forgiveness and tolerance, the Union Soldiers and Union Government officials did not try to hide their contempt for the former residents of the Confederacy. While passing a group of Union Soldiers, one of them spat a wad of chewing tobacco toward the coach Charles and Nadine were in as they passed.

"Look at the shit we were fighting and dying for boys." The offending Soldier said to his comrades.

Charles was tempted to produce his discharge papers to prove to the Soldiers that he did his share of fighting to defeat the Confederacy but quickly remembered how many of the Union Soldiers hated Black people more than the South did. For many white men in the North, freed blacks would be competing for their jobs and would be willing to work for much less than whites. Charles chose to stick to the business and allow the insult to pass unchallenged. Charles and Nadine thought it best to leave town immediately and travel to their Plantation. All along the road to their plantation, he could see the burned-out remains of once majestic plantation mansions and miles of unattended fields. The roads were also filled with blacks and whites moving aimlessly up and down the road. Most blacks traveled north, and the whites moved in both directions. The sight of the burn-out mansions caused the Sinclairs to fear what they would find once they reached their plantation home despite the many reports they had received to the contrary.

The first thing Charles noticed when he arrived at the border of his lands was how well his property was kept. Unlike most of his neighbors, his land seemed untouched by the war. He was surprised to see so many people working in his fields. As he and Nadine reached the gate to the entrance to the plantation, their presence was noticed by the workers, who stopped working and began to run towards them, singing and dancing. Charles wondered who all the people were because he made sure all the people on his lands were freed and sent North before the beginning of the war. Charles had a sick stomach, feeling that he had mistakenly left so many people behind. The closer Charles got to the mansion's front door, his ill feelings turned to anger. He hoped the senior Lawrence had a good explanation for why he did not ensure all his people were sent north out of harm's way.

Charles and Nadine were greeted at the door by Lawrence and the house staff.

"Welcome home, Mr. Charles. Look at you, Ms. Nadine. My, haven't you grown into a beautiful woman?" Lawrence cheerfully stated.

"Thank you, Lawrence. You have done a great job here. But who are these people, and why are they still here?" Charles asked.

"They just keep coming, Charles; the word got out about you freeing your slaves and sending them North, so they keep showing up looking for work and help to get North," Lawrence said.

"A lot of them were in the Army during the war and now have nowhere to go," Lawrence explained.

"Well, I'll be damned," Charles stated in disbelief.

"We are using the profits from the land to finance their relocation north, but now that you are back, we have no fear of losing the land to those damned Carpet Baggers," Lawrence said.

He could not help noticing the look of pride on Nadine's face, knowing her man was responsible for so many people's happiness. Charles took a moment to look at his land from his second-floor front balcony. He could not remember it being so beautiful or productive; busy people were rushing here and there without the motivation of an overseer's whip or stick. Each of these people worked for wages to finance their relocation north and was more motivated to bring the crops to market.

When Charles and Nadine went to town to visit the county magistrate, he was taken aback by the impoverished appearance of many of his plantation neighbors who sided with the Confederacy. A few of his former neighbors arrived at the magistrate's office with land deeds in hand, looking for any offer for their properties to save them from starvation and walking away homeless and empty-handed. His former neighbors looked at him with contempt for his decision to side with the Union; they found out much too late how Charles had freed his captives, which caused unintended slave revolts on the surrounding plantations. Charles and Nadine ignored their looks of hatred and contempt. They entered the magistrates 'office to begin their scheduled land rights meeting. Upon entering the room, he was surprised to find the Jewish plantation owner who sold Nadine to his father.

"Well, looksee here, Boy, you are done grown up." The red-faced white man stated.

"And who do you have there? Ain't that the heifer I sold to your daddy?" The man continued lustfully eyeing Nadine, licking his lips, recalling the nocturnal plans he had for her.

"It's good seeing you, Mr. Green," Charles responded, not acknowledging his attempt to insult him and belittle his wife.

"Why are the rights to my land being challenged?" Charles asked.

"Son, if it were up to me, there wouldn't be any of this nonsense, but everybody must prove they own their property and swear to uphold the Union.

Charles knew he was lying; his lawyers had submitted all the necessary documentation to Washington and the Mississippi State Office. However, the Regional Reconstruction Office demanded that each property owner be personally met to prove they were not imposters. Charles went along with the pretense of support the cheerful man tried to fool him with.

Charles was prepared for the demand and produced his military discharge papers and the land deed proving his ownership of his father's lands.

"Well, everything is in order, but do you really want to return here? I mean, a lot of folks won't take kindly to your helping the Yankees fight the Confederacy." The man said.

"My family has owned this land for almost a hundred years, and I am not going to be chased away by those foolish enough to fight the Union," Charles replied defiantly.

"Now, don't be so hasty now, son; you might want to consider listening to the offers I have been getting for your property." Mr. Green continued.

"Mr. Greenburg, I am not interested in selling my property, and you could have made your offer by telegraph and saved me a trip down here," Charles responded.

Charles used Greenburg's full name to make the man's face flush red. He knew using it would put the man on notice that he met business and would not back down.

"Listen here, boy, you can do with your property what you want; I was just trying to give you a little friendly advice." The visibly angered man replied, dropping all the pretense of friendliness.

"Mr. Greenburg, my name is Mr. Charles Sinclair, and I would appreciate it if you did not forget it, "Charles said sternly.

"As for my interest, from what I have seen, I have managed my lands better than most of you," Charles replied.

Charles could feel the hatred and animosity growing among the men and women standing in the office who could overhear their heated exchanges. Some of the men began to move closer to providing support for Mr. Greenburg and to intimidate Charles.

Charles could see the men closing in and braced himself for a fight; he had killed Southern White men during the war and was ready to defend himself if necessary.

"Come on, Charles, I think we are done here," Nadine said as she gently took Charles' arm to lead him out of the office.

"You might want to talk some sense into your husband, girl, before he does something foolish," Greenburg said, addressing Nadine.

"Thank you, Mr. Green, and you have a beautiful day," Nadine said as she pulled her husband towards the door.

It angered Charles to hear his wife speak so submissively to the rude man, but he quickly realized that she was trying to avoid anything happening to him.

Charles and Nadine pushed past the growing crowd of onlookers who had never seen a Black man speak so defiantly to a white man before. The couple ignored the angry stares and verbal insults as they left the office and mounted their carriage to return to their property.

"This place no longer feels like home," Charles said, breaking the silence.

"Now that I am back, neither does it feel like home to me either," Nadine responded.

"I can't believe I could have ever been comfortable here," Charles said.

"I know what you mean, Honey," Nadine responded.

"I am having a second thought about the children visiting here," Charles said.

"Charles, I promised them they could see our plantation," Nadine stated.

"Yes, I know, but I am having second thoughts," Charles responded.

"Everything went O.k. at the land office, so I don't see why they cannot come down for a little while and return to us when we are done with our business down here," Nadine said.

"Nadine, you don't know these people like I do; there could be trouble," Charles said.

"All of your papers are in order. Don't forget you fought for the Union, and nobody is going to be dumb enough to bother you," Nadine said, snuggling closer to him and putting her head on his shoulder.

"Baby, I just don't know," Charles responded.

"Ok, what about if they came down for the last week we are going to be here, and then we will leave right away after that?" She said, looking him in the eyes in the submissive and seductive way she knew would melt his heart.

"Ok, Baby, for only the last week, and that is it," Charles said.

"Thank you, Baby, and I am going to give you a special treat tonight for being so sweet." Nadine snuggled closer and kissed him on the cheek.

Charles's anger melted away as they enjoyed the beauty of the southern countryside on a sunny day as they traveled to their plantation. However, he secretly felt apprehensive about his encounter with Greenburg. He wondered who the interest was seeking to obtain his property. Perhaps he should give Greenburg's offer to sell the land more consideration.

The weeks spent inventorying and assessing the income potential of the Sinclair plantation went by quickly. More and more freed Blacks showed up to the Sinclair estate, causing the surrounding plantation owners to complain that he was taking all the available labor. The other landowners refused to change how they dealt with their former captives, causing many to seek better opportunities with Charles. Nadine took her role as the first lady very seriously; she would ensure the arriving refugees were fed, washed, and given a place to stay until they could arrange their passage North or for those who decided to remain on the plantation as laborers.

The children arrived as promised, and he enjoyed watching them run around the plantation grounds with the other kids as he had done as a child. Mamma Kate, of course, would not let the children come down without her and didn't miss a second before she started telling Charles what to do.

"Charles, if you think I'm going to wait all day for you to pick out the clothes you are taking back with you up north, you got another thing coming," Kate stated in her usual bossy manner.

"Ok, Kate, I will get to it right away," Charles responded light-heartedly.

"You done said that two hours ago, but all you have been doing is standing there watching them wild children play." Kate continued.

"I know, I know, I will get right on it," Charles said.

"Don't think you are so grown that I won't take a switch to your behind, boy." She said, faking anger, causing them both to laugh.

Charles grabbed her in a big bear hug and kissed her hard on the cheek. Kate pretended to struggle to get away.

"Boy, if you don't get your hands off of me and get to your chores, I'm going to tan your backside," Kate said as they both enjoyed reminiscing about the many happy moments they had together in the house.

One of the children came running excitedly, announcing visitors were coming down the road to the main house. Looking down the road, Charles could see Mr. Greenburg accompanied by two other men in his carriage and Union soldiers on horseback. The sight of the old slaveholder and supporter of the Confederacy riding alongside Union soldiers made Charles immediately apprehensive. He went to the front of the main house to greet them.

"Howdy, Mr. Sinclair, boy, you really got things looking good around here," Greenburg said without exiting his horse-drawn carriage.

"How can I help you, Mr. Green," Charles answered, still wondering who the men in Greenburg's carriage were and why they were on his property.

"I thought I'd drop by to see if you have had a change of heart about selling your property," Greenburg cheerfully declared.

"I am sorry you had to waste your time coming all the way out here, but I have not changed my mind," Charles replied.

"Well, that was only part of the reason for my visit; your neighbors have lodged a complaint against you for stealing their workers," Greenburg stated.

"I thought every man was free to work where he wished now that the war is over," Charles replied.

"Well, that may be true, but some of these darkees still owe their former master's money for loans and advances they received while working on their lands," Greenburg stated.

"The Captain and his men are here to search your property for runaways who still owe money to their former masters." Greenburg continued.

This made no sense to Charles; how could a man who had provided free labor all of his life owe the man who collected the dividends of his work without offering any compensation? However, Charles could see beyond the deception; he knew Greenburg had brought the Army with him to intimidate Charles and provide the clear message that the local government had endorsed the attempt to grab his lands.

"I am unaware of any fugitives living on my property or in my employment; however, if you provide me with a list of names of the people you are looking for, I will advise them to seek you out to resolve the issue," Charles replied.

"That's mighty kind of you, but since we are already here, why don't you gather up all of your darkees and let the Captain and his men take a look around?" Greenburg slyly asked.

"Do you have the warrant to search my property?" Charles asked.

"Look here nigger, I am sick and tired of your sassy nigger mouth." The Army Captain, who had sat quietly until then, watched the verbal dance between Charles and Greenburg.

"I beg your pardon, Sir. I fought in the Army of the Potomac for the right to live in peace without the fear of losing my property or being harassed by some trivial Army Captain." Charles shot back.

"I don't care who you fought for; you are nothing but a loudmouth fucking nigger who is about to get his brains blown out if you don't stay in your place." The Captain said.

Charles had seen many men like this Army Captain; had it not been for the war, this Captain would still be digging through the mud for a living. With authority granted to him by the Army, this man was determined to steal as much property as he could.

Several armed young men who were now living on the Sinclair Plantation arrived and stood behind Charles, ready to fight if the situation called for it. Seeing that Charles was not alone and willing to fight to protect his property, the Captain angrily held his tongue, fearing for his life.

"Mr. Greenburg, would you be so kind as to escort this man off my property and not return without a search warrant? Charles said, not trying to hide his contempt for Greenburg or the Captain.

"This is not over yet, you uppity nigger." The Captain said with all the bile he could muster.

"Sir, I can't say it has been a pleasure, and I hope that I never see you again," Charles said before turning away and entering his estate's front door. Nadine greeted him as he entered.

"Charles, I know this property has been in your family's name for a long time, but shouldn't we at least consider giving it up?" Nadine asked, fearing for their lives.

"I have killed many animals like them dressed in gray during the war, and I am not going to hesitate to kill more of them now that they have changed the color of their uniforms," Charles stated.

"But Charles, they are Yankees, and they have the courts to back them," Nadine warned. "They are nothing but a bunch of criminals hiding behind those blue uniforms, and I am not going to let them take my father's lands without a fight." Charles declared.

"More and more, I wish we never came here," Nadine said.

Charles secretly agreed with her, but had it not been for his presence here, his lands would have been confiscated as abandoned property, and no one would have objected.

"Honey, just continue to pack, and let's get away from this place as soon as we can," Charles said to Nadine, trying to ease her fears.

CHAPTER 40

Prelude to Damnation

It had been several days since Greenburg and the arrogant Captain had visited the Sinclar estate. Charles still felt apprehensive concerning the motives and intent of the two men. Charles initiated nightly security watches to safeguard the people on the plantation against vigilantes who may try to capture people who they claimed owed them money for being enslaved on their plantations. No one could sleep the night of the attack on the Sinclair plantation. A heavy sense of foreboding lingered in the air; the sentries were jumpy, and everyone walked around the dark camp wide-eyed and on edge.

Charles could hear distant thunder on the bright starry night. He looked up at the crystal-clear moon, and a sick feeling hit him in the stomach like a death-inflicting body shot by Mike Tyson in his prime.

"EVERYBODY, GET DOWN!" Charles yelled out as loud as he could just as the first artillery shells hit the Sinclair Estate. They were ready for a mob of angry men on horseback; however, Charles could not believe the Army would lend their artillery support to attack without provocation or justification. The precision of the artillery strikes testified to the military's duplicity.

"GET TO YOUR STATIONS!" Charles yelled out after recognizing the barrage pattern as a precursor to a ground attack.

None of the artillery shells hit a significant building or damaged anything of value.

Lawrence and his three sons took on the leadership role of directing those disoriented by the artillery strikes to their predesignated fighting positions.

The artillery barrage ended as suddenly as it began.

The eternal second of quiet was immediately filled with the sound of nightlife, the buzzing billion insects, the chilly wind blowing through the trees, and the moans and the screams of terror from dying men, women, and children.

Through the smoke and fire, he could see them coming. "Just as I thought, unsupported frontal Calvary attack." Charles thought to himself and prayed that enough of his men survived the artillery surprise attack and were ready to fight for their lives. He looked into each of their eyes, acknowledging his failure to anticipate the artillery attack while reassuring them that their defense plan would still work.

Charles now feared the Army's involvement in this land grab, i.e., if Greenberg had found some loophole to declare him a threat to the Union, he would have the entire might of the US Army stationed in the area. Charles knew no defensive plan could stand up to that kind of force. Luckily, his defensive plan was designed for an organized evacuation. From his concealed position, he could see the looks of confusion on the faces of the mounted attackers. They had expected to see people running wildly about in chaos and a handful of poorly organized defenders to contend with. Instead, they saw no one as they continued Gallup forward, firing wildly into the night.

After the riders had reached the predesignated kill zone, they were hit with a deluge of bullets from unknown locations. The attacking riders rode blindly in and out of predesignated kill zones without a plan to contend with organized resistance. The few surviving riders broke away and made a desperate attempt to escape the slaughter. Everybody knew their defense required that the enemy be fooled every time they attacked. The defenders could not afford any attacker to escape to reveal their defense positions and battle tactics.

A group of ten or more riders rode through a gauntlet of fire, refusing to go down despite the multiple gunshots they had suffered. One by one, the attackers dropped. Charles found himself sympathizing with the gallant horse riders riding for their lives. What a shame those excellent riders must die tonight".

The final three riders managed to hide within the pack of panicked riderless horses to escape the massacre.

All the people on the Sinclair Plantation cheered at the sight of the retreating soldiers. Still, Charles knew they had no time to delay the evacuation had to begin immediately. It would not take long before the attackers changed their strategy now that they knew what to expect.

"LAWRENCE, GET THESE PEOPLE OUT OF HERE!" Charles shouted over the cheering masses.

Jack looked at Charles in confusion. "Didn't we just whip them crackers a new asshole?' he thought to himself.

"Don't worry, Mr. Charles. Those fools aren't returning for more of that," Jack Lawrence cheerfully replied.

"LAWRENCE, THE ARMY IS COMING!" Charles shouted.

Lawrence looked at Charles in disbelief, then suddenly seemed to make a connection with the artillery barrage before the attack. Jack's face went blank.

"We will get right on it, Mr. Sinclair," Jack responded before calling his sons to organize the evacuation. To their surprise, most of the people on the Sinclair Plantation had already prepared for evacuation.

Charles noticed how the artillery strikes targeted open fields and avoided damaging standing structures. Unfortunately for them, that is where Charles had hidden his fighters. One other thing they had overlooked was that many of the Black men on Charles Plantation were Union Combat Veterans who had survived being used as shock troops for the Union Army.

Charles raced to the big house to check on his family. The two young men snapped to attention, beaming with pride as their victorious commander rushed past. Charles hesitated as he reached the door, then turned back to address the two young men.

"You, men, need to go and look after your families now. We are evacuating the Plantation," Charles instructed.

"No, Sir," Shot back the older of the two.

"We are not leaving your side until you and your family are safely away from here." Seeing the determination in the two young men's eyes, Charles knew trying to change their minds would be useless.

"Ok, let's get out of here as fast as possible," Charles commanded.

Charles and his two young companions turned and entered the house. At the top of the stairs were Nadine and their two children packed and ready to go. Charles could not have been prouder of how they handled this adversity.

Charles thought he heard the faint sound of thunder on the horizon. He turned to his two companions for confirmation, and their expressions confirmed his worst nightmare.

The roof of the house collapsed under the violent force of a direct artillery strike. Charles watched helplessly as the debris, shrapnel, and fire fell upon his family and consumed them. He could see the terror and confusion on their faces as they sank beneath the flames and smoke. The house was hit multiple times to destroy it. Charles fought his way to the last place he saw his family. Charles was suddenly hit by the concussion of an artillery strike that landed nearby, knocking him unconscious and flying through the front door and out of the house.

A few days later, Charles awakened out of his coma and tried to struggle to his feet, dazed, confused, and amazed that he was still alive. As his head cleared, he looked at the shocked and confused faces circling the campfire hidden deep in the Mississippi swamp. Charles remembered seeing these types of looks after each defeat during the war. He looked around for the faces of his family members, hoping any of them escaped the massacre, and wondered how he had managed to survive the attack. He tried to rise and was stopped by Jack.

"Now you sit still, Mr. Charles," Jack instructed.

"Where is my family?" Charles asked, already knowing the answer.

"There ain't nothing you could do for them now; you just try to keep still." Jack Lawrence instructed.

Charles turned his face away and wished he could cry instead of feeling the rage he felt in his heart and soul. He cursed everything in existence and all beings, gods, and deities that support it.

His heart pounded, and he could not catch his breath, but the rage held until he passed out.

Over the next few months, the ragtag group of survivors of the massacre regained their strength with the assistance of the still very active Slave resistance network; unfortunately, many were hunted down and tortured to death. Others fought to survive by being invisible in the swamps of Mississippi. As the months passed, they were forgotten, and Southern progress began to flourish again on the stolen Sinclair lands. The survivors of the Sinclair massacre were able to transform their grief and rage into a plan for revenge and redemption. The idea was simple: first, they would need to steal several barrels of gunpowder and other items from the Army depot. Secondly, they would need to provoke Greenburg and his Army Captain so severely that they must attack again. The years of Army training and war experience that most of the men in the encampment had enabled Charles to achieve results quickly.

The camp was alive like a beehive under attack on the night of the attack. After many months of planning and training, they were finally ready to begin their retribution to end the feeling of humiliation, grief, pain, and sorrow. Charles was under any delusion that any one of them would escape and live a long life to die with family and friends at their bedsides. Charles knew this attack would end with his death, but before he died, he would kill as many of them as possible.

Mr. Greenberg hosted the annual 4th of July ball at the stolen Sinclair plantation. All of the county's landowners and dignitaries attended the ball. It was not uncommon for dignitaries from far and wide to participate in the Greenberg Plantation balls, and it provided the opportunity Charles was looking for to persecute his revenge on those who killed his family and friends.

Three horse-drawn wagon trailers filled with barrels of gunpowder stacked neatly six rows deep and three rows wide sped through the fugitive camp hidden in the swamp driven by Charles's men wearing their newly acquired blood-stained Union uniforms. The riders were jovial, loudly boasting of the combat battles they survived during the Civil War; other rowdy exchanges were made as they drove their horse teams to their final locations. The small town constructed in the swamps that Charles and the survivors of the massacre at the Sinclair Plantation were generally under blackout conditions but was now glowed brightly from the numerous campfires. Wagons filled with women, children, and possessions were being loaded to escape North during the confusion of the attack Charles and his men were preparing to conduct. It was time to lay their trap and make the crackers pay.

The phone rang, bringing Charles back to the present. He was not expecting anyone to call him on his private line.

"Hello, how can I help you?" Charles answered the phone.

"Mr. Sinclair, I know you had left strict instructions for calling you at home, but Sir, I think your life may be in danger." Mr. Drake Ellington said in a calm, professional voice.

Charles was relieved to hear Ellington's voice proving that he had survived the earlier reported attack.

"It's good to hear your voice, Mr. Ellington. I need you to come to my estate immediately and bring a handful of your most trusted men." Charles instructed, getting straight to the point.

"Yes, Sir," Drake replied, welcoming Charles's direct command approach.

Charles had more direct experience in warfare than any living man. While he hated the destructive nature of war, he took advantage of every American war to satisfy his need for human blood. However, no one associates the current rendition of Charles Sinclair with the military and only knows him as a man who grew up in the lap of luxury.

Charles hung up the phone and sat back in his chair. "Why does it always come to this?" He asked himself, thinking of all the blood and slaughter he had witnessed in his existence.

It was just like the night he laid a trap for those who murdered his family and destroyed his life. He and his men quietly encircled the Sinclair plantation. Their agents had poisoned most of the guards; others, they used knives to make a silent kill. Music and laughter could be heard as they closed in on the house. On signal, all the doors and windows of the master house were breached, causing chaos and terror for all the guests at the Greenburg Ball.

Charles entered the front door with a security detachment on both sides. He scoured the room for two faces, i.e., Greenburg and his murderous Army Captain Smith. Greenburg tried to move to the back of the room to avoid being noticed by Charles, but his movement made him stand out. Charles pointed him out and instructed his men to bring him to his location. Charles sensed someone staring at him; he quickly turned and locked eyes with Captain Smith.

Charles smiled, and he waved the man forward. Captain Smith ignored his invitation and turned his back.

Charles quickly closed the distance between him and the back of Captain Smith; he drew his sword and plunged it up between the Captain's legs and up his body, impaling him on his sword. Charles was careful not to hit the man's heart, ensuring he had his attention.

"Excuse me, Sir, I didn't get that. Do you mind repeating it?" Charles whispered into the screaming man's ear.

Charles's attention was drawn to a thump on the floor; Greenburg had passed out at the sight of Captain Smith's impaling. Charles kicked him forward, completing the attack and getting the man off his sword alive.

"Wake that Mother fucker up!" Charles commanded.

Some of the men decided to piss in his face to wake him up, and it worked.

Charles grabbed him by the hair and began to beat him in the face with his free hand. The blows were purposeful and vicious, designed to kill. Soon, nothing was left to punch but a pool of red mud where Greens' head used to be.

Charles did not notice, but all the other survivors of the Sinclair massacre were acting out their dreams of revenge and retribution. The Green plantation mansion was turned into a house of horrors as the ball attendees were hunted down and slaughtered. It was at that slaughter that Charles first saw Dechontee and Stephany. Charles noticed Dechontee and Stephany standing calmly, witnessing the carnage. The well-dressed Black woman and White woman locked eyes with Charles, smiling, then turned and walked away unchallenged by Charles' attacking men. No one was spared; those who were not gunned down fell under the sword and knife. Those who managed to escape the master house ran into the woods with their beautiful clothing covered with blood, pursued by determined men drunk with hatred and vengeance.

The Army Captain was saved and brought outside the house before it was set ablaze to ensure all inside were dead. Charles instructed his men to put the Captain on a horse with a note telling where they could be found. Two of Charles' men took the Captain to the outskirts of the Green plantation before giving his horse a good slap, sending it racing into town.

Charles returned to his campsite to ensure everyone was ready for their guest. He was counting on their anger and low opinion of his mental capacity to help them fall into his trap. The grounds were well prepared, all the fighting positions were faced in the right direction, and the necessary number of weapons to defend the sector was shown. The attack from the town started as predicted, with an artillery attack decimating the camp sight, leaving nothing standing. Quiet fell over the night, and the distant roar of the cannon ceased. The bright moonlight revealed devastation no man could survive. Through the smoke and fire, they came; the massive Calvary charge comprising both soldiers and civilians was followed by the Infantry charging with fixed bayonets and civilians on foot seeking revenge. Charles knew to move his camp to an alternate location and observed the artillery attack from a safe, undetected position.

When the maximum number of men and horses entered the kill zone, he signaled a man standing by with a bow and fire-tipped arrow to send the signal to fire.

A single flaming arrow sailed through the sky, causing all the attackers from the town to look up and follow its bright path through the black sky. Unknown to the attackers, hollowed-out tree trunks had been placed in a circle surrounding the battle area and filled with grapeshot. Each tree trunk was reinforced with metal straps taken from water barrels to ensure they would not explode but direct the grapeshot in the desired direction.

The roar that followed violently shook the earth; thousands of steel ball bearings of death buzzed and whistled through the air.

The force of the blast knocked the breath out of Charles. After the last buzzing sound of the grapeshot that tore apart everything in the kill zone had fallen silent, Charles raised to assess the damage; what he saw sickened him. Nothing was left, no men, horses, trees, insects, but pools of blood and body parts dangling from the surrounding trees. He staggered backward in shock, dropping the sword that he was ready to fight to the death with. He didn't notice that the second wave of soldiers had already begun their assault. Bullets had whistled by his head before he was wrestled to the ground by one of his men who was near him.

"Sir, are you alright!?" The man demanded.

"It was good knowing you, Soldier; it's time for us to finish this," Charles said. All the attackers understood and accepted that it was their job to give their lives to buy time for the woman and children to make their escape while all of the attention was now on Charles and his men. Each man was instructed to escape, taking as many of the attackers with him as possible and trying to survive the best way they could. Unlike most other men, Charles was a billionaire by those days' standards and had the means to modes of transportation other men did not. Charles instructed them to try to make it to the nearby Mississippi River port, where a ship would be waiting for him to sail them away safely. The only thing he could not predict was the incredible speed at which the second attack wave was conducted. Charles depended on them to underestimate him and failed. A second wave of attackers quickly cut off his escape route to the port and cut down the men on the way to the harbor. He ran to a nearby saddled horse and promptly mounted it, giving the other man a parting wave as he speeded off in a different direction.

Charles could see the attackers' flanks converging, cutting off all chances of escape. He pressed his horse harder, racing to reach the road before the two now visible Calvary wings merged, cutting off his escape route. The attacking Calvary spotted Charles trying to avoid being entrapped, pushing their advance harder. The fastest horseback riders on both sides broke off to intercept Charles. Charles knew he had no chance against three or more attacking riders, so he decided to attack the main body of the Calvary column in the hope of catching them off guard. He drew his sword and pistol, then turned his horse hard left, charging into the exposed flank of the main body, cutting, slashing, and shooting anyone who was not caught off guard. Unbelievably, Charles could get through the other side of the Calvary formation and made a clean getaway through the dark woods. His heart pounding quieted, and he could not catch his breath. Charles realized he had not gotten as cleanly away as he had thought. It started with a burning sensation here and there, then debilitating pain. Charles touched the source of the pain and burning and felt thick streams of blood coming from too many places. His life is now in the hands of the horse he trained to go to the shipping docks for the arrival of the clipper La Morena.

Charles awoke still straddling his horse, drinking water from a barrel at a dock along the Mississippi River. He tried to raise himself but was instantly stopped by the pain. Charles rode the horse to the stable as quietly as possible; however, he noticed the docks were empty and the La Morena had not arrived yet. Charles had expected at least a caretaker to be available at the pier. He unlocked the stable door without getting off the horse because he couldn't. After closing the door, Charles navigated the horse to the enormous hay pile. He gingerly lowered himself off the horse, landing with a thump. He waved the horse away and fell into a deep coma.

The Liberty City massacre was a media sensation; the whole world was talking about everything that they heard and nothing about what they knew. The news was about a hoard of un-killable black savages that turned into a beast at night to murder innocent white men, women, and children. Charles was reported to have the ability to turn good niggers into bloodthirsty black unchristian savages. The Newspapers said the black monster was still on the loose, and a price of ten thousand dollars was posted for him, dead or alive. However, the reality was Charles had been wounded three days ago, and he was slowly bleeding to death as he fell in and out of delusion. He thought he felt himself being lifted off the floor. Still, when Charles tried to open his eyes, he saw one of the two women spectating the revengeful massacre at the Greenburg event. Charles remembers thinking no woman could be strong enough to carry him so effortlessly before falling back into darkness. Next, Charles remembered lying in the Dechontee's lap while riding in an ornate, lavishly decorated private stagecoach.

"My love, you are dying," Dechontee whispered into his ear as he lay helpless with his head on her lap as she ran her fingers through his blood-soaked hair.

"What, who are you?" Charles managed to ask.

"I only tell that to my dearest friends, lovers, and prey, my love." The woman seductively stated.

"Who are you, and where are you taking me?" Charles asked, suspecting she would turn him in for some reward.

"Since you must know, my name is Dechontee, and this is my sister Stephany. We are taking you home, my King," the woman said jubilantly.

"Charles managed a painful laugh, "Sorry lady, I'm not going anywhere but dead; I got more holes and cuts on me than any doctor could ever plug. So, go ahead and turn me in; I will be dead by dawn anyway." Charles managed to say.

"Not if you don't want to, my King," Dechontee said, lifting his face to look him in the eyes.

"Dechontee, don't do it, just kill the bastard and be done with it," Stephany said.

"Didn't you see him at the mansion?" Dechontee asked.

"Yes, I saw him beating the little man to death, but what do we need with him?" Stephany asked.

"I need him, Stephany!" Dechontee answered angrily.

"I'm telling you, Dechontee, this will not end well," Stephany warned.

"Don't be jealous, my sister; you will always be my first love," Dechontee said.

"Go ahead, fucking kill me, I don't care, I have nothing to live for anyway," Charles managed to say.

"What if you could live on to peruse your enemies and restore your family's name?" Dechontee asked.

"Isn't that what you want?" She asked.

The prospects of continuing his retribution on those who had killed the love of his life and their children cleared his head.

"Yes, that is exactly what I want." He said clearly.

"Hold your head back and rest," Dechontee said as she lifted his head and laid it on a pillow, keeping him in an upright sitting position on the floor of the coach.

He awoke momentarily and thought his wife had straddled his face and was grinding her clitoris into his mouth. He had the sensation of drowning and breathing at the same time. He felt the pain of his wounds melt away as he fell into a river of tranquility; Charles remembered thinking that he was finally dying and would join his family in the afterlife. However, he did not know that his nightmare was beginning.

CHAPTER 41

The Blind, Deaf, and Dumb

Julio and O'Bannon followed Floyd and Isoba back to the Waldorf, where Floyd was staying. They quickly followed the two men to Floyd's suite as discreetly as possible, hoping to avoid any security detail they could not talk their way past.

The detectives knew their visit would not go unnoticed by the FBI agents in the hotel lobby, who would immediately notify Agent Jackson of their presence. Julio knew they were working against time. He had to get as much out of Floyd Harrison before Agent Jackson arrived. O'Bannon suggested using the carrot approach to get Floyd to cooperate; Floyd may also be a victim. Matt O'Bannon had difficulty controlling Julio but understood Julio's need for immediate answers. The elevator opened on the 10th floor, and the detectives went down the luxurious hallway to Floyd's suite. The hotel manager escorted them to Floyd's suite and knocked on the door, announcing that he had visitors. Floyd opened the door with his well-rehearsed Tom Cruise grin, expecting it to be Rachel; who else could it be?

"Mr. Harrison, we are sorry to bother you at home, but we have an urgent matter we must discuss with you," Julio stated.

Floyd's face turned pasty white, and he stood speechless. Isoba remembered Floyd's apprehension about Detective Rodriguez, and now he was at their door.

"Yes, yes, of course, come in." He said after overcoming his shock.

"Will that be all gentlemen?" The Clerk asked, hoping to take his leave from the situation.

Choirs of yeses responded, and the Clerk sped away.

After entering the hotel suite, Julio quickly got to the point.

"We need to know everything you know about a woman named Dechontee," Julio stated.

Floyd and Isoba glanced at each other to see if they had heard the same thing.

"The woman is a bogymen myth," Floyd answered lightheartedly.

"Well, your bogeyman myth has kidnapped my wife and claims to have a fat friend of yours, and she wants me to take you to her in exchange for my wife," Julio said.

"So, if there is something you could do to help the both of us, I would advise you to do it quickly," Julio said.

"I don't have a fat, Oh my God!" Floyd continued.

Floyd's blood ran cold, "They must be talking about Belington, what the fuck he did now?" He thought.

Floyd was stunned. Was a woman holding Billington hostage and demanding he be turned over to her? Was this happening, or perhaps an elaborate joke being played on him? Could this possibly have anything to do with the mysterious women he was told about, who were associated with the disappearance of the brothers investigating the Sinclairs in the past?

"As Mr. Harrison has stated, we know nothing other than the myths; I am sorry we cannot further assist you," Isoba volunteered.

Isoba gave Floyd a stern look to stop him from getting involved with the Detective and Dechontee. Isoba knew that if Dechontee had the Detective's wife, there would be no hope of saving her. Plus, Isoba was warned to avoid the women at all costs.

"Kidnapped your wife and my fat friend?" Floyd repeated.

Julio's cell phone rang Melissa's ringtone, and he quickly answered.

"Hello, Melissa, is that you?" Julio hopefully answered.

"No, my lover, but you are standing in the room with the man who could bring you two back together again," Dechontee said.

"This bitch is watching our every move." He thought to himself.

"Ok, where do you want me to bring him?" Julio asked.

Floyd and Isoba's blood ran cold as they listened to the Detective receive the address of their execution.

Julio was given the address and a not-so-subtle reminder that they had his wife and unborn child as leverage. Julio knew he would not have a chance of sneaking Floyd out of the hotel even if he agreed to go with them voluntarily. His only hope was to seek the assistance of Agent Jackson in retrieving his wife safely.

"Put Mr. Harrison on the phone; his fellow Serapian wants to talk to him," Dechontee said.

Floyd reluctantly took the phone.

"Hello, this is Floyd Harrison." He answered nervously.

"Hey, buddy, I told them that I vouch for you as a real brother of the Craft and that you only came here on a secret mission about that nigger in New York; you don't have to worry about nothing," Belington said frantically before the phone suddenly taken away from him.

"You Serapians are scraping the bottom of the bowl these days for parasites." Dechontee mockingly stated.

"The jokes on you, lady; Belington is not a Priest and is useless to you," Floyd said, trying to diminish Belington's bargaining value.

"No, the joke is on you, my love; do you see that handsome Detective standing there watching you talk on the phone? All I must do is to tell him to blow out your brains to see his wife, and what do you think he would do? She asked.

Floyd remembered his first encounter with Detective Rodriguez and knew she was not bluffing.

"I would advise you to get here as soon as you can and tell me everything you know about Charles Sinclair, and I mean everything. And be a darling and bring all your notes." She said before hanging up the phone.

Floyd was speechless, in the twenty-first century, dealing with a fanatic who had taken this way too seriously. He wanted to tell Detective Rodriguez everything he knew to help him regain his wife and avoid becoming the next entry into the missing brothers' book.

"We will have to consult without superiors for the information you are looking for," Isoba stated more to Floyd than to the two detectives, secretly telling Floyd to keep his mouth shut.

"What the fuck is a serpent or whatever the fuck she was talking about? Julio demanded.

"I don't know what she was talking about or what she wants with me." Floyd lied as instructed.

"No, Lad, there isn't a Masonic Order with that name," O'Bannon stated.

Julio finally lost patience with Floyd and grabbed him by the throat with his left hand, pressing the muzzle of his 9mm pistol against Floyd's Temple.

"You want to try that again?" Julio asked Floyd.

O'Bannon did not want the situation to escalate this quickly to the threat of the use of deadly force. Still, he had to back his partner's move by pulling out his weapon and training it on Isoba, preventing him from going to Floyd's assistance.

"For the last mother fucking time, who the fuck are you people, and who the hell is Dechontee?" Julio demanded, still choking Floyd with his gun against the helpless man's head.

"Ok, I will tell you all I know." Floyd managed to say.

"Floyd, don't tell them anything!" Isoba demanded.

"You keep your fucking mouth shut!" O'Bannon warned Isoba.

"This has gone way too far," Floyd said, trying to bring sanity back into the room.

"Floyd, they can't make you tell them anything; let our superiors deal with them," Isoba warned.

"The next time you open your fucking mouth, I am going to put a bullet in it," O'Bannon warned Isoba.

"Isoba, some lunatic who believes all of the stories are true, has this man's wife; we got to help him." Floyd sympathetically stated.

Floyd sympathized with the detective and knew if someone held his wife hostage, there wouldn't be anything he would not do to get her back.

"Some lunatics? Floyd, you have been warned; keep your mouth shut!" Isoba warned.

"That's it, you are under arrest for obstructing a police investigation," O'Bannon stated as he turned Isoba around to put handcuffs on him.

"Take him into the other room and see if he will be more willing to cooperate," Julio instructed O'Bannon so he could be alone with Floyd.

O'Bannon dragged Isoba out of the living room; all the while, Isoba continued to warn Floyd not to talk and wait for instructions from their superiors.

Once alone, Julio released Floyd and put away his weapon to show Floyd that he meant no harm.

"Mr. Harrison, I need to know anything you can tell me that could help me get my wife back," Julio said, getting right to the point.

"What I can say is that the woman claiming to be Dechontee is a fraud," Floyd stated.

"What makes you so sure of that?" Julio asked, not revealing what information he had already learned.

"The actual woman named Dechontee died hundreds of years ago, and whoever we were talking to over the phone must be someone who has taken on her identity in some kind of role-playing game," Floyd stated.

"You mean like Dungeons and Dragons?" Julio asked.

"Exactly, just like Dungeons and Dragons, but this person has become lost in the role-playing game and has begun to believe it is all real," Floyd stated.

"Believe what is real?" Julio asked.

"Immortality," Floyd reluctantly answered.

"You've fucking got to be kidding me; you mean to tell me that the people who have my wife believe in all that crap?" Julio asked in disbelief.

"Yes, and they mistakenly believe that I know something that could help them achieve their quest; this is all a big game of history treasure hunt for men with too much time on their hands," Floyd answered.

"What does this have to do with Charles Sinclair?" Julio took the opportunity to ask.

"Frankly, we don't know, but the Sinclairs were being investigated the last time we encountered a female over one hundred years ago named Dechontee.

"Your friend in the other room seems to believe it's true," Julio responded.

"As I said before, some of us take it more literally than others; the information I have just given you is enough to have my family's membership in the organization revoked forever," Floyd responded.

"Listen, that is all fascinating, but we need your help to get my wife back." Floyd impatiently replied.

"I will help you as much as I can, but I have to warn you that the people holding your wife believe in this myth," Floyd said.

"The prospects of gaining immortality has led men to commit gross atrocities in the past," Floyd continued, trying to soften the reality that the detective's wife may be in the hands of mentally unstable people.

Julio called O'Bannon, who was holding Isoba in the bedroom, and told him to release him and escort him out of the hotel suite.

"We will not be able to protect you," Isoba said as he passed Floyd and left the hotel suite.

Floyd felt shame and remorse for revealing secrets of the Serapian Order to the detective; however, he felt morally obligated to help Julio rescue his wife from someone he believed was playing this game too seriously.

"Don't worry, Isoba, I will have New York's finest for protection," Floyd said assuredly.

"My friend, they may not be enough," Isoba said as he sadly left the hotel room.

"Mr. Harrison, I don't intend to turn you over to anyone, but I need your assistance to get my wife back," Julio stated.

"As I said before, I will do what I can to help you," Floyd compassionately replied.

"We will have to sneak you out of the hotel so the FBI agents will not follow us in the lobby," Julio said.

"FBI, what FBI Agents are you talking about"? Floyd asked, not realizing he was under law enforcement surveillance.

"Never mind that for now, we have to get moving as soon as my partner returns," Julio replied.

🙈🙊🙉

CHAPTER 42

The Final Mask

Charles Sinclair III still held on to the hope that he could somehow rescue Elaine and keep his secret from being revealed. However, he had started arranging to leave the country, disappearing, and reinventing himself to return as Charles Sinclair IV. Lawrence and other trusted individuals were well versed in making the legal arrangements and preparing his cover story to fit the narrative of a man returning to his ancestral home to visit a non-existing wife and adult son only to become ill and die, thus leaving everything to his fictitious inheritor. Lawrence announced Mr. Drake Ellsworth and Mr. Bowser's arrival. Charles decided to have the meeting in the dining room to give the session a more personal touch; after all, he would ask the men to accompany him on a mission they may not be returning from. Charles wondered how to express the danger the men would face in a way they could believe. Luckily, he would not have to tell them about any crucifixes or stakes through the heart like he had seen in Hollywood vampire movies, but the truth was just as unbelievable.

Lawrence entered the dining room, followed by the two visitors. The signs of the morning's ambush were visible on the faces and clothes of the two men. Charles's years of war gave him many examples of what people looked like in victory and defeat;

he could see that these two men were lucky to be alive and ready for some payback.

"Gentlemen, please have a seat." Charles requested.

Drake noticed Charles's change in tone and questioned why he was being so friendly with him now. Drake was surprised to see how fit Charles suddenly appeared. Had he not known, he would have never guessed Charles had just been shot and nearly killed not too long ago.

"What I have to tell you is almost too incredible, but Elaine Singleton is alive," Charles stated.

"That is impossible; I saw her body in the morgue," Drake responded in disbelief.

"As incredible as it may sound, my doctor who was recently abducted told me that he saw her alive and being held by the same people that were holding him," Charles stated.

A thousand thoughts raced through Drakes' and Bowers' heads; had Elaine planned this all along and not told them about it? He knew she was ruthless, but he believed he had won her loyalty and that she would not pull a stunt like that and expose him to the wrath of her multitude of enemies. However, he was relieved that she was alive because now the focus of her enemies' anger would be shifted back to her where it belonged and off him and potentially his family.

"So, tell us where she is, and we will go get her and make whoever is holding her regret their foolishness," Drake stated.

"I am afraid that it is not that simple, and you will need my help to get her back," Charles said.

"With all due respect, Sir, we can come up with all the money whoever is holding her is demanding, not that they will get the chance to spend one dime of it," Drake said.

"It is not a matter of money, Drake," Charles said.

"Then what in the hell do they want?" Drake asked.

"I can tell you that if we have any hope of seeing Elaine again, I must come with you to get her," Charles replied.

"I cannot allow you to put yourself in danger by helping us. Just tell us where Ms. Singleton is being held, and we will take care of the rest," Drake responded.

Charles smiled and found Drake's concern for his well-being sincere but amusing, given that Drake and his men would be in danger.

"Drake, I appreciate your concern, but there are things here that you don't understand, and you nor your men will be able to retrieve Elaine without my assistance," Charles replied.

The verbal admission of some unusual circumstances or situations validated Drakes's suspicion that something unnatural was central to last month's events. However, accepting some of his wildest ideas would start him down that slippery slope into insanity.

"Things like what?" Drake reluctantly asked.

"I can't tell you right now, but we will have to be prepared to fight a type of enemy that you have never faced before," Charles stated.

CHAPTER 43

The Perfect Mouse Trap

Dazed and confused, Paul Blacksmith emerged from Dr. Stanley Johnson's resurrection tank. His emergence from the resurrection tank was not as dramatic as Elaine's; however, his thirst for blood was just as extreme. Unfortunately, he had none of Elaine's enhanced abilities due to the immature state of his initial exposure to Dechontee's immortality disease. His attacks on the other creatures in Dechontee's ranks were easily fended off, and he now lay naked and shivering in a fetal position in a corner. When Dechontee approached him, he attacked in a hunger-crazed attempt to feed on her. Dechontee quickly slapped him back into the corner.

"Help me, why doesn't anybody help me"? Paul begged.

"My poor darling, I was afraid that I had lost you forever," Dechontee said.

"I am burning up inside; I need to feed." Paul continued to beg.

"Paul, my beloved, you know I will always care for you, and I have just what you need." Dechontee continued.

"Belington, would you be a dear and come over here and meet a lover of mine"? Dechontee said.

Belington had lost a massive amount of weight and was now a mindless slave of Dechontee, like all the other infected people under her control.

Belington approached unsuspectingly and stood by Dechontee's side. Paul immediately attacked and plunged his fangs deep into Belington's neck. The force of the attack knocked Belington onto his back, with Paul's naked body straddling him as he fed on Belington. Belington was powerless to avoid or defend himself against Paul Blacksmith. If not for Dechontee's intervention, Paul would have drained him dry. Dechontee knocked Paul off Belington before he could finish killing him. Paul rolled to the side and quickly went into a crouching attack position, snarling at Dechontee like a wild dog bearing his bloody fangs.

"That is enough for now, Paul," Dechontee said, ignoring his threatening posture but keeping her body between Paul and Belington.

Belington struggled to get to his feet, still holding his neck where Paul had bitten him.

"We will be having a guest this evening, and the both of you need to be ready," Dechontee announced.

"Stephany, would you be a dear and get some clothing for our good friend Paul? We can't have him running around naked like the others, can we"? Dechontee requested.

"By the way, how is our little jealous housewife doing?" Dechontee asked.

"A few broken bones and the loss of a lot of blood, but other than that, she is alive," Stephany replied unsympathetically.

"Don't forget, my dear, we need her alive just a little while longer, and we will have every one who could be a threat to us or my beloved in one place," Dechontee stated gleefully.

Stephany had learned the disappearing drill very well. The steps were monstrously simplistic, i.e., locate anyone who knew anything about them and kill them all. Of course, not every disappearance act yielded the gluttony of bodies as Dechontee's love spats with Charles Sinclair. Still, she was never disappointed in the number of fresh bodies to feed upon when the arguments were as vicious and passionate as this one. However, she had never held the pregnant wife of a police detective before but soon realized how quickly you can bend them to your will once you have something they hold dear in your hands. As unsympathetic as she was for Melissa Rodriguez's current situation, she could not help but feel some compassion for the unborn child. The thought of the child growing in Melissa's womb intrigued her. It led her to fully comprehend yet another side effect of the disease she was afflicted with. She would never know the secret of motherhood like the woman whose life was in her hands.

Stephany walked down the dimly lit hallway of the administrative office space of the abandoned factory they had relocated to as their final location before their disappearance.

Dechontee had mastered Dr. Stanley Johnson's resuscitation tank, and she had allowed her mistakes while learning the technology to live in a nightmarish condition of being neither living nor dead. The screams and moans of the creatures flooded the stagnant air, interrupted only by the rhythmic clicking sound made by Stephany's stiletto heels as she made her way to Melissa's location. What was once an office fish tank conference room was now converted into a holding tank for the undead. Stephany watched one of the weaker creatures being torn apart and eaten by the other stronger vampires. She watched in amazement how quickly they consumed the other creature and wondered what it must have tasted like; she hoped she would be allowed to have one once Dechontee had no more use for them.

CHAPTER 44

The Sacrificial Lambs

The emergency meeting with Mr. Choi was arranged quicker than Isoba thought possible. The location was unusual, but the circumstances were equally bizarre. He sat alone in a remote area in Central Park on a bench under a single light pole designed to look like the original gas lanterns waiting for Mr. Choi. As a Serapean Eidikoi Frouroi (SEF) or Special Guards member, Isoba was well-trained in most martial arts. However, he was not confident his fighting skills would be enough, so he came armed with an AR15-M4 Bull pup semiautomatic rifle concealed under his jacket and a Smith and Western 357 revolver in his shoulder holster. Isoba watched as his insignificant-looking Master slowly approached the deserted and dark park road. Isoba wondered if any criminal was stupid enough to try to rob this seemingly frail old if they would live to regret it. Isoba had never failed a mission before and struggled to find a rational way to describe the previous night's events.

"Greetings, Master." Isoba humbly greeted his mentor and teacher as he approached.

"How are you, Isoba? Thank God you are alive, for I had feared the worst." Mr. Choi said, trying to put Isoba at ease.

"Master, I fear Mr. Floyd Harrison and the Order may be in grave danger," Isoba spoke.

"You are brighter than you know, Isoba. We have been discovered and are now the hunted". Mr. Choi said.

"Can't the SEF protect us from this threat"? Isoba asked.

"The woman called Dechontee has caught wind of us, and if she stays true to form, she will try to kill us all." Mr. Choi stated.

"Master, whoever is pretending to be this woman could not possibly take on the entire SEF," Isoba said confidently.

"My young friend, no one is pretending to be Dechontee; it is her." Mr. Choi sadly said, knowing he was admitting to exposing his protégé to a certain death.

"Master, that cannot be. That would make her over 200 years old," Isoba said in disbelief.

"We believe she is older." Mr. Choi said.

"So why have we wasted so much time on Mr. Charles Sinclair." Isoba began to ask, and then suddenly, it dawned on him.

"Bait, we were used as bait." Isoba finally began to understand.

"We could not prove her existence until now." Mr. Choi stated.

"What about Mr. Harrison? He does not realize that Dechontee is real, and he has agreed to assist the police to get the detective's wife back," Isoba said.

"That was very noble of him, but unfortunately, Mr. Harrison has been disavowed and deemed a threat to the Order." Mr. Choi sadly said.

"A threat? Are you serious?" Isoba asked, understanding that "threat" was a code word for a target for elimination.

"He cannot fall into Dechontee's hands; he knows more than he realizes and could unknowingly provide her with enough information to kill us all." Mr. Choi sympathetically stated.

"How can we engage this creature without exposing more of our members to this danger?" Isoba answered.

"We have used our contacts in the law enforcement community to recruit the people we need to go after Dechontee and to eliminate any threat Floyd could pose to our Order." Mr. Choi stated.

"People, Master, who would be so stupid to go up against a monster like Dechontee?" Isoba asked.

"They think they are going against the late Ms. Elaine Singleton's drug cartel, and we will use the confusion to eliminate any threats to our Order." Mr. Choi stated.

"When will they get started?" Isoba asked.

"They already have; we have been observing Mr. Charles Sinclair's homes, business, and restaurants for any signs of Dechontee or anyone we can lead us to her." Mr. Choi stated. "We are also watching Elaine Singletons' operatives," Mr. Choi continued.

"Master, Ms. Elaine Singleton is dead, so how could any of her people be useful to us now?" Isoba asked.

"Once we suspected Dechontee was responsible for Elaine's corps disappearance, our operatives leaked a lie telling her enemies in Philadelphia that she was still alive and was planning to take over the remainder of their businesses. They believe we could help their assassins find where Elaine is hiding to eliminate her." Mr. Choi said.

"I guess that is the Serapian way of doing business," Isoba stated, trying to hide his disappointment.

"Yes, it is, and to ensure things go according to plan, I am putting you in charge of this threat to the Order." Mr. Choi stated.

Isoba trusted his mentor and teacher more than his parents, but the latest information he had received turned everything he knew and believed on its head. He was now told he had to eliminate a man who he had embraced as a brother and friend, plus deal with underworld scum to try to capture or kill an immortal. He questioned when he would be deemed a "threat" to the Order and whether they would be so quick to be rid of him as they were with Mr. Floyd Harrison.

"When will I meet these gentlemen?" Isoba asked.

"They were at Mr. Sinclair's' restaurant looking after you when you were there with Mr. Harrison." Mr. Choi answered.

Isoba remembered seeing a group of men at the Oasis restaurant who did not fit in despite their expensive suits. Isoba hid his surprise and suspicion after being told that he was being watched without his knowledge by underworld henchmen.

"I see. Is there anything else"? Isoba asked.

"Just one more thing: we have Mr. Harrison's hotel under surveillance, and a hit team is on standby, ready to strike as soon as the detective takes Floyd to meet with Dechontee. You will lead the hit team". Mr. Choi stated.

"And what about Mr. Harrison? Are we going to try to recover him," Isoba asked.

"Mr. Harrison had chosen his fate when he decided to speak to an outsider about our organization," Mr. Choi stated.

It saddened Isoba to hear the final adjudication of Floyd's fate. Isoba questioned if he was in Floyd's shoes, would he help the detective get his wife back or live with the knowledge that he left an innocent pregnant woman in the hands of a monster to protect his position in the Serapian Order? He knew Floyd to be a decent person and a dedicated member of the Order, but that would not be enough to save him. He prayed it would not be him that would have to take the life of a man he truly admired.

Back at the Sinclair estate, Clair entered the room with a look on her face, and whatever it was, Charles knew he was not going to like it.

She came to tell him that the evening news had just reported a city-wide search for Mr. Floyd Harrison, Detective Rodríguez, and his partner, Detective O'Bannon.

"You've got to be kidding me," Charles responded.

"The news mentioned that it was in connection with the disappearance of Detective Rodreguez's wife," Clair said.

Charles immediately knew who had the detective's wife and what fate Dechontee had already determined for her.

This could put Elaine's life in danger. He immediately thought to himself, Charles moved up the assault plan to rescue Elaine and to terminate any future threats to himself or his family if possible.

"But Charles, I have good news, too. The La Morena is ready for sea and will be waiting for you when you are ready," Clair said before hastily walking out the door.

Clair knew what Charles was capable of and continually tried to forget his hidden nature so their relationship could flourish. Clair had seen his face once after a fresh kill, and it terrified her. Yet the one thing Clair remembered the most about the encounter was the look of shame on Charles' face when their eyes met. At that moment, she understood who he was: a beast, a man, and her friend. She learned to forgive the monster that lived in Charles and to love the man as she prayed for his safety and the salvation of his soul.

Drake returned to the Sinclair estate with five other team members later that night. They were led into the dining room by Lawrence. The first-time visitors were amazed by the beauty and luxury of the luxurious dining room. However, what struck them the most was the assortment of blades, knives, and guns neatly displayed on the dining table. Charles stood at the head of the table dressed in a close-fitting black combat outfit. The closer the men came, the more impressed they were with Charles's battle gear.

They could make out the armor plate patterns as they got closer. Drake smiled and gave Charles a long inspection of his battle kit.

"Would it be presumptuous for me to ask if my men and I will get battle gear like that"? Drake asked to redefine their relationship now that they were about to go into battle. Drake felt vindicated about his suspicion of Charles; he knew another person was hidden behind the elegant image Charles presented. Drake had known many men who had killed men in combat and the mark it left on their souls. The first time he met Charles Sinclair, Drake saw that mark on him. Still, nothing in Charles's history justified his suspicion.

"Lawrence will show you gentlemen where you could change, and gentlemen, as a minimum, each of you will carry a sword and a combat knife," Charles spoke to the men as if he had known them forever, yet never dropping his guard.

"There it is again, the command voice," Drake thought. He could recognize the tone and pitch of a man accustomed to leading men into combat.

"Mr. Sinclair, may I ask you a favor?" Drake asked.

"Sure, what is it?" Charles replied.

"Do you mind if I step outside momentarily to make a phone call?" Drake asked.

"No, I don't mind, Drake, and please use the house phone," Charles said.

"Thanks, Mr. Sinclair," Drake replied.

"Drake, this may be the last day of our lives; I would like to end it by saying my first name, okay?" Charles said, half joking.

"Yes, Sir, Charles," Drake replied, giving Charles a broad grin and a half salute.

Charles returned the gesture as Lawrence was leading Drake out.

Once alone in the dining room, Charles struggled to find the words to help these men prepare for what they were about to face. Dr. Johnson had warned him that the resurrection machine worked, and now it was in the hands of a soulless monster. He could not imagine what types of monstrosities she would create for the pleasure of watching them suffer or worse. These men would face creatures Charles had never seen before, but he knew one thing: bullets would not be enough.

Meanwhile, Floyd and the two now fugitive detectives sat silently in a dinner on 21st Street, Long Island City, New York, waiting for Agent Jackson to arrive. No one spoke for a long while, each man tallying up their lives to see how they wound up in this situation. O'Bannon, who was a cunts hair away from full retirement, Rodriguez with a rough but loving marriage and a good-paying job, and Floyd, who could never go back to the South after this; how was he going to explain this to his wife? The painful silence was broken when Agent Jackson and the only other survivor on her team, Agent Todd Bostic, looked too young to be an Agent, but his poor taste in clothes made him fit right in. The tables in the back section of the diner had been prearranged to seat the large party.

"Well, gentlemen, I guess I have to hang around you two since a girl can't get away from this bullshit long enough to get laid." Agent Jackson said as she and Agent Baker took their seats.

Julio retold the events that led up to their current situation; Julio couldn't believe that he and his partner would have warrants put out for their arrest.

"What do you think they want with your information on Charles Sinclair?" She asked.

"My friend here believes she may belong to a larger organization seeking the secret of immortality if you can believe that. Floyd believes they were attracted by the story of Charles' miraculous survival of the attack on his life." Julio replied.

"So they naturally expect you to turn him over in exchange for your wife, right?" Wanda asked in disbelief. Some of the information she had learned during her investigation, but nothing indicated a motive for kidnapping the wife of an NYPD Detective.

"Look, I don't have the time for this bull shit; are you going to help us get my wife back or not?" Julio asked impatiently.

"So why did you call me here?" Wanda asked.

"We are going in to get my wife out of those lunatics' hands, and I am afraid that if I get the FBI or the NYPD involved, they are going get my pregnant wife killed!" Julio said.

"Unfortunately, I asked too many questions about the wrong people and got thrown off of the case, so I have limited access to any information that could help you," Wanda stated.

"However, you are reporting a kidnapping, and I am obligated to assist you. We will wait until we verify the suspected location before I call it in, and that is the best I can do for you." Said Wanda.

Sitting in a car across the street from the diner, Samuel Scales watched the unlikely dinner companions. He reported their location and activity to his security base on the Sinclair Estate. Samuel only reported urgent situations directly to Charles, and this situation was becoming more remarkable by the minute. Samuel watched as the group departed the restaurant in two cars traveling in the same direction. Samuel contacted Charles to report the groups' activities, especially their journey towards the Astoria industrial park, which caused Samuel immediate concern.

Charles knew he had a minuscule window to attempt to secure Elaine's freedom and eliminate Dechontee before Detective Rodriguez fell into Dechontee's trap. Hearing that Agent Jackson was now involved disturbed him.

CHAPTER 45

The Unmasking

At eleven-thirty that evening, Julio, Matt, Wanda, and Floyd arrived at the factory address given by Dechontee. The factory area was void of human and vehicle traffic. The incandescent street lamps cast long shadows, adding to the empty, eerie street atmosphere. The sound of a New York City Transit passenger train was deafening as it sparked and rumbled past one block away on the elevated train tracks. The building's red exterior added to the feeling of dread the group was experiencing as they sat outside of the address given to them by Dechontee. Julio and Matt decided to enter the Red factory building the next time the NYC passenger train passed to mask the sound of their entry. He and his partner Mathew O'Bannon had done this hundreds of times. They felt their experience and training gave them an edge over those holding his wife hostage. They instructed Floyd to stay behind them and out of the way. Agent Wanda Jackson and Agent Bostic waited outside as the FBI protocol required them to do. They called into the FBI night desk to report a kidnapping in progress and their current location. Julio and Matt entered the site with flashlights beaming into the darkness, guns ready to fire at any suspect, and lights illuminated.

The two detectives were immediately struck with an overwhelming scent of death, decay, and gasoline when they entered the structure. The smell of death and gasoline increased as they descended deeper into the darkness. The detectives found a stairwell at the end of the hallway leading up to the second floor where the business offices once were. As they climbed the stairs, they could hear screams and moans of agony coming from an unknown location within the building. The detectives braced themselves on each side of the door leading to the second floor before breaching into the abandoned hallway, ready to fire. The scent of death, human waste, blood, and gasoline made the two detectives gag and Floyd throw up. The executive floor was abandoned, but a few lights enabled them to make out the layout of the office floor, and the drums of gasoline lined up along the walls. They saw the expected empty cubicles and chairs arranged in the typical row fashion designed to squeeze as many workers into them as possible. The prominent feature of the office floor was the large, unlit frost glass executive meeting room.

Matt and Julio knew they were in over their heads but felt they had no choice if they had any hope of recovering Melissa alive. Matt thought he heard something coming from the glass meeting rooms as they passed. He turned his light to investigate and saw necked, bleach-white-skinned people on their knees, circling the unconsumed remains of what was once a human being. The light made all the creatures look up at once toward the trio with their glowing red eyes and blood-soaked faces. The naked, chalk white hairless skinned creatures growled like dogs at Julio, Matt, and Floyd with blood-red hungry eyes and mouths full of jagged teeth swimming in the victim's blood. The creatures immediately attacked, fighting one another, trying to reach the men. The two detectives instinctively began firing at the surging mass of death coming at them. The well-trained round only managed to knock the creatures back but not stop them. Julio and Matt tried to return to the stairway, hopefully out of the building. The two detectives' training kicked in as they fired their weapons as they retreated. Floyd never stopped screaming as he turned and ran towards the stairway they came up. The creatures were impervious to pain and had no fear of death. The detectives emptied clip after clip into the charging creatures to no avail. Agent Jackson and Agent Todd Bostic heard the gunfire. They called for backup before entering the building to assist the two detectives. They arrived on the second floor just in time to prevent the creatures from overwhelming the two detectives. Still, their added firepower only slowed the creatures down, not stopped their attack.

The creatures' frontal assault was so savage that they did not realize that some of the creatures somehow got behind them. The creature's rear attack went unnoticed until one grabbed Agent Bostic from behind and bit out the side of his neck, causing blood to flow out of his neck like a river. Agent Bostic's scream altered the others to the danger; Wanda and Floyd reached out and grabbed him, trying to prevent him from dragging him into the horde of creatures to be torn apart. Wanda looked into Agent Bostic's wide, terrorized eyes as she struggled to free her last partner from the grips of death. Agent Bostic continued to fire into the creatures as he blacked out from the loss of blood from the multiple bites he had suffered as Agent Jackson and Floyd tried to free him from their grip. Agent Bostic was finally violently snatched away by the creatures' sudden surge of savagery into the darkness. The survivors had little to no time to mourn, lament the Agent's death, or radio for assistance as they struggled to fight their way back to the stairway and out of the building. The protracted firefight was burning their ammunition, and they were no closer to returning to the stairway than when they began. Julio quickly realized this was a trap, and whoever had his wife had no intention of letting her go or for him to live.

The survivors had to find an alternate exit to escape the attacking creatures. They found a door leading away from the administrative area at the end of the hallway. When Julio, Wanda, Floyd, and Matt got into the stairway leading to the next floor, the creatures refused to follow them into the stairway.

"Shots fired, shot fired. Officers in need of assistance!" Julio frantically called over his radio but did not get any response."

Something frightened the creature so much that they would not enter the stairway to follow them.

"Matt, is your radio working? I am not getting any response," Julio asked.

The animals stood at the stairway entrance, hissing and snarling as their prey escaped into the area; they were too terrified to follow.

"I'm not getting anything," Matt responded.

"I'm on my last clip!" Matt warned.

"Me too!" Julio announced.

"We have to go back for Todd!" Wanda proclaimed.

"Forget it; he is already dead, "O'Bannon said.

"We don't know that!" Wanda angrily replied.

"We barely got out of there alive, Agent Jackson, and trust me, your man is dead," Julio said.

"What the fuck have you gotten me into?" Wanda rhetorically asked.

"Backup is not going to get here on time," Wanda warned.

Julio, Matt, Floyd, and Wanda climbed the stairs and entered the third floor, ready to continue the fierce fight. Standing almost within arms' reach, they were greeted by a beautiful, well-dressed white woman who was utterly out of place. Upon close inspection, they realized that she fitted the description of the woman seen on the surveillance videos at the morgue and the hospital where Paul Blacksmith was taken.

"Greetings, we have been waiting for you." Stephany greeted them as if they were there on a social visit.

"KEEP YOUR HANDS WHERE WE CAN SEE THEM." Julio nervously commanded; the trio aimed their guns as their hands shook uncontrollably.

Julio and the other group members surveyed the environment for additional dangers. The dark, massive shipping warehouse floor was abandoned except for hundreds of gasoline drums and one dimly lit empty office space in a distant corner hundreds of yards away.

"Who are you, and where is my wife!?" Julio demanded as they approached the woman who stood with her back to the darkness; Wanda, Julio, and Matt came with guns trained on her, ready to fire.

"My name is not important; what is important is that you and your friends are here," Stephany stated.

"Is your name Dechontee?" Floyd asked.

"You people don't know what you have gotten yourselves into." Stephany laughed, shaking her head in disbelief.

"Please follow me, and everything will become crystal clear to you," Stephany said.

"You are not going anywhere," Julio said as he tried to reach out and apprehend Stephany. No one saw her move, but she was suddenly behind them. They turned with their guns ready to fire, but she was gone. They looked at each other in disbelief and confusion.

"We are going to die here," Matt said.

"Stop that bull shit, Matt," Julio said.

"Where did she go?" Wanda asked in disbelief.

"I don't know, but this is some weird ass shit," Julio said.

"Julio, I think we better find a way out of here and come back with backup to get Melissa," Matt warned.

"I'm not fucking leaving this place without my wife!" Julio shot back.

"He may have a point," Floyd stated, scared out of his mind.

"You shut the fuck up; if it were not for you and your crazy-ass friends, we would not be in this mess." Julio angrily stated.

"This fighting is not getting us anywhere, gentlemen," Wanda said, trying to get the men to focus on survival.

"We can work our way around to that lit office space at the other side by hanging close to the wall, so we will not be surprised again," Wanda suggested.

Wanda realized that she was the most objective person in the party; yes, she had lost the last member of her team, but she had to focus these men on their survival if any of them were going to have a chance of survival.

"This way, your wife is waiting for you." Stephany's voice instructed from the darkness.

"Dammed, this bitch is in my head." Wanda thought to herself.

"Are you with me or what, Matt?" Julio asked his partner.

"Let's just get this shit over with," Matt replied.

"This is suicidal," Floyd stated.

"Just stay behind us," Julio told Floyd.

"We can't go back, so I guess we don't have a choice but to see where this direction leads," Wanda stated.

No one liked Wanda's situation assessment, but they knew she was right.

Charles and his assault team raced to the location. They parked several blocks from the red-painted factory building in Astoria, Queens; Dr. Stanley Johnson's nephew Samuel had followed Agent Jackson and the two detectives. The site seemed too opportunistic for Charles not to be suspicious of some subplot Dechontee was waiting to spring on him. Regardless of Dechontee's schemes, tonight will be the end of her meddling in his life and posing a threat to everything he held dear. Charles and his men parked a safe distance away to ensure their presence would not be detected until it was too late for a reaction from whoever was waiting for them inside. Charles was met by Samuel, who directed them to the last location where he had seen Detective Rodriguez and his companions enter less than an hour before. Samuel reported the sounds of a firefight coming from the abandoned factory building the detectives went into. He also told Charles about the two FBI agents who went into the building after the sound of gunfire could be heard. Samuel also expressed his confusion and concern from the most recent report from his FBI informant concerning a black operations FBI Strike Team arriving in the area. Charles was suspicious of how quickly the FBI contracted a Black Team and their deployment to the current situation. Despite his reservations, he hoped the additional manpower would turn the situation in his favor if Charles ran into an uncontrollable situation. Charles regretted Agent Jackson had gone into the building and feared for her life. Wanda's presence only made things more complicated and dangerous for everyone.

Far away, on the West Side highway outside of the visitors' entrance of the USS Enterprise, Mr. Choi Wu sat alone in a parked car. The recent chain of events had forced him to consider unspeakable measures. A dark sedan pulled up behind him, and a well-dressed man approached the passenger's door and got into Mr. Wu's car.

"Hello, Peter. Thanks for coming out so late." Mr. Wu greeted the FBI Regional Director.

"Master, how could I not be as concerned as you about the recent chain of events?" Director Peter Lynn replied.

"Do you believe they know the location of Dechontee?" Mr. Wu asked.

"Yes, our wiretaps of Mr. Harrisons' hotel room and the surveillance following Mr. Samuel Scales verify that." Director Lynn replied.

"This information must never reach the public." Mr. Wu warned.

"I agree, Master. Mr. Scales led us to a meeting with Agent Jackson, Agent Bostic, the two detectives, and our brother, Floyd, in Astoria Queens," Lynn replied.

"How well do you know the two Agents assigned to this case?" Mr. Wu asked.

"Agent Jackson was one of our rising stars, and no one was more resourceful than Agent Todd Bostic," Director Lynn regretfully stated.

"The two NYPD Detectives had also received high praise." Mr. Wu replied.

"We have Isola's warning to Brother Floyd Harrison not to speak to the police on record." Director Lynn reported knowing the Serapian Order would demand a full review.

"Yes, that is regrettable; however, my heart goes out to him and the family of the police detective." Mr. Wu replied.

"Whoever is behind this is ingenious; they created a condition they think could be controlled." The director added.

"Once we have Dechontee in our possession, we must erase all evidence of our involvement," Mr. Wu rhetorically stated.

Director Lynn said, "The kill team has already been assembled and is ready to enter the structure."

"The price for immortality seems to be a question our late Brother, Floyd Harrison, is about to learn." Mr. Wu sadly said.

Back at the factory building, Julio, Wanda, Floyd, and Matt inched closer to the dimly lit corner of the warehouse floor. They could make out medical equipment and recently used items scattered haphazardly on the floor. Stephany suddenly appeared out of the darkness; Matt turned and fired, only to watch her float out of the line of fire and close in on him with blinding speed. Stephany slapped Matt, knocking him off his feet towards the pitch-black center of the warehouse floor. Julio immediately ran toward his partner and friend, who had disappeared. He used his flashlight to pierce through the thick darkness, looking for Matt. Flashes of light from wild gunfire momentarily illuminated Matt, crawling backward on the floor, trying to escape Stephany, closing in on him in the blackness. Charles raced in the direction of the gunfire flashes in search of his friend and tripped over Matt's gun, lying on the ground. A deafening silence and the smell of burned gunpowder filled the air.

"Matt, Matt, where are you?" Julio called out into the darkness.

The thick blackness consumed the light beam of Julio's high-illumination flashlight, which he used to search in all directions to find his friend.

"Matt, you son of a bitch, answer me!" Julio yelled into the darkness.

Julio's heart sank as he tried to find a reason to expect to see his long-time partner alive again.

The sound of a bone-chilling female laugh echoed out of the darkness.

Matt suddenly walked slowly out of the darkness; his shirt was covered in blood. He walked towards the bewildered group with a blank look on his face. Matt was followed by a different woman they all intuitively knew, Dechontee. Julio and Wanda raised their guns in Dechontee's direction.

Floyd was hysterical with fear. He frantically looked for somewhere to run, but the only place to go was to the pitch-black factory floor where only God knows what awaited him.

"Halt, put your hands where I can see them; this is your final warning!" Julio called out.

"Kill him," Dechontee said into Matt's ear.

Matt raised his secondary weapon and fired in Julio's direction. Julio rolled out of the line of fire and raised on one knee, ready to fire his gun. Julio never knew Matt to miss and realized whatever hold this woman had over him that Matt was struggling to refuse her order to kill him.

"Matt, What the fuck are doing!?" Julio demanded.

"Stop, that's enough, dear," Dechontee whispered into Matts' ear, smiling as she looked into Julio's wide, terrified eyes.

Julio slowly got to his feet, still holding his gun trained on Dechontee.

After moving out of Matt's gunfire direction, Wanda also refrained from returning fire.

"Matt, what the fuck is going on? Answer me!" Julio tried to get Matt to respond.

"Can't you see, my dear, you are only alive because I want you to be?" Dechontee seductively stated.

"You must be that bitch, Dechontee," Julio said, recognizing the female voice he heard using his wife's phone.

"Yes, my love, you will soon learn who you are," Dechontee said with a bone-chilling laugh.

"What have you done with my wife!?" Julio demanded.

"Your wife? Oh yes, I told you, my dear, you two will be reunited if you do what I say." Dechontee stated.

"Well, bitch we are here, now where is my wife!" Julio responded as he stared down his gun's iron sights, fighting the urge to fire.

"Now, is there any reason for that kind of language, Detective Rodríguez?" Dechontee asked in a scolding voice.

"Bitch, I will blow your brains out in the next two seconds if you don't tell me where Melissa is!" Julio treated.

Matt moved in front of Dechontee to protect her, still holding his gun trained on Julio.

"I can't let you do that, Julio," Matt said.

"Matt put your gun down and move the fuck out of the way," Julio warned.

"I can't." Matt implored.

"Go ahead, dear, move aside so this young man and I can get to know each other better," Dechontee told Matt.

Matt obediently complied and stood silently by her side.

"Lady, I don't know what you did to my partner, but you are going down tonight." Julio threatened.

Dechontee let out another high-pitched laugh.

"You don't know what is happening here, do you? Didn't our Serapian friend, Mr. Harrison, tell you who and what I am? Dechontee asked.

"Yeah, you are some crazy bitches who has lost any connection to reality and is about to go to jail for life or get a needle in her arm to end it all," Julio said.

"Well, my dear, the only person who has lost connection with reality is you, but don't worry, I am about to give you all the reality you will ever need," Dechontee said.

"Whatever, lady, just keep your hands where I can see them and get on your fucking knees and interlock your fingers behind your head," Julio demanded.

"I have a better idea; why don't I take you and Mr. Harrison to be reunited with your friends?" Dechontee stated as she began to approach Julio and his companions.

"Lady, I am not going to tell you again; get the fuck on your knees and interlock your fingers behind your head!" Julio demanded, ready to shoot.

Dechontee continued to approach without fear. Julio fired four shots, two at her head and two at the center of her chest as he was trained. Dechontee moved like a blur out of the line of fire while Matt moved to protect Dechontee and was hit in the heart, falling to the floor dead.

Julio rushed to his partner Matt's side, who was bleeding out on the dirty warehouse floor.

"Matt, Matt, what the fuck, why did you do that!?" Julio cried as he cradled his dying partner in his arms.

Julio reached for his radio to call for backup and medical attention for his partner. Dechontee knocked his radio from his hands. Julio fired again, only hitting the air. Dechontee laughed, clearly enjoying herself.

"Well, you really messed that up, didn't you, my dear? Dechontee said.

"You better focus on Melissa and put that toy away before someone else gets hurt." Said Dechontee.

"My partner needs help!" Julio said, trying to reach any level of humanity Dechontee may possess.

Wanda tried to use CPR to save Matt, as Floyd used his hands to try to stop the blood flowing from Matt's dead body.

"Your partner is dead, thanks to you and your toy; now, who else has to die before you realize that you are not in control of this situation?" Dechontee unemotionally asked.

Julio reluctantly accepted his helpless situation but could not make any sense of what was going on, nor believe that he had just killed his partner and friend of over ten years.

"Ok, lady, you win for now, but I swear you will pay for this one day." Julio, on his knees in front of his dead partner, threatened, barely able to hold back the profound grief and rage he felt as a result of his partner's death.

"Yes, perhaps one day I will pay for all that I have done, but I am afraid you and everyone you know will be dead before that happens." Dechontee boldly stated.

"Stephany, bring our other guess here so that I can greet them like civilized people," Dechontee requested.

The other two survivors, Floyd and Wanda, stood up hesitantly after witnessing the unbelievable chain of events.

"Well, who are you, my dear?" Dechontee asked Wanda.

"I am FBI Agent Wanda Jackson, and I must warn you that anything you may say will be held against you in a court of law; you have the right to remain silent, and you also have the right to an attorney and…" Wanda said before being interrupted by Dechontee.

"Aren't you the professional?" Dechontee said mockingly.

"Have you met my lover, Mr. Charles Sinclair?" Dechontee rhetorically asked.

Agent Jackson was taken aback by Dechontee's blatant claim of a relationship with Mr. Charles Sinclair, but this was the first time the Agent had been able to collaborate a direct connection between the buzzard events and Mr. Charles Sinclair.

"What is the nature of your relationship with Mr. Sinclair?" Wanda impulsively asked.

"Like I said before, he is my King and lover, my dear," Dechontee said.

"What does he have to do with the kidnapping and all the deaths associated with Ms. Elaine Singleton?" Wanda asked, hoping Dechontee would provide the evidence she was looking for.

"Dechontee laughed again and said, "Everything."

"I am sure he took an immediate liking to you," Dechontee stated.

"Why would you say that?" Wanda asked, knowing how much she looked like the woman in all the paintings she saw at the Sinclair estate.

"Don't you know that you look like his murdered wife?" Dechontee asked.

"Mr. Sinclair has never been married." Agent Jackson stated.

"You people really don't know anything, but you are here now, and we must make sure this doesn't go any further," Dechontee said.

"Listen, Miss, we can resolve this peacefully before anyone else gets hurt," Floyd said, trying to contain the terror reeking from every pour of his body.

"Mr. Floyd Harrison, right?" Dechontee asked.

The mention of his name made Floyd feel faint.

"Yes, you requested that the Detective bring me here, so here I am," Floyd said nervously, trying to hide his terror.

"Floyd, it was our friend, Belington, who suggested bringing you here," Dechontee stated.

That stupid, dirty son of a bitch, Floyd thought to himself.

"Where is he?" Floyd asked, hoping she would say dead.

"First, I have to warn you that you may not be able to recognize him after all the weight he has lost," Dechontee said.

"Enough of this bullshit, where the fuck is my wife!?" Julio demanded.

"Young man, you really need to learn more patience, but I think my lover has arrived, and we must conclude our business here. Stephany, would you be a dear and escort our friends to their loved ones?" Dechontee said.

Stephany began to move away with Floyd, Julio, and Wanda when Dechontee suddenly stopped them.

"Wanda, my dear, would you be so kind and stay here with me for a moment?" Dechontee asked.

Wanda's heart stopped with fear at the thought that she would be left alone with this woman. However, she still had her gun, even though it had proven almost useless against creatures that killed Agent Bostic. If she played her card right, she could still get the upper hand on the woman calling herself Dechontee if she caught her off guard.

"I have a few more questions to ask you if you understand your legal rights," Wanda said, trying to hide her fear.

"Do you think being left alone with this woman is wise?" Julio asked in a low voice close to Wanda's ear.

"I will be alright; go find your wife," Wanda said in a firm voice, knowing she had no choice.

Julio and Floyd reluctantly followed Stephany, leaving Wanda alone with Dechontee and Matt's dead body.

Melissa Rodríguez was awoken by the sound of gunfire somewhere in the vast factory building where she was being held captive. For the first time, she allowed herself to believe that she and her unborn baby would get out of that place alive. Outside her door, she could see the creatures lurking, waiting for something to happen. One of the creatures, in particular, scared her more than the others; Paul would stare into her room through the small triangle window as if looking for a steak that was taking too long to cook. Never in her medical career had she seen a man that looked like he should be dead than this creature. The other creatures bared their long fangs and made animal-like hissing sounds to keep Paul away from the door. She examined the two holes on the side of her neck and was concerned that they were not closing. She also could feel other physical effects of conditions she could not explain. All that she knew was that Dechontee had bitten her for some unknown reason, causing her to blackout, only to awaken with the taste of blood in her mouth. She feared for her unborn child, who grew more and more restless in her womb. She felt fragile and lifeless. Melissa knew medically that she required a blood transfusion but could not understand her desire for raw, bloody meat. She never lost faith in her husband and knew he would never stop until he had rescued her and their child. Still, after what she had witnessed since being captured by

Dechontee, she secretly prayed he would not be in danger by coming to this place.

It had been several hours since Paul had emerged from the resurrection tank, and his need for blood still caused him unbearable pain. He could not wait for this cat-and-mouse game Dechontee played with Detective Rodriguez, and the others were over so that his need for blood could be satisfied. He still could not understand why Dechontee did not allow him to finish off the fat redneck, Belington; however, she was not around now, and he was hoping that Belington would be stupid enough to give him another chance. Paul studied the new disciples of Dechontee, who were waiting for instruction for any sign of weakness to enable him to attack and steal their life's blood. Paul also searched the crowd to ensure Elaine was not among them. His heart would fill with fear each time he would think of Elaine. Elaine had killed him once, and Paul wasn't confident that he would be able to return the second time. Elaine still lay in a coma in the room next door to Melissa, and Paul made sure that he did not go anywhere near it. Paul looked again in Belington's direction, who immediately sheepishly hid behind the other vampires for protection. Paul could hear another round of gunfire, but this time, it was much closer. His stomach began to growl in anticipation, but after seeing what Elaine was capable of, he feared the noise would awaken Elaine out of her sleep and kill them all.

Knowing the imminent arrival of the contracted kill team, Charles and his team quickly moved to the building and threw a flash grenade before entering. The sound of the flash grenade caused the creatures blocking the ground-floor stairway entrance to turn around to investigate the noise source. The zombie-like creatures attacked each other as they desperately tried to reach Charles and his team to satisfy their hunger for blood. Charles and his men opened fire, but like Elaine and her fellow Agent, they quickly realized their guns were not able to stop the naked albino-looking creatures that attacked with reckless abandonment. Drake and Bowser had been in many gunfights, but this was something out of a nightmare. Charles and his assault team were surprised at the creatures' speed and savagery; they emptied their automatic shotguns into the charging mass, but despite blasting off limbs, it did not faze them. A group of the creatures broke through and swarmed two of his men, firing frantically to keep the monsters off them.

"The guns are not working; use your swords and knives!" Charles yelled out to his men.

Charles began hacking his way through the creatures with blinding speed. His movements were so fast that Drake and the other men who accompanied him stood in awe as Charles almost single-handedly hunted down and killed at least ten creatures before the remaining creatures melted back into the darkness in fear. After the last attacking creatures were dead or had fled into the darkness, Charles approached Drake and the other surviving members of his team to check on them.

Drake, Bowser, and a surviving member of the assault team cringed in fear and horror when they saw Charles's face, which had been transformed into the mask of a demon. After witnessing him in action and seeing his true face, Drake and his men cringed in fear of Charles.

"Drake, you and your men have nothing to fear from me." Charles tried to reassure them, knowing his true face of death was finally exposed.

Drake did not answer. He stood in shock, not realizing he had his gun trained on Charles and ready to fire.

Nothing could have prepared Drake for what he had witnessed. Charles Sinclair's true face dwarfed the shock and horror of the creatures Drake and his men were fighting.

"Get your men ready to move, Drake," Charles commanded, ignoring the gun pointing at him.

One of Drake's wounded men moaned loudly, breaking Drake out of his terror of Charles. The three other surviving team members went over to the dying men to provide what assistance they could, but not taking their eyes off Charles. Charles inspected the bodies of the dead creatures. He was amazed to see that they had lost all their skin colors and were filled with a mixture of blood and some unknown milky-white substance that oozed from the wounds on their dead bodies. He knew they had been human at one point but could not believe their transformation. Charles, whose tactical radios were set on low-frequency channels to avoid being jammed, radioed Samuel to send in a medical team to recover one of the dead creatures to be studied by his son, Dr. Stanley Johnson. Samuel informed Charles that his request could not be followed due to the arrival of the black operations assault team. Charles was also told that the black ops team was getting ready to enter the building. Charles had to quickly locate Elaine and determine if she would be rescued or destroyed. If his beloved friend Elaine had undergone the same procedure to be brought back to life as the creatures Charles had just fought, he knew she would not want to live that way. He had to be ready to end Elaine's suffering.

On the warehouse's third floor, Wanda was startled to hear more gunfire from the lower floors progressing to her location. The gunfight continued heading in the same direction she and Detective Rodriguez, Floyd, and the other two dead members of their party traveled. She was relieved to hear that help was on the way. Yet, she was concerned because she did not hear any radio traffic or commands to surrender that would be associated with an assault by a law enforcement agency. Perhaps the attackers were local police operating on a different radio channel that prevented her from hearing their transitions. Still, regardless of who they were, it gave her reasons for hope to be rescued from this nightmare.

"Don't worry, my dear, that's just Charles and his friends coming to pay us a visit," Dechontee said as if they were best friends or shared similar concerns.

"Now you are being ridiculous; Mr. Sinclair is in no physical shape to be here tonight. I guess you have not been keeping up with the news," Wanda said.

"He had gotten you all fooled," Dechontee said after a long, humiliating laugh.

"No one is trying to fool you, lady; Charles was shot and almost killed during the attack that took his friend, Ms. Elaine Singleton's life," Wanda said, trying to get Dechontee to continue the conversation in the hopes of getting more information and to stall for time.

"Yes, that was not supposed to happen. I only wanted to scare Charles and to let him know that I knew all about his affair with Elaine, but the bitch attacked first and was killed; plus, the bitch almost got my Charles killed as well." Dechontee said.

"Do you realize you have just confessed to being an accessory to murder?" Wanda asked.

"Yes, I know, and I cannot wait to see the look on Charles' face when I show him that I have brought her back to life," Dechontee said like a child waiting to show her school project to her parents.

"Lady, you need some serious psychological help," Wanda said, shaking her head.

"I often wondered if that would help me feel better, and I even tried it once, but it did not end well for the Psychiatrist," Dechontee said.

"Did you have a conflict with your therapist?" Wanda asked.

"Oh no, he was delicious," Dechontee said, smiling.

Wanda could see flashlights emerging from the doorway of the stairway she and her party had used to enter the empty, massive factory production floor. She wanted to warn whoever it was that had come to rescue her from the danger she had witnessed but feared the potential for violence that was ever present with Dechontee. The distant lights did not try to avoid the vast darkness that separated Wanda's current location in the dimly lit corner of the warehouse floor but came straight in her direction. Suddenly, the flashes of gunfire and the sounds of a savage battle could be heard coming out of the darkness. She could hear men yelling and the sound of wild animals fighting in the dark, and just as suddenly as it started, it was over. Some gasoline drums ignited, causing bright explosions and turning the blackness into a hellish inferno. The screams of wounded men filled the blackness, followed by others offering words of encouragement and comfort to the wounded. Out of the fiery inferno, three male figures emerged, one walking boldly forward, followed by two others supporting one another as they struggled to walk due to their wounds. As the men approached, Wanda was shocked to see Charles Sinclair leading the two other men who were covered in blood and that white fluid.

"You see, what did I tell you? My lover, Charles, has finally come to visit us," Dechontee chirped.

Wanda stood in shock. How was it possible for Charles Sinclair to make it past the monsters that killed Agent Bostic and her? How was it possible for him to be here? Is it possible that Dechontee was telling the truth about Charles Sinclair? Are Floyd and his secret society right about Charles?

"Dechontee, what the fuck have you done?!" Charles demanded.

Wanda stood dumbfounded and amazed to see Charles Sinclair standing before her, fully recovered and armed.

"What have I done? Do you have the nerve to ask? I told you there will never be another woman in your life unless I say so!" Dechontee shot back.

"Dechontee, you have gone too far this time!" Charles shot back.

Drake and Bowser collapsed onto the factory floor from exhaustion and blood loss.

"Agent Jackson, take these two men and get out of the building," Charles commanded, paying no attention to the shocked look on her face.

"This bitch is not going anywhere," Dechontee said with her voice full of malice.

"Dechontee, this has to stop; let them go," Charles demanded.

"Charles, you know I cannot do that," Dechontee responded.

"I will ensure our secret is safe; just let them go." Charles tried to appeal to Dechontee.

"Enough, Charles! I don't have the time for this shit; I will allow you to leave with your whore, but that is it. I will not allow your sentimental attachments to these people to jeopardize Stephany or me!" Dechontee said as she grabbed Wanda by the throat, choking her as she lifted her off of her feet. Wanda struggled to break free, shocked by Dechontee's strength.

"Put her down, Dechontee; I will not tell you again!" Charles demanded.

Dechontee could detect that more than a resemblance to his dead wife motivated Charles' desire to protect Wanda.

"I am trying to do you a favor, my love; Elaine will not be as merciful with this bitch once Elaine realizes that she was not even cold in her grave before you found someone to take her place," Dechontee said.

Charles knew in his heart she was right, but he still could not allow anything to happen to Wanda. He rushed forward, knocking Dechontee and Wanda to the ground to enable Wanda to break free. Charles and Dechontee quickly jumped to their feet, ready to continue the fight.

"Wanda, get these men out of here!" Charles commanded Wanda as he placed himself between Wanda and Dechontee.

"You ungrateful son of a bitch, you are willing to fight me over this bitch!?" Dechontee said as the pretentious mask of civility dropped from her face. Her long canine teeth were now exposed as she snarled at Charles.

Dechontee's death face horrified Wanda, causing her to cover her mouth and fight the urge to scream.

Wanda felt her mind rush headlong into insanity. Nothing she witnessed could be real. No rational mind could accept what she was experiencing.

Dechontee rushed forward and slapped Charles across the face, knocking him so hard that he slid several feet across the floor when he hit the ground. Charles was quickly on his feet and rushed at Dechontee in a flash, grabbing her by the shoulders and trying to restrain her long enough for Wanda and the two wounded men to escape.

"Get out of here, Wanda. I will not be able to hold her for long!" Charles commanded.

"I don't believe this shit, so you don't give a fuck about that bitch Elaine. I was a fool to think that giving you your space would be enough for you to come to your senses. I should have left your stupid black ass in that filthy shed that I found you dying in, you god damned fool. What do you think that bitch is going to replace your dead stupid ass wife?" Dechontee screamed before breaking free and rushing at Charles again.

Wanda, Drake, Bowser, and the other injured man took advantage of Charles and Dechontee's struggle to make their way through the flames toward the stairway leading back down towards the awaiting creatures on the lower floor.

Julio and Floyd could also hear the sounds of a struggle coming from the direction they had just left and wondered if whoever was being engaged was having more success than they had. At the very least, they were reassured that they were not alone and that rescue was possible. Stephany paid little attention to the sounds of battle. She continued to escort the two men away from the factory production floor.

"Hey, what was that?" Julio inquired about the noise of violence coming from behind them.

"No need to worry yourselves about that," Stephany said disinterestedly.

"I thought I heard the sound of gunfire," Julio said.

"Do you want to see your wife or not?" Stephany asked coldly.

"Ok, where is my fucking wife, bitch?" Julio reluctantly responded.

Julio knew that his life as a police detective was over after accidentally killing his partner. Julio knew it was an accident, but how would he get anyone to believe what happened there?

"That's better, we are almost there," Stephany said.

Stephany, Julio, and Floyd turned the corner, and the two men froze with fear. Ahead of them was an assembly of ghoulish-looking people awaiting them. Julio instinctively reached for his pistol but found the holster empty. He felt more vulnerable than ever but was determined to find his wife and unborn child no matter the cost. Floyd was equally traumatized at the prospect of going any further towards the macabre assembly ahead of them. One of the creatures Floyd thought looked familiar; it was lurking behind the others, awaiting them.

Unlike Julio, who was motivated by the love for his wife, Floyd had no love for Belington and was not inclined to risk his life for BB's safe return; unfortunately, he was too far into the snare to get out, and he knew it.

"Floyd, old buddy, I told them you would come." Belington greeted Floyd as if it was a festive occasion.

"Belington, is that you; what the hell happened to you?" Floyd asked Belington, not believing what he was seeing.

Belington was under half the size he last saw; he was now dressed in the same clothes Floyd last saw him in, but now they were falling off his emaciated body. The flesh on his pasty white face sagged as he stared back at Floyd with blue eyes sunken back into the dark eye sockets of his skull. Floyd was amazed at how much Billington had changed. His clothes hung off him like a scarecrow. There was always something menacing beneath the fake Southern charm Billington tried to fool people with, but now, BB's filthy soul was worn on his sleeve for the world to see. Belington flashed his usual insincere broad smile, revealing the same elongated canine teeth all the creatures in the building shared. For reasons beyond Belington's understanding, his stomach began to growl, and his mouth watered at the sight of his old friend. He could almost smell and taste the blood flowing in Floyd's body and knew that he needed his blood more than Floyd did.

"Don't be afraid, gentlemen; they will not harm you unless I want them to," Stephany said.

"Fuck them and fuck you, where is my wife?" Julio demanded.

Julio struggled to find the courage to continue his quest to find his wife. How he was going to get her out of this hell hole, he did not know.

"That's right, where are my manners? You still think Melissa is still your wife?" Stephany said sadistically.

Stephany's words hit Julio like a ton of bricks; he dared not try to read the negative undertones of her words and held onto the hope of seeing his wife and unborn child safe.

As Julio and Floyd approached the awaiting macabre assembly, Julio could not believe his eyes—Mr. Paul Blacksmith himself. Finding Blacksmith here was not surprising; nothing else would make sense. Julio wanted to say something to Paul but could not find the words. Paul warned him, but his pride and arrogance did not allow him to listen; now, he, Melissa, and their unborn child would pay the price.

The creatures in Paul's ghoulish assembly were more human-looking than the ones he and his late partner fought on the warehouse's second floor. They retained their hair and some skin color, but they all looked pale and emaciated. The night had so many twists and turns. Julio began to believe he was having some elaborate nightmare and would wake up safe and sound at home if he could find a way to wake up.

"I warned you, pig, not to say her name. No, you would listen, and now you and your bitch are dead." Said Paul as Julio and Floyd approached.

"Now, boys, let's not get ahead of ourselves. First, we have to reunite our good friend Julio with his wife as promised." Stephany flashed a nonverbal warning to the other creatures lurking around with fiendish intent in their eyes.

Meanwhile, the battle between Dechontee and Charles took an unexpected turn when Dechontee made the motion of slapping him with the back of her hand from several feet away. Charles was knocked violently off of his feet by an unseen force. Charles quickly got to his feet, dazed and confused, only to receive another much harder phantom blow, causing him to almost black out when he hit the ground hard. He got on one knee and suddenly felt a vice grip on his throat, but Dechontee was still too far away to be choking him, but she was clenching her fist in his direction.

"I told you before, you nappy-headed fool, no other woman has anything on me." Said Dechontee as she gestured like she was lifting Charles off of his feet, and his body floated off of the ground as Charles struggled to break free of the invisible hands choking him. Charles felt himself floating towards Dechontee until he was face to face with her. Dechontee kissed Charles lovingly as he gasped for air.

"How am I doing this, you may ask? I told you, Charles, your abilities will get more and more powerful the older you get; that is if you don't let one of these bitches get you killed first." Said Dechontee into Charles's ear before he blacked out.

Wanda, Drake, and Bowser took advantage of the battle between Charles and Decontee to the stairway they first used to enter the warehouse floor. The stairwell and walls were covered in blood and that other white shit those Zombie-looking creatures were filled with. Wanda and the two other survivors prayed that no more creatures were waiting for them on the lower floors, which they had to battle to get out of the building. The group retraced their steps down the stairway and into the administrative area, where they lost Agent Bostic. Upon entering the lower floor, they were amazed to find the level littered with the butchered remains of the creatures they had fought earlier. Their disembodied remains were scattered everywhere, forcing Wanda, Drake, and his injured companion to step over their bodies cautiously. Wanda felt compelled to look for Bostic's body but quickly remembered the savage cannibal behavior of the creatures and knew there would not be much left. She swore to herself that she would get justice for Todd and all the other deaths that crazy bitch was responsible for. Wanda did not care how fast Dechontee could move; she was determined to put a bullet up her ass one day.

"Charles, this is Sam, come in, Charles, this is Sam, come in." A radio transmission announced somewhere in the dimly lit administrative office's hallway.

Wanda searched for the sound of the broadcast and found one of Charles's team's tactical radios that must have been dropped during the fight.

"This is FBI Agent Wanda Jackson; identify yourself," Wanda said in the most professional voice she could muster.

"Where is Mr. Sinclair?" Samuel demanded.

"Listen, I have a police emergency; there are multiple people dead and injured in need of immediate medical attention. Do you understand me?" Wanda announced.

"Is Mr. Sinclair injured?" Samuel asked.

"I am not sure, but I know he will be dead unless you place that call for immediate assistance," Wanda stated.

"You are in luck; your friends have arrived and are preparing to enter the building. They look trigger-happy, so I would not make any sudden moves if I were you." Said, Samuel.

"Thank God," Wanda said out loud. Still, she was amazed that a tactical assault team could be assembled quickly and dispatched to her current location. She instantly realized she must have been under surveillance and followed her to this factory building. Wanda was happy to hear they had come, regardless of how and why they arrived. Wanda had mixed feelings about leaving Charles Sinclair, Floyd, and Detective Rodriguez alone to face Dechontee, but she did not have a choice. Charles's bravery had allowed her to take the two injured men to relative safety, and she was determined to return to rescue Charles and the others as soon as backup arrived. Wanda changed the radio channel to the FBI emergency frequency to communicate to her colleagues who had just come and were ready to enter the building. She wanted to alert them to her presence and warn them about the creatures she had encountered.

"This is FBI Agent Wanda Jackson, badge number 5588, in need of immediate assistance." Wanda broadcasted but only received static.

That's strange; she thought that channel should be alive with radio traffic at this stage of a rescue operation.

"Something is not right," Drake said.

"Don't be ridiculous; we are just experiencing a technical glitch. We will be safe in a few minutes." Said Wanda, not convincing anyone.

"This is FBI Agent Wanda Jackson, badge number..." Wanda was suddenly interrupted in the middle of her transmission.

"We know who you are; stay off of the radio." Some unknown male voice broke into her transmission.

"This is Agent Jackson; identify yourself," Wanda demanded, and the radio went dead.

"Come on now, what the fuck now!?" Wanda said out loud.

"I told you that there is something wrong," Drake repeated.

Wanda knew he was right but could not imagine what to do about violating FBI communications protocols. Wanda, Drake, and Bowser continued to push their way out of the warehouse. She noticed flashlights entering the stairway from the main floor below.

"Up here, we are up here. Be careful; some assailants are in the building," Wanda called out as she held out her FBI identification. A barrage of gunfire responded from the floors below that would have killed Wanda if Drake hadn't snatched her out of the line of fire.

Meanwhile, on the factory's third floor, Dechontee effortlessly dragged Charles's motionless body behind her as she joined Stephany and the other creatures surrounding Julio and Floyd.

The flames and smoke from the ignited gasoline drums continued to build. Dechontee and Stephany were unconcerned by the exploding gas drums.

"Stephany, we are going to have a slight change of plans due to the unexpected guest's arrival," Said Dechontee.

"Yes, I sensed them as well," Stephany replied.

"Why don't we take Julio to his wife and allow Floyd some time alone with his good friend Belington? After all, I am a woman of my word." Dechontee coldly stated.

"Dechontee, you promised me a fresh kill!" Paul Blacksmith barked out in protest as he hungrily gazed at Julio.

"I promise you that if you open your mouth again, you will be the next one dead," Dechontee said, getting tired of Paul's blundering.

Floyd looked around the factory floor in horror and disbelief. Was this what the Bishops warned him about? Was this the price they were willing to pay to live forever? Floyd thought to himself. What he witnessed defied everything he understood as physically possible; could everything he believed to be fantasy be true? Could these women before him be over 200 years old and immortal? Whoever, or whatever they were, he did not want to be left alone with what was left of Belington. Floyd could sense a new malevolence radiating from Belington and knew he would be dead if he were left alone with Billington. Floyd wondered why he seemed only concerned with the exploding gasoline drums and the spreading fire. Floyd began to realize that he was being used as a sacrificial lamb by the Order, but was determined to escape to see his wife again. He always loved Carol; now, she was the only thing he could think of at death's door. What a fool he had been to put the Order before his relationship with her, and now he would die for that mistake.

"Where is my wife?!" Julio demanded.

Hearing her husband's voice outside the door of her room, Melissa was filled with dread instead of joy. She knew something about her had changed, and she did not trust herself to be alone with him. She pulled her knees to her chest and squeezed them into her with her arms as hard as she could as she cowered in the furthest corner away from the door as she could, praying her beloved husband did not enter. She was horrified by the thought of holding him in her arms as his hot blood flowed down her throat.

"Stephany, would you be a dear and put our friend here in the room with his wife?" Instructed Dechontee with a broad, sadistic grin on her face.

"It is about time," Stephany said as she roughly grabbed Julio's arm and dragged him past the other creatures to the door where Melissa was being held. She unlocked the door, threw him in, and then locked the door behind him.

"Melissa, are you in here? Where are you?" Julio called out as his eyes adjusted to the dimly lit room. He could hear crying coming from one of the dark room's corners.

"Julio, you should not have come," Melissa said as she tried to melt herself further into the corner of the room, fearing for Julio's safety.

"Murania del mi corazon; ¿Cómo podría mantenerse al margen?" Julio said as he approached his cringing wife.

"Mi, Corazon, I should have trusted you; this is all my fault." Melissa cried as intense hunger pains increased while she continued to avoid her husband's touch.

"Let's not worry about that right now, baby girl; let's just get the fuck out of here," Julio said as he slowly approached his wife, who looked battered but seemed otherwise unhurt.

"Julio, please stay away. They did something to me, and I don't know if I can control myself!" Melissa warned.

"Whatever they did, we can fix it after we get the fuck out of here." Julio encouraged.

He could finally see his wife's condition as he brought her into the light projected from the hallway outside the door. He was immediately filled with rage and fear when he saw her pale, drawn skin and bruised arms and legs.

"I'm going to kill all of these mother fuckers for this!" Julio said, not trying to control his anger and outrage.

"Julio, you got to get out of here now; one of us has got to make it," Melissa said with tear-soaked eyes.

"Stop talking crazy; I am not going anywhere without you, Melissa," Julio said as he pulled her close, wrapping her in a protective embrace.

Melissa, fighting the urge to plunge her teeth into his neck, pushed him away and rushed back to the corner where she had initially hidden when he had entered the room.

"Julio, you got to leave now; it is too late for me," Melissa struggled to warn him.

Julio could hear laughter from the hallway and turned to see the sickly-looking creatures crowded around the door, witnessing Julio and Melissa's encounter.

"What the hell did they do to you?" Julio asked, knowing he did not want an answer.

Outside in the hallway, Floyd Harrison was seized and brought to Dechontee.

"It seems we have captured the wrong person; I could not begin to tell you how embarrassed we were when we found out that your fat friend knew nothing about you and your Serapian Brotherhood," Dechontee said.

"What do you want from me?" Floyd asked defiantly.

"We want the names and locations of all of your brothers, of course," Dechontee said casually.

"That is not going to happen," Floyd said, trying to project courage he did not possess. The thought of providing all the information he could muster to these monsters for the Orders sending him here to die crossed his mind, but his oath to his father forced him to keep his mouth shut. He also knew once they got the information they needed, he would be killed.

"You will talk; you people always talk. It is time for you and Belington to talk heart-to-heart, and I am sure he will convince you to be more cooperative." Dechontee said after laughing mockingly at Floyd.

The thought of him being given to Billington enraged Floyd. Two of Dechontee's creatures took Floyd away, followed by Belington, who eagerly followed.

"Are you sure you want to wake that bitch up? "You saw what she did the last time," Stephany asked Dechontee asked once they were alone.

"I am sure the sight of Charles will bring her fully back, and I have given her my blood, which should bring her totally under my control," Dechontee replied.

"You take too many risks trying to get that fool, Charles Sinclair, to dedicate himself to you. Girl, when will you cut your losses and move on?" Stephany asked.

"I can't explain why I love him so much, but I know him better than he knows himself; he will come around, but for now, let's put him in the room with that bitch so they can be reacquainted," Dechontee responded.

"What about Melissa and the baby? Dechontee asked.

"I think it is time for us to expand our family. After all, you are getting on my last nerve bitch, with all this Charles Sinclair bullshit." Said Stephany humorously.

"What do you think the infection will do to the baby? Do you think it will not come out deformed?" Dechontee asked, having never been confronted with new life, only death and destruction.

"Bitch why are you asking my ass; I'm not the one choking mother fuckers out from across the room," Stephany replied.

"Don't ask me how I do it because I don't know. I know I am getting more and more abilities as I get older. And yes, I could hear that last smart-ass remark you just thought of bitch," Dechontee said, causing both women to laugh.

A low-flying helicopter flying at window height suddenly flashed a searchlight, catching the two women off guard. The two women were blinded by bright searchlights beaming into the large factory windows. A hail of gunfire from twin-mounted Gatling guns mounted on the tactical helicopter fired, spraying bullets across the factory floor. Some of the rounds from the machine gun fire hit the drums of gasoline that were not already on fire, causing a massive explosion that engulfed the attacking chopper, causing it to crash into the building and setting off secondary explosions. The second wave of attack helicopters filled with heavily armed military-trained assault teams wearing black unmarked uniforms and gas masks repelled onto the roof and into the windows of the burning warehouse.

The sound of the heavy gunfire and the explosion woke Charles. He looked around to get his barring in strange surroundings. After his eyes adjusted to the dark room, he discovered Elaine lying unconscious on a bed. He quickly rushed to her to see if she was alive, as reported by Dr. Johnson. To his amazement, Charles found that Elaine had a pulse; he then put his head to her chest in disbelief and heard a heartbeat. Unlike the other creatures Charles had confronted earlier, Elaine had not lost her hair. Still, her skin had an unhealthy gray look to it. Charles was confident that Elaine's resurrection, supervised by Stanley, was the difference between Elaine's recovery and those unfortunate creatures created by Dechontee. Charles reached down to pick Elaine up to get her out of the building. Charles's touch caused Elaine to wake from her deep sleep suddenly; she looked at Charles with a blank look in her eyes. He could feel her body tense and braced himself for her attack.

The wall behind them exploded from a missile strike from one of the attacking helicopters hovering outside the warehouse. The blast knocked them both to the floor; Elaine quickly got to her feet and locked her cold, predatory eyes on Charles.

Additional missile strikes knocked Charles and Elaine in different directions. Getting to his feet, Charles strained his eyes, trying to find Elaine through the fire and smoke. Following the missile strike, the floor was assaulted by men wearing black uniforms and gas masks who had repelled through the windows, throwing stun grenades and firing their weapons as they entered.

Dechontee and Stephany were soon on their feet after the missile explosions and the premature gasoline explosions they planned to use to destroy any trace of their existence. As they quickly cut their way through the attacking men, they noticed some attackers standing off with strange weapons. The next moment, they saw nets flying in their direction. The women quickly maneuvered out of the net's range.

Dechontee and Stephany rushed forward, killing the men holding the net firing guns, but they kept one alive.

Dechontee knocked the gun from the man's hands and then grabbed him like a rag doll. She plunged her teeth into his neck, then crushed her mouth into his, forcing her bloody tongue down his throat. Once the man's twitching stopped, she questioned him.

"Who sent you!" She angrily asked.

"The agency," The man answered.

"What fucking agency" Dechontee demanded.

"The FBI," the man answered.

"Give me a name," Dechontee demanded.

"I don't know", the man said.

Dechontee, frustrated, thrust her hand into his chest and tore out his heart.

"I am going to kill all of them," Dechontee proclaimed.

"They know who we are," Stephany said.

"Yes, I know, and now they think they can catch us like animals with fucking nets!" Dechontee said.

"The Serapians have made their last mistake; not only do we have one of their brothers, but a clue to one of their hiding places in the FBI," Dechontee said. If Floyd Harrison managed to survive, she would hunt him down and learn every secret he had before finally killing him.

The two women made their way to the rear of the building to the cargo elevators to make their escape. Dechontee and Stepany had all the information they needed to track down the Serapians who could threaten them. Infuriated, Dechontee did not care if Charles lived or died in the fire. She had finally had enough of him and would no longer try to get him to understand her value to him. Her only concern was eliminating the Serapians as she and Stephany had done before.

Outside the building, on a nearby rooftop, Isoba monitored the attack through a high-powered rifle scope. He watched as the helicopters maneuvered around the building, now in flames like angry bees, firing Gatling guns and missiles into the upper floors of the building. He watched as the teams armed with firearms to capture wild animals in nets descended on ropes and entered the building. Isoba carefully watched the building exit for the witches trying to escape or any sign of Floyd escaping the building. Isoba regretted Floyd's decision to help Detective Rodriguez and struggled with the mandate he was given to kill Floyd Harrison. Isoba also noticed a caravan of SUVs parked a block away that did not challenge his operations.

Inside the building, Floyd lifted his head to survey the damage as he lay prostrate on the floor to avoid the choking smoke from the growing fire, the shower of bullets, and rocket explosions. He was shocked to see that two of the creatures knocked to the ground by the missile strikes and gunfire were on fire but still alive. The creatures began to crawl towards Floyd with their fangs exposed, ignoring the flames consuming their bodies. Belington came out of nowhere and slit the throat of the two injured creatures from behind and drank the blood gushing from the knife wounds.

Belington then locked eyes with Floyd and smiled, then said, "You don't feel so uppity now, do you?"

"Keep the fuck away from me, you filthy animal," Floyd warned.

"No, not this time, Mr. Harrison, you are mine," Belington said as he slowly approached Floyd.

After being knocked down by the missile strike, Paul Blacksmith rolled over onto his back and looked up to a ceiling filled with fire and smoke. Paul thought for a moment that he was finally dead and safe in hell but was brought to his senses by a fresh round of gunfire. Paul could smell the blood of the attacking men before he could see them and prepared himself for the assault. The first man through the door was dead before he could realize it. Paul grabbed him and took him to an isolated dark corner to finish him off before any of his team members could react. The other attacking men fired blindly, hoping to hit anything; another man cried out as he was snatched into the darkness, followed by more untrained gunfire.

With each victim, Paul could feel his strength and power increasing. He wondered to himself if this was what Dechontee had planned all along. Paul could not care less; he was focused on not letting any of these men leave here with the blood he needed in their veins.

Julio awoke deaf from being knocked unconscious by a round of explosions; he frantically searched the room for Melissa but could not find her through all the smoke and fire. He took out his detective shield to enable whoever was conducting this rescue operation to identify him as a member of the NYPD. Julio could see the dead bodies of several of the assaulting men and monsters scattered about. Julio picked up one of the discarded AR15s and several magazines of ammunition before resuming the search for Melissa. A team of men wearing black combat uniforms and gas masks turned the corner and immediately opened fire. Seeing the muzzle flashes of the guns, Julio dove for cover in disbelief.

"Hey, you stupid mother fuckers, I am a Cop; hold your fire!" Julio, still temporarily deaf, managed to yell out.

"Throw out your weapon, and come out with your hands over your head," the masked man instructed.

"Who the fuck are you!" Julio demanded.

Julio's question was answered with a massive barrage of gunfire. He shook his head in disbelief. Now the fucking police are trying to kill me; what the fuck could go wrong next?! He thought to himself.

"Hold your fire, you stupid son of a bitches. I am a cop!" Julio declared as his hearing began to return.

The gunfire intensified, making it apparent the men were trying to kill him. Julio returned fire, causing the attacking me to take cover long enough for Julio to attempt to run across the warehouse floor and to the stairway he came upon.

More gasoline drums began to explode, leading to a massive explosion that shook the building violently.

Meanwhile, Elaine was killing her way down the hallway towards Floyd Harrison. Belington noticed her coming from behind Floyd and prepared to defend his prize prey, Floyd. Belington sprang at her past Floyd with his mouth wide open, flashing his razor-sharp teeth. Elaine grabbed Belington by the throat and effortlessly lifted him off his feet with one hand. Belington swung windmill punches at Elaine, trying to break her grip on his throat. She then reached into his abdomen with her razor-sharp claws, pulled out his liver, and began to eat it as Belington looked on in shock and horror. He tried to dig into her bloody mouth to pry the remains of his liver out of her mouth. His last vision was Elaine pulling out his heart and biting into it. His final thoughts were amazement at how someone could quickly consume so much flesh.

Floyd turned and cringed backward, watching with horror the grotesque spectacle of Elaine eating Billington alive. Floyd hated Billington but didn't believe anyone should suffer the fate that fell upon Billington. He did not try to help him despite Floyd's sympathy for Billington. Floyd took advantage of the woman feasting on Billington and the surrounding creatures, cowering in fear of Elaine to escape for the nearest exit.

Across the warehouse floor, Charles noticed Floyd racing towards an exit at the rear of the warehouse floor. While never seeing Floyd before, Charles suspected he was one of the Serapians lured into Dechontee's death trap. Charles chose to ignore Floyd, who was looking for a way out of the building, hoping his problem would take care of itself. Charles visually traced the path back from Floyd's escape path and saw Elaine feasting on Billington. Charles did not want to let Floyd escape. However, he finally relocated Elaine in the fire and smoke and was still determined to rescue her. Despite the flames and the death squad trying to kill them all, Charles raced through the fire and bullets, attempting to get to Elaine. Charles knew Floyd Harrison sealed his fate when he joined the Sapien body snatchers. Now that Dechontee and Stephany knew Floyd's identity, Floyd could run, but nothing could save him.

Charles cursed as more gasoline drums exploded, knocking him to the ground and temporarily blinding him, causing him to lose track of Elaine. When the ringing in his ears caused by the explosions died down, Charles could hear another gunfight nearby. He turned in that direction and was amazed to see Julio turn the corner, firing his weapon at the perusing masked men determined to kill him. Charles struggled with allowing the gunmen to kill Julio to protect his secret or helping the detective, a man Charles came to admire. Charles also weighed the benefit of keeping Julio alive and having two sets of eyes to search for Elaine, knowing he could deal with Julio's fate later.

"Mr. Sinclair, can you hear me? This is Samuel, come in." Charles's radio finally came alive.

"Sam, where in the hell have you been?" Charles demanded.

"Our radios were being jammed. I think the jammer was knocked out when that burning helicopter landed on it," Samuel said.

"There is a kill-on-sight order for the Detectives, Floyd Harrison and Agent Wanda Jackson," Samuel announced.

"Sounds like the Serapians are trying to cover their tracks," Charles said.

"Gunmen are covering the front of the building, but we are a block away and will provide you cover when you are ready to exit the building," Samuel stated.

"Ok, I will let you know when we get there," Charles concluded.

Julio was now pinned down by the superior firepower of the death squad that was pursuing him. Charles realized he might need his help to find Elaine if she managed to get out of the burning building.

Julio thought he felt something rush past him and crash into the men who were trying to kill him. The attackers were now on the defense, fighting for their lives against a blur, holding two short swords and cutting them to pieces. The last attacker was the most unfortunate; whatever had attacked the others had now seized the previous attacker and was savagely biting into his neck, beating him senseless every time he was able to manage any resistance. The man caught in the grasp of the creature finally went limp and was thrown aside by the thing that had attacked them. Through the smoke and fire, Julio could see the beast standing and coming in his direction. Julio raised his weapon and fired but was disheartened to notice that this monster also could avoid bullets like the woman who was responsible for Matt's death. Julio turned to run but was instantly hit in the face by the heat of the burning inferno that was increasing with intensity. Julio lamented his choices: confront this thing that just effortlessly took out five fully armed men or the flames and smoke. Before Julio could decide his next course of action, he was seized and pinned to the floor littered with the dead, thousands of bullet casings, body parts, gasoline, blood, and smoke. Julio struggled to break free and then realized that he was staring up into the bloody face of Charles Sinclair.

"Mr. Sinclair, what are you doing here? Did these people kidnap you? I've got to get you out of here!" Julio said, trying to make sense of Charles's presence in the building.

"Never mind that, for now, Detective, I need you to trust me if you ever want to see your wife again," said Charles.

"Have you seen my wife!? Where is she? I lost her in the explosions." Julio said.

The question to Charles made no sense: why would the detective's wife be there?

"No, but I know who does, and if you hope to see her alive again, you better let me help you," Charles stated.

"Don't tell me that bitch still is holding my wife," Julio said.

A sinking feeling turned in Charles's stomach, followed by sympathy for the detective, knowing Julio's wife was already dead or worse.

"There is nothing you could do for her if you are dead, Julio," Charles said.

"I need you to trust me, Julio, to leave here alive and return with help to get your wife." Charles continued.

"Ok, I got to find a way for us to get out of this burning building and avoid these mother fuckers trying to kill us?" Julio stated.

"Just hold on," Charles said before grabbing Julio by the arm. Julio felt himself being carried through the flames to the stairway, down a flight of stairs, and to the building entrance. Julio's mind could only process the movement in slow motion. Charles and Julio seemed to materialize out of thin air when they came upon Wanda, Drake, and Bowser in a gunfight at the building's exit.

Wanda turned, ready to fire, and was stopped when Charles took the gun from her hand.

"Charles, thank God you are still alive!" Wanda said, knowing she and the other two injured men owed their lives to him.

"How in the fuck did you do that!?" Julio demanded.

Suddenly, the stories Paul Blacksmith told him about Charles Sinclair could not be denied. However, Julio still struggled to find a rational way to explain everything he had witnessed that night. Was it possible for Charles Sinclair to be everything Paul said he was? Most importantly, was Charles Sinclair immortal, and is Charles Sinclair a Vampire?

Regardless of what he turned out to be, Charles had proven he was on their side, and his presence renewed their hopes of getting out of the burning building alive. Drake and Bowser lay unconscious while Wanda kept the Kill Team at bay. The Kill Team was strategically located outside the factory building, preventing Wanda and the other men from escaping the fire and allowing the fire to do its job for them.

"Samuel, this is Charles come in." Charles broadcasted over his tactical radio.

"This is Samuel; go ahead, Charles," Samuel responded on the radio.

"We are at the front entrance and ready for an exit," Charles announced.

"We are ready for you, Charles, wait for our signal," Samuel concluded.

"Stand by to move, stay close to me, and try not to get separated if you want to live." Said Charles. The sound of stun grenades and gunfire could be heard coming from outside the entrance of the building.

"Ok, this is it, let's go," Charles commanded.

The group rushed out to the building into the firefight; Wanda and Julio dragged Drake and Bowser away from the building in the direction of Samuel and his men, who had caught the attacking men off guard. Charles quickly killed any attacker who turned to try to stop Wanda and the other people from escaping. Charles and the four survivors returned to the black Cadillac Escalade where Charles had arrived. Looking back out the rear window, Wanda was amazed that none had left the burning building alive.

It was still being rocked by massive explosions from the hundreds of gasoline barrels stored there.

Isoba watched from his root top position as the men exited their SUVs positioned a bloc away from the factory building and lobbed flash grenades at the entrance of the building, temporarily blinding the men who were covering the exit. Isoba was relieved that he was not given the directive to kill anyone other than Floyd or the suspected witches. He was amazed to see Charles Sinclair but was more astonished to watch his unnatural speed and movements. Were their suspicions about Charles Sinclar correct? Was he witnessing the one they had been searching hundreds of years for?

Isoba swung back his scope, and a man ran in the opposite direction, but before he could get a clean shot, the man turned the corner. Isoba prayed it was Floyd Harrison.

Drake, Bowser, and the other surviving team members were receiving trauma medical treatment from one of Charles's rescue team members. Julio and Wanda sat back quietly, still shocked by what they had witnessed and experienced. No one knew what became of Mr. Floyd Harrison but doubted that he could have made it out of the building alive. However, there was still a chance that Melissa Rodriguez was still alive, and Julio was determined to find her.

Wanda did not know where to start; was she now a fugitive with a shoot-on-sight-kill order on her head? Someone did not want the public to learn about what she had accidentally encountered. The information had caused the life of Agent Todd Baker, Detective Matt O'Bannon, and all the men who came to rescue them. The most intriguing question for Wanda was who and what the elusive Charles Sinclair was. She remembered Dechontee's statement that

Charles was not who he claimed to be and that he had them all fooled. Was he immortal, as Dechontee suggested? Could he be killed? Was he a vampire?

"I know you have many questions that I can't provide answers that you will understand. Know this: your lives are in danger, and they will not stop until each one of you is dead," Charles said, breaking the uncomfortable silence.

"Who were those men trying to kill us?" Julio asked.

"Friends of Agent Jackson, I presume." Said Charles.

"But that does not make any sense," Wanda replied.

"Agent Jackson, I know you have come across the name of an organization called the Serapians. Mr. Floyd Harrison was a member of that group. They are dedicated to learning the secret of immortality, even if it means creating creatures like we fought inside that burning building. I guess that Mr. Harrison had signed his death warrant when he decided to help Julio rescue his wife." Said Charles.

"I was told to drop my investigation as soon as I mentioned that organization, and now my own Agency is trying to assassinate me to keep their secret. Just how influential are the Serapians? What do we do now?" Wanda asked.

"No one knows how dominant the Bishops are or how far their influence goes. The Bishops have a firm control over the FBI and other governmental officials, and they are willing to kill their own to keep their activities secret." Charles stated.

The vehicles stopped along a deserted pier section along the Franklin D. Roosevelt East River Drive in Manhattan. Samuel made a cell phone call and then reported it to Charles.

"Clair is bringing in the La Morena now," Samuel stated.

"Samuel, I want you to take these two men to the estate; they will not last much longer without additional medical attention. Spare no expense to get them out of danger and on their feet again. Make sure your uncle Stanley gets that creature's body to figure out what it is and how to kill them better the next time we run into them." Charles instructed Samuel.

"You said that you would help me find Melissa." Julio reminded Charles.

"Julio, you, and Agent Jackson are wanted people with a shoot-on-sight order on your heads. You should come with me until the heat blows over; then, you can return to look for your wife." Charles said, allowing Julio to hold on to his little hope of finding his wife and returning to any resemblance of normalcy.

Charles knew that if Melissa were lucky, she would already be dead along with their unborn child; however, he knew that was too good to be true when Dechontee was in the picture.

"You will be safe at my estate along with these two other men if you like," Charles said.

"Yes, but what about Melissa? We can't leave her out there like that!" Julio said.

"I have a vast information network and a few connections of my own that I will put at your disposal to help you find your wife, but for now, we have to get you off the street." Said Charles.

"I need to get back to the Agency to clear up this mess," Wanda said, still not grasping the immediate danger she was in because of the information she had stumbled upon.

"Wanda, they will kill you on sight. You know too much and will not be allowed to live long enough to share your discovery with anyone." Charles stated.

"Can you hear yourself, Mr. Sinclair? Do you honestly believe someone could have that much influence over the United States Law Enforcement Agency?" Wanda asked, not wanting to consider the possibility of it being confirmed.

"Samuel, call your friend at the Agency and let Agent Jackson hear it for herself," Charles instructed.

After the call was over and the order to have her killed was verified, Wanda sat in silent disbelief.

"Do worry, Agent Jackson; I am going to keep you safe until we can find a way to get you out of this," Charles said.

The vehicle occupants could see a luxury yacht slowly approaching their position along the pier. A smaller watercraft was lowered into the water and came towards the dock.

"Clair and the La Morena's shuttle craft is on the way, Charles; you need to get ready to get on board," Samuel announced.

"Wanda, you need to go with me on board the ship," Charles demanded.

With a heavy heart, Wanda agreed. Her life as she had known it was over, and her future was uncertain for the first time.

Charles and Wanda boarded the shuttlecraft, and after a short time, they were aboard the La Morena. The ship immediately headed for the open sea.

The night yielded to the early New York City rush hour as the black SUVs with Samuel, Drake, Bowser, Julio, and the surviving team members disappeared into the dense FDR drive traffic on their way to the Sinclair estate. Standing on the deck of the converted clipper ship, Wanda welcomed the warm rays of the morning sun that brought renewed hope for a better day.

Charles appeared on deck carrying two hot cups of coffee. He handed Wanda one of the cups and silently stood beside her, enjoying the fresh smell of the ocean and the morning mist coming from the water. The La Morena cleared the East River and entered the Atlantic Ocean.

"Where are we going?" Wanda asked.

"Africa, where this nightmare began," Charles announced as the luxury yacht sailed into the rising morning sun.